Three Wishes

Gemma ENGLISH

GW00492600

POOLBEG

Published 2006
by Poolbeg Press Ltd
123 Grange Hill, Baldoyle
Dublin 13, Ireland
E-mail: poolbeg@poolbeg.com

13 5 7 9 10 8 6 4 2

A catalogue record for this book is available from the British Library.

ISBN 1-84223-237-1

Typeset by Patricia Hope in Bembo 10.75/14
Printed by Litografia Rosés, Spain

www.poolbeg.com

About the author

Gemma English is married to Mark and they have two children.

She works in Bank of Ireland Mortgages in the IFSC and lives in Swords, County Dublin. This is her third novel.

Acknowledgements

I would like to thank all the usual suspects; you know who you are.

My family were a great support while I was writing this book. They took Jack and kept him reasonably safe while I was too busy to watch him. They also fed him and changed his nappies – for the latter in particular, I am eternally grateful.

I would like to thank Paula and all the guys in Poolbeg who have helped and advised me from the beginning. And thanks to Gaye Shortland for editing so quickly and helping me not to panic five days before Christmas.

A very big thank-you to Orlaith who helped me write this novel. Without her input I would have had no story. Thank you and just for the record, you're much braver than I could ever be.

A special thank-you goes to Mark. I love you very much.

Not so much a 'thank you', as a "hi there" to Jack and Jessica. You guys didn't exactly help with writing this book. Why does the word 'hindrance' spring to mind?

Jessica, you have an excuse; you weren't born yet. Jack, darling, you *were* born and quite frankly we need to talk. You guys may not have been much help but I still think you're wonderful, both of you.

A special 'hi there' goes to Matthew.

*This book is dedicated to
my mother, Dee.*

1

Julie Fennel and Sinéad Kilbride had been friends since the day they both got detention for smoking behind the high wall at the back of the school. Julie was fourteen, Sinéad had just turned fifteen and they had never as much as said hello to one another before that day. They were bunking off science class, each for her own reasons, and found themselves together behind this high wall at the back of the school grounds looking out onto the playing fields. After five minutes of kicking the ground and pulling little pebbles up from the tarmac they were bored.

Julie looked over at Sinéad and flickering smiles were exchanged. Julie leaned over, holding out a bashed-up packet of John Player Blues.

"Want one?" she asked.

Sinéad was all set to refuse but something made her hand reach out and take one.

"Thanks."

She took the cigarette and put it between her lips.

Julie handed her a packet of matches and they both lit up. Neither of them was very experienced and they both had to stifle a fit of choking. They sat closer and began to talk.

It turned out that Julie was bunking because she hated the science teacher and didn't want to sit through a full class. Sinéad hadn't done her homework. She was finding science a difficult subject and only three weeks into the year was already falling behind. She knew bunking the class was not the way to catch up but right now she just wanted out of the whole school.

They sat in silence for a moment, watching the grass shimmering in the empty playing fields. They were so far back from the road, the sound of the cars passing by was completely muffled. It felt as if they were in the middle of the country and not in the centre of Dublin. The late September sun broke though the clouds and shone down on the girls. The momentary heat was wonderful. They sat silently, backs against the wall, heads raised, eyes closed, taking in the sun's rays.

A sudden shrill voice broke the silence. "What am I witnessing? What is going on?" It was the assistant head, Mrs Hartley.

The girls jumped and threw their cigarettes away. They arced in the air in front of them – a bright orange spark falling in slow motion watched by each horrified pair of eyes.

"And smoking!" Mrs Hartley shouted. "I can hardly believe my eyes!"

The girls scrambled to their feet. Mrs Hartley was on

top of them in a flash. Grabbing each girl by the collar of her blazer she demanded their names and classes.

"Julie Fennel, 2A."

"Sinéad Kilbride, 2C."

"Second years? Smoking and ditching class?" Mrs Hartley was becoming more and more high-pitched. "What are you like?"

She marched them back into the school and down the corridor to her office where she scolded them for a good half hour. Mothers and Year Heads would have to be informed. Had they any idea how dangerous it was to be 'out on the streets' without permission? The school was responsible for their welfare between nine a.m. and four p.m. – where would that leave the school if anything were to happen to them?

In deep shit, Julie thought to herself but decided to say nothing. Instead she watched Sinéad who was completely out of her depth, her face ashen and her eyes – really big at the best of times – doubled in size. She's taking this whole thing far too seriously, Julie thought. Julie was not so brazen as she pretended to be, but she knew that in the grand scheme of things bunking a class and sitting on the playing fields was not a hanging offence – they hadn't even left the school grounds for heaven's sake.

"I'm very sorry, Mrs Hartley," Sinéad was saying in a small voice. She was looking up at the woman, her face a picture of sorrow and innocence. "It was a stupid thing to do – we had no reason for it. Just a silly thing we all do from time to time. It wasn't very well thought out – I mean, if we'd planned this at all we'd have left the school grounds for starters, wouldn't we?"

It was then Julie realised Sinéad was playing the game, and doing it very well. Mrs Hartley looked at Sinéad and, for whatever reason, be it the look on Sinéad's face, the innocence or the obvious truth that they hadn't planned the bunk very well at all, she let it go. She promised not to ring their parents and not to tell their Year Heads.

"If this happens again, I will make sure the relevant people hear about it."

"It won't, Mrs Hartley," Sinéad smiled, pale blue eyes and jet-black lashes devouring the woman.

"I will, however, be looking for both of you this afternoon. I want you both here at four p.m. – there are several things that need doing in this office."

She opened the door and the girls walked out, just in time to hear the bell sound for their next class. Mrs Hartley's door shut behind them and they walked quickly along the corridor.

"Thanks," Julie whispered.

"No problem. I just didn't want my mother called to the school. She'd have killed me." Sinéad smiled, the colour back in her cheeks.

"What class have you got now?" Julie asked.

"English," Sinéad replied. "You?"

"Maths. I suppose I'd better go though!" she grinned. "If I was caught around the back of the school again I'd be killed!"

"Will I meet you back here at four then?" Sinéad asked.

"Yeah, meet you here and we'll head down to Hartley together."

They turned the next corner and split up.

They met up again that afternoon at four and spent the next two hours in Mrs Hartley's office clearing out presses, and emptying bins around the school.

This work had been intended to punish them, but they enjoyed it. They chatted together while they pulled out the contents of presses and looked through timetables and class lists going back to 1970.

They left the school that evening, having forged a friendship that would last many years.

Eight years later Julie and Sinéad were still the best of friends. They had both gone to college, Julie to Cathal Brugha Street where she honed her skills and became a very professional chef. She rustled up many meals from the ageing leftovers in Sinéad's presses. She loved cooking up a huge meal and dishing it out to a group of hungry pals. She would get a gang together and try out new recipes on them – Beef Wellington or Passion-fruit Cheese cake – and she shone with pride when the dishes came back licked clean.

She got a job in a small restaurant on Dawson Street. She loved it, cooking up dishes and playing around with ingredients, making new dishes and changing the menu, dish by dish. Her work was admired and sought after. Other restaurants would send people in to eat there and steal ideas. Julie would be called out to tables in the restaurant and congratulated about the dishes and the meals prepared. Before long these 'customers' were telling her about restaurants they owned, or were opening and how a head chef with her flair was just what they needed. She smiled but declined each offer. It was only when the money offered began to reach offensive proportions that she felt herself cave in and listen to the details of each offer.

Sinéad went to DCU and got a Degree in Business and Marketing. Much to everyone's surprise, she had proven herself to be the power-driven one of the pair. She had started working in the bank a year ago and had already landed herself a position of prominence. She was on the ladder both personally and professionally. She was well known in the office and well liked. She was aware that her manager was grooming her for a position that was about to be announced in the department. She was advised to take a place on a course that was completely unnecessary for her current role. She took the advice and signed up for the course in public speaking and report analysis.

A week after she finished the course, certificate of accomplishment in hand, the position of Deputy Supervisor of the department was announced. She went for the interview but it was privately confirmed that this was just a formality. The promotion was officially confirmed two days later.

Sinéad was on her way to the top. It was officially time to think about moving out of home.

Two years later both girls were enjoying the highs of life that come with being young, educated and employed in a city like Dublin. They were both still there for one another, still best of friends. It appeared nothing could change that at this stage. But they were now women and their lives, both professional and personal, had taken them down very different paths.

Julie was working in an exclusive and very plush restaurant in Blackrock. There was a waiting list to get a table on Saturday night and the month of December was booked up in early August. Julie knew her work played a huge part in the success of the restaurant but she was not the type to play on this.

It was around this time she met Gavin Hurley. He came into the restaurant at least twice a week at lunch-time. He brought clients in and always asked for Julie to come out and sit with them after the lunch rush had calmed. She always came out and had a Coke with him, discussing the business and asking how he had enjoyed the new dishes. He was always complimentary and there was no mistaking the attraction between them.

A few weeks into this, Julie would find herself checking the bookings. She had begun to recognise the flutters of anticipation when she saw his name on the list. The excitement built as the lunch-time punters began to arrive. And then, there was Gavin. He'd walk in, his smiling face and confident air filling the room as he was led to his seat. He'd glance behind the counter and then towards the kitchen and search her out. Their eyes would lock for a second and he'd grin that broad grin of his. Her stomach would flip in the most enjoyable way, then she'd head to the staffroom, tidy her hair and straighten her uniform in anticipation for the invitation.

Without fail the word would come.

"Gavin would love a chat before he leaves – he wants to thank you personally," the maitre 'd would say and then grin as she flushed and rushed out to Gavin's table.

It took Gavin about three months to finally ask Julie out. The entire staff body was waiting for the event and there were many bets placed about how long they'd last or if Julie would back out and say no to the first date. She didn't. She replied to his request with a resounding yes.

Sinéad was too busy for men; there was too much work and too many opportunities. She didn't need the hassle of being answerable to a man as well. She liked working until late, getting things sorted out, reports printed, accounts tidied and ready for the morning meetings. She always made a point of being the last one in the office at night and the first one at her desk in the mornings. That way she could see what was happening, who was doing what after hours. She knew people made use of the computers after work and that didn't bother her. But what they did with the computers bothered her. Were they printing CV's? Who was taking courses and what courses were they taking? Was anyone quietly on the move? She wanted to be the first to know, to be one step ahead, ready for the resignation with someone ready and willing to step into the new position. She was eager to be on top of everything. Once the last person had turned off their computer and left the floor, Sinéad was right behind them. She'd check the fax machine and the printer for forgotten pages. Then she'd turn off the lights and head for home, a glass of wine and bubble bath. She'd sit up in bed watching TV.

Her life was her own. She was busy but it didn't bother her. She had no one else to think about, to consider or worry about. Her time was her own and the TV remote was always in her hand, no one else's.

That's not to say she was leading a completely celibate lifestyle. She was a good-looking girl with money and status; the men flocked to her. Some stayed for a while but most were simply passing through. She liked it that way. After all, she was only twenty-five, and there was plenty of time for relationships when she was older. She would marry some time in her early thirties, have two children one after the other – a boy and a girl – and then go back to work.

She'd seen it all before – that was what all the girls in work were doing. They married and within a year they were off having a baby. They'd come back and the following year they were off again. A few busy years in the beginning and back to work. Life would return to normal and she'd have the husband and the children like everyone else.

At the moment she was only twenty-five and there was no way she was getting tied down just yet. She was too busy.

2

Six months later Sinéad went out drinking with Julie on a Wednesday night. It was an impromptu session, they drank far too much, spent far too much and stayed up far too late. In the morning she woke up with a hangover that would drop a horse and someone called Richard's mobile number. She lay in bed wondering who he was and if she'd given him her number. She rolled out of bed, turned on her phone and a text came through almost immediately. It was from this Richard guy, just checking that she'd given him a real number and not some ex-boyfriend's one. She had to giggle at the suggestion and, as she sat on her bed, getting later and later for work, she recalled what he looked like. If Richard was the guy at the bar last night, the one with the dark hair, then he was cute. Really cute.

She rang him back that afternoon and they arranged to go for a drink. She wasn't looking for a boyfriend, nothing serious, she told him.

"Perfect, I was just looking for some casual sex myself," he laughed.

"Jesus, you're not backward at coming forward!" Sinéad laughed despite herself.

"What's the point? Life's too short and if I'm remembering correctly you're far too pretty to let pass by."

"If you're remembering correctly?"

"Yeah. You *are* the blonde girl with the red top?"

"Yeah."

"The top that was open down to your waist?"

"Yes." Sinéad blushed. That was a really low-cut top.

"Then you're the girl for me. When would you like to meet up for a drink?"

"I don't mind . . . the weekend?"

"Perfect. Will we risk our Saturday night on a blind date?"

"All right . . . Saturday night then."

Sinéad hung up, wondering what type of a person she'd just agreed to spend Saturday night with and if she was going to have to change her mobile number on Sunday morning.

Not very often but on special occasions, Sinéad went out with the work crowd on a Friday night. She had some rules set out in her own head about how she should behave on these nights out. They never wavered, not for a second. She was always watching herself. She never allowed herself to get too drunk or to let her guard fall too far.

On this Friday night, like many Friday nights past, she watched as the new girls and some of the older ones drank shots and danced around in the bar after work. She could never do that – it looked so undisciplined. How could they ever expect to be taken seriously in the office if they threw themselves around like that in front of every one at the weekend?

"Come on, have a Slippery Nipple, Sinéad!" Ciara called over to her, shouting above the heads of crowds of men in suits. "They're gorgeous!"

"Just order her one – she'll have to drink it!" Yvette shouted, linking Sinéad's arm and walking her through the crowd. "They really are yummy, Sinéad. Wait till you try it!"

"What is a Slippery Nipple?" Sinéad asked as she was pushed toward the bar.

"It's a shot! Just taste it and let your hair down!" Ciara shouted, passing a tiny drink to Sinéad.

Sinéad took the drink, annoyed. Of course she knew it was a shot, but what was in it? She smelt it and recoiled in horror. Aniseed, she hated aniseed.

"Has this got aniseed in it?" she asked.

"No, it has sambuca with a little bit of Baileys in it," Ciara slurred after finishing hers. She stamped her feet and shook out her body like after a work-out. "Blah!" she giggled. "It's hot!"

"Come on. You have to drink it!" Yvette had noticed that Sinéad was still holding her glass.

Everyone turned around – seven faces all watching Sinéad, waiting for her to drink the shot. She could smell the aniseed and it turned her stoma... ...t she knew she had to drink it. If she was to have any stand... ...r in the office next week, she had to be able to get on with it and drink the shot. But aniseed!

"I hate aniseed," she said.

"Tough, I hate Mondays but I have to do them every week!" Ciara laughed. "Just drink the drink!"

Sinéad lifted the glass, held her breath and drank the shot. The hot aniseed flavour ran down her throat and made her stomach churn. The girls all cheered and danced on the spot. This was the closest she'd ever got to being in the centre of this group and she could see they were all having a really great time. She stood still as they danced and sang. There was definitely camaraderie here. They seemed genuine enough and they all seemed very happy. Sinéad stood alone, not quite wanting to be drawn into their crowd, not sure how far outside she wanted to be either. There was whooping and cheering as they all began to dance to some song they all loved. Sinéad listened but didn't recognise it. The circle drew in. Sinéad was on the outside, everyone else was dancing. She wondered about joining them and letting her hair down this once. What was there to lose? A bit of a dance on a Friday night, what was wrong with that? While she stood there thinking about it, the group moved just a foot to the left and away from her. That slight move suddenly made them impenetrable. They were too far away now; she'd have to go up and break the circle to get in. She couldn't do that; it wasn't her style.

She watched them for a few minutes, her face not

betraying any f.... Her practised face. A smile just
playing ....er lips, friendly yet reserved, ready to accept
an offer to dance, and if none came she looked nonchalant
enough to seem unfazed.

Sometimes she wondered if everyone else analysed
their every move as much as she did. Always wondering
how she was perceived by the outsider, always aware of the
on-lookers? Somehow she thought not. She ordered a
Smirnoff Ice and went back to where the rest of the staff,
the non-dancers, were all sitting. No one even looked up.
They made a space for her and she sat down.

Her manager, Ruth, was just leaving. "Ah, Sinéad, I
wondered where you'd got to," she smiled. "I just wanted
to let you know, I'll be in late on Monday. I have a date
with a nine-year-old and a very cranky dentist. Poor old
Robert needs a brace so we're expecting some tears. I
should be in by lunch-time. Sorry, but sometimes I have
to be mammy first and manager second – so you'll be able
to hold the fort, just in case?"

"Absolutely – don't be rushing in if Robert needs a
hug and a kiss!" Sinéad smiled.

"Thanks, I'll have the mobile on for a long as possible
if you need me," Ruth said, turning to hug the IT
manager goodbye. "Thanks for the help today, Steve – if
my system had been down for any longer we'd have all
been sunk!"

"No problem at all, Ruth!" Steve blushed a little and
watched her leave.

"Well, see you all on Monday!" she called over her
shoulder as she made for the door.

Sinéad watched her leave. If she was honest, Ruth Hogan was probably her role model in the office. She had exactly what Sinéad wanted: she was in her early forties, at the top of her personal career ladder, with the husband and three children. She had everything and she seemed so capable. Sure, Ruth was a bit scatty sometimes and seemed to have very little time for herself. Sinéad often heard her cancelling hair appointments when one of the children was sick or she had to be home for some crisis. But she seemed to love it and she was always on top of her work and dressed in the best of clothes. Sinéad watched her leave the pub, waving at other tables and stopping to shake hands here and there along the way. Sinéad would be Ruth. Before her fortieth birthday, Sinéad would be manager, mammy and domestic goddess!

She looked back at the crowd still dancing at the bar. Poor fools, dancing away their career prospects, she thought to herself – a little smugly if she was honest.

Life was treating Julie very well indeed. Her restaurant had just been awarded four stars in the *Restaurant Guide of Ireland*. She was personally named in the article and she'd just been talking to *The Irish Times*. They were coming to the restaurant to do an interview with her for their *Weekend* section. They would chat to her about her life and how she came to be a chef. They asked about her personal life and wondered if she'd mind them printing her age and some personal details. For once in her life she was happy to have it all emblazoned over every newspaper in the land. Julie Fennel was twenty-four years old and she was in love with Gavin Hurley. She could provide photographs of him and would be available anytime for messages of congratulations and good wishes for their future.

They'd been seeing each other for only six months but she could just tell he was 'The One'. From the moment he held her hand. His hand was the perfect shape for hers – not too big – her fingers were not lost in his. Not too small either – she didn't like a man's hands to be effeminate. Gavin's hands were perfect; he was perfect.

On their first date he met her in the Punch Bowl Pub. They had decided not to meet in the restaurant or anywhere too close – prying eyes would have been watching their every move. She wondered about asking him to call to her house but decided against it. Not on the first night – she might hate him and then he'd know where she lived.

She had no reason to worry – as it turned out, she adored him. He was funny and confident without being arrogant.

He was standing outside the pub when she got there.

"What are you doing outside? I thought we were meeting inside?" she queried, realising she was ten minutes late. She was being fashionably late; she wouldn't have been so mean if she'd thought he was waiting outside for her.

"Indulging my one very bad habit," he smiled as he lifted a cigarette from his side.

"I didn't know you smoked," she said, sort of

disappointed. Would this mean he was going to be forward and back from the door all night? Worse still, the smell of stale smoke – what a turn-off!

"I'm trying to quit. I know it smells awful but I was really nervous tonight and I needed a hit," he replied, his honest face cocked to one side.

"Nervous about meeting me?" Julie grinned. "I'm a pussycat!"

Gavin put out his cigarette, blowing the last of the smoke over Julie's head. "Pussycats have claws. I've seen you in that kitchen. You don't take any messing!"

"I'm a whole different person outside the kitchen," she laughed. "Come on, let's get a drink and tell each other lies to make us sound like better catches than we really are!"

Gavin followed her into the pub, nerves still unsettled but excited none the less.

They sat in the lounge, away from the door and secluded. They ordered drinks and waited. There was silence between them for a while, but it wasn't uncomfortable. Sure, Julie would have preferred if they were talking but the silence wasn't intolerable. Gavin glanced at her, his eyes shining; they were stunningly blue in certain lights. He held her eye for a moment and smiled. A schoolboy grin that made her instantly comfortable. She smiled back, stifling a giggle. She felt as if she was bunking school with a boy from the local Christian Brothers. They seemed to be living on the edge, taking a chance. Her heart was beating fast and she really had no idea why.

"What is happening with our drinks?" Gavin asked.

"I don't know. You shouldn't have ordered Guinness. They always take an age to pull them here." She smiled, still wanting to laugh although she didn't know why.

"I like Guinness, and the wait is half the fun. The anticipation!" Gavin grinned.

"Anticipation? Are you for real?"

"Yes, the wait for the wonderful pint. It's great. Anyway, I've waited a lot longer for food in your greasy spoon!"

"My greasy spoon! I'll slap you in the head!" Julie laughed, raising her hand, pretending to hit at him.

"Hey, watch it! Here come the drinks. Where's your money? Are you paying for these?" He grinned at Julie's surprised face as he handed over the money. "Don't be silly – I wouldn't have invited you out if I expected you to pay. I'd have dropped hints until you invited me."

Julie sat back, happy. Gavin was just as funny in real life as he was when she had those ten-minute chats with him in work. She hoped that he liked her as much as she liked him.

3

A year passed very quickly and Julie and Gavin celebrated their anniversary in style. It coincided with Gavin's twenty-ninth birthday and Julie really wanted to do something nice for him. Well, not exactly 'coincided' – in truth Gavin had turned twenty-nine three months before but because of work commitments they hadn't done anything much to mark the occasion. Julie wanted to make it up to him and have a bit of a weekend away herself. It had been really busy in work for the last month and she could do with a bit of pampering. A weekend break somewhere nice would be great, somewhere she could get a massage and he could have a swim. They could get breakfast in bed and have the papers delivered right to their rooms, order room service and drink the mini-bar dry every night. Yeah, she'd bring him off somewhere really plush.

She checked the internet for deals and found just the spot. They took Friday off and headed down to Dromoland Castle in County Clare. She decided to make it a surprise, so she never told him their actual destination. He looked stunned as they pulled into the driveway and made their way up to the castle.

"Jesus, Jules, this is really extravagant! What did it cost you?" he whispered as they walked up the steps into the reception.

"Not as much as you think," Julie whispered back. "Now shut up – they'll hear you and think we're trailer trash!"

They were shown to the most beautiful room with views out over the lake. There was a huge bed with big heavy furniture and huge windows. To Julie's eye it was perfect.

"My God, would you look at the size of this bed?" She kicked off her shoes and lay back on the huge expanse of mattress. "How many of us could sleep here side by side? Honestly, look!" She lay down flat and rolled along the bed. It took five full rolls to get to the other side. By the time she got there she was giddy and dizzy. "Wow, that was fun! I'll do it again!"

She began to roll in the other direction. Gavin came over to the bed and stopped her by placing one hand on either side of her body.

"Yes, it's a huge bed, Jules," he grinned as he leaned down to kiss her. "But I'm sure we'll make full use of the entire space! In fact, if I just close these curtains, we could make a start!"

He went over to the window and drew the heavy floral curtains tight.

That evening they went down to the restaurant and had

dinner. Afterwards they headed to the residents' bar and sat up on the couch close to the fire. They looked at the family portraits and talked about whether or not they thought the castle was haunted.

"Oh my God, it must be!" Julie kicked off her shoes and tucked legs under her. "I mean, look at all the souls that have lived here. At least one must have decided to stick around. If I owned a home like this I'd stick around for as long as possible!"

"I don't go in for this ghost business myself." Gavin said looking up at a particularly plain woman whose portrait was gazing down at them. "How come all these families are so plain? Look at her, for instance, and the man beside her. They're awful-looking."

"Yeah, and they're all the image of one another too," Julie agreed.

"Yeah, all as ugly as sin!" Gavin laughed. "In years to come, our family photos would be stunning compared to these."

"Um, yes, my family were always extremely good-looking," Julie smiled. She wasn't being serious, though it was often remarked that her family were good-looking.

"I wonder what our children might look like?" Gavin asked, looking at her.

Julie was not looking at Gavin so missed the earnest look on his face.

"I don't know, " she answered. "I would presume a mixture of us both. Your hair and my nose. God, I hope they wouldn't get my hair and your nose!"

"Julie, I was wondering about more than that – " He

stopped abruptly. "Wait a minute, what's wrong with my nose?" He put a hand up to his face and tipped his nose self-consciously.

"Oh nothing! It's fine on you but imagine if a little girl got it! You have to admit it's a bit on the big side."

"I never thought it was huge – it was never a problem."

"No, Gav, I love your nose, on you. It suits you. It might not suit a little girl as well as it does you though. Anyway, forget the nose for a moment. What were you saying before that?"

But Gavin's moment was well and truly lost. There was no way he'd ask her to marry him now. "Nothing, it's fine."

"No, you sounded serious. What were you going to say?"

"I can't remember now actually."

"Go on, Gav. Let's hear it! You sounded serious and you know you crack me up when you're being really serious!"

"No, I can't remember what it was now."

"Gavin, are you sulking? You sound like you're sulking!"

"No. Do you want another drink?"

"Yes, I'd love one. A Bacardi and Diet Coke. But you *are* sulking. I know you, changing the subject and pouting, a definite sulk."

"I'm not sulking. I was thinking about something and now I've lost my train of thought."

The lounge boy came over and took their order. It

turned out to be twenty euro for the two drinks. Julie immediately began to complain bitterly about 'Rip-Off Ireland' and how prices were sneaking up all over the place.

"Soon," she complained, "we'll find ourselves being charged a hundred euro for a sliced pan and we'll all still be paying it through gritted teeth! Then we'll go home and complain that our money doesn't stretch like it used to. And then we vote the fuckers back in at the next election and they'll keep putting the prices up! And we'll keep complaining to each other and it's all a fucking vicious circle! We should do something about it!"

"Go up for election yourself. Tell it like it is, for the ordinary punter, the ones without the expense accounts."

"Yeah, the ones who have to pay for everything or do without it!"

"Right on!" Gavin laughed, not thinking she was serious about this. "Go out and get yourself elected, be the first independent Taoiseach."

"Now how would I do that? How does one get herself elected?"

"You find a gang of people who are gullible enough to believe your promises and you tell them you'll look after all their needs when you get the power. They vote for you and then you promptly forget your roots and spend all the taxpayers' money."

"No, seriously, Gavin, if I was to go for it and try to get elected, where do I start?"

"Oh Jesus, you're serious! No, Jules, forget it! You cannot honestly think you'd get elected!"

"I'll try."

That was it. The rest of the evening was spent with Gavin trying to talk Julie back out of running an election campaign. Julie would get riled about some issue and tell him exactly what she planned to do about fixing it. By the time they finally went to bed at five that morning, Gavin was talking Julie out of closing all of Ireland's borders.

"You can't close them all."

"Why not?"

"People have to get in and out of Ireland."

"There are far too many people coming and going at will around here. No, everyone has to stay put for a while, until I decide what our next move should be."

"What about the people who are on holidays?"

"Who?"

"The ones who went on a fortnight to Majorca and when they come home they find the borders all closed?"

"What about them? They're just confusing the issue with all that travelling. They should stay put too."

"In Majorca or Ireland?" Gavin began to laugh despite himself. She really was a dreadful little Nazi underneath the kind face.

"Look, they'll have to stay wherever they are when the borders close. In fact – wait a minute – I'm not sure what to do about them. I'll have to come back to them – they'll have to stay in Majorca for another while. Leave them to one side. But I am closing the borders. I will not be moved on that one! Let's see, what else would I do? I'd put way more people in prison and I'd do away with appeals or suspended sentences. If you're convicted for ten years then you serve ten years, not three or five or anything else!"

Julie drank a bit more of her drink and began to complain about how liberal the country had become.

"People don't care! They drive with no tax or insurance. They have hundreds of babies with absolutely no means of supporting them. And they complain about everything!"

Gavin drank the last of his drink. He had gone from being slightly amused to downright shocked during the last few revelations. Julie was becoming something of a Hitler right before his eyes. In Julie's world people would be imprisoned for having children who mugged, played truant, robbed a car, or themselves had a baby before their eighteenth birthday. Julie could see she was being tough, but she felt that Ireland was becoming too soft on offenders and things needed to toughen up around here. She was just the girl for the job.

Finally she gave in to exhaustion and allowed Gavin to take her to bed. She was either too drunk or too disheartened to continue righting all of Ireland's wrongs. Either way, she went to bed.

As they were lying in bed, Julie woozy with alcohol and Gavin tired from listening to the ever-increasing number of complaints Julie had, she leaned across the huge bed.

"What were you going to say earlier on? Have you remembered yet?"

"Yes, I have. I was going to ask you to marry me," Gavin replied.

"Really?" Julie smiled.

"Yes, but then we got on to your election campaign and I never got back to it."

"That's a very large pity. I would have said yes."

"Would you?"

"Oh yes, I love you loads, Gavin." Julie smiled at him, her hair tossed and her eyes drooping with sleep.

"Well then, Jules, would you like to marry me?"

"Definitely. That's a definite yes, Gavin."

"Yes? So we're engaged? We'll go out and buy a ring and tell our families?"

"God, yes. You're my completely best boyfriend I've had. I'd love it if we got married. I want to have loads of children, a big dog and nice house and I want to be a Soccer Mom."

"What's that?"

"It's a stay-at-home mother who takes their kids to soccer, ballet, swimming and all that stuff and makes home-made dinners and little treats and brings the kids to the park and stuff."

"I see. We'll see how it pans out, Jules. If we can swing it you'll be a Soccer Mom."

"Deadly! Now I'm tired. I'm going to sleep."

Julie turned over and was asleep in no time. Gavin on the other hand was far too excited to sleep. He'd just asked a girl to marry him, and she'd said yes. It was the first time he'd ever asked anyone to marry him and it went fine. Not exactly how he'd planned it, but hey, she said yes and now they were engaged. It was the perfect outcome.

And they'd both been lying down so she couldn't tell that he was shaking like a leaf as he spoke.

Sinéad got the call on Friday afternoon: she'd been

promoted to manager in the Credit Lending Department. She couldn't believe it. The interviews had been really tough and there had been huge competition for the position – she hadn't expected there would be so many candidates for the one job. But she'd got the position and that was that.

She rang her mother and told her the news. Her mother was thrilled and insisted Sinéad come over for lunch that Sunday to celebrate.

"Oh Mum, I'll come over but I'm not staying for lunch."

"Why not? Your dad would love to see you and I'll give Patrick a buzz. He'd be delighted to hear the news. He'll bring Bernadette and the kids over. We'll make a day of it!"

Sinéad rolled her eyes at the mention of her sister-in-law's name. The oh-so-bloody-boring Bernadette!

Patrick and Bernadette had been together since they were both nineteen. He went to college and worked hard; she left school and worked as a shop assistant in Arnotts. Patrick became the chief accountant for Boots in Ireland; Bernadette remained in behind her counter at Arnotts. They married at twenty-five and went on to have Ella and Oisín, now aged two and five. Sinéad loved the children dearly but they were two of the most over-protected kids ever spawned. Constantly being washed down with baby wipes, everything they picked up was sterilised and everywhere they went Bernadette was watching out for stray dust or, God forbid, a cat or dog. The children were forever at the doctor's; they caught every cold and bug going. Maybe if they weren't washed so much they'd have some kind of immune system.

"Mum, seriously, I don't need a big party. I just rang to tell you the news."

"And I'm very proud of you, my love. I want to have the family over for a celebratory lunch!"

"Anyway, Bernadette probably won't allow the kids come over. They might be contaminated with germs!"

"Oh stop it! Bernadette is just a bit panicky about the children. They seem to be very susceptible to colds and flu."

"They have no defence against them. They're never allowed to get dirty!"

"When you have children you'll be just the same!"

"No, I won't. I'll let them get dirty once in a while."

"Look, you come over to me anyway. I'll ask the others and hopefully they'll come too."

"All right, see you Sunday, Mum."

Sinéad hung up the phone, smiling to herself as she imagined her mother's face. She would stand in the hall, puffing herself up at the thought of Sinéad's new promotion. She'd go straight in to Mrs Stanley next door and tell her the great news. Mrs Stanley had no children of her own and she looked on Patrick and Sinéad as her surrogate children. Both women would be very proud.

Ciara rushed from her desk and threw her arms around Sinéad.

"Well done, you!" she beamed. "I can't believe it! You and I started at the same time and here you are running the department!"

Ciara seemed genuinely happy, no jealousy in her voice. Sinéad was a little ashamed as she admitted to herself she might not be so sweet if it was Ciara being promoted.

"Thanks, I can't believe it myself. I was sure Billy in Finance would get it," Sinéad smiled.

"Billy? No way, he's a pen-pusher. No organisational skills, couldn't organise a piss-up in brewery!" Ciara sat up on the desk. "So, are you going out drinking with your friends tonight? Or is Richard bringing you out to dinner somewhere fab?"

"Em, no. I didn't really plan anything because I didn't want to jinx anything. You know, presuming I had the job when I didn't."

"Well, I'll get out of your way and let you get the drinks organised. I'm sure all your gang will be waiting to hear the news." Ciara slid off the desk and went back to work.

Sinéad watched her leave, and then looked at the phone. She had rung her mother; Richard was away at a stag weekend. God, she really hoped that wouldn't give him any ideas of his own. She couldn't get hold of Julie for some reason and to be quite honest there was no one else to call. She looked over at Ciara and wondered about coming clean, asking her to come to the pub with her after work.

She stood up and was just heading over to Ciara's desk when Ciara got up and hurried to the door. As Sinéad stood there, unsure of whether she should follow her, Ciara glanced back and saw her.

"Did you want me?" she said. "I'm just running to the loo."

"No, it's fine. It was nothing. Go ahead." Sinéad smiled and went back to her desk.

She'd really have loved to celebrate the promotion, but in her heart she knew it would be the same old story. A bottle of wine and a Chinese takeaway while she watched TV alone.

She was just beginning to realise that life on your way to the top could be very lonely sometimes. She wondered if it was any better when you actually got to the top.

On the bright side, with the promotion came a very substantial pay-rise. And now that the money was hers, she was about to blow a large chunk of it and buy that car she'd been eyeing for the last two months.

There was a large second-hand garage she passed every day on the way home from work. A 2001 black BMW was sitting in the front window. It was very expensive, but it had been calling Sinéad's name from the moment she first saw it. It had six-spoke, 17-inch alloy wheels, a leather steering wheel, a stereo system to die for and only 25,000 miles on the clock. She'd taken it for a test drive one evening after work and the deal was done. In her heart at least. She loved it and immediately began to save any extra money she got. She stayed in at weekends, ate in the canteen instead of getting sandwiches in the deli across the road. She had the deposit and now with the pay-rise she could just about afford the repayments. It would put an end to most of her extravagances but what the hell. Richard could shout her a few drinks now and again!

4

On Saturday morning she was standing outside the garage, trading in her VW Golf against the car of her dreams. It was the easiest deal the sales guy had ever made. She was not the least bit interested in how much she got for the Golf; she just wanted to get her finance approved for the Beamer. The finance came back approved in an hour and that was it. Sinéad was now the extremely proud owner of a BMW. She was twenty-six years old, the youngest ever manager in the bank, she had her own apartment, a boyfriend and now a BMW. She was the success story of her generation! Would they be having a school reunion anytime soon, she wondered?

She might just organise one herself.

She rang Julie to see if she could go visiting with the new car. There was no reply, just her answering machine. She wondered what Julie was up to, that she was out for two days running.

"Julie, it's me. Where are you? Anyway, I'm ringing to

tell you all my news! I am now the manager of Credit Lending no less! And I am calling you from my brand-new shiny black BMW!"

She hung up and rang her mother. There was no one at home either. She hung up the phone, more than a little bit disappointed. She drove on, wondering whom else she might phone. Finally she gave in and rang Patrick. The phone was picked up after three rings.

The sullen voice of her sister-in-law came down the line. "Hello."

"Hi, Bernadette. Is Patrick in?"

"Who can I say is calling?"

"It's me, Sinéad!"

"Oh hello, I didn't recognise your voice. You sound very nasally – have you got a cold? Are you calling over? With a cold?"

"I don't have a cold. I don't think I sound nasally, do I?"

"Not any more actually. It must have been the line or was that your phone voice?"

Bernadette laughed a little but Sinéad knew she was being nasty.

"No, Bernadette, I don't have a phone voice. It's usually shop assistants who perfect a phone voice." Sinéad smirked to herself, remembering Bernadette's stint in Arnotts.

"I'll get Patrick for you," Bernadette sniffed.

The phone was put down and Sinéad could clearly hear Bernadette telling Oisín not to touch the phone.

"It's just Aunty Sinéad, but she doesn't want to talk to you. As usual she just wants Daddy."

Sinéad sighed. That was a really mean thing to do. As if

any adult would ring a house and ask to talk to the five-year-old! Sinéad really loved her niece and nephew. They were constantly on antibiotics, but it wasn't their fault. They were a product of their upbringing.

"Hi there, Sinéad!" Patrick sounded jolly.

"Hi, just thought I'd give you a call and let you know the news."

"Yeah, I heard. Great promotion, Mum told me. So are you making more money than God these days?"

"Almost as much as you, but just a little less than God made last year!"

"Well, never mind, I know for a fact he doesn't pay all his taxes and he gets a lot of back-handers!"

"Brown envelopes flying around the carparks of Heaven, are they? Very interesting!" she laughed. "Listen to this." She held the phone away from her ear and revved the engine. "Hear that?"

"Yeah, it's a car," Patrick replied.

"It's my new BMW!" Sinéad beamed.

"A new Beamer! Did you get a company car? Is it the five series?" Patrick sounded really excited.

"No, it's my own car, but it's not a brand new one. It's an 01, but it's really gorgeous!"

"Bring it round! Let's see it!" Patrick said.

"Are you not going out? Will I come around now?"

"Get over here, I want to see it! Oh, hang on."

Sinéad could hear Bernadette whining in the background.

"Sinéad, sorry, I forgot, Bernadette has people coming over for lunch. I have to help get the kids ready. But we'll be over in Mum's tomorrow for lunch. I'll see you then and I'll get a look at the car."

"Okay, that's fine," Sinéad said, but her heart sank. She really wanted to show off the car and there was no one to show it off to.

She drove home and let herself into the flat.

Richard rang sometime after four to say he'd be staying an extra night in Kilkenny.

"So it was that good, was it?"

"It was great. We had a real good laugh, just the lads. We got the notion of making Luke dress up as a woman and sing 'Like a Virgin'!"

"And did he?"

"Yeah! He sang really well too. He has a surprisingly good voice. We were all amazed."

"Dear God, talk about hidden talents!"

"I know. Anyway, we're staying down the extra night, so I'll see you tomorrow afternoon."

"Oh, I'm going over to Mum's to have lunch. I got the promotion in work."

"Oh my God, I forgot to ask you about it! Sorry. So you got it? That's fantastic!"

"Yeah, and I did that thing I was talking about for the last few months too." Sinéad was suddenly nervous. It was a huge amount of money every month and, even though they were not living together, she felt that maybe she should have run it by him first.

"You bought the car? Without me?"

"Yeah – but what do you mean 'without you'?"

"I just thought we'd buy it together." Richard sounded disappointed.

"We're not joined at the hip, Richard. It's my money and my decision. I can trade up my car if I want to." Sinéad knew she sounded bad-tempered and defensive.

"I know that, I just . . . I don't know, I thought we'd go together and buy it."

"Well – sorry, but you weren't here. You were away with the lads and I was here all alone celebrating my promotion. I went out today and bought myself a car."

"Hang on, I'm at my best friend's stag night! Luke and I have been friends since we were four years old! Don't start on about me being away. You could have waited till Monday to buy the car!"

Richard sounded annoyed. Sinéad knew she was being unfair. She hadn't meant to pick on him, but she was just so disappointed that no one was around to share her excitement about the job and the car.

"Look, sorry," she said, hoping the olive branch would be taken. "I didn't mean to pick on you. I just thought you'd be pleased for me, about the car and stuff."

"Of course, I am."

She decided to change the subject. "I hope that stag night hasn't given you any bad ideas of your own!"

"What? Settling-down-type ideas?" Richard replied. "Not likely. I'm not even thirty yet. I don't plan to be up to my elbows in nappies for at least another five years. But why were you not out partying last night? Why didn't you go out with the work girls?"

"Nobody was going out last night. I couldn't get hold of Julie so I just went home."

"Why didn't you ask the work gang to go out and have a drink? You should at least try to be friendly with them."

"I am friendly with them. I just didn't want to ask them all out last night. It's a week away from pay day and no one has any money."

"Except you, who just went out and bought a luxury car on a whim. Sinéad, you are unbelievable! Your priorities are up your arse sometimes!" Richard laughed, but Sinéad didn't find it funny.

"What are you talking about?"

"You spend all your money and time buying the best of everything – the car, the flat – but you never go out for as much a pint at Christmas with the work crowd. It just seems odd to me. Some of my best friends are the guys from the office."

Jesus, talk about having the olive branch whipped from your hand and being beaten over the head with it! "All right, I'll go in on Monday and ask all the girls out for dinner this weekend. Would that help?"

"Ah, look, it was just an observation. Sorry, maybe the gang in your office aren't as fun as the guys in mine."

"Richard, seriously, we are not going to get into a 'my office is better than yours' conversation again. I'm sick of that particular topic!"

"Here, I'd better go, Sinéad. I'll give you a call tomorrow evening. We'll talk then."

"I look forward to it."

"Don't be like that!"

"Don't lecture me about who I choose to drink with!"

"All right! Goodbye, I'll see you tomorrow," Richard laughed as he hung up.

"Bye."

Sinéad went to the fridge looking for something to eat for lunch. She was so excited about the car she'd had no breakfast. It was now well after four and she was starving. She opened the fridge and looked in: a pint of milk, half a bottle of wine, an out-of-date yogurt, an onion, some peppers and a tomato. She opened the press and found some rice, a box of Special K, three tins of beans and a can of tomato soup.

"*And when she got there the cupboard was bare,*" she said aloud as she looked at the press. "Ah! Soup!"

She loved tomato soup with lots of bread and butter, but lo and behold there was no bread in the flat. She opened her purse and counted her change. Three euro, and she had twenty-five euro in the bank, but that was to do her until next Friday when they got paid. Thank God Mum was making lunch tomorrow afternoon – and she might just grab a packet of biscuits and a litre of milk from the fridge before she left. She put her coat on and ran down to the shops for bread. Was this how it would be for the foreseeable future? No money and no food? God, was it a bit rash to have just gone for it and bought the car? But then again, you have to buy these things; you have to stretch yourself now and again. If she never took a chance she'd never have the flat or the job, or Richard for that matter. He was a drunken fumble one Wednesday night, and look at them now, almost a year later and still going strong. As she passed the car in her parking space she smiled at it.

You are so worth it all! she thought as she looked at its shiny silver wheels.

She also wondered about ringing Julie again and inviting herself over for dinner. After all, she had nothing to eat and no money to order anything in.

Again she tried Julie but there was no reply. She was beginning to get a bit worried. She rang Gavin's house to see if she was there. It all became clear when there was no reply in Gavin's either. Wherever they were, they were together, and no harm would come to Julie if Gavin was around. Sinéad liked Gavin. Yes, he was childish and a bit clingy for Sinéad's personal taste, but he really liked Julie and he was good to her.

She'd wait till Monday and give Julie a call then – wherever they were gone for the weekend, chances were they'd be back for work on Monday.

She turned on the heating and lay down on the couch, remote control in one hand, glass of wine in the other. This was becoming the drill on a Saturday night. Most of the time Richard sat at the end of the couch and Sinéad rested her feet on his lap as they watched a movie.

Sitting there alone tonight she wasn't so happy about the situation. She was bored. The promotion and the celebrations that never happened afterwards were making her wonder about her life. She stood up and went to the window. Pulling back the curtain she looked down at the bus stop across the road. A small group of people were standing there, waiting for the bus to whisk them off to the city. She watched them for a while, remembering how that very same bus stop was listed as an asset when she was buying the apartment. *Close to the city, on the 46A bus route.* She remembered her father pointing out the bus stop.

"Look at that, a bus stop right across the road," he'd said. "That'll be very handy for you."

"Dad, I have a car. I never use the bus."

"When you're going into town on a Saturday night, love, you'll need it then," he replied, looking into the hot press.

"Maybe," she nodded, looking into the open cupboard.

"It's handy to have it there, even if you rarely use it. It's a lifeline for your social life," he said, nodding sagely.

She had laughed at him and told him she never went into the city centre any more.

"Well, you just wait. You'll use that bus stop more than you think!" he told her.

She had never once used that bus stop.

While she was standing there, lost in the memory, the bus arrived. She watched the punters pay their fares and find seats. The bus pulled out and she watched it until in disappeared around the corner. She looked at the empty bus stop and felt a pang of loneliness so strong it stung in her chest.

The car, the job and the apartment were all fantastic, but were they worth the sacrifice? Standing at the window that night with no one to talk to or giggle with, she felt like Rapunzel locked in her tower, looking down at the world below. She had always presumed she had lots of friends. There was no end to the number of people she went to lunch with at work. The managers and supervisors from other departments, people she was at meetings with – they'd regularly all head for the canteen together. She and Richard went out all the time. She had people over for dinner; they drank wine and told all kinds of embarrassing stories. Who were all these friends? And where were they now that Richard was away for the weekend? She knew she'd met a lot of new people through Richard, but she hadn't noticed how much she relied on him for company, both him and his friends. She was realising she had a lot of acquaintances but, other than Julie and Richard, she had very few real friends.

She stepped back from the window and picked up her glass of wine. She was not getting melancholy tonight – she wasn't getting melancholy at all – it was no use. It just wasted tears and energy and it really achieved nothing. She opened the newspaper and looked at the TV listings. She had just got that Sky mini-dish installed. There had better be something worth watching.

The phone rang.

"Sinéad!"

"Hi, Julie, did you get my message?" Sinéad sat back in her chair, ready for a chat.

"No, I'm not at home," Julie sounded excited, in fact she sounded drunk. "Listen, I'm just giving the quickest call to tell you my news!"

"What news?"

"Are you sitting down?"

"Yeah, what's the news?"

"Gavin and I got engaged!" Julie practically exploded with excitement.

"You what? Oh my God, Julie, that's fantastic!" Sinéad was thrilled for her – she knew in her heart this was what Julie had always wanted. "Where are you? When did he ask you?"

"Last night! Down in Dromoland Castle – County Clare."

"Oh Julie, I'm thrilled for you, for both of you! Have you told your mother yet?"

"I rang her this morning. She was crying – she wanted us to come straight home so she could have a party!" Julie laughed. "You know my mum. She cries over everything!"

Sinéad knew Julie's mother of old. They hated each other. Julie and Sinéad both knew it but they never mentioned it. "Yeah, but her baby girl is getting married! What about Lynn – have you told her yet?" Sinéad picked her words carefully. As much as Sinéad hated Julie's mother, Julie hated her sister Lynn. Lynn was jealous of Julie's career and boyfriend. She was a nice-looking girl and only her bad attitude stood between herself and everything Julie had. Lynn was basically a lazy person. She wanted an easy job, then complained because it paid a pittance. She wanted to live in Glasnevin, but couldn't afford the house prices. She didn't want to live in an apartment; she wanted a garden. She didn't want to save though and as a result was still living in her mother's and complaining about Julie and her 'big job and her bigwig of a boyfriend'. The main bone of contention was that Lynn was thirty-three and single. Julie being only twenty-five and already getting married would not be taken well.

"She came on the phone, said 'Congratulations' and gave the phone back to Mum. She's such a wagon, couldn't be happy for me just once!" Julie sounded annoyed and Sinéad was sorry she'd brought it up.

"Forget about her – I'm thrilled for you, Jules. You found your Prince Charming and you bagged him. Well done, you!"

"I always said I would, none of this hanging around. Meet them, marry them, have babies, get a dog and make apple-pies for the rest of your life!" Julie smiled down the phone.

"Retire, have babies and make apple-pies? At twenty-five? I'm thrilled for you, Jules, I really am, but I won't be chasing you up the aisle, that's for sure!"

"I know, not your cup of tea, plenty of time for that malarkey! Right, Shinners?"

"Well, it's not on my agenda, but we're not discussing my agenda. Have you talked dates or any details yet?"

"Next year sometime, maybe around September or October. We haven't really discussed it in too much detail. I'll need you to be available for discussion and wedding-dress shopping!"

"I'd be hurt if I wasn't asked! Can't wait to get stuck in!"

"Thanks, Sinéad. Oh listen, I better let you get back to whatever you were up to. What were you up to?"

"Nothing, I'm just watching a bit of TV."

"Where's Richard?"

"In Kilkenny with Luke and the guys."

"Oh yeah, the stag. And you're all by yourself?"

"Yeah, I've just opened a bottle of wine and I'll be toasting your health in a few minutes as I watch something on Sky Movies," Sinéad replied, happy that it didn't sound the least bit sad to be home alone on Saturday night.

"You're drinking, alone in your flat on Saturday night?"

Now it sounded sad.

"You make me sound like a loser, Jules!" Sinéad smiled as her heart ached.

"Oh, I didn't mean it to sound like that – I just felt sorry for you! No, not sorry for you, you know what I mean!" Julie rushed over the words, trying to make it better.

"It's all right. I'm not the least bit lonely," Sinéad lied. "I'm just having a glass of wine to celebrate my promotion and the fact that I bought my new car today."

"Oh my God! That's fantastic news! The BMW? Is it gorgeous?"

"It's better than gorgeous, it's really expensive!" Sinéad laughed.

"Are you now my 'rich bitch of a friend'?"

"I most certainly am, although only on paper. Until my next pay cheque I have not got a brass farthing. I have to go over to Mum's to be fed tomorrow!"

"Oh that happens to me all the time, but I haven't a Beamer to show for it! Just a clapped-out Punto!"

"Well, now you have a rich fiancé to buy you a new car. Are you going to be calling yourself Julie Hurley, or Julie Fennel-Hurley?

"Will I hyphenate? Will I sit around practising my signature all day long?"

"Will you spell the hyphen?" Sinéad asked, taking a sip of her wine.

"I might – how do you spell hyphen?"

"H-Y-P-H-E-N, I think."

"I'll have to think about that. I'll get back to you on it."

They both laughed for a minute and fell into a comfortable silence.

"Wow, Jules, that is fantastic news," Sinéad smiled.

"Yeah, it is," Julie said absent-mindedly, looking at Gavin as he emerged from the bathroom, towel around his waist, muscular shoulders, dark hair tossed after he'd towel-dried it. "And your news is fantastic too! I'll give you a shout when I get home. I'd better go."

"Yeah, see you next week. Give my love to Gavin!" Sinéad hung up, her mood lifted until she remembered Julie's mother.

Frances Fennel was one of the rudest women alive. She had once accused Sinéad of being one of the stupidest and worst-mannered people that she'd ever met. To add insult to injury she had then taken Sinéad by the arm and run her down the path in front of a gang of their neighbours. Sinéad was mortified and furious. Julie had rushed up the road after Sinéad and apologised again and again. Sinéad accepted the apology but never set foot in the house again. The woman was clinically insane. She shouldn't have been allowed out alone.

Anyway, she was the one who'd started it all. It wasn't

Sinéad who had looked for help in locating a stupid book and then thrown the helper from the house.

The woman was mad and now Sinéad was going to have to spend a lot of time in her company. A thing she bloody well hated doing.

Sinéad would have to meet and greet her at the wedding. In fact, she'd have to meet and greet her at the engagement party, the hen night, the wedding shower and every other get-together they could think up before the actual wedding took place.

"Oh crap, that's just what I need. Frances fucking Fennel back in my life," she said aloud as she poured the last of the wine into her glass and began to flick stations again.

5

Sinéad sat in the church behind Julie's Aunt Una and her cousin Erica. She studied their hair-dos as she sat there. Erica had her hair in a fat French plait, with flowers worked through the plait itself. Sinéad could never do French plaits; she didn't have the coordination or the upper-arm strength. She looked at the flowers, white tiny roses, then at Erica's dress. It was bright pink, with lots of layers. Each layer was a different length and had a different cut. It gave the dress a floaty, airy feel to it. She looked lovely but to Sinéad's eye the plait was all wrong.

Sinéad had spoken to Mrs Fennel twice over the last three months, and had been in her company seven times. There had been hen nights, house parties, wedding showers and girly shopping expeditions. All of which the bride's mother and the bride's best friend had to attend and had to appear to be best of pals throughout. They smiled for cameras, hugged in front of other guests and generally gave winning performances at each get-together. Sinéad hoped no one could see the frozen smile or the stiff arm around Frances' shoulder. Just now outside the church they had posed for a photo together. Sinéad was hoping that was her duty done. They would never have to spend so much time in one another's company again and life could get back to normal.

"What time is it?" came a whisper from where Richard sat beside her.

"Half past one," she whispered back.

"I hope she's not too late. It's freezing in here."

"She'll be another few minutes I suppose. Anyway, it's the bride's prerogative to be late," Sinéad replied, stifling the urge to thump Richard. He was such a whiner lately.

"Look at that girl over there. I don't think she's wearing any knickers," Richard whispered.

"Where?" Sinéad looked around.

"Over there," Richard surreptitiously pointed at a skinny girl with a tight, low-cut dress and no VPL at all.

"Oh yeah. Ah though, she must have knickers on. It's the middle of winter – she'll freeze."

"Look at her outfit, Sinéad. I think knickers are the last things on her mind."

"How do you buy an outfit like that without at least wondering what kind of underwear to wear with it?"

"Sinéad, look at her! Really, do you think she cares about knickers?"

They both began to giggle.

"Seriously, she'll get a cold in her kidneys," Sinéad said, sounding exactly like her mother. "She'll be peeing all through the reception."

"I was always told sitting on cold surfaces with no underwear gave you piles," Richard whispered.

"Piles? Dear God, who told you that, and why had you no underwear on?"

"Not me! Vanessa was always being warned about it by my mother," Richard confirmed.

"Vanessa? Your sister wore no knickers?"

"I don't know, I just remember Mum giving her that advice a few times. Maybe it was to scare her into keeping them on!"

"That would work!" Sinéad laughed.

"Someone should tell that girl – pass her a note as you're going up for Communion!" Richard began to laugh and snorted. That made them both laugh harder. They doubled up, trying to laugh in silence. Every now and again Richard snorted.

"*Shh!*" Sinéad thumped him. "Stop doing that!"

"It's not my fault!"

Suddenly the organ warbled into action. Sinéad bit her lip to stop herself laughing. She could hear Richard breathing heavily beside her, but she was afraid to look at him. She could see him shuddering out of the corner of her eye. She looked around just as Julie's two sisters walked past them down the aisle.

A moment later Julie walked by on her father's arm. She looked like an angel, gliding down the aisle. Brown curls swept up in a pile on top of her head. White tulle and lace, with pale pink roses. She looked like an ideal drawing of a bride. Her face shone with happiness.

Sinéad stopped laughing as she watched her walk by.

She looked up at the altar. There was Gavin – a nervous smile, arms held out to take his bride in an embrace. They were in love; it was there for the whole world to see. Sinéad settled back as best you can on a church pew to listen as her best friend got married.

The priest was nice, but he seemed to like the sound of his own voice. He spoke about the sanctity of marriage, then about how lucky Gavin and Julie were to have found one another, then about how tough the years ahead might be and how they would always be blessed with loving friends and family. Sinéad could see Richard pulling up his sleeve casually and glancing at his watch. She looked to see what time it was. Two o'clock and they hadn't even begun the Mass yet. The priest was still rattling on about richer and poorer and sickness and health. Sinéad had by now zoned out completely. This priest was ruining the day. Sinéad hadn't wanted to daydream through her best friend's wedding, but what choice did she have? The priest would make have made the Pope yawn.

She made an effort to wake up. The priest was telling them that he was about to bind the two souls in front of him for the rest of their lives and perhaps all eternity. When they died they would be buried together – and what a wonderful thought – they would be there to greet each other on the other side! They would be raised together on the Last Day.

Now Sinéad really woke up. The Day of Judgement? Souls bound for all eternity? What if you married the wrong man? What if you married the man you *thought* was the man of your dreams only to meet the *actual* man of your dreams a few weeks later? Were you then bound for all eternity to the wrong man? Looking for all eternity at the better man across the road and wishing you'd waited another three months to tie the knot? According to this priest, not even death could untie you from the wrong man. She began to fidget in her seat. She glanced sidelong at Richard. Did his ears stick out? How come she'd never noticed that? And how many chins did he have anyway? Oblivious to the fact that he was being watched, Richard looked up from his leaflet and lost three chins. Sinéad breathed a sigh of relief but it was short-lived. He looked away from the altar, took a tissue from his pocket and wiped his nose. Sinéad knew she was being silly, but that one action turned her stomach. Why was she being so superficial? So he wiped his nose. At least he hadn't sniffed really loudly.

Richard realised he was being watched. He looked at her. "What?" he queried.

"Nothing." Sinéad looked back at the altar, glancing back only when she was sure he'd stopped looking at her.

Why was she being like this suddenly? Could it be anything to do with the thought of 'the rest of their lives and perhaps all eternity'?

Gavin and Julie honeymooned in New York, San Francisco and Las Vegas, spending four nights in each city. They had their photo taken at every tourist spot along the way and Julie bought silly souvenirs in every tacky shop they passed. She was every gift-shop's favourite customer. She bought snow-globes, T-shirts, pottery yellow cabs, tiny Golden Gate bridges and cable cars.

"They're tacky, Jules!" Gavin smiled as she picked up a large yellow cab.

"We'll never be on honeymoon again, and who knows when we'll be in New York again?" Julie told him as she made for the tills. "Anyway, I heard the yellow cabs are being phased out. I want to get one before they're all gone."

"That's the London cab you're thinking of," Gavin tutted, taking the ornament from her hand.

"Is it? I thought it was the yellow cab?"

"London." Gavin put the car back down and headed to the door. "Can we go now?"

Apart from the buying of souvenirs, they had a wonderful holiday. They spent far too much money, went to a Broadway show, ate in the best restaurants and drove for hours to get to the Grand Canyon. They took a helicopter flight across the Canyon. Julie pressed her nose to the window. Gavin sat still, gripping his seat until his knuckles were white. It was only when they were over the Canyon that he realised he hated heights.

6

Julie and Gavin had been married nine months to the day. Julie had been wondering for about a week now and today was the day. She didn't want to get her hopes up – after all they'd only been trying for three months, but this month she just felt different. She was excited, jumpy. In her heart she seemed to know something was new. For no reason at all last night she slept on her side instead of her stomach, wrapping her hands around her waist in a protective way. And she was sure she'd felt a little nauseous yesterday morning. She put the test on the back of the cistern and washed her face and hands. She brushed her teeth, silently praying there would be two lines. Her stomach was in knots as she turned to look at the test.

"If it's negative then you can get twisted tonight and start again next month," she told herself.

There were two lines.

She picked up the stick, then the packet and read the back. She knew it was a positive result, but just to be sure she checked it again. Her heart pounding, she raced down the stairs. Gavin would be home in an hour so she jumped in the car and went to the chemist. She bought another two tests, just to be sure.

They were positive too. Julie was pregnant. She sat on the side of the bath, shaking as she looked at the white sticks in her hand. She was having a baby. No going back now.

Gavin got home just after seven.

"Hello!" he shouted as he closed the hall door.

"Hi, Gav!" Julie called from the bathroom. She wasn't sure exactly how she was going to approach this with him. Blurt it out? Tell him over dinner? Wait until she saw the doctor?

Gavin came up the stairs and headed for the bedroom. Julie stayed in the bathroom, her heart and thoughts racing a mile a minute. He came back out a few minutes later; she could hear him stopping on the landing.

"Are you okay in there?" he called.

"Yeah, fine," she said.

"I'm going downstairs. When do you want to order the food?"

"I don't mind," she called, still sitting on the edge of the bath.

"You all right?" Gavin repeated.

Julie stood up and opened the door. Gavin was standing in the landing, his tall frame leaning on the banister, his face curious.

Julie stood at the bathroom door and held out the three white sticks. Gavin stepped forward, taking them from her.

"What are these?" he asked as he took them.

"Pregnancy tests," she smiled. "I'm pregnant."

Gavin looked at the tests for a second, then took her in his arms and hugged her.

"Fantastic, Jules!" he whispered as he hugged her.

From that moment on, everything in Julie's' life revolved around the baby. She made her doctor's appointments, rang the hospital and booked herself in with a consultant. She bought books and magazines, checked her dates and counted her weeks. Four weeks down, thirty-six to go. The baby would be due on the fifth of April. They had agreed to keep it a secret for the first three months.

"Anything could happen. Let's not get ahead of ourselves just yet," Gavin warned.

"I know, one in five pregnancies ends in a miscarriage," Julie chorused.

Gavin had been reading her books and had latched on to that particular piece of information. He kept telling Julie and then tipping wood. "It happens, so we need to be realistic about it."

"But you're being so pessimistic, Gavin. You have to believe things will be all right. You'll drive yourself mad otherwise," Julie complained.

"Yeah, but you have to just be aware of it."

"I am aware of it, but I really don't want to think about it all the time."

Finally the twelve weeks were over and it was time for the

first hospital appointment. Gavin took the afternoon off work and met Julie outside the hospital. After what seemed like hours Julie's name was called and they went into the doctor's office. They introduced themselves and the doctor asked Julie all about her medical history.

He took her blood pressure, checked her weight and felt her stomach.

"Well, Julie, you appear to be the perfect specimen of health," the doctor smiled as he turned on the ultrasound machine. "I just have to put this gel on your tummy – it'll be a bit cold – and then we'll have a look at your baby."

"Yippee!" Julie clapped. She was suddenly mortified. "Sorry – I'm a bit excited," she smiled as the doctor looked around at her.

"Well, you have every right to be," the doctor smiled, "and there is your baby."

He pointed at the screen.

Gavin and Julie leaned forward, but they couldn't make out any of it. The doctor took measurements and pointed at the heart, the head and the body.

They left the hospital, reassured that their baby was the perfect size and kicking around like Pelé in there.

They went straight around to the parents to tell them the news. First Julie's, then Gavin's, and it took a lot longer then they had anticipated.

There was wine to toast the baby, tears and hugging as the news sunk in and the scan photo was shown around. The date was memorised and discussed. Two hours after leaving the hospital they made it home. Julie sat down on the couch. It was half past seven when she got around to ringing Sinéad with the news.

"Surely that can wait till the morning, Jules? Why don't you have a bath and take an early night?" Gavin said as she took in the phone in her hand.

"I have to tell Sinéad. I've never kept anything from her for so long in my life! I have to tell her the news."

The phone rang, once, twice, three times. Julie was suddenly nervous, almost embarrassed to be telling her news. Why on earth was she embarrassed? She didn't know; she just felt it for some reason. The phone rang a fifth time. Where was she? Julie's nerve was just about to go when someone picked up.

"Hello?" Sinéad sounded breathless.

"Hi, Sinéad?"

"Hi, Julie. Sorry! I just ran for the phone!" Sinéad was breathing heavily down the phone. "I could hear it just as I was opening the door and my hands were full and then the key got stuck in the door and I was battling with that, and I dropped all my shopping in the hall, so I couldn't close the door anyway and you know how it is. The phone kept ringing and I was sure I'd miss it but I couldn't stop fiddling with the bloody key. Anyway, enough of all that – any news with you?"

"Yes, actually I do have some news," Julie grinned.

"I think I know what it is," Sinéad smiled.

"What? What do you think it is?"

"Well, if I'm wrong just say so, but I have a feeling you're pregnant, aren't you?"

"Yes! But how did you guess?"

"How did I guess? You found out in July, just before my birthday, didn't you?"

"Who told you that?" Julie looked over at Gavin, ready to kill him for spilling the beans.

"Oh come on! You suddenly stop drinking – completely! You're tired all the time, even though I know you went to bed at nine o'clock three nights in row last week! You have that happy glow and Gavin is constantly asking you how you're feeling!"

"My husband can ask me how I'm feeling without there being an ulterior motive!" said Julie.

"Not like this he doesn't. He's been doing some serious clucking lately."

"So you guessed and you never said a word?"

"Come on, I'm not that bad. I was waiting for the big announcement. Oh Julie! I could not be happier for you. Congratulations! When are you due?"

"April fifth."

"How have you been feeling? Oh, hang on, let me close the front door and then I want all the gory details!" Sinéad raced to the door and slammed it shut. "Right, I'm back. Tell me everything!"

Julie sat back on the couch, "Right, so I just had this feeling I was pregnant. Nothing I could put my finger on, just a weird feeling. So I bought a test on the way home from work. I was only a day late so I wasn't really sure if it would show anything."

Gavin listened in as he watched the television. My lord, women really do tell each other absolutely everything, he thought to himself.

7

Sinéad was delighted for Julie. But the thought of a baby right now! My God! There was no way that was happening to her. She was only twenty-seven, and life was far too good.

She was working hard but she loved it. Her life was a merry-go-round of meetings and projects. She had built up a trustworthy team. They worked hard and got the job done. They all worked well together. Yes, she still watched them like a hawk. She was still the first in and the last out most evenings but she was the boss. She was the top of the heap now and this December her bonus was going to be close to six thousand euro, after tax.

It meant that all those late nights, getting home from work just before the nine o'clock news and leaving the house in the morning just as the seven o'clock news was about to start had been worth it. It meant she could splurge six hundred euro on a new suit for the office and two pairs of shoes for 'after hours' as she liked to refer to her time at home.

She was off this weekend to have her hair styled and coloured, she was then getting her make-up done professionally, she was meeting Richard in the Westbury at seven and they were having dinner with Gavin and Julie at eight thirty. Julie was now five months pregnant and feeling great, so they could finally go out after dark without Julie falling asleep.

Sinéad had agreed to have a rich chestnut colour streaked through her blonde hair, and her natural hair colour softened to a honey blonde. She'd got her hair cut to her shoulders and they'd put rollers in to give it a little body. It really suited her naturally thick hair. She knew she looked good; she had caught the envious glances from the other women as she left the salon. She wore her new little black dress and her stalwart black coat. She had bought it three years ago, but because she was always careful not to buy clothes that would date too quickly and looked after her clothes well, the coat still looked brand new.

She walked into the reception and headed for the bar. Richard was sitting on a couch by the fire reading the paper. He looked up as she walked in and watched her walking over. He stood up as she approached and kissed her.

"Wow, you look . . ." he paused and took her in, "you look like a movie star!"

"Thanks!" she smiled. "That's always nice to hear!"

A lounge girl came over and they ordered drinks.

Richard couldn't take his eyes off Sinéad. "Your hair, what's new about it? It looks different."

"I had it done today – they put a little brown through it. It's nice, isn't it?" she replied.

"Yes, it certainly is."

Richard stared at her and suddenly Sinéad felt a little nervous. It was nothing he'd said or done, but Sinéad was getting the distinct impression Richard was getting broody. He hadn't asked her to marry him or even talked babies to her, but there was something in the air lately. He was edging towards it, she could just feel it. Yes, Richard was wonderful – she had long since got over the doubts she had suddenly had about him on Julie's wedding day. He was good-looking, funny, gainfully employed, all the things that would make him the perfect catch. He *was* the perfect catch, but it just so happened that Sinéad was not fishing at the moment. She was only twenty-seven and she was working on her career. She didn't want to get married just yet. Maybe she'd feel different in a few years, but until then she was happy as she was.

"Do you like my shoes?" she said, jumping in with conversation before Richard could speak.

He looked at the foot she had kicked up in front of them. He pretended to be interested in the shoes. "Very nice. Where did you get them?" He'd pose his question some other time, he thought as he listened to her chat about a pair of black high heels. Who cared if they were Prada? Anyhow, didn't Prada make handbags? Did they make shoes too?

Julie and Gavin arrived just after eight, all commotion and hugging. Julie was looking all rosy-cheeked and healthy. She was just five months pregnant and she was blooming, Richard thought. She was wearing a black shirt-dress with black knee-high boots. Her hair and make-up were pristine.

But all Sinéad could see was the weight she'd gained around her face and the spread in her hips already. Sinéad was secretly appalled, but she threw her arms around her friend and told her how well she looked.

"Sinéad, I'm huge!" Julie smiled.

"Don't be silly! You're pregnant!" Richard leaned in to hug her.

"I have months to go and I'm already up two dress sizes," Julie replied.

"Jesus, two sizes, how's that? Are you eating all round you?" Sinéad blurted, instantly regretting the comment.

"God, I'm trying really hard and I'm eating properly but I'm starving. All of the time! I wake up hungry, I eat all day and I go to bed hungry."

"Never mind, it'll be worth it in the end – a brand-new baby," Richard enthused as they finished up their drinks and headed for the restaurant.

They were seated in the window, given the menus and the waiter took their coats. Gavin watched as he disappeared around a corner carrying all the coats and scarves.

"Do you ever wonder what they do with the coats? Does anyone else kind of wonder if you'll ever see them again?"

"What do you mean 'what they do with the coats'?" Julie replied. "They put them on hangers and walk away."

"Do they go through the pockets? They've never seen us before, and we've just handed them a bundle of black coats – how do they know at the end of the meal which coats belong to which table?" Gavin looked around the table. Blank faces stared back at him. "Does no one else wonder about these things? Am I the only one?"

"Yes, you are," Julie tutted. "They don't go through your pockets. They probably have a section of rail for each table. They go back to that part of the rail at the end of the meal."

They studied the menu.

"So, Julie, have you had a scan yet?" Richard asked.

Sinéad looked at the wine menu.

"Yeah, I've had two. Everything is perfect," Julie grinned.

"Will you be finding out about the sex?" Richard asked.

"No, we thought we'd wait and see."

"There are so few true surprises in life, and this really is one," Gavin put in. "And your first baby, who cares if it's a boy or girl? It doesn't matter!"

"Have you a preference?" Richard put down his menu.

"Have you decided what you're having for starters?" Sinéad asked him.

"No, not really. I was too interested in Julie and the bump," Richard replied.

"I don't care. As long as it's healthy I really couldn't care less," Julie said.

"Me neither," said Richard. "Men are always saying they want a son, but I really wouldn't care. A baby is a baby – you'll love it either way."

"God, yeah!" Julie agreed enthusiastically.

"Gavin, do you have a preference?" asked Richard.

They all put their menus down and discussed the merits of boy versus girl.

Sinéad could feel her blood pressure rise. She really had no interest in whether the baby was a boy or a girl. As they said, once it's healthy who cares about what sex it is?

"Are we ready to order wine?" she asked, trying to catch the waiter's eye.

"Not for me," Julie groaned.

"Oh, poor you! How's the no-alcohol diet going?" Richard said.

"Not so bad, but nights like this you really miss a few glasses of wine with dinner. I don't want to even think about Christmas!"

"New Year will be tough too," Sinéad remarked, having ordered a bottle of red wine. "Lord knows you need to be legless to enjoy that night!"

"Thanks, Sinéad!" Julie laughed. "But after Christmas things are going to be moving really fast. January is always over in a heartbeat and then February is so short, then it's really only March and the 'baba' is here!"

"I always think January is so long," Sinéad said.

"Jesus, Sinéad! Talk about making her feel worse!" Richard laughed.

"Sorry! Sorry, Julie, I didn't mean to make it sound so bad. I just talk then think sometimes. Baba will be worth a hundred dry Christmases! And surely you can have a glass of wine with your Christmas dinner?"

"Yeah, but my heartburn is so bad these days, it's not even worth it. Anyway, I wouldn't like to chance it. I'd feel so guilty if anything went wrong and I was drinking."

"Nothing's going to go wrong, Julie," Sinéad smiled. "You're taking such good care of yourself. I'd be more worried that they couldn't give you an epidural if you have alcohol in your bloodstream. Imagine having to do a natural birth 'cos you had one glass of wine!" She began to laugh, but no one else found it as funny as she did.

Richard turned back to Julie. "Have you felt any kicks yet?"

"Yeah, just a few, but nothing you can feel from the outside yet."

"When you start to get big kicks, could I feel one? Would you mind?" Richard asked, his face lighting up.

"So, Sinéad, I think Old Dickie here has caught the bug," said Gavin smiling. "Will you be following Jules into the Rotunda, do you think?"

"Oh, not for a while yet!" Sinéad laughed, but she could feel her stomach flip and the colour drain from her face.

"Sinéad's too busy with work. But I'll get working on her!" Richard said.

"Are we ready to order, people?" Sinéad asked, trying to change the subject.

It was no use. They ordered dinner and went straight back to discussing what Julie could and couldn't eat. Sinéad listened, but really, was the baby all they were going to talk about until April?

8

Christmas came and went, Sinéad got thinner and Julie got bigger. Sinéad had found the South Beach diet and was following it to the letter. The weight was falling off her small frame, but she loved it. Julie was blooming all over – her face and legs swelled, her stomach was huge and the kicking was an all-day affair.

"This baby never stops dancing!" she laughed, holding Sinéad's hand over her stomach one morning. "It's constantly leaning on my pubic bone and toe-dancing on my bladder."

"While I do appreciate the descriptive prose, that's a little too much information for me there, Jules!"

"Sorry, but it is. And look," Julie held up a tag from a pair of trousers she was ironing. "I'm a size eighteen. Eighteen! I have another seven weeks to go and the last month you get really big. What am I going to do?"

"Nothing. You'll have the baby and then I'll give you this South Beach Diet book. You'll lose it all again, don't panic."

"I'll never lose this ass! Look at how big I am!"

"I would much rather not look at your ass, thanks," Sinéad smiled. "There are some things even a best friend shouldn't have to do!"

"So, enough about me. What's going on with you?" Julie said, putting down the trousers and starting to iron a large white shirt.

"What about me?"

"You and Richard. Is he still pricing wedding rings?"

"I have no idea. He's not so broody any more. He will actually allow us to discuss something other than your bump when we're alone, so that's a step in the right direction."

"Poor old you!" Julie laughed. "Are you still adamant about not getting married?"

"Yes, I am. Not yet, I really don't want to get married yet. I know you're really happy, but marriage and babies aren't for me. Not just yet anyway – I'm only twenty-seven! I'll marry him when I'm thirty-three or four! I swear to God I will."

"You'd marry him the morning of your thirty-fourth birthday if he'd just piss off till then?"

"In a way, yes. That's how I feel about it!" Sinéad laughed, but she knew it sounded cold. "Am I such a bad cow?"

"No, not really, but have you thought about saying yes and then having a long engagement?"

"No, I hadn't."

"Well, it might be just what you need." Julie shrugged, pulling a T-shirt out of the pile of ironing. "He'd be happy to know he's engaged and you'd be happy not to get married until you're heading for your mid-thirties!"

"That makes sense, in a calculating kind of way. It's not exactly romantic, is it?"

"Not everything in this life is," Julie replied, a resigned tone to her voice that Sinéad hadn't heard before.

"Are you all right?" Sinéad asked.

"Me? Of course, I am. I'm just dying to have this baby already. I feel like an elephant."

"If you were unhappy, you would tell me, wouldn't you?"

"If I was upset you'd be the first to know," Julie lied, although she didn't realise at that moment that she was lying.

It was Julie's due date. The date that she and everyone around her had been counting down to for the last forty weeks. All eyes were on her as the minutes ticked by. The calls came, a flurry of them around eleven that morning. Everyone wondering the same thing.

"Are there any twinges yet?"

"No, there aren't."

The sighs were heartfelt.

"Have you tried eating a spicy curry?"

"Yes, lots of them." None had worked.

"Washing the floor, on your hands and knees? Have you tried that?"

"Yes, but Gavin came home and the ensuing row was too awful to repeat."

"There's always sex – how about that? As a last resort."

"Not even if I begged. Gavin wouldn't hear of it."

"Any twinges while I've been on the phone?"

"Not a one, other than the up-chuck when sex was mentioned."

"Well, as soon as you have news, give me a call."

They all went away disappointed.

She sat up until midnight: no twinges, no water breaking, no 'shows' or anything else for that matter. Not even a hiccup. She lay flat on her back on the couch. Gavin flicked stations confirming that there was nothing on worth watching.

"So, I'm officially overdue. This baby will be late," Julie announced.

"Most babies are. Only about twenty per cent of babies come on the right day."

"I know. I know. But I wanted our baby to be one of that twenty per cent!"

"It might come tomorrow – a day or two is no big deal."

"Easy for you to say, you're not lugging around three extra stone in front of you."

"It'll all be over in a few days."

"But what if it's not? What if it goes on and on?" Julie tried to pull herself up to a sitting position, not an easy thing to do at nine months pregnant.

"It won't go on forever – in two weeks it'll all be over," Gavin smiled.

"Two weeks!" Julie was furious. "I'm not waiting another two bloody weeks. I'll do my nut. I may actually be a basket case if this goes on much bloody longer!"

"Come on. Let's go to bed," Gavin replied, turning off the TV. "You're just getting yourself all hot and bothered."

"Help me up," Julie reached up a hand and Gavin helped her to her feet.

They headed up the stairs. Julie first, Gavin following close behind.

"I know I've just invited you to bed, but I can assure you it is only to sleep. I will not be getting involved in any jiggery-pokery in order to get that baby moving," Gavin announced.

"If this baby has not vacated the premises by next weekend you no longer have a choice," Julie advised him as they rounded the top of the stairs and headed for the bedroom. "You're taking one for the team next Saturday night."

Julie headed for the bathroom and went to the loo before washing her teeth. She was standing at the mirror putting moisturiser on her face when she realised she was peeing slightly as she leaned forward.

"Oh dear God!" she said aloud. She could hardly believe such a thing had happened. She rushed to the toilet, but when she moved to walk water just gushed down. She had no control over it and very quickly realised this was not urine but something else. She was in such shock that it took a moment for her to register that it was her waters breaking. When she did finally realise it, she became a blubbering mess. She was excited and terrified at the same time. She wanted her mother, she wanted it to be all over and she wanted to remember every second of it all at the same time.

"Gavin!" she called, sitting down on the side of the bath. "Gavin, quick!"

Gavin came in, all ready with a tissue, so sure was he that she was screaming about a spider.

"Where is it?" he asked.

"No, Gav, my waters just broke!"

"Where?" Gavin looked at the floor and at the puddles around the room. "Did you walk around?"

"I ran over here from the sink. I got a fright!"

"All right, no worries. What did they tell you to do if this happened?"

"Go straight to the hospital."

"Well then, where's your stuff? Let's get going!"

"The bag is in the bedroom, under the window. But hang on, I have to change."

The drive to the hospital was fraught. They seemed to hit every red light between Griffith Avenue and Parnell Square. There was a lot of traffic on the road for such a late hour. The journey was not helped by Gavin asking if there were any pains every two seconds.

"Gavin, if I'm in bloody pain you'll be the first one I'll shout at."

"I'm just checking. We need to know so that you can tell the doctor."

"I'll tell the doctor not to allow you into the room if you carry on with this lark!"

Just as they rounded the bend from Gracepark Road to Richmond Road, a ring of pain burned Julie's abdomen. "Oh Christ!" she breathed.

"What, was it a contraction?"

"I hope so. If they get worse than that, I don't want to know."

The contractions came fast and hard. They burned her stomach and made her wince. They got to the hospital just before one and were seen immediately.

Julie was in agony – she gripped Gavin's hands as the nurse spoke to her. In her mind she kept repeating what the woman in the antenatal classes told them: "Each contraction is one less contraction." She was counting them: she'd had thirty-three so far. How many does the average woman have? She wondered about asking, but another pain gripped her and she gripped Gavin's hands hard again.

The nurse carried on talking. "That was a strong one," she said, looking at her print-out. "What do you think? Are they getting stronger or are they just the same?"

"Stronger!" was all Julie had time for before the thirty-fifth contraction began.

"I'll just do a quick internal and see how far along you are." The nurse sounded far too jolly, as if she was enjoying the fact that Julie was in pain.

Gavin immediately scuttled outside the curtain that had been pulled around the bed.

The nurse stuck her hand under the bed-sheets and then stared at the ceiling. Julie stared at the curtain. It looked like the curtains her grandmother had in her sitting room in the late seventies.

"You're only one centimetre dilated. It'll be another while yet," the nurse smiled. "I'll just ring the doctor and let him know you're here."

Julie lay back. This was it; this was labour. How odd. It was painful, no denying that, but it was a bit exciting. She

71

was about to have a baby. They'd all be shouting push and she'd be pushing and then there'd be a baby, and the baby would be washed and weighed and given to her to hold. They'd all congratulate her and wheel her off to be alone with the baba. Gavin would be so grateful to her, perhaps for the rest of his life. Her daydream was jolted by another contraction, just as Gavin nervously returned to his post beside her bed.

Some time later, a different nurse popped her head around the curtain.

"How long does this usually take?" Julie asked her.

"Is it your first?"

She nodded.

"It can take about eight to twelve hours. So get comfy," the nurse smiled.

Eventually the original nurse came back with Julie's chart. She glanced at Julie's face as a contraction began to subside, then looked at the monitor beside the bed.

"You've had a few big ones there. How are you feeling?"

"A little bit sick actually."

"That's quite normal, but I'm just looking at this print-out," the nurse showed Julie a graph that was printing out from below the monitor. "Each peak is a contraction. You've had six really big ones in the last five minutes. I think I might just have another quick look to see how things are going. Do you mind if I have a check?"

"Be my guest."

Julie was realising why women talk about dignity going out the window during childbirth. Julie's was just waving back as it headed for the door. It and Gavin.

The nurse's expression changed and Julie's heart began to race.

"What's wrong?" she asked, suddenly wanting to burst into tears.

"Nothing, you've just dilated five centimetres in about four minutes. You're six centimetres – we need to get you upstairs to the labour ward."

The nurse grabbed a wheelchair and asked one of the other nurses to call the labour ward and tell them they were on the way. She also told them to have an epidural ready – this was going to be quick.

Julie heard the quick part and honestly – if somewhat naively – thought she'd be back in her room holding a baby in her arms within the hour.

In reality it took about four more hours to get to ten centimetres. Gavin sat silent as a mouse beside her for the entire time. So much for rubbing her shoulders, wiping her brow or whispering encouragement in her ear. He just sat there, watching all the nurses and the student doctors fussing and checking around her. The only 'helpful' comment he made was when he saw the epidural needle. He folded his arms, let out a whistle and said: "Rather you than me, Jules."

"If you thank God for making you a man or some such crap, I'll castrate you with something blunt and rusty," Julie replied.

Not too surprisingly, Gavin shut up after that.

At five o'clock she was finally ten centimetres dilated and the midwife uttered the magic words.

"Now with the next contraction I want you to push hard. Three hard pushes."

In the middle of her first push the consultant walked in.

"Hello there, how are we getting along?" he asked and completely put Julie off.

He was brought up to speed by another midwife and then to Julie's surprise he stepped back, folded his arms and glanced at the clock above his head. It was a completely normal thing to do, but Julie had imagined he'd come in, sleeves pulled up and ready to help.

Another four pushes and Julie thought she was about to die, right there on the bed. She wished she'd worked out more often than she had – maybe it wouldn't be such a hard slog if she was more fit. If only she did aerobics like Sinéad, or ate less crap. Finally the midwife told her the head was crowning.

"Only crowning!" Julie blurted out. "It's not out yet?"

"No, but you're doing really well!" the consultant laughed.

"Oh shut up, what would you know? You've just got here. *And you're a fucking man!*" Julie shouted suddenly.

For the longest five seconds of Julie's life, you could hear a pin drop. The midwife's eyes were out on sticks while she tried without much success to keep from giggling. The consultant's face was a picture for a moment, but then he gathered himself together. He smiled and raised his hands in a gesture of surrender.

There was a sound of choking to Julie's left side. Gavin might just have fainted but Julie was too consumed in her own misery and mortification to even look around at him. Let him lie there. He wasn't being much help in any case. He hadn't counted to ten for each push or offered her a sip of water or anything. And now she'd gone and insulted the doctor. She had to fix that before she worried about Gavin.

"Oh my God!" said Julie. "I'm so sorry, I can't believe I just said that. I'm sorry!"

"It's all right. It's not the first time I've been shouted at," he smiled.

"Yeah but I'm really sorry."

"That's fine, Julie. Now let's keep moving on this, will we?" He returned to staring at her nether regions.

"All right."

"Give one more big push for me, Julie," the midwife put in.

Another three pushes and then she was told to pant. Julie clamped her mouth shut. She was not a performing monkey; she had been prodded, poked and threatened with an episiotomy. She had pushed till her heart was about to burst, but she drew the line at panting for the room.

One last push was all that was called for and the sound of crying filled the room. The consultant stepped forward and took the baby in his arms.

"Do you want to cut the cord, Gavin?" he asked.

Gavin shook his head, terror in his eyes. So the consultant took the scissors and cut the cord. The baby was taken off to the side where it was weighed and wiped clean.

Julie lay back on the bed, completely exhausted and overcome. Gavin sat back in his chair beside the bed. It was the first time Julie had actually looked at him since the pushing began. He was snow-white. Exhaustion and excitement mingled in his eyes.

"What is it?" Julie asked. "Is it a boy or a girl?"

Gavin eyes widened for a second. "I never looked. I was so shocked by all the hair."

"*What?*" Julie was suddenly aware of her bikini line. Her hand shot down to cover herself and it collided with the consultant's hand as he cleaned her up.

Their eyes met for a second and he smiled.

"The baby has a big head of black hair," he told her. "And you have a beautiful baby girl, born at seven fifty-two a.m. on Sunday the sixth of April."

"Can I see her?" Julie asked, suddenly overwhelmed by the pure happiness in the room. So this is why people decide to become gynaecologists, these little moments of happiness, every day of your working life. Nothing to do with looking up girls' skirts all day.

Two hours later Julie was sitting up in bed, showered and rested. Gavin was holding the sleeping baby. Julie sat there texting everyone in her phone book.

Introducing the one and only Annabel Jane Hurley.
Born 7.52 a.m., Sunday 6th April 2004.
Weighing 8lbs 4oz.
I am the greatest!!

The consultant came in to check on her as he was doing his rounds that morning. Just as he walked in the texts began to pile in, in reply to the good news. Julie ignored the beeping as she apologised again and again for shouting at him. He ignored the phone too and told her again and again that it was all right. Then he had a look at her chart and asked her how she felt. The beeping carried on. They both tried to ignore it and the fact that the phone was jumping around the locker as it beeped. Finally the phone buzzed itself to death by falling off the locker and crashing to the floor. The doctor bent over and picked it up.

"Christ, ten new messages. You'll get cramp in your thumb!" he commented as he handed the phone over.

9

Sinéad got the text when she turned on her phone on Sunday morning. She was lying in bed thinking about getting up when her phone buzzed. Her first thought was that it was Richard complaining at her again.

He'd gone home last night with a flea in his ear. Yet again he'd been banging on about the fact that they should get married.

"Oh Richard, for God's sake! I'm twenty-seven! I have no intention of getting tied down this early," she tutted at him.

"Getting engaged at twenty-seven isn't exactly unheard of. Look at Julie, she's twenty-six and she's married and having a baby. No one fainted when they announced that. You're not that young, you know!"

"I'm young enough! Richard – I do not want to get married. I'm really busy in work and I'm enjoying myself." She refilled their glasses of wine. "What's wrong with having a little fun while you're still young?"

"I just thought you might like to move up a level," he replied, taking the wine with a heavy heart.

"Move up a level? Like in PS2? On the Game of Life?" Sinéad laughed – she meant it to sound light-hearted but it came out as a snigger.

Richard looked her up and down. Sinéad saw him doing it and felt her hackles rise.

"You think this is all about you," Richard said. "How much you want things, how it affects your plans, your career, all about you. Has it never crossed your mind that I might have plans for the future too?"

"Yes. I've always assumed you had plans. I never realised your plans were so caught up in mine, Richard," Sinéad replied, her tone cold.

"We've been together for nearly three years, Sinéad! We practically live together, we do everything together. Of course, my plans are caught up in you! I love you, you selfish cow!"

"Well! When you put it like that, how could I refuse?"

"I will ask you once more, Sinéad. Do you plan to ever get married?"

"Yes." Sinéad took a mouthful of her wine. If he was going to play stupid games like this she'd just have to get drunk.

"When would you like to get married, in a perfect world, where everyone played your game?"

"When? When I'm heading for my mid-thirties. Next question."

"Do you see me in your future at all?"

"Yes, I see you in my future. You're waiting on the table

79

my handsome husband and I are sitting at in the year 2025!" Sinéad giggled.

"Sinéad, please, at least try to take this seriously. I'm thirty next March, and to be honest if you're only killing time then kill it with someone else. I'm sick of this game. I want to settle down, I want to have kids and just relax. If you don't want the same thing, then tell me."

Sinéad stopped for a moment. Richard was serious, very serious. Shit, this was not what she needed right now. She was not ready to settle down. Why was that so hard for everyone to comprehend? She was happy with Richard but why was he so eager to carve their names in stone? She looked at him, his face completely earnest. He was a nice guy but she didn't want to get married. Not to him, not to anyone. Every fibre of her being wanted to run away and hide.

"Richard, please, why do you keep pushing this? Can we not just leave things as they are?"

"I need to know."

"I don't want to marry anyone just yet."

Richard looked down, his face hurt. Sinéad was truly sorry for him. She loved him, she really did, but why couldn't he understand she was not ready to settle down?

"So that's a 'no' then," Richard sighed.

"It's a 'not yet'."

Sinéad didn't like how this conversation was shaping up. She could see Bridget Jones and her bottle of wine just waiting at the sidelines ready to welcome her back to 'Singledom'. She didn't much want to be single though. It was hard enough to meet someone these days, she worked long hours and anyway she really liked Richard. Yes, he annoyed her at times – he was always flicking stations while they watched TV and he was basically a lazy bastard at times, but he was *her* lazy bastard and she didn't want to lose him, not just yet. She had to think fast. He was liable to walk if she didn't say the right thing here.

"Listen to me, Richard. Listen to everything I have to say before flying off the handle." She was playing for time, unsure what exactly she was going to say next. "I'm not ready to get married just yet. That does not mean I will never want to get married. I will, of course I will. I want children and a husband and a dog and a family car and all that stuff, I do! But not just yet. I know you think twenty-seven is pushing old age, but I don't. I think I'm in my twenties and I'm working on my career and I'm having a lot of fun in the process. My plan has always been to marry when I'm in my thirties and have babies immediately, within a year or so. Have a baby or two and then go back to work. My job is really important to me – you have to understand that at this stage. You know me, my job comes first always. And as a result I have this apartment, my car, a healthy bank balance and all the perks we enjoy every day! Do you understand? Does it make any sense to you?"

Richard had been staring at her while she spoke. He made a move to interrupt a few times but kept quiet. Now it was his turn. "I hear what you're saying. I think you're making a huge mistake by saying that the job comes first – your job is just your way of making a living. That's what anyone's job is – all it does is pay the bills – remember that, Sinéad. They could fire you in the morning and then where would you be?"

"I'd be living off my savings for a while until I got another job. At least I have savings to live off."

"It's just money, Sinéad. You could go on the dole while you job-searched. Money would still be paid to your account each week."

"I don't think so," Sinéad smiled, her snobbery getting the better of her. "I would never go on the dole, thanks. I'd sooner move back in with my parents."

"You really do live up your own arse sometimes, Sinéad. It's not a matter of choice sometimes – you have to survive. I was on the dole for a while after college and there's no shame in it!" Richard replied, his heart speeding up. This was a subject close to his heart. He hated Sinéad's gold-card mentality. "Look, I can't talk to you at the moment. I have to go home."

"What? You're leaving?"

"Yes, we're getting nowhere here – we're just going around in circles and fighting about the bloody dole. It's ridiculous."

"I wasn't rowing about the dole! You were up on your high horse about that one!"

"Sinéad –" Richard stopped and looked at her. He wasn't sure what he should say next. He wanted desperately to wake her up to herself. To make her see that her bank balance was not the most important thing about her. "I'm going home."

"Oh fine, go home then," Sinéad said, filling her glass with the last of the wine. "Call a taxi then."

He did. The taxi arrived very quickly and he was gone.

Sinéad was left on her own again. This was not how she expected the night to pan out. Stupid Richard, why was he always looking to get married? Couldn't he see that they were happy as they were? He was always bringing up the whole marriage and babies thing. She turned on the TV and found that *Muriel's Wedding* had just started. She sat up and watched it, putting all thoughts of Richard to the back of her mind. She went to bed at 2.30 and slept soundly.

She woke just after ten and turned on her phone. She was expecting the usual text apology to be waiting for her. Richard was the Text King – why say it when you can text it? Her phone buzzed and she smiled. There it was. She looked at the phone and pressed 'read'. Julie's name came up; her heart skipped a beat. She sat up in the bed.

"Oh my God!" she said aloud.

When she read the message she couldn't believe it. Her best friend was a mammy! Tears sprang to her eyes. A baby girl! That was lovely. She set about texting back. She would give them an hour of two and then she'd give Julie a call. She had to get up and buy some baby presents and she should get something nice for Julie, then she'd ring the hospital and find out the visiting hours. She should really tell Richard as well. He'd be really annoyed to miss that news. She'd hop in the shower first. Then she'd call him.

10

Richard was over the moon to hear about the baby. He appeared to have forgotten that they had been arguing the night before and that suited Sinéad down to the ground. She really didn't need the hassle of opening that can of worms again. They decided to meet in town and head up to the hospital together. They waited until late to give the grandparents time to stare at the baby before they interrupted.

They got to the hospital at 7.30 and gave Julie's name at reception. They were directed to her room. On the way up in the lift Sinéad's heart was pounding for some reason. She couldn't understand quite why she was so nervous about seeing Julie, but she was.

"Some babies are really ugly when they're born. So if this one is, say nothing," Richard told her as they stood watching the floor numbers pass by.

"Richard, as if I would!" she replied.

"I'm just saying, babies can be very ugly and you sometimes open your mouth without thinking."

"I will not say the baby is ugly. I have a brain in my head. Anyway, Julie's gorgeous so why would her baby be ugly? Do you think Julie is ugly?"

"It's nothing to do with the parents. Babies sometimes look wizened and old for a few days," Richard said as they got out of the lift and headed for the private rooms.

"Okay, enough. I know some babies are ugly and if Annabel is one of them I won't mention it," Sinéad said, motioning that the conversation should now end. She was very aware they were talking quite loudly and they were fast approaching Room Number Five. "Not that she will be."

"She might."

"She won't. Now shut up!"

They knocked on the door and walked in.

The first thing that hit Sinéad was the smell of a dirty nappy.

Oh Christ! she thought to herself as she plastered a smile on her face.

Poor Julie was standing at the bed, a clean nappy in one hand, a ball of cotton wool in the other and baby poo on each of the fingers on her right hand. She looked confused and sickened. She turned around to them and smiled. Sinéad wondered how on earth they were going to be able to sit there for twenty minutes and say nice things about the screaming and pooing bundle on the bed.

"Let me see her!" Sinéad said in her best excited voice.

"Hi, you guys! Great! Can you just keep your hand on her while I wash my hands?" While Sinéad hesitated,

Richard rushed forward and put his hand gently on the baby's chest.

Julie ran for the bathroom and remerged a minute later all smiles and clean hands.

"Sorry, it really gets everywhere and I'm new at this! So here she is!" Julie put the new nappy on the baby and closed her sleep suit. She picked her up and held her out for them to inspect. Richard stepped forward, his head in Sinéad's way and big hands touching the baby. Sinéad found she was being left in the background but to be quite honest it didn't bother her too much. She just stood back and looked at the cards dotted around the room.

"I got you these little things for Annabel and just a little gift for you in here too," she said, putting her parcel down on the bedside locker. "They're only small and when things settle down you can tell me what you really need."

"Oh my God, she's the most beautiful baby I've ever seen, Julie!" Richard enthused.

"Where's Gavin?" Sinéad asked.

"He's walking his mother to her car. She left her car around by the park and she was nervous going back there. He'll be back in a minute."

"Why was she alone? Did his dad not come in too?" Sinéad asked, looking out the window at the bus stop across the road.

"He's in Sweden for a week, some work thing. He was on the phone this morning – I think he was actually crying when he found out he'd missed the birth. He expected me to go over the due date, he said," Julie said. "Here, Sinéad, don't you want to hold Annabel?"

Sinéad spun around from the window. She hadn't wanted to look like she wasn't interested.

"Oh, has Richard finished? I just didn't want to crowd you," she smiled, coming over to the bed. "Yes, of course, let me hold the baby!"

She sat down on a chair beside the bed, feeling nervous, and Julie handed over the tiny bundle. Sinéad kept a smile pasted on her face, doing her best to appear confident – she couldn't remember when she had last held a tiny baby or indeed if she ever had. Needless to say, Bernadette hadn't allowed anyone's germ-ridden hands to touch her babies. And, in any case, Sinéad had never felt any desire to.

The baby was heavier than Sinéad expected her to be and there was something really satisfying about holding her. She was just the right size – she fitted perfectly into the crook of your arm. Sinéad stared down at the baby; the baby opened her eyes and stared back. She was not an ugly baby, anything but. She was the most beautiful baby Sinéad had ever seen. Her blue eyes blinked lazily at Sinéad as they surveyed one another.

As Sinéad gradually relaxed, a wonderful sensation crept over her like a feeling of deep contentment. She was amazed to feel a strong surge of protectiveness towards the tiny helpless creature in her arms. Then Annabel yawned and spanned her fingers wide. They were really long thin fingers, with sharp little nails on each one. She smelled of talcum powder. And her lips, what a pout! Sinéad stared at her perfect mouth and chubby cheeks. She was so perfect, just a perfect tiny person. Sinéad was mesmerised by the small face that blinked up at her. There was something truly amazing about that face. It was extraordinary, as if they'd always known each other. She stared at the baby, oblivious to everyone else in the room.

Had she been wrong all along? Thinking she had no great interest in having a baby? Listing it away down her list of priorities, like a duty to be attended to as efficiently as possible so she could then get back to the real business of life – her work?

"I see you like each other," came Julie's voice.

Startled, Sinéad glanced up to see her friend smilingly gazing at her and Annabel. "I've never seen such a cutie, Julie! My God, she's wonderful!"

Gavin walked in, breathing heavily, complaining about having to run up three flights of stairs.

"You should have taken the lift, you eejit!" Julie laughed as she kissed him on the cheek.

He walked around the bed to Sinéad and looked down at the baby in her arms, grinning from ear to ear. The proud dad.

"Do you want to hold her?" Sinéad said, though she was reluctant to let her go.

Gavin nodded and held out his arms. Taking the baby, he walked around the room with her.

Sinéad still felt emotional. The depth of the feelings aroused as she held Annabel in her arms had taken her completely by surprise.

She watched Gavin and Richard as they looked at the baby. Then she looked at Julie as she sat proudly on the bed, beaming to herself.

She had to admit it: Richard had a point. A happy family life was more important than money. She couldn't see it yesterday but she could today.

She loved the independence her career gave her. She was not ready to give it up. But she would have to seriously rethink her priorities.

11

Three days after the birth Julie and Annabel were officially discharged. Julie couldn't wait to get out the doors. She was looking forward to the excitement of pink balloons and champagne waiting for her at the door when she got home. She couldn't wait to be at home with Annabel in her carrycot and all the family *ohhing* and *ahhing* over every little hiccup and sigh.

Instead of all these things, she got home to a pile of washing and a house that looked dusty and shabby from three days of Gavin living there alone and not wiping a single counter down. The carrycot was upstairs and all the dirty clothes she'd given him to bring home were piled on the landing. There was no champagne and the only balloons were the wilting helium ones that her sister had brought to the hospital on Sunday night. To add insult to very considerable disappointment there was no food in the fridge, not even a can of Diet Coke to quench her thirst. And suddenly she was very thirsty indeed. She looked around her; Gavin was holding the baby and jigging her up and down. Annabel was fast asleep but beginning to wake and her face was 'scrunching', Julie knew the signs: she was about to cry.

"Gavin, you'll wake her up and then she'll think it's feeding time."

"I just want to hold her. She's so gorgeous," Gavin smiled.

"I know. I just want to get her into some routine. I don't want to feed her till three, and it's only a quarter past one. Will you put her down?" Julie could hear the edge in her voice.

"I just wanted to hold her. She's my baby too!"

"Well, if she cries you deal with her."

Julie went up the stairs and sat in the bedroom. She looked around her; there was so much to do. What to do first? She looked at the baby's room, full of baby gifts and torn wrapping paper. She looked at the wash basket and it was overflowing. She heard the baby begin to cry downstairs and fought the urge to go down to her. She was Gavin's baby to sort out. He'd woken her up. She filled a basket of washing and went through some of the baby presents. It was clothes mostly, all for three to six months. They seemed huge. She found a dress for six to nine months in among the gifts. She held it up and gasped. Tiny little Annabel would some day fit into an outfit that size? She put away as much of the baby stuff that she could, but there was far too much and far too little storage space in the nursery. She did her best, then closed the door; she'd try to work on the rest tomorrow.

She picked up the wash basket and headed to the kitchen. She threw a few things in the washing machine and wiped down the counter tops. She put a few bits into the dishwasher and suddenly the kitchen looked like home again. She could still hear the baby crying and glanced into the sitting room.

Gavin was walking around with Annabel in his arms, jigging her now with an urgency that was missing earlier. Her tiny head was all red from the exertion of crying and her fists were flaying around in rage.

"Does she have a dirty nappy, do you think?" Julie asked.

"I don't know. She's just screaming here. What were you told to do if she cried?"

"Check her nappy, feed her or burp her. That's pretty much it. Do want me to take her?" Julie asked, knowing she shouldn't offer, but she wanted Gavin to go to the supermarket for her.

"That'd be great." Gavin handed her over without a second glance.

Julie took her and headed back up the stairs to change her. "Gavin, I need you to go to the supermarket for me," she shouted back downstairs.

"When?"

"Now."

"All right, what do you want?"

"Everything – there's nothing in the fridge. Why didn't you go while I was in the hospital?"

"I was in with you most of the time, and I was in work," Gavin called back, his tone defensive.

"Well, there's nothing in the fridge – can you just go now then?" Julie was irritated and her voice was sharp.

"Fine."

Gavin went to the shops and came back with five bags of groceries but nothing to eat for dinner and no baby stuff at all, not even a nappy. Julie bit her lip. She rubbed her itchy nose. At least he'd got a six-pack of Diet Coke. She sat down at the kitchen table and drank almost an entire can without stopping. She could hear Gavin going into the sitting room.

"Touch her and I'll knife you," she shouted. She kept her voice light, but she meant every word.

At three o'clock in the morning Julie was sitting at the bottom of the bed, Gavin snoring beside her, Annabel at her breast. Her head was heavy with sleep. It kept jerking awake from dreams. She opened her eyes – perhaps if she kept them open she wouldn't drift off like that. She looked down at the tiny baby in her arms. She was beautiful: her perfect face, her tiny nose, her hand so tiny, her fingers so long, her skin so soft. Julie was so overcome with love for this baby that tears sprang to her eyes. She smiled to herself as she wiped them away. She unlatched the baby and burped her, kissing her head and smelling the baby smell that seemed to cover everything in the house since Annabel came home.

"I love you, Annabel," she whispered into the baby's ear. "I'll love you even more when you start to sleep through the night!"

Annabel burped loudly and spat up some of her milk.

12

A few days after the hospital visit Richard and Sinéad went out for dinner. There was a bottle of champagne waiting for them at the table when they arrived. Sinéad saw it as they were being walked to the table and wondered what it was doing there. She thought about asking him but then left it. No doubt she'd find out sooner or later.

They sat down, the waiter said something to Richard and he nodded his head. The waiter opened the champagne and poured two glasses.

Richard picked up his glass and tilted it up towards her. "Cheers!" he smiled.

Sinéad took up her glass and gestured back at him. "Cheers!" she replied.

They both took a sip and then fell back into a silence.

She glanced at Richard now, as he sat equally silent across the table, sipping his champagne. What was *he* brooding on?

"Why are we drinking champagne?" she suddenly asked, to break the silence.

"Well, it's a funny thing . . ." Richard sat back and cleared his throat. "Remember we had that little chat last Saturday?"

Sinéad nodded.

"Well, don't worry, I heard what you said and I will not be opening that can of worms all over again. The fact is, I had planned to ask you to marry me that night. I thought we'd be going out tonight to celebrate the whole engagement thing. I had booked the table and the champagne a while ago. Then the 'chat' didn't go too well. I thought about cancelling the whole thing: you, me and the dinner! But then I thought again. I know you don't want to get married for a few years, and that's all right. I can wait. And then I thought: why not just celebrate *not* getting married? Let's set a trend, let's live together forever more and never get married! We can call each other our 'partner' and have one very over-indulged child just before you go into menopause. Perhaps wait until you're forty-three to start trying and surprise everyone when we announce you're pregnant! What do you think?"

Sinéad looked at him, astonished. He was joking, wasn't he? Winding her up? He was smiling but he sounded serious. "What are you going on about?"

"Well, you don't want to get married. You keep saying so. So let's never marry. Let's spend all our money on a really expensive house in Dublin 4 and buy the best of everything – new cars, expensive furniture and foreign holidays. What do you think?"

Sinéad felt utterly confused. "Richard, are you serious about all this? Waiting until we're in our mid-forties to have a baby? A house and expensive cars! Are you just trying to get at me 'cos I don't want to get married yet?"

"No! Not at all. I want to be with you, Sinéad. That's for granted. I would forego the wedding and put the babies on hold if you really want it, but I want to be sure you want me. There's no point in us sitting around here for the next five years and then having to start the whole process over again with someone else. What do you think?"

Sinéad sat back in her seat. She looked at Richard, appraising the situation. On the surface, it wasn't a bad offer. It sounded to her a bit like having your cake and eating it – not that she had any intention of waiting for near-retirement to have an Annabel! The truth was, she wasn't hugely into weddings anyway. She was not the type of girl who wrote her name with her boyfriend's surname. She didn't spend hours wondering what her wedding dress would look like or what colour she'd put her bridesmaids in. But was this a trick question? If she agreed to this, would he then turn the tables on her and claim she didn't really love him if she didn't want to marry him? And even if he meant it all at this moment, would he later be hurt that she was willing to live with him, have a child with him but never give up her independence by marrying him – 'taking everything he had to offer bar his name' so to speak?

She looked at Richard. Was he the type of person who needed to get married? He did love weddings. He was always first on the floor after the meal and last to leave the residents' bar – not that he was a drunk or anything like it – he just loved the atmosphere of a wedding!

Sinéad began to see the bigger picture. Maybe it was time to be a bit more flexible for Richard. Did he need to get married? Did he need the security of a wedding ring on his finger? It wasn't unheard of. Usually it was women who wanted above all else to get married, but in this relationship it was Richard who did.

"Well, Sinéad, what do you say? This isn't very flattering, you know – this huge hesitation on your part!"

She took a deep breath. "Richard, I hear what you're saying and I appreciate the fact that you're willing to change your plans and not get married just for me. I know you always planned to get married." She stopped, searching for words. She still wasn't quite sure what she wanted to say.

"I always assumed I'd get married, but that's all right," said Richard. "You're much more important to me than a day in front of the altar or even a child. I would love to marry you and have children with you, but having you with me through thick and thin for the rest of my life is far more important – on any conditions."

"All right, I know I want all the things you've just listed. The house, the car, the holidays and, believe it or not, the babies at some point! And, believe it or not, I don't want to wait until I'm menopausal to start thinking about having them. I know in your heart you really want to get married." She paused again, afraid to commit herself to anything, afraid whatever she proposed it might be the wrong move. "So let's get engaged, let's buy the house in

Dublin 4, probably gut it and rebuild it from the foundations up and get settled in. Then let's see where we are and think about babies and weddings. I'm twenty-seven now. Let's say that by the time I'm approaching thirty-three we look at things and decide if we're ready to marry and have children. If we're not, we wait a while. If we are, we get on with it. But we'll be together. We're not going to have to start from scratch with someone else in five years' time."

Richard looked at her. "Get engaged? With no real plan to get married for at least five years? That doesn't make any sense." His face darkened and he looked away from her.

Was she being selfish? Was she looking for things all her own way as usual? She honestly didn't think she was. But she might be wrong, yet again.

"Why get engaged if we have no real wish to ever get married, Sinéad?"

"We *will* plan to get married – we just won't set a date tonight! I thought the main thing was to confirm for ourselves that we're happy together, that we're committed to each other. I thought that was what you wanted!"

"I do, but I want to get engaged with a view to marriage within a few months."

"A few months? Are you nuts? No one gets engaged and is married within a few months! You have to book hotels, bands, churches and order dresses and everything. It's a huge undertaking!"

"That's true I suppose. I never really thought about how long it takes to organise these things."

"Then there are the church forms and that. They take a while too."

"All right, since you appear to have this all thought out, I bow to your superior knowledge!"

"Thank you very much, but there really is no need. It's just the fact of the matter – we'd need at least a year to sort out a wedding! A few months is just ridiculous!"

"OK, OK, I take your point – but we're getting off track here. You're not talking about needing a year, you're talking about needing *five or six* years!"

"So what, Richard? Did I dream it or did you not just propose that we never get married at all – that we just live together? Did you not just say that being with me forever is more important than a marriage cert or having a family? And now you're pouting because I *agreed* to commit to you *and* consider marriage in five years' time!"

"Sinéad, I –"

"Is that not a contradiction – big-time?"

"No, I –"

"Or were you just winding me up? Trying a bit of reverse psychology?"

Richard looked a little shamefaced at this.

"You were, weren't you?"

"No, no, not really – or not consciously – but –"

"Look – all I'm saying is let's wait a while. Let's get engaged, then give me a few years to get my career well off the ground. Then we might be the wedding of the year or we might have changed our minds completely. Either way we'll be together and hopefully have a very clear picture of how we want to the future to pan out."

Richard was silent for a while, eyes downcast, thinking. Then he looked in her eyes, smiled and took her hand. "I can't argue with that. We'll be together, and engaged. Yes, I'm happy with that."

Richard raised a toast to their future and Sinéad relaxed. They were engaged. She'd given Richard the commitment he'd been longing for and she was starting to come round to the idea of getting married. Perhaps this marriage thing wasn't quite the prison sentence she'd imagined. All in all this was a wonderful evening! She'd just got engaged and decided to buy a house – in Dublin 4 no less. The materialistic Sinéad was jumping for joy.

"And before you know it we'll be knee-deep in nappies and breast-feeding equipment!" grinned Richard.

The bottom fell out of Sinéad's dream lifestyle. "Breast-feeding? I hope to God you're joking? I have no intention of breast-feeding anyone!"

"Come on, Sinéad! It's the best thing you can do for a baby – everyone knows that!"

"The best thing you can do for a baby is take folic acid and never name it Shania or Heathcliff or something ridiculous like that. Especially if your surname is Brady or O'Reilly."

"You're not breast-feeding then?"

"Absolutely not."

Richard sat back, looking again as if he should rethink his entire life plan. "All right – I just assumed that every woman wants to breast-feed."

"No."

"But Julie did."

"Julie wanted a baby and a mortgage far too young if you ask me. Anyway, Julie is Julie, I'm me. I do not want to breast-feed our imaginary baby. If you're so concerned about it, *you* breast-feed it."

"Well, that's just ridiculous, Sinéad."

"This whole thing is ridiculous. In case you haven't noticed, we have no children, we have no immediate plans for any and so this conversation can safely be postponed for another year or two anyway."

"I suppose you're right," Richard shrugged. "Anyway, we're engaged and we're buying a house together. That's a result anyway."

"It surely is," Sinéad smiled. "But the real question here is this: when are you taking me out to buy me a huge diamond?"

"Anytime you like. How's about Saturday?"

"Now that's what I like to hear!"

13

At Annabel's six-week check-up she had put on two pounds and the doctor was delighted with her progress.

"Wonderful!" she smiled as she watched Julie dress the baby. "And how are you feeling?"

"Fine. I'm fine."

"You look tired. I know you have a brand-new baby in the house, but are you getting any sleep?"

"Some. I'm still feeding her myself, and she's waking up twice a night. But I'm doing my best to rest when I can." Julie was shocked to realise her voice was wavering.

"Is Gavin helping you enough?"

"He's doing a bit, but what can he do?"

"Everything barring breastfeeding," the doctor smiled. "Are you taking any vitamins?"

"In fits and starts. I have a jar in the press but I forget to take them."

"Well, will you try to take one every day for the next

fortnight and we'll talk again when she's in for her jabs at eight weeks?"

"Yeah. I think I'm just tired more than anything else," Julie smiled.

"That's allowed, but don't let Gavin away with too much. Teach him to use the washing machine and hoover."

"I will," Julie said as she walked out.

Julie walked home, pushing Annabel in her pram. It was all right, this motherhood thing. She was good at it, she seemed to have the knack and she was having a good time. Annabel was thriving and she was as cute as a button – Julie had seen women in the local shop pointing at her and smiling the other day. She got home just as Annabel began to stir. It was time for a feed so Julie sat down – at least it gave her time to sit and listen to the radio.

Three weeks later and Julie had done enough breast-feeding. She had only meant to feed Annabel for the first few weeks and then a few more but now she was almost ten weeks old and it was time Gavin got acquainted with the three a.m. feed. Yes, she was still waking up at three and then again at seven. Sinéad had bought her a book that promised to get your baby into a routine by day five or you could ring up the author and she'd come over to your house and train your baby personally. They were on Day One.

Annabel moved on to the bottle with no great upset at all. As long as the food was coming from somewhere she didn't seem to care. Gavin read the instruction on the tin of SMA and Julie measured out the formula. They sterilised everything in the kitchen, even the counter tops the bottles were never going to be anywhere near, 'just to be on the safe side'. 'Better safe than sorry' and 'If in doubt sterilise it' were becoming buzz words in the Hurley household.

The bottles were made and put in the fridge, the steriliser washed out and put back together, the kitchen swept and the counters wiped down. They both sat down at the table. Julie picked up the book and realised that Annabel should have been out of bed and playing on her kick-mat if she was to keep to her routine.

"Oh shit, Belle should be up and playing on her mat, but she's just gone to sleep fifteen minutes ago and she should have had two hours' sleep already according to this book." Julie read the relevant paragraph.

"Forget the book. Let sleeping babies lie is what I say."

"But she should be awake, otherwise she won't go down at seven – she won't be tired."

"She'll sleep. Just don't panic about it," Gavin reassured her. "I'm making a cup of tea. Do you want one?"

A week later and true to the book's word Annabel was sleeping and eating to a routine. She should have been playing, resting and dressing to one as well but Julie didn't have the heart to insist she play on her kick-mat when all the baby wanted to do was sit on Julie's knee and stare up at her. Anyway, Julie liked staring down at her too. It was a win/win situation and one Julie was not about to disrupt.

With the baby in a routine, the atmosphere around the house relaxed. Gavin and Julie knew that by eight o'clock most nights Annabel would be asleep and they would have a wonderful three hours to themselves before one of them would have to feed the baby while the other headed for bed. Then one night Gavin offered her a glass of wine when the baby was settled. A little while later he led her up to the bedroom and they resumed their marital relations. Twice.

14

Annabel was back with the doctor for her sixteen-week jab.

"Are you feeling any better now that she's sleeping through the night?" the doctor asked.

"Yes, I'm still tired, but I feel a lot better and Gavin has come on in leaps and bounds!"

"And how are you? The last time we spoke you were still waiting for your cycle to regulate – have things settled back to normal?"

"Yeah, perfect. Everything's back to clockwork, thanks," Julie smiled, always embarrassed to talk about these things, even to a doctor.

"Good. So, what contraception are you taking?"

"I was going to go back on the pill for a while."

"Will I prescribe you some?" The doctor started to type on her computer. "You know the drill: wait until your next period and then start."

"Thanks," Julie replied, taking the prescription.

Julie looked at the calendar: it was the tenth of September. She was racing to the clinic to have Annabel weighed and on her way back she was going to walk down to Tesco's. Something about the date struck her, and it was not the 9/11 thing – it was something else. She went down to the clinic and then to Tesco's. On her way home she remembered what it was she'd forgotten. Her period – she was three days late. She hoped her periods weren't going to become irregular now after she had given birth.

Three days later there was still nothing, and now she was feeling a little queasy.

"It's nothing," she told herself aloud. "You're only imagining it."

The next day she went out and bought a pregnancy test, just to put her mind at rest. It was going to be negative of course, but just to be sure she'd better test.

It was positive.

She sat on the side of the bath, just as she had the July before and stared at the two blue lines.

"Not what I expected to see," she said aloud.

She went to the kitchen and opened her diary. She looked back at August and saw that her last period was on the fifth. She was six weeks give or take a few days. She counted forward nine months. May? April? She wasn't sure. She'd just gone through the whole process and she still wasn't sure about it. She went to the bookshelf and took down her book. She went to open it but closed it again. What difference did it make when it was due? It was another baby before she'd even started this one on solids. She'd be nine months pregnant at Annabel's first birthday.

"Bloody hell, this is not what I wanted!" she whispered to herself. "Damn Gavin and his 'just once won't matter'!"

She watched the clock until Gavin came home. When he did she met him in the hall.

"Hi, you," he smiled as he shut the door. "Is Annabel awake?"

"Yeah, she's just about to go down. Could you look after her? I'm not feeling too good?"

"Sure. Are you all right?"

"I just feel a bit tired and worn out. I'm going to run a bath and get to bed early. Can you watch her tonight?"

"Course I can," Gavin said as he headed to the sitting room. "I love a bit of time with my girl."

Julie lay in the bath, her head spinning. What would she tell Gavin? How would he take it? What would happen? She knew what would happen: she'd get fat again and give birth again, this time with another small baby hanging from her shirt-tails as she did it. But this was a new baby, a new life and she should have been delighted. She always wanted a family, lots of children, a house full of laughter and noise. This baby was just as worthy of a celebration as Annabel had been. But dear God, why did it have to arrive so soon after Annabel? Could she not have enjoyed the first year without this added hassle? Added hassle? This baby was a hassle, was it? She chastised herself for the thought. No, this baby was a new person and she was just as much to blame as Gavin was. No – stop that, no one was to blame. It was an accident, one night of passion and this was the outcome. Nothing more. Weren't we all the outcome of one night's passion? From here on in, it was a fact, she was pregnant. It was not an accident, not a mistake, not a tragedy, just a fact and this baby was a part of the family. She would love this baby and never let it know she had cried when she found out it was on the way.

The following morning she got up before Gavin and made him breakfast.

"Sit down and have a slice of toast, Gav," she said when he walked into the kitchen.

"What are you doing up and dressed?" he asked.

"I want to go to town today, so I'm up early."

"That's the life, head off to town or out to the beach if you feel like it, while I'm out earning the mortgage!" Gavin smiled. This was an old line, repeated ad nauseam. He didn't mean a word of it and Julie knew it.

"I wanted to tell you something too," Julie sat down.

"Sounds ominous," Gavin stood at the door. "But make it quick, I'm really late."

"I did a test yesterday and I'm pregnant again," Julie blurted.

"Pregnant?" Gavin's eyes were wide. "But how?"

"Oh, I don't know, Gavin. How do you think?"

"But we hardly ever . . ." his voice trailed away. "Shit, Julie."

"'Shit, Julie'? Is that how you feel about the impending

birth of your second child?" Julie was annoyed by his reaction, ignoring the fact that she'd felt just the same way yesterday.

"No, I'm just surprised." He sat down, looking pale. "I thought you were on the Pill."

"I was waiting for my period to go on it," Julie sighed.

"Oh Christ, I can't think about this now, Jules." He stood up again and just as he was about to leave he said, "I can't believe this. Seriously, Jules, at this rate we could have a litter on our hands in five years."

With that he shut the door and headed for the office. He had been smiling at her when he said it but Julie was stung by the remark.

She sat at the table and cried.

Then she went to the bathroom and threw up. And so another pregnancy took hold. One in which Julie got very well acquainted with the toilet bowl.

15

The engagement announcement went out in *The Irish Times* two weeks later. Sinéad got the engagement ring of her dreams. Her sister-in-law was struck dumb with jealousy when she saw it. The girls in work stood around her desk just gaping at it. A large square-cut diamond in a high setting with four small diamonds on either side set into the band.

Julie was thrilled for her but understandably she was preoccupied with the new arrival.

"Sinéad, I am thrilled for you!" She grabbed Sinéad in a bear hug. "I knew you'd cave in sooner or later! It was Annabel, wasn't it? She made you go all gooey for a baby?"

Julie was joking but Sinéad's heart skipped a beat just the same.

"Look at the ring!" she said, holding out her hand.

"Talk about your rocks!" Julie took the ring and made a wish on it. "Well, best of luck to you, Sinéad. I hope you get everything you wish for!"

"Oh, I think we have it sussed," she smiled. "Did I tell you we were looking at a house in Ranelagh last weekend? Very expensive, but absolutely gorgeous. Red brick, bay windows, steps up to the front door. Big back garden, mature trees and parking in the front garden. We're putting in an offer so fingers and toes crossed!"

"Oh my God, how much?"

"They're looking for excess of nine hundred thousand, so we offered eight fifty. We'll be paying it off for the next fifty years, but so will everyone else! We'll all be flat broke together."

"Jesus, Sinéad, what kind of money does the bank pay you?" Julie felt a small stab of jealousy towards Sinéad for the first time in her life.

"A lot. They seem to think I'm worth holding on to, so they pay me well. Anyway, it's Richard who's made of money. He makes twice what I do and he doesn't work half as hard."

Sinéad looked at her ring under the spotlight in Julie's kitchen. The spotlights always made it sparkle.

Three weeks later the vendors got back to Sinéad and said they would accept eight eighty for the house, no lower. She rang Richard and they agreed that as it stood they had saved twenty grand; they really wanted the house so it was madness to hold off and lose the whole thing for such a small amount. They reminded themselves, when buying a house on the south side anything up to fifty grand was a small amount of money.

112

So, on the fifteenth of September, they signed on the dotted line and became the proud owners of a house in Ranelagh.

"Step one on Sinéad's plan to conquer the world!" Richard had laughed as he raised a toast to them that night.

"Now that that's all sorted out," said Sinéad, "we really have to start thinking about what work needs to be done to the place. The kitchen needs to be gutted and we should get it rewired. We'll go up to the house on Saturday and have a good look at what we need to do."

"Oh my God! Does it ever stop?" Richard sighed in good humour. "I thought we could just savour the moment for now. Enjoy the fact that we're officially homeowners before we start gutting and rebuilding the whole thing!"

"You forget I've been a homeowner for a few years already. I know you need to get these jobs started and the price agreed quick before there's another jump in the housing market and the prices all go up again!"

"Okay, let's get in there on Saturday and look around. See what really needs doing and get it started. After all, the quicker we get settled in, the quicker we can start thinking about weddings and babies."

"What!" Sinéad looked at him, stunned. "Richard, don't you remember our agreement? Please don't push things too fast there. We agreed to put off any such decision-making for the next few years!"

"I know. I know! Slip of the tongue!" He grinned at her and she relaxed a little.

But it was worrying. She'd thought they had an

agreement but now she suspected Richard had a secret plan to chip away at her opposition until it crumbled. God, since Julie got pregnant and definitely since Annabel was born, Richard had become very clucky. He kept slipping phrases like 'when we have kids' into the conversation – even 'Our children are going to do X,Y or Z'.

It was fine, she supposed – it was the average kind of talk for a man heading into his thirties. He was looking to the future with the same expectations as most men his age and in his circumstances.

She wished he weren't quite so obsessed about having children, though.

Because, besides her reluctance to give up her career and independence, there was a new worry nagging at Sinéad. Something she had never admitted to Richard. Or anyone else. Hardly even to herself . . .

And then it had surfaced in recent weeks, as if it had waited to emerge until she'd finally accepted the idea of marriage and children . . . this little memory . . . something that had been said to her many years ago, said almost in passing . . .

Her doctor had noted that her periods were irregular and quite heavy. She was in his surgery every few months, suffering from cramping and in some cases fever. She would often require a sick cert for a few days. The doctor had tried to put her on the Pill but it hadn't agreed with her so he took her off it again.

Then he had said something about her fertility. She was only nineteen at the time and she hadn't taken it too much to heart. Now it seemed as if the fear had just hidden itself away until it emerged all these years later to become a tiny but constant voice in her head.

"We really should get this investigated," the doctor had said. "It may, and I don't say this lightly or to scare a young girl, but this may affect your ability to have children in years to come. It should be investigated. It might be nothing but it's best to know for sure."

She had shrugged and told the doctor it was nothing to worry about. She was in college and was enjoying the social life. Babies and marriage were a million light-years away.

Had a million light-years passed by already?

Sinéad wasn't ready to face all of this just yet.

So she set a few obstacles instead.

She called to Julie a few weeks later. Inevitably the conversation turned to babies and this time Sinéad let it continue instead of rolling her eyes and demanding alcohol. She said nothing incriminating, nothing to make it sound like she was fishing. She just asked a few questions and listened intently to the answers.

"So, when did you decide it was time to have a baby?" she asked, watching Annabel, careful not to make eye contact with Julie.

"Oh God, I don't know. We decided before we got married that as soon as we were settled we'd talk about it. And then all of a sudden Annabel decided to surprise us."

"So you were trying?"

"Well, yeah, I suppose. But, God, I hate that saying, don't you? 'Trying for a baby' – it makes it sound like you're just constantly having sex, and then saying to each other, 'God, I hope it worked this time!'. It wasn't like that at all."

"But you weren't on the Pill when you got pregnant?" Sinéad looked up at Julie for a second, judging the expression. "I'm just interested. I never really got the full story at the time."

"We were thinking about it, so I came off the Pill and I was waiting for things to calm down, you know. Then a month later she was on the way."

"It took only a month? Well done, you!" Sinéad laughed.

"No, a little longer than that I'm sure, but not much," Julie replied. "Why all the questions? Are you thinking along those lines yourself?"

"God, no!" Sinéad smiled. "Not until I'm married and settled in my nice new house. Not for at least another two or three years."

"Well, whenever you decide, there are some great books out there and believe it or not the internet is great for information."

"Oh please! Books? I think I know the basics!"

"Just so you know – you never have to tell anyone you read them!"

"I think I'll be all right. Anyway, this is not something I have to worry about any time soon."

Sinéad left that evening feeling happier. Julie had been on the Pill for years and years and surely that messes with your hormones? Sinéad was never even on the Pill, she just had that diaphragm thing. Getting pregnant would be as easy as just not putting it in, no hormone problems or anything. Julie had had no problem having Annabel. It'd be fine.

Now that that was put to rest Sinéad applied herself to getting some real work done.

She opened the Golden Pages and looked up builders. She spent an hour ringing around each one. Most of them were dismissive until they heard it was a seventy-year-old house that needed to be gutted and rewired. They all got very excited as they heard Sinéad's plans for the house, pulling up carpets, sanding floorboards, plastering old walls and pulling out kitchens, bathrooms and bedrooms. They could see only too well that Sinéad was going all out on this house. And that money was only an afterthought.

16

"Sinéad! Thanks so much for agreeing to mind Annabel for me," Julie smiled as she opened the door.

"My absolute pleasure! Where is the baba?" Sinéad passed Julie in the hall and headed straight to the sitting room. "Is she in here?"

"Yeah, she's just there on her play-mat." Julie followed her in. "Now, I'll be about an hour. She's just been fed but there are bottles made up in the fridge, and there's stewed apple in there too. Give her a spoon or two if she's hungry."

"No problem. I'll sort her out. You should get going. You'll miss your appointment."

"See you! I'll be on the mobile if you need me."

"But I won't," Sinéad grinned and shut the door behind Julie.

Julie got into the car and drove off. She'd told Sinéad she was going to get a prescription renewed. It was the first time she'd ever deliberately lied to Sinéad and she felt guilty about it. Oh, it's just a white lie, she thought to herself. Sinéad doesn't know and doesn't care. It gives her more time to spend with Annabel and she loves that baby, there's no doubting that. But she still felt guilty about it.

The doctor called her name and Julie followed her into her office.

"What can I do for you today?" the doctor asked.

"I'm a bit embarrassed about this to tell you the truth," Julie began, her face flushing. "I'm pregnant again."

"Really?" the doctor eyes widened for a moment. "How old is Annabel?"

"She's almost five months old," Julie's cheeks burned.

"Would I be right in saying this wasn't planned?" The doctor had chosen her tone carefully.

"You would be exactly right."

"Well, basics first. Let's talk dates and then health care."

They went through all the details – last period, whether she was taking folic acid – and finally came the big question.

"How are you taking the news?"

"It's sinking in, I think. I've been getting morning sickness, so that helps to focus your mind."

"That'll do it. And what about Gavin? How has he taken the news?"

"He was surprised. It took a few days to get his head around it, but now he's got used to it." Julie looked at the height chart on the back of the door. "In fact, I don't really know how he feels. He doesn't say anything about it."

"Nothing?"

"No, he hasn't even asked me about our hospital appointments yet. Last time he was all set to ring the Rotunda himself, but this time . . ." She let her voice trail away. She didn't want to finish the sentence, she didn't like where it was going.

"Do you think he might need to come down and see me?" the doctor asked.

"What would that do?" asked Julie.

"Well, he needs to be there for you. This is going to be a physically exhausting pregnancy for you. Your body has just been pushed to its limits and hasn't had much time to recuperate. Now it's doing it all again. You need to look after yourself, and Gavin needs to share the responsibility here."

"Oh God, was this madness?" Julie asked, her eyes stinging suddenly as the reality hit her like a wave again.

"It was what it was. These things happen sometimes and we just have to work with it. Tell Gavin you've been to see me and that you need to take it very easy this time."

"Thank you."

"I take it you're going back to the same obstetrician this time round?"

"Yes, I suppose I am. I hadn't given it much thought."

"I'll write him a referral letter – he might want to see you earlier this time."

The doctor got to her feet and, taking her cue, Julie rose too.

"Will everything be all right?" she asked.

"I'm sure it will, but just to be on the safe side I'll send the referral off today."

The doctor gave her a reassuring smile – but Julie didn't see it. She was already out the door, her eyes filling with tears that she didn't want the whole surgery to witness.

When Julie got home she found Sinéad and Annabel watching *Dr Phil*. Sinéad was sitting on the floor and Annabel was sitting in her bouncer in front of the TV. Between them they had finished the last of the stewed apple and Sinéad was licking the spoon. Annabel was mesmerised by the television. Neither of them looked up when Julie walked in.

"Well, there goes any possibility that she'll ever go to college," Julie announced. "Sinéad, daytime chat shows? Did you drop your brain on the way over?"

"What did you say?" Sinéad said, her eyes still on the TV.

"I think I've made my point."

Julie walked through the room and into the kitchen. Sinéad stood up and followed her out.

"What's wrong?" she asked.

"Nothing, I'm fine," Julie replied, far too quickly as she began to make them tea.

"You didn't even say hello to the baby when you came in. Something is very definitely up."

"No, nothing's wrong," Julie said. She handed Sinéad a mug and caught her eye. Sinéad held her stare.

There was real concern in her eyes and Julie felt her will weaken.

"If I tell you something will you just listen and not pass judgement?"

"Has Gavin hit you?"

"No, of course not! What kind of person do you think he is?"

"Sorry, it just sounded like it was going that way. I'm sorry, I would have been completely stunned, and I would never have thought it of him or anything. Sorry, just go on."

They went into the sitting room. Annabel was still watching the television, *Dr Phil* had ended and there was some courtroom drama starting. Julie vaguely wondered about Annabel seeing anything graphic but it seemed a little over the top to change the station.

Sinéad sat forward. "Come on. What's wrong?"

"I'm pregnant again," Julie said, bluntly on purpose. She wanted to see the real reaction.

Sinéad started to laugh. "Jesus, Jules, there's no stopping you, is there?"

"You don't seem appalled. Are you not shocked?"

"What can I say? It's not for me to say anything."

"But you don't think I'm completely mad?"

"Oh, as a fucking hatter! But everyone does it, don't they?"

"Not usually five months after the last one!"

"Ah sure, what can you do about it?"

They both looked at Annabel who had stopped watching TV and was sucking her fingers, staring back at them. Julie stared at her for a long time, taking in the tiny hands and wisps of hair. The mass of hair she'd been born with had fallen out within days and now it was growing back much lighter. She was going to be someone's big sister very soon.

"Oh bloody hell, Sinéad, what am I letting myself in for?"

17

Six months later and things were very different. For starters, Sinéad and Richard were living on a building site. They'd had to sell Sinéad's apartment and then the new owners wanted to move in. How inconsiderate of them! They had to move out of the comfort of a fully furnished apartment and into a shell of a house. They had got a builder in to do all the work: pull up floors, plaster walls, gut the kitchen and rewire the entire house. It sounded like a clever thing to do, get it all done at once and have it all finished in no time. Just shows what they knew. Six months in and the house had just been rewired, the kitchen was outside on the road in a skip and the bathroom had a big hole in the wall. You could be seen using the toilet from halfway up the stairs. They had put a big sheet of cardboard up over the hole but it didn't help – builders would shout in and poke the cardboard to see if anyone was in the bathroom. Sinéad wouldn't go to the bathroom between eight and six while the builders were there. They were always very polite to her and they never actually poked the card if they thought she was the one in there, but after seeing one poor apprentice having a staple-gun shot through the hole at him while he was in the bathroom she decided it wasn't worth the chance. She hung out in her parents' house until the builders went home. Richard had no qualms about using the facilities and so stayed around to watch over things and help out if needed.

Finally, seven months after buying the house and five months after moving out of the apartment, their builders left. In fairness to them they left the house in very good condition. There was a new kitchen, bathroom and a downstairs toilet. They had painted all the walls and polished wooden floors. The kitchen and hall were tiled and there were new light fixtures all over the house.

Sinéad and Richard had bought some lovely new furniture: a heavy chandelier, a huge mirror for over the fireplace and a mahogany sideboard, all for the sitting room.

Sinéad bought a floral rug that almost covered the entire surface of the room – about a foot of varnished floor was visible around the edge. Richard had hated it at first when Sinéad brought it home. He complained loudly and often about it until it went down and he suddenly saw the full effect.

They got a huge couch and big wide fireside chairs, they hung a painting on the wall above the sideboard and placed a bowl of flowers in just the perfect position. The room was painted deep red and, with light that flooded in through the bay window, the room was bright and airy.

Sinéad sat on the couch and looked around her. This was her kind of house. She looked out the window. A Spar around the corner, a park up the road and the sound of children playing in a garden nearby. This was her kind of neighbourhood. This house was worth every penny and all those months of living in the bedroom afraid to go to the loo for fear of being seen by some random builder. As she stood at the window looking out, a truck pulled up outside the house and a delivery-man got out and knocked on her door.

"Richard Greene live here?"

"Yes."

"I have a delivery from DID Electric."

The man walked off and opened the back of the truck. Another guy jumped out and they began loading up their trolley again and again. Sinéad stood back and watched. A home cinema system, fridge, cooker, dishwasher, washing machine, dryer, microwave and mini stereo system were unceremoniously dumped in the middle of the kitchen and the men left. Sinéad stood looking at the huge boxes. She had been very excited when all the stuff was being delivered but now that it was here she could see there was no way she could move it or install any of this. She had to wait until Richard came home. And even though the kitchen was big, this amount of packaging and boxes made it tiny and crowded-looking.

She decided to shut the door and go back to the sitting room – it was clean and tidy in there. She made herself a mug of tea, laid a few biscuits on a plate and went back to the sitting room, ready to sit back and relax. She got comfy, put her feet up and balanced the tea on the arm of the couch. It was a thing she'd have shot Richard for doing. She sat back to read the paper. Sadly, it didn't take as long as she'd anticipated. There appeared to be no news at all that day, and so ten minutes later she was back to staring at the walls again.

She watched the end of *Oprah*, cursing herself for forgetting about it. It looked as if it had been a good one. The entire audience was sobbing and there was a woman telling everyone about her husband and how wonderful he was. It appeared he was shot after going to investigate a noise in the middle of the night. While Sinéad was very sympathetic to his wife, who in God's name goes out to the garden – for it was in the garden he confronted the two teenagers – to investigate a noise? Look out your window, put on a light, but never go to investigate! Anyway, this man had confronted the teenagers and told them to get out of the garden. One of them had pulled a gun and shot him at point-blank range, hitting him in the chest and stomach. Sinéad shuddered – if they get the stomach you're a goner. Everyone knew that. Perhaps if she ever met this woman, on second thoughts, she'd let the whole 'Why did you let him go to investigate the noise?' thing pass. She was sure the woman had asked herself the very same thing umpteen times in the last six months.

Oprah ended and Sinéad found herself again at a loose end.

She rang Julie.

"Are you around today?" she asked.

"Always. Why aren't you in work?"

"Holiday. Could I come round?"

"Please come! You can help with Annabel! She's a nightmare today."

"Great! I'll be over as soon as I can."

Sinéad felt very sorry for Julie. She had no real right to feel that way but she couldn't help it. Julie was happily married and Annabel was a doll of a child, but Sinéad couldn't help but notice that this was not the life Julie had thought she was getting when she married Gavin. Julie made no secret of the fact that this pregnancy was unplanned and that Annabel was a handful. It was plain to see that Julie was not getting the support she needed from Gavin – he was working all the time and Julie was having a hard time controlling and keeping up with Annabel. She was a year old now. She was just starting to walk by herself. She wanted to walk everywhere but needed to be carried too. She was a ton weight. The last time Sinéad picked her up she was shocked by the weight of her and Julie was lugging her up and down stairs, putting her in her tall chair, in her car seat, in shopping trollies and generally just carting her around all the time. No wonder Julie was so stressed. Now her back was beginning to give way and the last time they were out together Sinéad could see that she was in pain even though neither of them mentioned it.

When she got to Julie's she wasn't at all surprised by what she saw. The house was turned upside down. There were toys on every surface, all over the floor, on the couch and chairs. All the books from the bookshelf were on the floor, most of the framed photographs from the shelves in the sitting room were scattered around the floor in the hall, Julie's wedding photo and a photo of her grandmother were on the dining-room table, obviously rescued from small hands. The blind had been pulled down too far on one window and it was bent where it hit the windowsill. A bowl of Weetabix was overturned on the floor in the dining-room, alongside a half-finished bottle that was spilling out the last of its milk on the wooden floor. There were three glasses on the mantelpiece, a varying amount of water in each one, each there so long there was dust floating on the water. The washing machine was open and there were clothes thrown around the kitchen floor. That stupid Dinosaur Barney was on the DVD singing some inane song about the colour of a flower and somewhere in all of the mess there was a toy that kept shouting "Wiggle wiggle!". Sinéad was going to find it and break it before the day was out.

Julie was walking in circles, holding hands with Annabel, dodging the toys, bottles and pictures as they walked around the hall, kitchen and sitting room. She looked sick with exhaustion.

Sinéad looked around, grabbed a bucket that was lying on the ground and filled it with toys. She grabbed the bottle and the Weetabix and put them in the sink. She grabbed a cloth and cleaned the floor where the bowl and bottle had been. She picked up the books and photos and put them back on the shelves. She pushed the chairs back to where they should have been and pulled up the blind. Things were beginning to look a bit better around here. She took the glasses from the mantelpiece and put them in the sink too, then wiped down the counter tops. She threw all the clothes from the floor back in the washing machine and fished the phone back out when she realised it was in there among the clothes. She looked around: the place was a lot better – at least it looked clean now. There was still Liga or something mashed into the floor in the kitchen and more of the same in the dining room – but at least it was better.

She grabbed Annabel's other hand and carried on the circuit with her.

"Julie, sit yourself down, make a cup of tea and put your feet up. Does she have a nap at all?"

"She's only up twenty minutes. This is what happens when she wakes up. Everything gets flung around," Julie said as she flopped down on the couch. "Thank you so much – my back is killing me!"

"Is there anything you can do to make things easier for yourself?"

"Not really – things are as easy as they're going to get around here. Annabel is getting better at walking and any day now she'll walk by herself. I'm assured she won't want my hand so much then and she'll content herself with walking around the room by herself."

"Yeah but, Jules, you look so tired."

"It's just the way it goes when you're eight months pregnant – you ache and you're tired and sick of being pregnant. And poor old Annabel, she's only a baby. She's very good really, but she's hard work. She never stops going all day long – and this bloody walking! God help her, she's delighted now she's realised she can get around on two feet, but she never sits down any more. All she wants to do is walk and all I want to do is rest my back!"

Sinéad walked around in circles with Annabel, while Julie lay on the couch chatting to them as they passed each time and all the time Sinéad asked herself: did she really want this? Did she want to give up work for a year to walk around in circles with a small child? She had to admit she didn't think so. She looked down at Annabel. As cute as she was, this was the most boring pastime ever invented.

18

A month later Julie found herself experiencing déjà vu. The contractions began and the memories just came flooding back.

"How could I have forgotten about them?" she asked again and again.

"Are they awful?" Gavin sympathised while not taking his eyes from the road.

This time the baby had decided to arrive just as rush hour began on a Friday afternoon. And while the traffic appeared to be at a standstill, the baby was in rather a hurry to get started.

"I swear, I'll be ten centimetres dilated by the time we get there. I'll be having this baby in the carpark!"

"I'm going as quick as I can."

"Go down the bus lane – you have an excuse made in heaven!" Julie gripped the door handle as another contraction began. "Gavin, get a move on!"

They pulled in outside the hospital and Julie jumped

from the car. She was sent into the emergency room and seen by a very pretty midwife. Julie looked after her as she went to page the consultant, taking in her tiny waist and the way her uniform hung loose on her hips. She wondered if her own hips would ever be the same again? Would anything ever hang loosely from them again? Other than a child, that is.

The midwife came back, Julie's file in her hand. "The doctor's on his way. I'll just run this trace for another few minutes and the doctor can check you over when he comes in."

"Have you any children?" Julie asked, realising as she spoke that it was a very personal question to just blurt out like that.

"No, I'm only twenty-seven. I'm not even married, so no babies just yet."

"I'm only twenty-eight and this is my second one," Julie replied, feeling very young to be having a second child.

"Really? What did you have the last time?"

"A girl."

"How old is she?"

The nurse was friendly but Julie could see that this was just a professional interest. Their lives could not be further apart.

"She's a year old," Julie said.

"Wow, you'll have your hands full!" the nurse smiled as the doctor appeared around the curtain.

"Hi there, Julie. So, it's show time, is it?" He looked at the nurse and she handed over the file and flitted off.

The doctor looked at the chart, called after the nurse

and then disappeared around the curtain after her. Julie could hear them talking about something. She looked down at her stomach – the stretch-marks and the belly-button and then the monitor strapped across it. She lay there hooked up to the bed and watched other people walking in and out of the room. It was the emergency room so most of them moved at a quick pace, grabbing surgical gloves and patient files before disappearing behind screens. Their pace and the idle chat of the doctor and the nurse were in stark contrast, Julie thought. She was hooked to the monitor, lying in the bed unable to get up and leave now even if she wanted to. She felt it was very symbolic of her life. She was stuck: two children, a husband and a mortgage. She was only a year older than that pretty midwife yet she felt a hundred years older than her. She was just beginning to wonder if you could get postnatal depression while still being 'natal' when the doctor came back. He looked at the monitor and within ten minutes Julie was upstairs in the delivery suite, Gavin at her side, and the 'epidural man' was on his way.

Five hours later Julie was handed her baby daughter. She looked down at the tiny face, at the eyes blinking slowly. The baby yawned and Julie found herself involuntarily nodding approval and 'ohhing' at her. The baby looked up at Julie, her eyes skimming over her hair, eyes and chin before settling back to sleep.

"Any names chosen?" the doctor asked as he wrote up her chart.

"We hadn't really discussed it much. I think it was a toss-up between Emma and Anna." Julie looked at Gavin.

"Whichever one you want. You pick," he said.

In her head she knew he was being nice; it was just a kind gesture in acknowledgment of her hard work. They were very similar names – if he liked one, chances were he would like the other. But Julie couldn't help feeling this was another way in which Gavin was distancing himself from this baby. She felt very acutely during the pregnancy that Gavin was not as interested this time around. This was 'her baby', as if she'd tricked him into having her. She looked at the baby, so perfect, so pretty, just like a tiny blonde Annabel. She took a deep breath and sighed. It seemed to come from her toes and was so heartfelt that the doctor looked up.

"I think I'll call her Genevieve. Genevieve Kate Hurley," Julie announced.

"Genevieve?" Gavin and the doctor chorused together.

"I thought it was Emma or Anna. Where did Genevieve Kate come from?" Gavin asked.

"Well, I just looked at her and she looks like a Genevieve. I really like it." Julie looked down at the baby. "Hello there, Genevieve!"

"Genevieve Hurley, Genevieve, Eve, Vieve, Gene," Gavin played with the name for a while. "What's the shortened version?"

"There is no shortened version." Julie looked up at him, at his face frowning as he concentrated on the new name.

"Well, hand her over then," he announced. "Let me get my hands on Genevieve!"

He took the baby and held her for a very long time, staring down at her.

"I think she looks like me," he finally said. "Genevieve is the image of me."

19

At times throughout Julie's life she had looked at her mother and envied her. When they were young she used to get up when she felt like it, do the housework, light the fire and make the dinner. She'd be there in the house waiting for them when they got in from school and some days when the weather was good she'd meet them from school. They'd have ice creams and walk through the park on their way home. They got dinner from the chipper on a Friday night and her mother would go to town in the mornings while they were at school if she felt like it. Julie had wanted her mother's life. She didn't see the dull monotony of it at the time. Or the thanklessness of it. They complained when their uniforms weren't cleaned and ready each morning and they complained about the dinners that were waiting for them each evening. They fought among themselves and threw books and toys at one another. They drew on the wall beside the phone and didn't understand why their mother was angry with them when she found out. Now she understood what her mother was complaining about. How unrelenting the days were. Every day the same thing. The routine that everyone was talking about was useful but it was also painfully dull and when you were living your life ruled by someone else's sleeping and eating routine, you really felt so helpless and completely bored with your own life.

At times Julie had wondered about how busy she would actually be with two small babies. She had imagined things would be hectic but there was no preparing for just how hectic things were. Strangely, from the moment Genevieve came home from hospital the girls became synchronised in their crying habits. When one cried, the other joined in. Annabel was feeling put out about the new baby. She began to poke her on the top of the head, always finding the soft spot and poking hard. She would slap her in the face when they were in the supermarket trolley together. She was missing the full attention she used to get from Julie and was being bold for the first time ever. She would throw her toys at the baby and slap her on the head whenever the opportunity presented itself. Whenever Julie shouted at her to stop, Annabel would throw herself on the ground and bawl crying, even for the smallest admonishment. She threw tantrums on a regular basis.

Julie was exhausted and found her patience running very thin when it came to Annabel's moods. She kept having to remind herself that Annabel was still only a baby herself – she was barely fourteen months old and perhaps Julie was expecting too much to expect her to take a new baby in her stride. The sleep deprivation wasn't helping either and, even though this time around Julie knew it wasn't going to last forever, it was still very hard to get through it.

Gavin was back in work a week after Genevieve was born and it was all down to Julie again. Gavin would be up and gone by 7.30 each morning. Did he leave a slumbering Julie behind him? Dear God, no.

She woke up at 6.30 each morning with Gavin. She'd jump in the shower, throw down a cup of tea and be ready with the bottle just as Genevieve began to cry. She fed her and at half past seven Annabel would wake up, full of the joys of a full night's sleep. Once Annabel was awake the whole house was awake, she was just that type of person. She was loud and playful and full of talk, not that she had that many words – Mama, Baba and 'cat' were her only real words, but she was trying and as a result there was a constant babble coming from her general direction most of the time. It was a terrible thing to admit but Julie wished she'd just keep it down sometimes.

Genevieve slept for an hour between nine and ten. That gave Julie just enough time to bathe Annabel and get her dressed. She'd leave Annabel in her cot with a few toys while she dressed the baby and then it was time for Genevieve to have her bottle, while Annabel got a drink of juice to keep her quiet. Then Annabel got her lunch around midday and she was put up to bed for a nap. The baby would be put on her kick-mat and she'd dance wildly for an hour before tiring herself out and falling asleep where she lay. Julie knew she should move her to her cot but she never wanted to wake the beast upstairs. She'd usually leave the baby sleep on her mat with a blanket over her. While they were both asleep Julie had her lunch, tidied the kitchen, hung out washing, swept floors and caught up on anything else that needed doing around the house.

Around 2.30 they both woke up, drank a bottle and the whole thing started again. Julie began to take them out in the afternoon. They spent hours in the supermarket and walking around the shopping centre, Annabel slapping Genevieve as they walked aimlessly around the shops looking at clothes and trinkets Julie had no real intentions of buying.

Thankfully, in the early months, for the most part Genevieve was a quiet baby. She cried when she was hungry or tired but the rest of the time she was quiet. She didn't get the hang of feeding though and she ate very little – as a result she was still waking throughout the night long after Annabel had been sleeping through. She was over sixteen weeks old before she began to sleep through. By the time that happened Julie was like a zombie.

Genevieve began to 'coo' very early on, perhaps because Annabel never stopped talking in the house, but the cooing was getting progressively louder and now, when she woke at night, instead of looking for food she lay there and cooed to herself. That wasn't a problem in itself but it was very hard to get any rest with a constant 'coo' sound coming from the corner of the room, no matter how cute it sounded.

By the time she was four months old the gentle, quiet

baby was well gone. In her place was a baby who screamed when she didn't get her way and spat up her bottle. She'd been looking for food from thirteen weeks. At fifteen weeks Julie had given in and fed her some baby rice. She ate it hungrily and lost all interest in the bottle. Feeding times became a four-hourly battle. Genevieve shook her head from side to side, chewing on the teat and spitting up any milk she actually got into her mouth. Feeding went on for hours each time and Julie was at her wit's end. She found herself repeating "This too shall pass" in her head as she forced the bottle into the baby's mouth.

Then one morning it did. Genevieve took her bottle, then her breakfast. She drank her bottle at lunch-time and ate all of her puréed carrot. That was it: they had fought the good fight and come out the other end, Julie a little more ragged around the edges and Genevieve a little chubbier around hers. Once she got the hang of food and the delights of custard and stewed apple there was no stopping Genevieve. She ate for Ireland. Her face was caked in food, from her chin to her hairline. Turnip hung from her eyelashes and broccoli could be seen lodged in her ear as Julie bathed her at night.

One morning the alarm went at 6.30. Julie could hear the loud cooing from Genevieve in the other room and suddenly she couldn't move. She was too tired and the day ahead looked like an eternity. Gavin got up and began to get ready for work. She watched him from the bed, her head heavy with sleep.

He showered and came back into the room, the smell of shower gel and aftershave mingled.

"You should get up. She's already awake," he smiled at her as he took a shirt from the wardrobe.

Julie rolled on to her back, finding herself in a very comfortable position. "I know. I will."

Gavin went downstairs and Genevieve began to cry. Julie looked at the clock. It was seven. She had lain in bed instead of getting up and having her shower and breakfast, and now there was no time. She'd have her hands full until after midday. There'd be no time for a cup of tea until then – she'd be gasping with the thirst.

"Christ," she sighed.

She pulled on a tracksuit and went into the bedroom. Annabel was asleep, her nappied bum sticking up in the air as she slept on top of her covers. Genevieve was awake and waving her arms. As soon as she saw Julie her face lit up. She smiled up and Julie found herself on the brink of tears. That tiny face, those huge green eyes and the blonde hair already curling, how could you not jump from the bed with a song in your heart every single day? Knowing such a wonderful sight awaited you, how could you not be deliriously happy? She picked her up and carried her out of the room.

It was 7.05. For the next twelve hours the noise, confusion, joy and tears would be unstoppable, no matter how much Julie would dearly love it to stop.

That afternoon they were all up after their nap. Julie took a chance and put Genevieve out on her kick-mat, which she never usually did when Annabel was walking around.

Annabel was very sturdy on her feet at this stage but accidents happened and Julie would never take the chance. Today for some reason she did. Perhaps she hadn't thought about it. The baby was put lying on the floor on her kick-mat and seemed perfectly happy to kick like a small wild animal for a while. Everything was bliss until a song came on the radio and Annabel danced to it. She bounced up and down, throwing her head from side to side, but she was still not completely steady on her feet. Her nappy made the balance tricky and she hovered very close to the baby, like a very unsteady tree ready to fall on a small flower.

"Annabel, not so close to the baby!" Julie screeched.

Annabel got a fright, toppled, steadied herself and then fell to the other side, crashing to the floor with only her small arm to save the fall. The baby woke with a start and began to cry. Annabel heard the baby cry, thought she was in trouble and began to whimper. Then she realised her arm was sore and now Mammy was going over to the baby first and no one loved her at all. She began to howl, grabbing her arm and shivering. Genevieve heard the commotion and began to cry louder. The room was practically vibrating with the noise.

Julie sat with the baby in one arm, hugging Annabel with the other. "It's all right, honey. Mammy's not angry with you. Sorry I shouted at you. You just can't dance so close to baby Bella."

"Baba!" Annabel wailed.

"Baba is fine – I just got a fright – I was worried that's all." Julie hugged Annabel and it seemed to do the trick.

Annabel shuddered, her face stained from the tears. "Ow!" she said, showing Julie her arm.

They inspected the arm. It was a little red from the bump but nothing more serious. Julie kissed it. "All better," she smiled.

Things became quiet and Annabel played her games a safe distance from Genevieve that day.

Gavin came home from work at seven. Julie always had the girls fed and ready for bed by the time he got home. He needed to spend some time with them each night so he would come in and read them a bedtime story before putting them both to bed. Well, in theory this is what Gavin did.

In reality, when he came in, Annabel danced at his feet until he picked her up and put her on his shoulders. Genevieve would stare up, shaking with excitement as she watched them walk around the sitting room, almost tipping the ceiling as they walked. Gavin would put Annabel down and pick up Genevieve and walk from room to room making her look in each mirror they passed and then he'd blow on her tummy and make her squeal with laughter. Annabel would hear the commotion and come running, looking for the same performance on her tummy. Gavin would lay both girls on the couch and blow on both their tummies until they were hysterical with laughter and all thoughts of sleep were completely gone. He regularly got Annabel so hyped up and giddy that she actually threw up and Genevieve would get overtired and end up crying from sheer exhaustion.

It would often take more than an hour to settle them

and it got to the point that Julie would find her blood pressure rising at the sound of Gavin's key in the door at night. She complained to Sinéad that she would actually see the blurry lights whizzing in her eyes, just like she did when her blood pressure rose during her pregnancies, from the moment Gavin came into the room.

Sinéad thought it was funny. "The sight of your husband makes your blood pressure rise. Is that a good or a bad sign?"

"I would imagine it's very bad," Julie giggled.

"And you got these blurry lights in your eyes when you were pregnant? For the whole nine months?"

"No. Just towards the end, when my blood pressure rose."

Julie wondered if Sinéad was thinking about having a baby. She'd asked a few loaded questions recently. Julie wondered if it would be impolite to ask her about it. They had been best friends all their lives, but this was a very personal decision and Julie really didn't want to seem as if she was prying. She decided against it; when the time was right Sinéad would tell her if there was any news.

"Not that I should really care about what symptoms you get when you're preggers. I have no intentions of being that way for a very long time," Sinéad laughed, but her laughter sounded hollow and at that moment Julie knew.

Sinéad was thinking of babies, and maybe she wasn't as happy as she claimed to be.

20

Genevieve's first birthday was coming up. Things were beginning to look like Julie's life would get a little easier. They could finally pack away that damn steriliser for starters. Julie hated that machine. She was sick of her sisters-in-law laughing at her and telling her she 'didn't know she was born' whatever that was meant to mean, that they had never had electric sterilisers when they had their babies. They'd had to boil bottles in Milton fluid and fish them out of the boiling water with tongs. They also never had these new fangled Rock-a-Tots; they'd had to carry their children in their arms for the first year of their lives. They had none of these seats with buzzers or bells and lights. Their children had to learn to read if they wanted to entertain themselves.

She tried not to listen to them. If they were to be believed their children were born before the advent of electricity or the epidural. Although maybe they were –

both of Gavin's sisters were a lot older than he was and they both married ridiculously young. One of them was only twenty-one when she ran down the aisle. It was never discussed but from what Julie could make out she had run up the aisle eating dry crackers to stave off the morning sickness. Gavin was only ten at the time, and that coupled with the fact that he was a boy meant that he missed the entire row. This was a terrible nuisance as Julie would have dearly loved to have had the lowdown on that particular story.

Her sister-in-law was one of those really annoying people. She was always advising Julie on little cost-cutting ideas.

"Just a thought, you really don't need to buy the girls' winter coats in Arnotts. Dunnes have a beautiful range in their Children's Department. Now that you're all living on Gavin's wage, that is. I thought you might appreciate the tip."

Julie would smile, biting her lip as best she could.

Her sister-in-law was always the one who 'just happened to notice' when one of the girls had a dirty face or stuffed nose. As if none of her children ever buried their faces in the potted plants or caught a cold once in a while.

But actually the steriliser business had nothing to do with Gavin's sister and her irritating personality. Julie just hated it and everything it stood for. It stood as a reminder that she had a tiny baby, one that was defenceless, completely and utterly, who had no defence against the normal dirt and bacteria on the surfaces of the house, who couldn't yet take a chance with just normal dishwashing, who was too young and defenceless to even stomach ordinary milk. Then there was the monotony factor. Julie had to make up formula, then as time went on they progressed up the ladder of formulas, but it was formula just the same and the same rigmarole was involved. Standing in the kitchen, washing bottles, loading the steriliser and boiling the kettle. A little later you burned your hands on the plastic bottles as they came out fully sterile. You then dropped the fully sterile bottles all over the kitchen floor while the skin on your fingers actually stuck to the bottles. You then picked the bottles up from the floor, cursing as you put them back on the counter. You filled the now germ-laden bottles with boiling water, let it cool and measured the formula, scoop by scoop. In fact a lot of the 'bottle-making' shenanigans made a complete mockery of the whole sterilising procedure. The bottles would be carrying every possible type of germ by the time the baby actually put the teat in its mouth.

Julie had a neighbour, Ellen, who 'just loved making the bottles'. She said it gave her a sense of fulfilment; it was another job to tick off on her task list and when it was finished she didn't have to think about it again. Julie felt the opposite: it was a job that hung over her – the endless washing, measuring, shaking and knowing that it was a fruitless task – it would just be done all over again the following day, and the day after that and the day after that.

It was the monotony that got to Julie most of all and not just the monotony of the steriliser process. The girls needed routine. They got up at the same time each day, napped at the same time each day, ate at the same time, got hyped up by Gavin at the same time each day and went back to bed at the same time each day.

It was just so monotonous. She sometimes didn't know what day it was. What difference did it make to her anyway? Every day was the same. Christmas Day, birthdays, anniversaries, Easter, Halloween. Without fail, the babies were awake before seven each morning, got up and had breakfast, had baths and got dressed, had lunch at midday and went for a nap, woke up at two and had a drink and a rusk each at about three, had tea at five and bed with a bottle at seven. It was a great routine and it gave her and Gavin an evening together each night but, Christ, the monotony of it all! And the fact that it was three hundred and sixty-five days a year, twenty-four hours a day.

Like on Christmas Eve, they had opened a bottle of wine when the children went to bed. They couldn't go out, Santa was coming and all the people they knew were either busily awaiting his arrival or out from midday, drinking and singing in crowded bars in the city.

Julie and Gavin couldn't get too drunk because the children would be up at seven in the morning. The girls were just that bit too young to even 'get' the whole Santa thing yet. It didn't stop Santa coming down the chimney and leaving gifts, but it meant that when they all got up the next morning Gavin and Julie were the only ones who would be in any way excited about the arrival of the Man in the Big Red Suit.

At 8.30 the next morning, after breakfast and dressing, the family headed into the sitting room to see what was under the tree. While the girls' faces lit up when they found a cartload of gifts with their names on each one, they didn't completely understand why they were getting them.

Annabel kept tugging at Julie's leg and asking, "But why, Mammy?"

"It's Christmas, honey. Santa Claus brought them for you. You were a really good girl this year."

"But why?" Annabel shook her head as she walked away. She really didn't get this whole Christmas thing.

Genevieve neither understood nor cared. There were lots of new toys and lots of cardboard boxes. She didn't care where they came from or who delivered down the chimney – they were hers and she was going to spend the day in the largest box, the one that had a plastic window in the front. That window had shown off Annabel's newest doll. Now the window was covered in Genevieve's sticky finger-marks and wet patches from where she had licked the plastic from both inside and outside the box. Ten minutes later Gavin and Julie were entertained with the sight of the girls' fist-fighting over the box. It may have been the first ever fistfight between the two. It was a dirty fight and there was no real winner. The box was ripped during the seventeenth round, a particularly vicious one where Genevieve bit Annabel and Annabel pulled a clump of Genevieve's hair out by the roots. At that point Gavin intervened and box was thrown away.

Early in the New Year Julie got her brother Paul to look

after the girls for the night while she and Gavin went out for a meal together. She asked Paul to stay the night so that they could stay out late. She had also meant for him to get up and give the girls breakfast the next morning, giving her and Gavin a lie-in.

Paul had been only too delighted to oblige when he heard there was a bed for the night. Julie could hardly believe her luck. He'd even told her to put away her purse, that he'd look after the girls for free. In hindsight she should have guessed that there was something in it for Paul. When he showed up that evening with a new girlfriend and both of them were carrying an overnight bag, Julie realised just what was in it for him. She tried to ignore the bags, telling herself that Paul was now twenty-three and entitled to have a girlfriend if he wanted. Still, when she looked at him he still only looked seven years old to her. And this new girlfriend looked like a six-year-old wearing her mother's clothes and make-up. They looked too young to be left in charge of themselves, never mind two small girls as well. Having said that, Julie was determined to go out and so left the children looking after each other.

Gavin and Julie had a wonderful night and stayed out until after three. They came home, drunk and giddy. They looked in at the girls and chatted far too loudly to each other about how wonderful they were. They woke Genevieve up with all the gushing. She cried for a few minutes before they managed to settle her back down. It seemed the mixture of their drunken good humour and their grinning faces was too much for a tiny girl at four in the morning. After tucking her in and kissing Annabel, they headed for bed.

Julie had only shut her eyes when the alarm went off. It was seven, she could hear the girls in their room laughing and playing, but as she listened the laughter turned to tears and calls for Mammy and breakfast. Julie lay there wondering if there was any chance of the girls going back to sleep. As she lay there she heard the unmistakable sounds from the spare bedroom. Paul and his new girlfriend were getting better acquainted. She lay there for another few minutes until the sound from the spare room was too much for her. He was her brother after all. With a very heavy heart and a splitting headache she got up and brought the girls down for breakfast. At nine Gavin got up and Julie passed him on the stairs as she went back to bed. As she lay there trying to get back to sleep, praying she could sleep through the rest of her hangover, she realised again that this was not the life she'd signed up for, when four years ago Gavin had proposed to her in Dromoland Castle. She wondered if Gavin felt the same way. Tears stung her eyes suddenly. She wasn't even thirty yet. Surely that was too young to be so disillusioned with her life? She wondered what would become of her. Was this her life? Was this it?

She got up just after eleven. Her body ached the way it does when you're very tired and hung over, but the headache was gone. She felt better for the sleep and she knew the girls would be going down for a nap soon. She had a shower and went downstairs. There they were, playing in the sitting room, all the same faces, doing all the same things. She looked around her and longed for some excitement. Something out of the ordinary, a break from the routine. She wished for a day when she could just head off to the cinema or get a DVD and sit on the couch, drink a bottle of wine and eat chocolate till her stomach was sick. But she couldn't; she had to keep an eye on the clock: it was time for a bottle, it was time to change a nappy, to put them down for a nap, to pick them up and kiss cut knees, to bandage cut knees, to have lunch, to have tea, to bathe them, to put them to bed – on and on it went. She was in charge of two tiny people's days. Their lives, their experiences, what they saw, what they did and where they went was all up to her every single day. No wonder she felt overwhelmed most of the time.

On a stressful day she found herself looking at the clock around four and counting down the hours until they went to bed. She was glad to see the back of them both some days, days when they had played tag team on her only surviving nerve, screeching and shouting, in good and bad spirits all day. Then of course there were the days they all sat on the floor in the sitting room, surrounded by toys, and they all played together for hours. She showed the girls how to press the buttons and push the shapes through the different holes. She loved to sit with them and watch their faces as they worked out something new, the unabashed delight when a square went through the square hole. Genevieve would smile, look up at Julie and bat her eyes when something went right. She would exude quiet satisfaction; she looked somewhat smug, if a baby could be described as smug.

Annabel on the other hand was a whole different story. She would screech, clap her hands and do a victory dance when the toy had succumbed to her greater powers. She would sometimes take the toy and fling it on the floor as proof that it was defeated. There was never a dull moment when things were going well for them.

As Genevieve's birthday approached, Julie could feel some of the tension fading away from her shoulders. The girls were no longer babies, they were toddlers. They could be reasoned with up to a point. Julie could tell them not to touch something and sometimes they didn't touch it. She was beginning to see light at the end of the tunnel and it made her think about going back to work. She was still friends with the manager and he was always complaining that Gavin had taken the best chef in Dublin and made her a housewife.

She approached the subject one night, about a week after Genevieve's birthday. Gavin was reading the paper and Julie was watching TV.

"Gav, can I ask you something?"

"Mmm."

"What would you think if I said I was considering going back to work?" She watched the paper as she spoke.

"What? Why?" Gavin lowered the paper.

"I never intended to leave work for good. I just meant to take maternity leave."

"We don't need you to go back to work. We're doing fine as we are. Think about it, Jules. We'd have to get a childminder, or a place in a crèche for them – that'd be ridiculous money."

"We might not — my mother could take them. It's not so much about the money anyway. I just think I'd like to get out of the house for a while. Talk to some adults for a while."

"If you really want to, we'll look into it then," Gavin replied getting back to the paper.

"No, Gav, 'we' will not look into it!" Julie suddenly exploded. "*I* will look into it and *I* will decide if it's something I want to do. I put my career on hold for two years. I never said I'd give up work. That was never the deal."

"Okay, okay — no need to overreact. I said okay if you really want to."

But Julie was furious. What gave Gavin the right to be such a chauvinist? He was the one who was outnumbered in this house, three to one.

21

Well, the inevitable happened. Richard's younger sister Vanessa got engaged, then got married and eleven months later gave birth to a huge baby boy. He tipped the scales at a whopping 11lbs 3oz. They got inundated with names from friends and family. Some memorable ones were Buster, Big Boy, Tyson and John Charles Bobby – no one understood that one until it was explained: JCB.

A day or two later and Vanessa wasn't laughing any more. Her stitches were killing her but, more to the point, he was her baby and, monster or not, she loved him and was going to defend him to the ends of the earth.

"His name is Liam," she announced.

The following evening, at Richard's parents' house, the subject of baby names was high on the agenda.

"Liam? Is Liam not a bit, well, sort of . . . ordinary?" Richard said.

His mother was fuming. This was her first grandchild and she was going to enjoy him no matter what they were calling him. "Give it a rest, you! She can call the baby whatever she likes."

"But 'Liam'? Mum, that's a crap name."

"I know that, but she likes it."

"So you think it's a shit name too? And you're not saying anything?"

"Your aunt Christine hated the name Richard but I didn't care. And I'll say to you what I said to her."

"'Shut up, you bitch'?"

"No, I said when she had a baby of her own she could call it whatever she liked. But I was calling my baby what *I* liked. So, Richard, when you decide to have children you can call them any name you like. We'll say nothing at all."

Sinéad, who has been watching the exchange with an amused grin, suddenly froze. The look on Richard's face was unmistakable. The 'Baby' topic would be back on the table tonight and she was running out of excuses about why they should wait a while longer to get married and have children. The net was tightening.

Eleven months earlier things had got tough between them. Genevieve had been born late at night, just before they were heading to bed. Richard had sat up talking about his plans for children. It turned out he was thinking three was a good family size, with two to three years between each one. He figured that they should really think about having all the children before Sinéad was thirty-seven or so. He didn't want to leave it too late and get into that whole issue of Down Syndrome and stuff like that. If they were destined to have a sick or disabled child then so be it, but he wasn't going to 'court disaster' as he put it. They should have the children while Sinéad was in her early to mid-thirties.

Sinéad was irritated that a lot of the conversation was 'about her' and not necessarily 'to her'. Richard was discussing her and her age and the fact that they should have children before 'she' got too old. There was no mention of Richard being older than her. She argued the point for a while but it was futile. Richard was speaking the truth: it was better to have children earlier. There was no denying it and there was no denying that her age was a bigger factor that his age was. She was only twenty-nine though and time was still very much on her side. They sat up for an hour talking it over and that night Sinéad had dodged the bullet. They turned out the lights and went to sleep, no closer to setting a date and no closer to having that elusive baby that Richard was dying for.

To her surprise Richard didn't say a word about babies or weddings after they left his mother's house. Sinéad had been expecting it and was ready for the row that would no doubt ensue. But it never came. He never said a word. They just went home, she made curry for dinner and they sat in the sitting room watching TV until midnight. There was no unspoken tension in the room. There was nothing.

The following day they went to work and when Sinéad rang Richard in the afternoon they chatted happily until Richard had to go to a meeting.

By Wednesday Sinéad had all but forgotten the baby issue. She was thinking about other things, like whether or not to book some time off next month for Richard's birthday and what exactly he wanted to do this year.

That was why it such a shock when Richard came home on Thursday night and told her what was going to happen. He didn't ask, he told her.

"Right, we've pussyfooted around this thing for too long now."

"What thing?"

"This wedding, the babies, our future."

Sinéad stomach lurched. "But we have an agreement. We decided to wait for a few years and *then* decide if we want to marry or just go on living together. Don't you remember? You promised!"

"Forget all that. I know what we decided. I thought I could go along with that but I can't. I think we know by now we want to be together, have children together, and it doesn't make sense to wait. So this is what's going to happen: we're getting married next year. Anytime you like between January and December. You pick a date and then do whatever it is you girls like to do. Book hotels, bands, flowers and dresses. Whatever. But we need to set a date and we need to get married. I want to move on here. I want to have children and pick baby names. And this has been going on too long for me."

"Well, this is all a bit sudden, Richard, I can't just pick a date out of the blue," Sinéad began to gabble.

"It's not the least bit sudden – you've been wearing that ring for eighteen months now. All my friends are settling down and having kids, even James and he was the most confirmed bachelor of the lot of us. He has two kids now. I want marriage and children, Sinéad. I have no idea what you have against it."

"I have nothing against it. I just want to wait a while."

"Then pick a date in December. But, please, Sinéad, we're picking a date tonight."

Sinéad knew she was cornered, and she knew he had a point. She did want to be with him and she couldn't risk losing him. She was wearing the ring a long old time; the house was perfect, they had the cars, the jobs and lifestyle. It was time to set a date.

They sat up until after two talking about it all in detail. What they wanted and what they didn't want. They wondered about the first Wednesday in June. You could always be one hundred per cent sure that it would be a scorcher on the first day of the Junior and Leaving Cert exams. Alternatively, they could make it early September, the week the schools reopened where the same good-weather rule applied. It would be in Dublin. They weren't going down the country and they weren't going abroad. They'd have an old-fashioned family wedding, with cousins and drunken aunts telling them they were wonderful, the residents' bar and flower girls sleeping on the altar. They were having the works and it was all going to be caught on video.

By the end of the night Sinéad was just as excited as Richard. Why had she put this off for so long? What had she been nervous of? She was marrying Richard not a complete stranger. If the worry about her fertility crossed her mind, she quickly pushed it away.

As for Richard, he was beside himself with delight. They'd be married and within a year they'd be parents. He'd have the baby he was so looking forward to holding.

22

It turned out that June was all booked up, so Sinéad and Richard decided on early September. They put the deposit down and circled *September 3rd* on the calendar as the day they would get married.

So on the first Saturday in March, Julie and Sinéad left their homes just before sunrise and headed for the city. This was no ordinary shopping-trip: they were looking for the Wedding Dress of the Century.

Sinéad had wondered about asking her mother along but then decided against it. Her mother could never ever tell anyone that they didn't look well; you could be dressed in sackcloth and she'd tell you that you were beautiful. This was a lovely quality but Sinéad needed someone who would tell her the truth and worry about the consequences tomorrow. Her mother was also the type of person who found it almost impossible to make a decision. She was so bad that Sinéad's father had chosen both his children's names. Sinéad decided to go out on the first trip with Julie and only get her mother involved when she had actually decided on a particular dress. It would be easier for all involved if the decision was already made by the time her mother came into the picture. She still felt a little bit guilty as she left the house that morning and met Julie at the Stephen's Green Shopping Centre. Her mother had no idea she was indecisive and she'd be heartbroken to think Sinéad was choosing a wedding dress without her. Sinéad had to put these thoughts out of her mind as she headed for the first shop.

Luckily, once in the door of the shop she found it hard to think of anything but what cut, shade and design she wanted. The shop assistants were over to them like moths to a flame. In turned out Sinéad was just the type of bride all the shops were dying to get their hands on. She was young, skinny, pretty and had money to burn. She was hurried into the changing rooms and dress after dress was paraded in front of her. She tried on seven in the first shop, each one more expensive than the last. Julie looked at the price tags and almost choked. Had things gone up that much in just three and a half years? Her dress had been half the average price in this shop and she hadn't visited any bargain basements. She wondered about saying it to Sinéad, but the look on her friend's face confirmed that she was having the time of her life and for now expense was the last thing on her mind.

They took the names and style numbers of dresses and tiaras and headed for the next shop. Once there Sinéad tried on another four dresses, and made the decision that veils didn't suit her.

"I look like the Virgin Mary in this veil," she announced.

"You do not!" Julie laughed, but in fact she did.

"Yes, I do, look," Sinéad joined her hands and made her face look serene.

"Stop, you'll be struck by lightning for comparing yourself to the Virgin Mary!"

"I will not. I bet God's up there saying, 'Isn't that girl the split of Mary when she was younger!'"

"Sinéad! That's blasphemy!"

"It's not!" Sinéad laughed. "All I'm saying is that I look like Holy Mary in this particular veil."

"Then take it off before we're kicked out," Julie replied, looking at another rail of dresses.

She was aware that the assistant was becoming annoyed at the amount of giggling. Sinéad was not the least bit fazed by the look on the assistant's face. "Hi there," she smiled. "I really don't think I'll bother with a veil. Can I see some tiaras instead?"

The assistant raced off and dug out all the tiaras they had in the shop. The girl could obviously smell money from Sinéad and was damned if she wasn't getting her commission on this sale. She was almost conducting a spending spree in her head.

After trying on twelve dresses, eight veils and seven tiaras they decided they'd done enough shopping for one day. They headed for Arnotts café and discussed the merits of each dress in turn, not forgetting to consider suitable styles and colours for the bridesmaids' dresses to match each potential choice. Julie was to be bridesmaid of course and Annabel and Genevieve were to be flower girls.

Two hours later they were all talked out and tea was coming out their ears. The good news was they had narrowed down the choices to four dresses. Sinéad decided it would be best if she went home and thought about them some more, then perhaps next week her mother would come with them and they'd all have a look at the last four dresses together.

In the meantime there was plenty more work to be done. Sinéad and Richard had chosen the hotel. They now had to look at bands and DJ's and decide on which type of car they wanted for the day. Sinéad wanted a vintage Rolls-Royce but Richard was visualising a top-of-the-range Jaguar roaring up the drive and delivering them to the hotel's front door.

23

It was seven weeks to the wedding. The house was crumbling at the foundations under the weight of all the wedding gifts coming in on a daily basis. The invitations had all been posted last week and the last of the preparations were well underway. Sinéad had got her way with the car: she was being picked up from the house at one o'clock the afternoon of the wedding by a vintage Rolls-Royce. She was sick with excitement about the car. Thoughts of Audrey Hepburn and Cary Grant danced in her head when she saw it and she knew she had to have it. Richard could see instantly it meant the world to her and so agreed to the Rolls without complaint.

She had gone to have her make-up and hair done for a trial run. It was nerve-wracking, especially when the woman applying the make-up announced that she never allowed a bride to wear mascara on the big day.

"No mascara?"

"No, it might run if you cry, love."

"I won't cry."

"Every bride thinks they won't, but they all do. It's a very emotional time."

"No, seriously, I won't cry. I'm not that kind of person."

"They all say that and then they all cry."

"Get some waterproof stuff then." Sinéad felt she was stating the obvious here.

"There's no such thing. It all runs."

"No, it doesn't – you practically have to chisel mine off some nights. Seriously, I'm not walking down the aisle without mascara."

"You're the first bride I've ever put mascara on. Don't blame me if you cry and it runs."

"I won't cry and it won't run."

"You're the only bride that's ever had a problem with not wearing mascara."

"I doubt it. I'd say the other brides put some on in the car on the way to the church."

Sinéad was wondering about telling the woman not to bother with the make-up at all but then she couldn't be sure how well it would turn out if she did it herself on the morning. So she went ahead with the make-up artist who claimed that she never used mascara, never ever, not even once, on a bride.

Her hair was a huge success. It was swept up high on her head with the tiara holding back what looked like a waterfall of blonde curls with tiny hair ornaments like diamonds in her hair. She was glad she had decided against a veil. It would have been such a waste to cover this creation!

She had taken her mother's advice and asked her
cousin Avril to be her other bridesmaid. With Annabel and
Genevieve as flower girls they needed two bridesmaids to
balance things out. Anyway, poor Julie would have been
run ragged on her own, trying to keep the flower girls in
order – she dreaded the thought of the long march up the
church aisle and was relieved to hear she'd have Avril's
help to shepherd the girls.

Avril was thrilled to be asked and completely agreed
that Julie had her hands full enough with two toddlers, so
she had done all the small odd jobs that Sinéad needed.
She collected the stationery from the shop and helped print
up the Mass booklets. She was constantly available for any
little odd jobs Sinéad needed to have done. And there were
lots of jobs that needed to be done. Sinéad felt bad for
calling on her but Avril so much enjoyed being in the
middle of everything that Sinéad soon felt fine about it all.

The day of the wedding finally dawned. Sinéad was back
at home, Avril had stayed overnight and the house was
buzzing. All too soon the car arrived and it was time to
leave the house she'd grown up in. She looked around her
– this house held so many memories for her.

"Are you all right, love?" her father said as he stood in
the sitting room with her.

"Yeah, I'm just a bit nervous. Next time we have a chat
like this, I'll be a married woman!"

"I've thought about that a lot over the last few weeks.
But look at Patrick, he's never changed a hair since he got

married. It's not the life-altering event people say it is. You'll still be my girl and we'll still laugh at all the same things."

"I know, but I just hate not being in control! From now on I'm at the mercy of the priest, then the hotel, then the band. You know what I mean?"

"They're all professionals, love – they've done this a hundred times over. You're not at their mercy; you're in their capable hands."

"Okay, you're right. Now we better go. I don't want to be too late for poor old Richard."

They arrived at the church just after two and everyone was waiting outside. She got out of the car and smiled as she heard the gasps. Her dress was cut to perfection, the waist was nipped as tight as possible and her flowers were the most vibrant orange, standing out against the white dress. And the snow-white dress brought out her tan wonderfully. It was topped off with a gold tiara and a diamond necklace. She knew she looked every cent of the three thousand it had cost to dress her up that day. She knew that people were stunned. And she couldn't wait to see Richard's face when she got to the altar.

She wasn't disappointed. Both Richard and his brother, who was his best man, looked amazed when she walked up the aisle. Richard blinked twice and then smiled as he took her hand.

As soon as they got a chance to sit back and listen to the readings Richard leaned over.

"You look wonderful," he whispered, his breath hot on her shoulder.

She looked at him and drank in the look in his eyes. This wasn't lust, this was love. If he looked at her with that emotion for the rest of their lives she was going to be very, very happy.

"I love you," he smiled.

"I love you too," she replied, and at that moment she meant it with all her heart. She was honest enough to admit she hadn't always felt that way, but today, and from this day on she would love him. He was the only man in her life and they would be very happy together.

The wedding was a complete success. The guests lined up outside the church to compliment Sinéad on her dress. They hugged and kissed her, telling her again and again how wonderful she looked. Julie and Avril fussed over her and kept the flower girls' hands away from the snow-white dress. Julie would look over at her from time to time and wink at her. She would appear at her shoulder every now and again and tell her how beautiful she looked. Sinéad would glow with pride and hug Julie. Then she would find her eyes were filling with tears, which was a very un-Sinéad-like thing. And of course her mascara ran a little.

The hotel was wonderful, the band got everyone dancing and the night was a huge success. The only problem Sinéad had was that the day went by in the blink of an eye.

The next day Julie and Sinéad were sitting in the bar of the hotel. Julie was eating her lunch and cutting up pieces of food for the girls. Gavin was at the bar chatting, watching the table, ready to come back once the girls were settled and eating their lunch. This was a trick he'd perfected during Julie's last pregnancy. He'd hover around until Julie had sorted it all out, whatever it was, and then he'd come back and ask if he could help, safe in the knowledge that things were all sorted out and no further fixing was necessary. Julie was on to him and this time he wasn't getting away with it.

"Gavin, come over here please!" She tried to ignore the irritated tone in her own voice.

"What's wrong?" he called from the bar.

"I need help with the girls. Annabel needs you to help her cut up her fish fingers."

Gavin knew he was cornered. He sloped back to the table and cut up the lunch, blew on the fish fingers to cool them and watched as Annabel devoured them. Julie noted that he was well able to help out when he had to. He was just being a lazy bastard, and she notched it up in her mental notebook. They'd row about it later.

Sinéad was sitting on the other side of the table, watching all that was going on. She ate a tuna sandwich and drank her Diet Coke. Again she found herself wondering about the whole baby thing. She was afraid her face was betraying her thoughts and she'd somehow offend Julie. She decided to change the subject.

"Oh my God, it's all over. That's it. It's completely over!" she sighed.

"Yeah, it flies by, doesn't it?" Julie smiled as she took a bite of a ham sandwich.

"I can't believe I'll never wear that dress again," said

Sinéad, "after all the dieting and stitching it took to fit into it, and now it's an ornament."

"Well . . . you could sell it," Julie replied.

"Did you sell yours?"

"No, I'm keeping mine. I'll give it to Annabel or Genevieve when they're getting married. One of them can wear it if they like or make it into a christening robe for their children."

"What?" Sinéad dropped her sandwich.

"What?" Julie looked up.

"You're going to tell the girls to wear your wedding dress? Unless they make some dodgy choices and marry as teenagers, it'll be over twenty years old by then!"

"Watch it! No child of mine will marry as a teen! What I mean is I'll give it to them and if they want to wear it, they can. If they want to throw it in the bin they can do that too."

"I think that's very unfair – they'll feel obliged to wear the bloody thing for fear of offending you!"

"I don't know about Genevieve yet, but I really think Annabel will be no shrinking violet when she gets older. If she doesn't want to wear my dress she'll come out and tell me!"

24

Julie looked into her options. She wanted to go back to work, but she also wanted to be with the girls as much as possible. She gave birth to them, she wanted to be the one to bask in their reflected glory when they won the three-legged race, knew their ABC and counted to ten unprompted for the first time. She wanted to be the stay-at-home-mom most days, but also get out to work and back to normality every once in a while. She decided to go back to work part-time. Monday to Wednesday would suit best but she was willing to be flexible. She rang Liam, the manager of the restaurant in Blackrock.

"Jules, I can't believe it! We'll take you back in the morning, darling! When are you coming back to us?"

"Well, I was wondering if I could come back maybe in a fortnight. I need to talk my mother into taking the girls."

"Perfect, this is a dream come true, Jules! We need a talent like you in the kitchen – there's a real shortage of expertise these days."

"Just one thing, I was really looking to come back on a part-time basis. Maybe three days a week, or five mornings? I'm willing to be flexible with the days."

There was a silence down the line. "Part-time? What do you mean?"

"I know it's a bit unusual for a chef, but the girls are still so small and I don't want to miss out on them altogether. I just want to work a few hours and get out of the house for a while. You understand the situation – you have children, Liam," Julie said, sensing that this career path was becoming overgrown very quickly.

"But Jules, you know we don't do part-time in a kitchen, never. It just wouldn't work. I need staff that can stay late if we need it and will be on hand every day. That's seven days a week, not three, not a few half days midweek. We would need you to commit to a full-time job. No matter who you are," Liam sounded like he was sorry, but there was no way he could have a part-timer in his kitchen.

Julie couldn't understand why not. She tried to get around him, but it was no use.

"There's no point, Jules. If you decide to come back full-time the door will always be open to you. Part-time is a no go. I'm sorry."

"That's a pity, but there is no way I want to go into the kitchen full-time, Liam, not while the girls are so young. It wouldn't be fair."

Julie was sick with disappointment. Maybe she was being silly but she had been so sure that Liam would have her back and that she'd just slot back into work with no problem. Now that he'd said no she was right back to square one.

Never mind, she thought as she sat at the kitchen table. There were plenty of jobs out there and she was well qualified. Time to dust off the old CV.

She sent out copy after copy and cover letter after cover letter. Each time she was careful to put down that she needed to get a part-time position.

A few weeks later the phone calls began and then the letters came back.

Again and again, there were no positions to offer her. The kitchen was fully staffed at present or they needed a full-time chef. When she said that she was only looking for a part-time job the reply was always the same. There was nothing on offer. She was unemployable – four years of college, five years' experience and she was unemployable.

She sent out a new round of CV's, this time emphasising her management skills, her bookkeeping and organisational skills. This put a new twist on the CV and she hoped it would work. It didn't. They wanted an accountant to do their books and she had to admit she only took accountancy as part of a course, not in depth. She was not an accountant. They didn't want a manager who worked only three days a week, they needed a manager who was available day and night. She was not available day and night. She was unemployable. She had no office experience and no retail experience and they were the only ones even interested in part-time workers. There was always the likes of Dunnes Stores or the local

Spar and although the money she'd earn there would buy just the same amount as the money she'd earn anywhere else, she didn't want to work there. Perhaps she was being a snob; she didn't mean to be though. And Lord knows she'd worked her way through college on just such jobs and they were fine, but she wasn't a student any more. That wasn't the only problem. The local Spar opened until midnight seven nights a week and Dunnes were looking for night-shift workers. It just wasn't possible for her to take these jobs and they were the only ones that seemed to be willing to even interview her.

After all those years in college she was unemployable? What about her degrees and certificates? In silent fury, Julie gave up.

Gavin was sympathetic but non-committal about it all. "Well, maybe it's for the best. I like you being at home with the girls, and the childcare fees would have been a joke," he told her as he waited for the kettle to boil.

"It was really nothing to do with money. I just wanted to get out of the house, to earn a little money for myself. I wanted to contribute. Even if it was just a few hundred euro, it would have been my contribution."

"You do more than enough as it is, Jules. You take care of the girls and that is contribution enough to the house. Believe me!" Gavin smiled and squeezed her shoulder as he passed her on his way to the sitting room.

"You know, you say all the right things, you make all the right noises at me about the value of a stay-at-home mum, but you still manage to sound like a condescending prick, Gavin!"

"What?" He stopped in the hall, turned around and stood there with an amused look on his face.

"You heard me," Julie replied as she passed him and went up the stairs. "I look after the kids and run the house; you bring in the money. Welcome to the fucking 1950's! I'm the little woman and you're the condescending pig. Don't we make a happy little union? Now excuse me while I go upstairs and see to our little piglets."

Julie could hear Gavin snigger at the piglets comment, which had been a step too far. She had felt a smile creep across her face as she said it. That was a nuisance. She was always pushing the point just that step too far and making it sound comical.

She went into the girls' room and giggled to herself for a moment before she gathered her thoughts and checked on Annabel. She pulled the sheets back up over her and tucked them in at the sides. As she turned to check Genevieve, she noticed the monitor. Damn, he'd heard her laughing and now he thought he was off the hook, that she wasn't being serious when she said he was a condescending pig.

She was being serious; Gavin was becoming a complete chauvinist. Just the other day he told her he was paying for her to join the AA. That he was worried that she would be stuck somewhere with a flat tyre or she might lock her keys in the car.

"Do you know what to do if you ever did lock your keys in the car?"

"I won't lock my keys in the car. You need the keys to actually lock the car."

"It can happen. What would you do, Jules? You have to think of these things, what with the girls and all."

"Gavin, if I had a brain freeze and locked my bloody keys in the car, even though with central locking that is a near impossibility, I would either break a window to retrieve them or I would call the AA."

He sighed. "Have you ever changed a wheel, Jules?"

"No."

"Do you know how?"

"Yes, you stand by the side of the road and bat your eyes at passing motorists. One of them always wants to stop and show off for a while."

"Please tell me you're joking. You are aware of how dangerous that is?"

"Gavin, lighten up, you eejit! Of course I know how to change a wheel, but you got me that stuff that you can spray into your tyre and it'll get you home."

"Even so, you need to know."

A week later he insisted that he bring her car down to the local garage to get it serviced. He would be able to talk to the mechanic better than she would. Julie would be done out of their entire life savings, they might even have to remortgage if, God forbid, the car needed some new bulbs.

She would definitely have to talk to Gavin, lay it straight to him that sometimes, believe it or not, she was completely capable of living and breathing out in the real world.

Then two weeks later she got a call from a Mr Lynch in Dunnes Stores. He wondered if she wanted to come for an interview. They weren't looking for anything too mind-boggling and it was part-time. They needed shelf packers in the Grocery Department. Julie's heart sank. She really didn't want to stack shelves for a living. She didn't want to work in her local supermarket, but beggars can't be choosers and this was the only job that had come her way. She really wanted the money and the outlet. Her heart was heavy as she agreed to go in for the interview.

She walked into the shop, dressed in a suit, and asked for Mr Lynch at Customer Services as she'd been told to. They paged him over the loudspeaker and he came from behind some swinging doors. He was pleasant and good-humoured as he led the way back to an office behind the staff area. It was quiet and surprisingly tidy back there. Julie had expected to see stock and boxes stacked up around the place.

The interview went well and she got offered the job before she left the room. She accepted it, telling herself that it would be fine: it was only three days a week and it paid well.

She started the following Monday. She worked Monday to Wednesday from eight to four. As jobs went, it wasn't the worst. It was monotonous, the irony of which was not lost on her either – it was, however, lost on the girl she told as they stacked shelves of beans for the third day running. It was also very tiring. But most of the girls she worked with were very nice – they chatted together and passed the day quite happily.

When she got her first pay cheque she was sorry she'd bothered opening it. She'd got one hundred and seventy-three euro after tax – that meant she'd be making the grand total of about seven hundred euro a month. Her mother, as it happened, couldn't take the children for three days a week and neither could Gavin's mother. Julie had put them in a small crèche in a housing estate close to the house. It cost six hundred euro a month to have them both there part-time. Julie was working for the grand total of a hundred euro a month.

Gavin couldn't believe his eyes when he saw the money and his ears when she told him about it. He sniggered at first and told her to keep her pocket money for herself.

"Aw honey, I wouldn't take your few euro from you!"

"Shut up, Gavin, it's a hundred euro we didn't have last month and we're not that bloody rich."

"We're doing all right. We do not need you to put that money in the kitty – you're welcome to it."

"Chauvinist!"

"Perhaps I am. I still don't need your hundred euro."

He followed her into the sitting room and then carried on talking. "So let me get this straight: you mean to tell me you get up at 6.30 three mornings a week, you pack the kids up and send them to the crèche, then go to work and stack shelves until four in the afternoon and they pay you a whopping one hundred euro a month? They saw you coming."

"No, Gavin, I don't make one hundred euro a month, I make seven hundred a month."

"But you have to put the children in a crèche and that costs six hundred, leaving you the grand total of one hundred euro a month."

"Don't worry about it, Gavin. I'm paying for them to be in the bloody crèche – it comes from my wages."

"But why are you going to work? It makes no sense! Your money's gone on childcare!"

"I need to work, I need to feel I'm making a contribution. I need to make some money of my own!"

"But you're not! You're making a few hundred euro a month and then creating a new bill that negates the entire pay packet! It makes no sense."

"Gavin, I need to get out of the house. I have been looking after babies, changing nappies, making bottles, washing clothes and watching fucking *Barney* for over two years now! I need to get out of here. Before I lose my mind!"

"Then why didn't you join a mother-and-toddlers group? Why take up a job that doesn't actually pay you anything?"

"Gavin, do you hear yourself? Do you hear what you've just said?"

Gavin stared at her. He obviously hadn't heard himself.

"I didn't join a mother-and-toddlers group because I actually wanted to get away from the girls for a few hours every week. And as for taking up a job that doesn't pay me anything, that's what I've been doing here for the last two years. I've been working around the clock for free. At least working in Dunnes I manage to get a few hours of adult interaction and I get a lousy hundred euro at the end of the month. It's actually a better deal than the one I've had here for the last few years!"

Gavin was stunned into silence. As hare-brained a

decision as it was to go part-time in the local supermarket, he could now see what she was doing it for.

After that he shut up about her decision to go back to work. He finally realised it wasn't about the money. It was about Julie getting back to being Julie again, not a mother, not a wife, just Julie. Maybe she wasn't working as the chef she'd trained to be, she certainly wasn't working to her full potential, but she was getting out of the house, getting out there without the girls. When she went to work she was being treated as 'Julie', not Annabel and Genevieve's mother, not as Gavin's wife, but as Julie. That was all it was about. She didn't want to change the world or how the local Dunnes Stores did business. She didn't want a huge pay-cheque or a job where she had to stay and work after hours. She just wanted to get out and about, be in adult company again. If the pay was lousy, so be it; it was never really about the pay anyway.

29

Sinéad and Richard were almost a year married. The year had really flown by. There'd been a huge reshuffle in the office and everyone thought they were for the chop. Some people were but Sinéad had come through it. She was still there. She had a new office, a new title and about ten extra people who reported to her, but for the most part it was just the same job. Things had been a bit fraught for about four months but they were settling down and Sinéad was enjoying her first day off for over five months. Richard was in work and she had the house to herself. She had no plans at all; she just lay on in the morning, walked to the corner to get the paper and a croissant for breakfast and pottered around the house. She read the paper from cover to cover and drank mug after mug of coffee. She lay on the couch watching *Oprah* and eating biscuits. At about four there was a break in the daytime entertainment. The talk shows were over and the children's programmes began. She sat there and watched

Sponge Bob Square Pants for a while. Then she flicked stations for about twenty minutes before she had to concede there was in fact nothing on worth watching.

"Goddamn!" she complained to herself. "Three hundred bloody stations and there's nothing on!"

She turned off the TV and rolled off the couch. She wandered around the house for a few minutes – nothing doing in the kitchen – the sitting-room was clean, as was the dining-room. She thought about sitting in the garden for a while, so she went out there – but it was too cold and she had to go back indoors. Maybe this was why she never took time off? Maybe it was just a bit boring hanging around the house on your own. She headed upstairs and decided to clear out her wardrobe. She opened the doors and decided against it – it seemed like too much hard work. She decided to clean out a drawer under their bed. If it was too boring she could fling all the stuff back in the drawer and go back downstairs. Pulling the old clothes from under the bed was such a trip down memory lane – old jumpers and T-shirts. A T-shirt from Julie's hen night, all washed out and raggedy but it went into the 'keeper' pile, as did her Wham T-shirt, the one with a big photo of George Michael and Andrew Ridgeley on the front. It was yellow with age, really baggy and ridiculously short but she loved it. Julie had one just the same in black and they had gone to various school discos wearing them together. She couldn't help but smile when she looked at it. They really thought they were the bee's knees, as her mother used to say, in those T-shirts. She wondered if Julie still had hers. Then there was a big jumper she'd commandeered from Richard a few years ago and had forgotten all about. She remembered exactly what she used to wear with it, a particular pair of jeans and pair of boots with heels. She had loved herself in that outfit. It was so dated now, but at the time she looked so cool.

While she was pulling out all these old jumpers and T-shirts she felt a hard box right at the back of the drawer. She looked into the drawer and saw a black box tied with an elastic band. She fished it out. The box was familiar but she couldn't quite remember what was inside it. Upon opening the box she discovered a few of her old diaries. If there was one thing she was really good at, it was keeping a diary. They were completely worth their weight in gold. She sat down on the bed and emptied out the box. She looked at the years and found one from two years ago. She opened it to see what had been happening that very day two years ago.

Nothing much had happened. She was complaining about Stephen in work. She wrote that she wished he'd find a new job and fuck off. Well, he had found a new job, and the last she heard he was living it up in Edinburgh and running some IT firm.

She looked at the rest of the year and could hardly believe her eyes when she found an entry on the day they got engaged. She had listed all the things she had wanted out of life: the house, the car, the holidays, a baby. She had a second list of things she wouldn't mind getting but they were secondary to her first list: on this list were a Louis Vuitton bag and a Christmas tree decorated only with ornaments from BT. The only thing on the list she hadn't got yet was the baby. She was thirty-one now. Maybe she should think about having a baby soon. Again the memory of what that doctor told her came back. Maybe she shouldn't leave it too long to get the ball rolling on this one.

She sat there and ticked each item on the list. They had the house that everyone else they knew wanted. They both drove brand-new company cars. This year they were off to Switzerland for a fortnight and then later in the year she and Julie were heading to Rome for a girls' weekend. The only item on the list that they hadn't got yet was the baby. She hadn't thought about it for a while but now she remembered that feeling, that excitement in the pit of her stomach as she held Annabel for the first time.

Maybe she should stop putting it off. Stop putting up the obstacles – work, wedding, house, travel. She closed the diary and lay back on the bed. She would be thirty-two in eight months, just about the time she'd expected to be when she was having her first child. The more she thought about it the more she realised the time had come to start talking babies again.

Richard came home that night just after eight and Sinéad was waiting for him, a glass of wine in one hand and some fancy lingerie under her clothes.

"Hi, Richard," she smiled.

"Why, thank you!" he replied, taking the glass of wine and sitting down.

"I was thinking about a few things today and I've come to a conclusion."

"Sounds ominous," Richard smiled. "What have you been thinking, and how much will it cost us?"

"Nothing at all. I thought we might start thinking about a baby."

"A baby, and you say it won't cost us?" Richard laughed.

"Well, not for a while anyway. What do you think?"

"You know what I think!" Richard's face showed a mixture of relief and delight. "When are you thinking of starting?"

"You know me – once I get an idea in my head I don't hang around."

"So what are you saying? From tonight?" Richard's eyes widened.

"No time like the present. Agreed?"

"Yeah, why not!"

And so that night they began. The following night they continued and the night after that they worked a little harder. A few weeks later they had got themselves into a routine – not the most exciting routine but it was all for a good cause, Sinéad would remind herself. Richard seemed to be enjoying himself completely. Three weeks later it became apparent that it hadn't worked. Sinéad shrugged it off and carried on with life. It never works the first month, she thought.

The second month they began again, business as usual.

The routine hadn't changed and they sort of fell into it again. They didn't really discuss it; they discussed other things but never the routine. And again, at the end of the month they waited. When Sinéad got her period they didn't make much comment – there was nothing to say about it.

So they began the third month. The doctor's words rang in her ears but she ignored them. These things always take a while, she told herself. It by no means meant there was a problem – three months was completely normal. People were always saying that they tried for months and sometimes years for various babies you saw crawling around the floor or pulling at Waterford Crystal and the like. People try for ages; most people don't get pregnant immediately.

After their sixth month of trying Sinéad still wasn't pregnant. She wasn't overly concerned but it was getting harder to ignore the tiny voice in her head. The one that kept telling her she should have been checked out when the doctor had advised her. She dismissed the thought. How was it ever going to work if she was panicking every month? She needed to relax about this. So what if it was taking longer than expected? So what if she was nearing her thirty-second birthday and her best friends' children were old enough to be her flower girls? Thirty-two was not old to be having a baby these days – it was the about average, wasn't it? There were always the girls who got pregnant after the Leaving Cert, but she knew she was never going to be one of them. Most women were having babies in their thirties now. She hadn't left it too long. That was not the problem here.

So what was the problem here? Why was it not happening?

Sinéad was in Easons one Monday evening. She was looking for a new book to read. She'd just finished *The Da Vinci Code* and was in the market for something a little less taxing. She really wanted to be entertained, a 'boy meets a girl and they all live happily ever after' type of book. She wandered about looking through the shelves and before long found herself in the Health Section. Lots of medical books and a fair bit of self-diagnosis going on. Books that promised to heal everything from brain tumours to broken nails. Then there it was: *A Complete Guide to your Fertility*. A book that '*lifts the lid on myths, fact and taboo*'. She picked it up, glanced at the back, then the index, flicked through the pages and put it back down. She picked up a book about pregnancy, then one about getting pregnant. The first chapter in that book was 'How to Choose a Partner'. Sinéad smirked to herself; there really were books on every topic imaginable. She walked away and back to the novels. She found one that fitted the bill, a bright yellow cover with a drawing of a pair of sparkly shoes on the cover. It ticked all the boxes: boy meets girl, boy dumps girl, boy spends the rest of the novel trying to get her back. Perfect. In a brain–dead sort of way.

She stood in the queue to pay and looked at the woman on the register. She was working away, not stopping to look at what anyone bought or even to look at who was buying it. Sinéad looked back at the Health

Section. It had been six months . . . what if there was something small they were doing wrong? It might just take a pointer to send them in the right direction. It might not be such a bad idea to have a look at one of the books, just to be sure. It wasn't as if she had to study up on the whole process, but it wouldn't hurt to have a quick refresher course. She was only thirteen when the nuns had taken them into a small room after school and shown them an educational video and explained to them how a baby was conceived. She knew there was more to it all than they had let on all those years ago. She made a spur-of-the-moment decision and left the queue. She went back to the baby books and picked up the one about fertility. Then she saw the one about trying to get pregnant, but that one started with a chapter about finding the right man. *Dhaw*! She didn't need that much help. She bought the one about fertility. She rejoined the queue, hiding the cover of the book with her handbag, running a very fine line between disguising the cover and looking like she was about to steal it. She saw the security guard looking at her. She looked him in the eye but never moved the book.

She got to the top of the queue. The woman scanned the books, took the money and threw the books in a bag. Their eyes never met during the entire transaction but Sinéad's cheeks burned none the less.

She went home and read the book. They recommended that getting to know your cycle was the most important thing and the key to getting pregnant. The more Sinéad read about her cycle, the more she realised she didn't have the faintest idea what was happening from month to month. She went out and bought some ovulation-predictor kits. Armed with them and her new-found knowledge, she was optimistic that next month things would be very different. She took the tests every morning and then, just like the book predicted, thirteen days into her cycle the test showed a happy face, meaning she was ovulating. Now was the time to grab Richard by the ear and lead him to the stairs. She did, and he wasn't exactly dragged kicking and screaming.

She was sure it had worked this month; there was really no reason for it not to. She had never been so sure of anything in her life.

That was why, two weeks later, it almost broke her heart to find she'd got her period. She wondered for a day or two if it could be those implantation pains that she'd just read about in her new book. She got the book and read the symptoms again. She counted the days since ovulation and read about the other symptoms that should be making an appearance if she was in fact pregnant. Sore, swollen breasts. Was she sore? Swollen? Not really, she had to admit. A need to pee more frequently – did she have that? Did she wake up at night and have to use the bathroom? No, but wasn't that just a symptom of old age? Didn't you get a weak bladder as you got older? Anyway, the answer was no – she wasn't waking up at all during the night. So maybe the pains were just plain old period pains.

A few days later it was confirmed that yes, that was exactly what they were. Still, never mind, these things take a while. And seven months was not a long time to wait. Still, she might run out quickly to Easons and buy that other book she was looking at, the one that told you to choose the right partner. Maybe she'd put it back too soon. That book was especially for people who wanted to have a baby; this one she had was about your fertility. That wasn't quite the same thing. Was it? It wouldn't hurt to have a quick read and see what the other one had to say.

She bought the new book and raced home. It was a very good book – lots of information, easily laid out and quick reference guides after each chapter. This book would be her salvation! It became her bible. It said that if you took a cross section of a hundred couples, ninety per cent would be pregnant within one year. Of that ninety per cent there would be some who got pregnant in the first month, some after three months, some more would take six months and another group would take a full year. Then there was a final group who would not be pregnant within a year. Some of them would take eighteen months; some would have problems and need help. She was just finished her seventh month of 'trying'. She understood what Julie meant now: the word 'trying' had long become distasteful to her. It conjured up thoughts of people obsessed with having sex, sex at the right time, lying flat on your back afterwards, tilting hips with cushions. Too much work, no love, just functional sex. Baby-making, sperm and eggs, timing and temperatures. God forbid she and Richard ever got that bad!

"Please God, let us never get that way!" Sinéad prayed as she read the book.

She wondered if she was already obsessing just a little. The book, the tester kits and just last night she had lain flat on her back for twenty minutes, even though she was uncomfortable that way. She decided not to do that again. Buying and reading the books made sense; the kit was just a tool – a help rather than anything else; but lying on the flat of your back after a bit of passion was a step too far. That was crossing the line to obsessed.

26

Sinéad sat in the toilet cubicle in work, her head in her hands. She'd just got her damn period again, together with the cramping and the heavy feeling that she hated. She had hated it as a teenager but, Jesus, she loathed that bloated feeling now. She felt let down by life, by her body, by everything. Her body was letting her down each month and now it was letting her down again. She was a woman after all; she was meant to be able to do this. This was what she was put on this earth to do, was it not? To go forth and have bloody babies! Was it not in the Bible that the purpose of a man and a woman coming together was to have children? Was she not playing her part in this? Was she not following all the rules? Why was she not pregnant by now? She should be pregnant a million times over that this stage. They must have had sex five million times this year and still nothing. What was wrong with her?

She tortured herself with the all the 'ifs'. If she'd got

pregnant in her first month, her baby would be three months old now. If it had taken three months she would be due any day now, maybe she'd be in the hospital now. Even if it had taken six months to get pregnant, she'd be six months gone now.

She was thirty-two now, not that thirty-two was old, but she was a year older. It was taking longer than she'd anticipated. It was stretching into years. If someone asked her how long they'd tried for their baby, she'd have to admit it took over a year. What if it took two years? What if there was another year like this? Another year of testing and watching and hoping? What would she do? What would happen if there was nothing to show next year? It hadn't worked so far. Who said it would happen at all?

All the time she could hear the same sound in her ears. The doctor's voice repeating again and again, "We should get this checked out, Sinéad. It might be nothing but it's best to know for sure."

How sorry she was that she'd never agreed to have herself checked. It could be too late now, over a decade later.

She pushed the memory from her head. There was nothing she could do about the last ten years – she had to deal with the here and now. What did the book say? She'd have a look at it tonight, and while she was looking at it she'd have a glass of wine. There was no use abstaining for the next week.

When she got home she had a look at her book. She knew what it would say; she'd read it cover to cover a hundred times over. She was the most knowledgeable person in her postal district. She could go head to head with a consultant from any of the maternity hospitals in the country. There'd be very little new they could tell her. If she was asked to go on Mastermind she wouldn't have to think about her chosen subject. 'The joys of trying and failing to get pregnant' – that's what it would be.

She knew what the book was going to say, but she read it none the less.

The books said that after a year of trying you should refer the problem to your doctor. Refer it to a doctor. Admit defeat and ask for help. Admit to a stranger that you need help in this most basic area. She couldn't believe it. She didn't want to. Why should she? Why was she having these problems?

She had read all the books. She'd played by the rules.

In fact she'd done everything possible to get pregnant. She had changed her diet, cut back on alcohol and stayed away from colleagues who smoked. She'd taken the folic acid, cut back on caffeine, she even drank that hideous green tea and what's more she was beginning to like the taste, that's how brainwashed she had become. This was not funny any more. She had spent the last year buying those ovulation kits and they weren't cheap. She'd waited day after day until she finally got that stupid smiley face. That stupid face on a plastic stick that made her giddy with excitement when she saw it and two weeks later broke her heart. All that meant a year of baby-dancing until she was quite frankly sick to death of the whole procedure. Richard would sometimes tell her to take a month off. To stop the damn testing and counting days, just go with the flow and if they felt like going to bed early just go with it. She would agree to relax about it. She knew he was sick of her watching how many beers he drank on a Friday night. She could see his point about having a glass of wine and letting go for a night, but when push came to shove she just couldn't relax that much. She was always thinking about the baby they might have. She read that if she lay on her back, her hips tilted upwards with her legs in the air, it helped the 'swimmers' get to their destination. So while Richard lay back and relaxed, she turned upside down on the bed and stuck her legs in the air. As she lay there watching the clock and looking up at her feet as she wiggled her toes, it often occurred to her that Richard was very relaxed about the whole thing. He would make jokes about her while she lay there and grab her ankles to overturn her. She wondered why he didn't seem to care. Was he not bothered by his inability to get her pregnant? Did it not make him wonder at all? Month after month?

He didn't seemed too bothered about the books and guidelines. He glanced through them and listened to Sinéad as she read out parts that she felt were important. But he never really seemed too concerned about it.

"Don't be panicking yourself – it'll happen," he kept saying to her.

"But listen to this part – it says men shouldn't wear cycling shorts – it gets various places too hot."

"When have you ever seen me in a pair of cycling shorts, Sinéad?"

"You used to cycle all the time when you were in your teens – you told me that yourself."

"I know, but I was wearing my school uniform or a pair of jeans. I wouldn't be caught dead in a pair of cycling shorts!"

"Then what's going wrong here? Why am I not pregnant yet?"

He would hug her and laugh. "Sinéad, you are a gas little worrier sometimes! It'll happen, sooner than you think."

"How do you know? What if you're firing blanks? What if my tubes are blocked?"

"I'm not firing blanks and I'm sure your tubes are just perfect. It just takes some people longer than others. No worries."

"You seem very sure of all this."

"I am. Don't be worrying about this. I'm on the job, Sinéad!"

He always seemed so jolly about it, so sure it would happen. Sinéad sometimes wondered if he really understood the whole process, but she didn't trust herself to ask him if he did. She just encouraged him to read the books. He never did though – he just smiled and nodded when she read aloud to him.

She watched him night after night; he didn't think twice about it. He joked with her for while, then turned over and fell fast asleep. What was so different about them? He had wanted a baby more than she did. How come he could just switch off and go to sleep as she lay there praying quietly that it would work, this time please let it work? She looked at him as he lay there, snoring contentedly, and it all became clear. She was obsessed by the baby and he was not. She realised that at some point in the last six months or so, she had crossed that line and Richard hadn't. In fact she'd crossed it and kept on running, and now the line was a speck on the horizon behind her somewhere. Richard was not even in sight of the line yet, he was so far behind her in this thing. She was obsessed. Against all her own best intentions she was now obsessed. She hadn't meant to become this person, she hated the very thought of it, but she was. She thought about it constantly. She saw pregnant women all around her, women pushing prams, pregnant women pushing prams. The world was going through a population explosion, everyone was having children. People in work were coming in week after week and announcing the good news. At last count there were six girls in the building. People who weren't married and weren't even thinking about it, they were four months gone before they noticed their tummy was sticking out a bit. They weren't taking folic acid or watching their alcohol intake! It was so unfair! She'd been so good. She'd taken all the vitamins and the rest that was required. She'd never even looked into a pub, never mind sat around drinking in one. Whenever someone came in and made the magic 'announcement', she would smile and congratulate the person. They would order some cakes from the canteen and have a cake at their desks in the afternoon. She would listen to the due dates, the tales of morning sickness and the shock when the second blue line appeared on the

Clear Blue test. She would come home that night and, like a banshee, she'd cry, shout and then order in a huge Chinese and open a bottle of wine. She'd down the whole thing. Richard would sit with her while she sobbed, drank and got more and more bitter. She'd count the months they'd been trying and cry. Richard would sit quietly holding her hand, but he never said anything.

She heard people come into the bathroom, one of them was complaining about something. She sat in the cubicle with her head in her hands. She was not ready to come out just yet and definitely not if there was a group watching her. She could hear the girls talking but she wasn't listening to them and was not at all interested in whatever they were saying. She had problems of her own.

But then she heard her own name in the conversation. She lifted her head and listened. It was Tracy and Yvette – she recognised their voices.

"And that Sinéad Kilbride bitch! Don't get me started on that cow!" Tracy was saying.

Sinéad sat up and listened. What had she done to call down the wrath of Tracy?

"I know, Little Miss Fucking Hospital Corners," Yvette complained. "You know she was only here a wet weekend when she got made manager. That was an inside job if ever I saw one. Someone gave her the heads-up on what to do and who to kiss ass to. She was sleeping with someone in here. She must have been. How else could she come so bloody high up the food chain so quickly? She only started here a month before me and now she's my manager. There was something going on there, I'll tell you that now!"

"Sinéad? Sleeping with someone? No chance! That'd mean some sort of emotion. Sinéad doesn't do emotion," Tracy tutted loudly. "I'd say now that marriage is a real passionless affair. She's married to her job and by all accounts he's even more career-orientated than her. I bet they sleep in separate rooms."

"That's what I'm saying – she's not getting it at home, so she's in here sleeping with management. Getting the heads-up on where to be seen and whose ass she should be seen kissing. I have to say though, whoever she's sleeping with he's obviously crap. She's still going round here with a fucking poker up her arse. Stuffy cow. "

"Shush! Be careful no one hears you!" Tracy laughed as she opened the door. "But I couldn't agree more!"

Sinéad sat in the cubicle, tears streaming down her face. It wasn't so much the fact that they were talking about her, it was what they said. They'd been horrible about her, and Richard. Saying her marriage was a sham was rotten – how dare they say such a thing? They were never very chatty with her but to be honest she hadn't realised they didn't like her. And they didn't just dislike her – they seemed to hate her. She sat there a while longer, her shock turning to anger. She wondered about calling them into the office and telling them she'd overheard them. Threatening them with a trip to Personnel and a warning on both their files. She'd love to see the look on that Tracy's face – she'd have a heart attack, trying to backtrack and panicking. Sinéad would be well within her rights to do it, and it would prove for once and for all that she was top of the heap because she was a strict and shrewd manager. It would also confirm that she took no shit from her team – they were not at liberty to step out of line. But as her anger subsided she began to wonder what that would solve? They'd just be a bit cleverer about where they went to bitch. It would change nothing and to be honest it wasn't the fact that those two fools were talking about her that was making her cry. It was far more personal than that. She was coming to the conclusion that she would need help if she was to get the baby she by now so desperately wanted.

Finally Sinéad decided that enough was enough. This situation has been going on far too long. She looked at Julie and Gavin as her example. They had the two girls no bother at all. She had been trying for a whole year and was still empty-handed! This situation was going to have to change. She would sit Richard down and have a word with him that very night. She rang him from work to make sure he was coming straight home after work.

"Before you even start, I know what this is about," Richard began, taking the glass of wine and putting it on the coffee table.

"What is it about?" Sinéad put the bottle down and sat down beside him on the couch.

"It's this whole baby thing. Sinéad, you're a woman obsessed."

"Well, maybe I am, but I think I have good reason to

be at this stage," Sinéad defended herself. "I'm thirty-two and we've been trying for a year and a month now."

"A year and a month? At the ripe old age of thirty-two you want to call in the experts for our fertility issues?" Richard was joking but his heart was sinking in his boots. He didn't want this. He didn't want to go to some doctor's surgery and talk about his sex life. He'd heard all the stories about sperm tests and performing into tiny plastic cups. His blood ran cold at the thought. He just wasn't that kind of person. He was actually very private about his personal life. He always was. He hated doctors, he was rarely sick and if he was he'd just dose himself up on Lemsip until he felt better. No matter what was wrong with him, his answer was Lemsip. And it usually worked.

Why couldn't Sinéad just wait and see what happened? Surely she'd be pregnant in no time if she just stopped panicking about it. Didn't she realise that she was being her own worst enemy here? Doesn't everyone know that obsessing about having a baby can make it even harder to conceive?

"Richard, I don't think this is as funny as you do." Sinéad could feel the tears well up in her eyes and fought to keep her composure. The last thing she needed was to cry now, before she had even made her point.

"I do not find this funny," he said. "I think you're overreacting and I'm trying to keep a lid on the whole situation. I'm trying to remain level-headed here."

"Well, I have been level-headed. I've read all the books I could lay my hands on, I've done those stupid tests every month and I've lain up in that bed with my legs in the air night after night. I've tried very bloody hard to sort this out. Now I think we need to get some help."

"What kind of help? What do think we're doing wrong here, Sinéad?" Richard complained.

"We're doing something wrong – otherwise I'd be pregnant."

There was silence for a moment while they both dissected that comment. Was Sinéad assigning blame here? Not really, but Richard knew things were closing in on him slightly. She'd read the books, she'd taken the vitamins and of course there was always the legs thing. He decided to listen to her before he said anything else.

"What would it involve, this help you're looking for? Would you have to go in and be examined by some doctor?" Richard asked.

"I don't really know. I suppose they'd have to have a look at some point."

It wasn't the first time Sinéad had thought about what might be involved. She looked it up in her books and tried the internet but it was quite vague about what exactly would happen. They listed a few tests and then said that every couple would be treated as individuals and the treatment received would vary according to their needs. So she had no real solid information for Richard.

"I've looked it up on the internet and read everything I can about it, but it's very vague. They do some tests, take blood samples, sperm samples and stuff like that, but after that I don't know. I suppose just thinking about it from a business point of view, they'll go for the simplest and cheapest fix first and then get into the nitty-gritty later. I mean, they probably wouldn't bother sending out for a load of tests and expensive drugs without checking a few basics first. Would they?"

"No, of course they wouldn't. They'll just ask a few questions first and take it from there I suppose."

Richard still didn't want to go. Why couldn't she just relax? He was sure everything would be fine if she just relaxed a bit. But she was so wound up – of course tonight was not the night to point that out to her – so instead he listened, hoping that she might just talk herself out of this idea. It was no use.

"So are we agreed that going to the doctor is the next step for us?" Sinéad asked, feeling happier in herself.

Richard felt his stomach lurch. "Us? Do I have to go too?"

"Yes, why wouldn't you come too?"

"I just thought you were getting seen first," Richard said.

"We can get seen at the same time. Maybe there are easy little tests they can do on you right there in the surgery."

"Like what? Toss off in a plastic cup? No thanks!" Richard said.

"Oh for God's sake, Richard, please! You have to come with me. This is scary enough without having to face it all alone. The problem might not even be mine – it might be you after all!"

"I doubt that," Richard tutted.

"What makes you so fucking sure? Have you had your sperm tested before?"

"No," he replied curtly.

"Then, please, come with me and at least listen to what the doctor says then. Please?"

They looked at each other.

Sinéad's face pleaded with him, her eyes wide, her expression scared, and finally he gave in. He could see why she wanted to go and get it sorted out. If there was a problem they really needed to know about it sooner rather than later. He just didn't want to though. He wanted to carry on as before and happily ignore the fact that they were trying for much longer then any of their friends had been. He just wanted to bury his head for a little while longer.

"All right, I'll go with you. But I do not want to have to head off to the bathroom by myself in the surgery."

"I don't want to have a doctor reach up my skirt, but if I have to I will."

"That's not the same thing. You have to just lie there – I'll have to perform and then it'll all be examined."

"I have to lie there with a complete stranger inspecting my bits, and they never come back and tell you what a lovely bum you have. They just pull off the gloves and tell you to get dressed while they try to keep themselves busy in the corner with their back to you. You have no idea what shame is until you realise you've lost your knickers down the leg of your jeans and they walk in while you're bare-assed searching for them!" Sinéad smiled as she relived a particularly embarrassing smear test two years ago.

"What did you do with your knickers that they ended up down the leg of your jeans?"

"Everyone hides their knickers at the doctor's. I have no idea why, but we all do it."

"Do doctors think that girls all go around wearing no knickers?" Richard started to laugh.

"I'm sure they know we all hide them, and the mad thing is we all wear nice new ones when we go for a smear or anything like that, and then we hide them under all our clothes instead of showing them off!"

"So you'll be wearing your best pair when we go to the doc's?"

"Most likely," Sinéad smiled, taking a sip of her wine.

"I see." Richard topped up her glass and sat back. He watched her as she relaxed and drank her wine. Maybe tonight would be the night and all this baby obsession would be over for once and for all. He prayed that things would ease up around here, very soon.

27

Richard got the call on Wednesday afternoon. Sinéad had made them both an appointment for the following afternoon with her doctor. The appointment was for 4.30 and Richard was to meet her beforehand. From the moment he heard her voice on the other end of the phone he could feel his stomach begin to flip. The last thing he wanted was some doctor asking him all kinds of questions about his life before he met Sinéad. He was only twenty-six when he met her, and so what if he lived the high life before he settled down with her?

He stared at his computer for a while before he took a walk to the coffee shop on the corner and ordered a black coffee and a Danish. He sat at his desk and nursed his coffee until it was stone-cold and tasted like poison.

Sinéad was sitting at her desk on the other side of the city, smiling from ear to ear. They were finally getting things sorted out. By this time next week the ball would be rolling and she'd at least feel they were one step closer to having that wonderful baby she longed for. She hoped that they would get some answers tomorrow. She knew it was a little wishful of her but she couldn't help it. She looked at her screen but she couldn't concentrate. Ciara came over to her desk and asked if she was free to talk.

"Sure, what's going on?" Sinéad smiled.

"Well, I thought I'd let you know the news before I announced it to the whole floor," Ciara grinned, her brand-new wedding ring shining brightly as she put her hand nervously to her neck.

Sinéad's heart plummeted. Why today? "What is it?" she asked.

"Well, it was a total surprise to us I can tell you, but I'm pregnant."

And with that there were seven girls pregnant in this building.

Sinéad slapped on the fake smile and bit her lip as her stomach churned. "Well done, you! When are you due?"

"I'm due in October, so I'm just thirteen weeks tomorrow. I was going to say something last week but I was so sick I just couldn't face the thought of all the fuss. I've been so ill – I've been living on Silvermints and ginger snaps!"

"Really? I never noticed a thing!" Sinéad grinned. "Well, are you making the announcement now or later?"

"Oh God, I'm so embarrassed – what do people usually do?"

"It's up to you. You can tell a few people and tell them

to pass it on or you can stand up and tell the room here and now!"

Sinéad was pushing Ciara to announce it and get the hell away from her desk. She knew she was being unfair but to be honest she'd had enough of people gushing about the shock and the morning sickness.

"Oh God, I'd be too embarrassed to stand up and shout. What if no one came to congratulate me? I'd die of embarrassment."

"No, you wouldn't. It'll be fine. Here – stand there." She took Ciara by the arm, led her out of her office and stood her in front of the other desks at the top of the room.

People looked up, sensing there was something going on, more importantly something that would involve a bit of time away from their desks.

"Ciara has a bit of news!" Sinéad announced, then turned to a scarlet Ciara. "Go on! Tell them all your news."

"Well, I'm, em, I am, eh, I'm pregnant!" Ciara announced.

There was a huge cheer and people came running from desks all over the floor. She was surrounded in seconds, everyone hugging her and asking her how she was feeling. She was pulled over to her desk and put sitting down. Then the questions began. Sinéad went back to her desk but she could still hear everything. When was she due? Was it planned or a surprise? Had she got pregnant on honeymoon? Had she any craving yet? What had Stephen thought of the news?

Sinéad sat at her desk listening and being more and more amazed by each question. Had these people no tact? Was it planned? Who on earth would ask a question like that? She looked out and saw Evelyn Smith. That was who would ask a question like that, and worse.

The following afternoon Sinéad left at three. She went straight to the surgery and waited outside in the car park for Richard. It was 4.20 when he showed up, as always cutting it fine. He parked and came up to her. He looked a bit nervous, but that to be expected. He hadn't ever met this doctor and it was a bit of a personal issue to discuss. They walked in and took a seat in the waiting room. Half an hour later they were called.

"Hello there, Sinéad. And you must be Richard?" The doctor smiled over his glasses as he shook their hands. "What can I do for you both?"

"Well, it's a bit embarrassing actually," Sinéad began.

The doctor made a shrugging gesture. "I've heard all sorts in here," he replied.

"We've been trying to have a baby for a little over a year – and nothing. I'd like to get things checked out if I could."

"I see," the doctor smiled sympathetically. "All right so, let's get this sorted. You've been trying for a year?"

"About fourteen months now."

"And you're what?" he looked at his computer. "You're thirty-two and Richard is what?"

"Thirty-five."

"You're both still young. Tell me what have you been doing? Run me through it."

So Sinéad began to tell the story – the ovulation tests,

legs in the air, folic acid, caffeine and alcohol banned from the house and green tea by the truckload.

"And these tests show that you're ovulating every month?"

"Yes."

"And your periods are regular?"

"Yes, now they are. When I was younger they weren't though. My doctor at the time thought I should get it checked out. But I never did."

"Any reason why you didn't?"

"When I got into my late teens I was told to tick the calendar whenever I got my period. I did and after a while I could see the pattern. I just had a long cycle, about six weeks. But for the last four years it's been a perfect twenty-eight-day cycle."

"That's fine. A young girl's body will often take a few years to adjust to menstruating. There's no need to worry about that for now." The doctor looked at his computer screen for a moment, then he asked, "Sinéad, have you ever been pregnant?"

"No."

"Have you ever had a miscarriage or abortion?"

"No, nothing at all."

"Richard, have you ever had a child?"

"No, I've no children."

"Have you ever got anyone pregnant and had it end in a miscarriage or abortion?"

There was a pause.

Sinéad looked over at Richard – idly at first. Then she saw his face.

"Richard?" she said.

"I did once." Richard was looking at the doctor, not at Sinéad.

"What?" Sinéad spun around in her chair. "Who? When?"

"Okay, Sinéad, calm down now." The doctor held his hands up to try to calm things down. "Go on, Richard. This is important. We need to know the full history."

"Years ago, I was in college. I was only nineteen and we decided to go to England." Richard could feel Sinéad's eyes burn into him. He didn't look at her.

"And she had an abortion?"

"Yes." Richard was so ashamed. It was a period in his life that he never spoke about. He had pushed for the abortion. He knew the girl was not happy to go through with it. After the initial shock she had wanted the baby; it was he who didn't want it. He had made the phone calls and booked the hotel for the weekend. They had stayed together for a couple of months after the abortion. Richard had stuck around to make sure she was all right and everything had gone back to normal for her. Then when things had settled back down and it was all over, there was no need for them to stay together. They both finished college and got their degrees. They never spoke again and nobody, not even Luke, his closest friend, had ever found out about the abortion. Now here he was, announcing it out of the blue in front of his wife. There'd be hell to pay tonight.

Sinéad looked down and he sneaked a quick look at her. She was crying. He wanted to scream. One stupid mistake and it was back to haunt him.

The doctor was writing on his notepad and nodding. He looked at Sinéad and smiled at her. She said something quietly to him. Richard looked at her but she didn't look up.

"That's all right, Sinéad, nothing to be sorry for," the doctor replied and put the pen down. He stood up and looked at a book from his shelf, then came back to his seat. "All right, this is what we need to do. We need to get a few tests done: blood tests and a sperm test. Do you have private health insurance? VHI, Bupa?"

"Yes, we both have."

"Would you plan to go private then?"

"Yes, I want this all done as fast as possible," Sinéad said.

"All right. You have a choice: there's the SIMS clinic or the HARI Unit at the Rotunda."

Richard and Sinéad looked at each other for the first time since the abortion announcement.

"The Rotunda will be fine. At least if this all works out I'll be familiar with the place for the ante-natal visits," Sinéad sighed.

"I'll give you a referral letter – you can ring the hospital and make an appointment with them. I have to tell you, even if you go private, there are waiting lists. You are by no means alone in all of this. There are very many couples in just the same situation." He smiled. "Pick up the letter from reception tomorrow – I'll have all your information listed."

"Thanks," Sinéad smiled.

The doctor stood up and walked then to the door.

Richard couldn't get out quick enough. He jumped off his seat and bolted for the door. He headed straight to the reception and paid for the visit, then stood outside the door and waited for Sinéad to come out.

She had lagged behind with the doctor.

"Do you want to come and see me alone in a week or so?" he asked her.

"No."

"Have a talk with Richard tonight and find out the full story. As he said, he was nineteen and at college. It was just one of those things. They happen to more people than you think, Sinéad."

"I know, but he should have told me. I shouldn't have found out like this." The tears began to sting again. "I have to go."

"Sinéad, let me know when you get an appointment with the HARI Unit. Between us we'll get you sorted out."

"All right. I'll ring next week." She rushed to the door, tears streaming down her cheeks again.

28

Richard was standing beside her car. He looked ashen.

"Get out of the way," she said, not meeting his eye.

"Please let me explain."

"No. I don't care. It was years ago. It was nothing to do with me and obviously you feel it was none of my business or you would have told me about it."

"I've never told anyone about it, Sinéad! Not even Luke!"

"You're not married to Luke! We shouldn't have secrets, Richard!" Sinéad sobbed and thumped his chest. "Now get out of my way!"

Richard stepped to the side. "Will you be all right?"

Sinéad opened the car door. "I'll be fine."

"Please, are you fit to drive?"

"I'm fine."

Sinéad reversed. Richard had to step back so she didn't hit him. He followed her home in his car. When he got in, she had locked herself in the bathroom and he could hear her sobbing. He heard the bath water running a few minutes later. He put a bottle of wine in the fridge and lit the fire. He checked the TV pages and found that *Moulin Rouge* was coming on at nine. He hated it but Sinéad loved it. He would pour her a glass of wine, light some candles and they'd watch Ewan McGregor dance and sing all night. He opened a bottle of beer and tried to read the paper but he couldn't concentrate. As awful as it was for Sinéad to hear the news like that, it brought back some long suppressed memories for him too. He had wondered as he got older how it had actually affected the girl – her name was Joanne. He had hung around thinking he was doing the right thing. He waited and made sure that she wasn't sore and that her periods were back to normal – as if that was any real indicator as to how she was feeling. He thought that as long as she was back to regular functioning that she'd be fine. It was years later, after he finished college and had lost touch with Joanne completely that he realised things were not as simple as he had once thought. He knew she was upset and that she cried a lot during their weekend in London and when they got back. She had become reserved and quiet. They had both agreed to tell no one about the abortion.

Before they had gone, Joanne kept referring to it as 'the baby' and Richard had fought with her, telling her it was a clump of cells, nothing more.

"Cancer is a clump of cells and if you found you had cancer you'd be straight over to there to get it removed!" he shouted at her.

"Our baby is not cancer! It's not a clump of cells! It's

a baby, it'll grow up to be a man or a woman and it'll have children of its own and a life of its own! It's a living being!" she had cried.

"It's not! Look at the books, Joanne! It's a clump of cells and it's about the size of a pinhead! It's not a baby!"

"It is to me and you're asking me to kill it! You're sending me off to London to kill my baby!"

"This is not what we want, Joanne!" Richard hated the sight of her at this stage, the eyes always red from crying, the face snow-white from throwing up, the cold hands shaking constantly. Now at the age of thirty-five, he could see clearly she was only eighteen and she was frightened. Frightened of the sickness that took over her body each day, frightened of what would happen to her in the city, alone with a baby. She was from Carlow and had come up to UCD after her Leaving Cert. It was her first time away from home and she looked to Richard for support and help. He was older, living at home, used to the city and if he said so himself very popular on the campus. If his friends had seen how he behaved about the baby he wouldn't have been quite so popular.

"It's not what I want. I don't want to kill this baby. What about adoption? People want babies all the time. Give this child a chance at life, please, Richard!"

"No, it's all booked and sorted out. It's for the best, Joanne. Look at us – we're teenagers for fuck sake. We can't have a baby. We're in college – it'd be madness to give it all up to have a baby now."

"I want this baby, Richard. I don't know why but I do. I don't want any help from you once the baby is born. Just go with me to the hospital for check-ups. That's all I want from you."

He looked at her, her eyes watery, her hair limp in a ponytail and her face glowing white it was so pale.

"No. I don't want this baby. I've arranged for the abortion next weekend. I'll pay for everything, but, Joanne, we are getting rid of it."

He remembered the look of astonishment on her face; she looked down at her shoes and then back up at him. She looked at him wide-eyed for a moment and then she nodded. She said nothing else, just got her coat. She said she'd meet him at lunch-time on Friday on the campus and they'd go together out to the airport. She left.

They met up on Friday, travelled to London and came home on Sunday night. They passed time with one another for a couple of months until Joanne came to him one day and told him they needed to talk.

She told him that she would never forgive him for making her kill her baby and that she wanted nothing more to do with him. She knew he was only staying around to look like he cared. And that from this moment on the pretence was over. They were finished and she never wanted to speak to him again, not one word.

It was his turn to look stunned. He just nodded and that was it. They never spoke to each other or anyone else about the baby. Richard now realised it was very much a baby they had clinically arranged to remove from their world. And now fifteen years later it was back to haunt him. The baby would have been about fourteen now, just in its teens. How different life would have been around here if they had a fourteen-year-old coming over at weekends, playing loud music and fighting with them.

He heard the sound of Sinéad moving around upstairs, then the sound of her coming down. She walked into the sitting room, her eyes tired and her face tight with pain.

"I don't want excuses. I want the facts. What happened, who was she, why did she have the abortion, where and why and . . ." she trailed away.

Richard went to the fridge and came back with the bottle of wine. He started from the beginning and told her the whole story, warts and all. It took three hours to talk it all out and in the end they had both gone through anger and hurt and tears. At 12.30 there was nothing more to say.

Sinéad finished her wine and went to bed. Richard turned off all the lights and followed her up.

29

Julie was sitting at the kitchen table thinking that things were finally getting easier for her. The girls were settled into the crèche, they had both made little friends and everyone's horizons were broadening. They had both come on in leaps and bounds with eating and drinking. They had to drink what they were given; there was no time for tempers and mollycoddling in the crèche. Julie had had a dreadful time trying to get Genevieve to drink from a cup. She loved her bottle and was adamant that she would never give it up. A fortnight in the crèche and she was drinking from the cup with no big fuss at all.

Julie liked her job too. She was in a routine, she had a few friends that she went to lunch with and had a great giggle with them all. Yes, it was a boring, thankless job but at least she was paid and she got an hour's break at midday. An hour off when she was looking after the girls was unheard of. And she could run around the shops after work without a buggy or a dawdling child. Anyway, she was used to thankless jobs – she was a mother after all.

Three months into her new job Julie had a new lease of life. She was feeling in control and better able to deal with the tantrums and doldrums of dealing with the girls, especially as Annabel had entered the Terrible Threes.

Julie and Gavin had decided to stay in the house on Griffith Avenue and get an extension. They were now stuck on Griffith Avenue until they died. But let's face it, there were worse places to be stuck. Their mortgage had almost doubled and all they really had to show for it was new carpet throughout the house, a bigger kitchen, a utility room, a playroom and a decked patio. They also had paved the front drive and paid off Julie's credit card, but really for the amount they paid they had very little to show for it.

Gavin came home one day after the building work was all finished and the house still looked like a bomb-site. He stood in the kitchen and surveyed the extension and the patio.

"Jesus we've been done!" he announced. "Surely we should have got more than a square foot of kitchen and a utility room for fifty grand!"

"I know, as soon as you have an extra room you fill it. Everyone said it when we were doing up the plans, but what can we do?"

At least the girls' toys were out of the sitting room. They had a playroom now that Julie could leave them to howl and run in – the real beauty of it was that no matter how awful it looked she could just shut the door and forget about it. They had games laid out that would go on for days and days. She would just look into the room, and see the game in progress, their small heads down playing together and working on the various ideas. She would smile as she looked in at them – she could see them from the kitchen and dining room and so could keep an eye on them as she carried on with her housework. Things still got too quiet on occasion and she'd make the mad dash from the kitchen to see what was happening, but they were usually just busy breaking some toy to pieces.

"I used to have to tiptoe around that mess!" she'd say to herself as she tidied the sitting room.

There were of course the days when she wanted to bang their heads together. They would cry and shout at each other and constantly want her to sort out their quarrels. Well, Annabel would want Genevieve taken away and put in another room.

"Breaked, breaked!" she'd cry and point at Genevieve.

Genevieve would look up from where she lay, on top of whatever toy Annabel had been playing with. The toy would not be broken but it would be flattened or bent out of shape. Julie would pick it out from under her and reshape it before handing it back to Annabel, who would then fling it against the nearest wall and scream. Genevieve would smile at her from where she still lay, and sometimes, to add insult to injury, roll over, pick up the thrown toy and shuffle off with it in her mouth.

Then came the days when the girls just wanted to hang out of her all the time. They wanted stories. They wanted to be watched while they danced or sang or played with their toys. For a while about two months ago, they both suddenly decided they wanted to be carried everywhere they went. They could be a complete handful at times but most of the time they were plain sailing at this stage. They fed themselves and went to bed without too much fuss. A bath, bedtime story and they were gone for the night. Julie was starting to greet each day with a smile again. It was still hard work and the girls were still very much little children but things were looking up. The job and the crèche were helping Julie not feel so housebound any more.

One night Gavin came home and produced a bottle of expensive wine. They sat back and drank it while they watched a movie. Then came the crunch.

"I was thinking, Jules," he said.

"What about?"

"Having another baby," he said and looked straight over at her.

Her stomach flipped. Her life was just getting back to normal. She had a job and some semblance of normal life. Another baby was the last thing she needed to be dealing with.

"You must be joking!"

"Why would I be joking? I thought you wanted loads of kids?"

"Not likely, Gavin. I've just got back to work. The girls are happy in the crèche. Things are finally getting easier for me. We need some time to just relax for a while."

"What time to relax? Genevieve is two. If you get pregnant again in say two or three months, she'd be three when the next one arrives." Gavin was sitting forward – he'd turned down the TV to make his point.

"I'm not ready to start that whole shebang again, Gavin. Honestly, the girls are a full-time job and I'm happy in Dunnes. I'm finally getting things back to normal. I'm not ready to start all over again." Julie put down the wineglass and shook her head.

"This would be the perfect time to start again. Do you want to wait until you've forgotten how it feels to be up at night? Until they're both in school and then start all over again? No way – get it all over and done with in one sweep."

"No, Gavin. I think you're being selfish asking me to give up my job and my independence just as I'm beginning to get it back," Julie replied.

"It makes complete sense to go again now. While we're still used to nappies and toys and bottles and all that. Don't wait until we're older and less able to cope with the sleepless nights."

"Gavin, I'm thirty-two and you're thirty-four. We're not pushing old age here – we have a few years left in us yet. Wait a while and we'll be talk about it again."

"That's madness, Jules, and you know it. We should get it over and done with now, while we're still young!"

Julie could hear the tone of his voice: he was set in his plan. She would have to argue hard to get her point across.

"Gavin, I don't just want the kids to be 'over and done with'. I want to enjoy them, each of them, for who they are and get to know them. Not just rush through their lives until they're going to school and then college and that's it, they're raised and gone!"

"You know what I'm saying. I'm not saying rush through the children. I'm saying get the pregnancies, the sleepless nights and nappies all over in one big swoop. Then relax and enjoy the children, knowing in your heart we'll never have to this again."

"What are you talking about? Never have to do it again? We might have to do it all again. We might want to. A lot can happen in ten years. We might just want another baby in five years – we might both want one in five years."

"What do you mean 'both want one in five years'?"

"As it stands, Gav, I don't want a new baby right now. I'm happy as we are and I'd rather wait until we both wanted to have a baby, not just you."

Gavin was not listening to her – either that or he was just so hell-bent on having a third child that he blanked out her argument.

"Come on, at least think about it, Jules! Imagine, a little fella running around upsetting the girls!"

"A little fella?" Suddenly things got as lot clearer to Julie. "You want a boy, do you?"

"Well, we have the girls – it'd be nice to have a son."

"And what if the next one is a girl? What then?"

"We'll love her, the same way we love the girls upstairs." Gavin took a sip of his wine "There's no shame in hoping for a boy after two girls, Jules."

"I know. But this idea of going again in the hopes that it's a boy – I don't like it. What happens if we have a girl? And what happens if we never have a boy? Do you plan to keep trying until I hit forty odd? Seven little girls and we're still trying, Gavin?"

"Come on. Don't be ridiculous. I never said any such thing. If we only ever have girls then that's fine, but I really would love a boy."

"You'd love a son, but it's me that has to go through with the pregnancy and the birth and then look after the children when they're born. I feed them day and night and sit up at night dealing with the teething and the fevers. As I recall you didn't do too much pacing of the floor at three a.m. with the girls when they were teething. It's not just one more child to me. It's night feeds, nappies, doctor's appointments and juggling three small children instead of two. Quite frankly I do not want to juggle any more children. I have enough on my plate."

"So you don't want any more children? You've finished having children at thirty-two? That's it?"

"No, that's not what I'm saying, Gavin, and you know it!"

"It sounds like that to me." He sat back and turned up the TV.

He was sulking. She hated when he did this. He didn't get his way straight away and now he was going to give her the silent treatment all night.

They sat in silence for two hours. Julie could live with the silence just fine; it was the sighs and the tutting she couldn't bear.

"Oh, Gavin, shut up!" she finally shouted.

"I haven't said a fucking word," he retorted.

"I'm going to bed."

She got up and left him sitting there, all sulked up and no one to sulk at.

A few days later Gavin came home from work with a box of chocolates and sorry smile.

"I've been thinking about what you said and I can see your point."

"What? Why the change of heart?" Julie was delighted but she wondered what was behind the sudden change.

"I would love another baby, but I was talking to Áine and Jenny in the office today. They were talking about babies and stuff. I said that I was trying to talk you into having another baby. They practically turned lynch mob on me when they heard about your new job and everything. Maybe I was being selfish."

"You listened to the girls in the office before you listened to me?"

"No, not exactly. I was thinking about it for a few days and then they said exactly the same stuff you said about it. About it being so tiring, and juggling three babies and all that."

"But why did you take it seriously when they said it? Why didn't you hear me when I said it?"

"Jules, I was a bit drunk that night. I was being pushy. I thought you just needed a nudge in the right direction. Now I can see I was wrong. Please don't give me a hard time over it."

"Gavin, I really need you to start thinking about me for a change! I need to have some life of my own before I can give it over to the children. I need to be out there without them every now and again. That's why this job, crappy as it may seem to you, is so important to me. It's my lifeline. It gets me out and away from the girls for a few hours each week. God, do we really have to go into this all over again, Gavin?"

"No, we don't! I just told you I can see your point of view, or didn't you hear me? I know exactly how you feel about that bloody job."

"All I'm saying is that when the time is right we'll have another baby. But only when the time is right for both of us, not just you!"

"I already said I agree. But I just want you to know this. I really want to have another baby. I would love to have another one tomorrow, but I'm willing to wait. This is postponed, not cancelled, all right?"

"The jury is still out on this one, Gavin. But the jury will not be back for at least six months. Understood?"

"All right, I understand."

Gavin dropped the subject after that. In fact, he studiously ignored the subject. That was fine with Julie. She was busy with work and the children, but happy with her life for the first time in a long time. She felt good about herself.

She lay back in the bath one night after the girls were in bed, music on the CD player, lavender-smelling bubbles and lots of steaming hot water. She was relaxed. It didn't take long for her mind to wander. It wandered back to Gavin and 'Babygate'.

Gavin really had no idea how much work was involved in raising children. It was a wonderful experience and Julie would not have traded places with anyone when it came to looking after the girls, but it was a full-time job, mentally as well as physically. And she was just getting back to having some Julie time. Now Gavin shows up with his 'Let's have another baby' – and now she felt guilty for saying no. It wasn't that she didn't want another baby – it was just that she wanted a year or two more of a break. She was only thirty-two after all – they weren't exactly running out of time here. Just this afternoon, she'd been looking at the girls while they played in the back garden. They were self-sufficient most of the time; so she could deal with another baby. But why should she?

Recently she had taken a good look in the mirror: her hair was pulled back in a pony-tail and it could have done with a wash, she was in an old pair of jeans, a baggy pink hoody and a pair of old runners. For the first time in her life Julie looked shabby. She looked like someone who had given up on her looks. But she hadn't given up on her looks. She still cared what she looked like and wanted to look fabulous and smart when she ran to the shops, called to a neighbour's house or went to work. But the fact was she didn't. Her hair needed to be cut and coloured and she badly needed a bit of make-up. She didn't have to wear make-up in work. She was just stacking shelves and going back and forth from the stockroom. There was no point to it. But the problem was that between work, looking after the girls, supermarket shopping and housework there was no time or call for dressing up and wearing make-up. She just didn't have the time to look after herself, and she really didn't have any reason to dress up.

She fussed over the girls. She was adamant that they would look clean and beautiful every day; then she made sure the house was clean and tidy just in case anyone called in. There was always food in the press, clean windows and freshly cut grass. All the trimmings were just right; it was Julie herself that didn't quite fit the picture. She looked dowdy, she felt dowdy. There just weren't enough hours in the day to allow her the time to get her hair done or make-up sorted out.

She cringed as she thought back to the last time Sinéad had called over. Gavin had taken the girls to the park and then to McDonald's. Julie had the house to herself and they spent the afternoon chatting over coffee and biscuits. They just sat in the kitchen refilling coffee mugs and eating all the nice biscuits in the press. Sinéad looked like she stumbled out of a fashion catalogue; Julie on the other hand had looked like she stumbled backwards through a hedge and then fought her way through undergrowth on her way to the table. She had looked at Sinéad, her hair and her clothes. When they were younger Julie had always been the pretty one of the two. That was not vanity talking; it was just the simple fact. She had a prettier face and better legs. Sinéad was pretty too, but she helped it along by wearing the best of clothes and having her hair done regularly. But lately, when they were together, Julie looked at least five years older than Sinéad, instead of ten months younger. She hated it. She had always been proud of her looks and she was right: she used to be beautiful. Not any more though, The fact that Gavin and herself rarely went out socially was not helping matters. If she didn't go out socially, she didn't need make-up. And as time went by her make-up bag got old and battered, not helped by the fact the girls played dress-up now and again and had begun to use her make-up for those sessions.

She had found them just three days before: Annabel
had drawn all over their faces with Julie's lipstick and put
eyeshadow all over their chins and cheeks. When she
walked in and found then she shouted at them to stop.

"Aunty Sinéad!" Annabel protested.

"This is Mammy's make-up, not Aunty Sinéad's. What
are you doing? Give me that lipstick!" Julie took the
eyeliner from out of Genevieve's mouth. "Ah ah! Don't
swallow that!"

"Not Mammy – Aunty Sinéad!"

Julie started putting her lipstick away and closing her
foundation while trying to ignore the fact that her make-
up was old and sticky and that the stickiness had nothing
at all to do with the girls' hands. Then she heard Annabel
again, properly.

"We're not being Mammy. We're being Aunty Sinéad."

They didn't see Julie in the same league as Sinéad; they
didn't equate Mammy with make-up and looking well. It
was a wake-up call Julie didn't like getting.

That evening as she had run their bath and scrubbed
both the dirty faces, she made herself a promise. Enough
was enough. Gavin had been smart-ass enough to tell her
that her hundred euro wasn't needed in the family kitty, so
from now on she was not throwing it into the kitty. She
was sorting out her hair and getting a facial, then she
might even get a manicure. So a hundred euro a month
wasn't going to pay for them all at once, but so what? It
might not be a huge pay packet but it was enough to get
her hair done and her legs waxed. She was making an
appointment to have her hair coloured, cut and restyled.

And she was having a facial and a massage in that new beauty salon near the park.

Next morning when she'd dressed and fed the girls, she gave them both an apple juice and put on a Barney video for them. It bought her twenty minutes to make a few phone calls. She made a booking in the hairdresser's. It would cost over a hundred euro for the hair-do. She'd never spent that kind of money on her hair before, but she was worth it. She confirmed the appointment and hung up. Then she called the beautician and booked a massage and a facial. Again, it would be over a hundred euro, but she was assured that it would be three hours of sheer bliss and the girl on the phone had promised her that she'd feel like a new woman after the massage. It would be worth it just to feel normal again. With a new hair do, relaxed muscles and a wonderfully cleansed face, Julie would be ready for anything.

Then Gavin arrived home and announced that what this house needed was another bloody baby. All her good intentions were in danger of going up in smoke.

Now lying in her bath, she felt her neck stiffen under the pressure. She sank down deeper into the water, letting the bubbles tickle her chin and nose. She was so tired and her head was sore from thinking all the time. She just lay there, too tired to move.

30

Sinéad collected her referral letter on the way home from work the following day. She wanted to get the ball rolling as quickly as possible. They had done the hard part, and had the heart-to-heart about Richard's past. Hopefully that was it; they would never have to talk about it again. Sinéad prayed it would never come up again. Among other things it had revealed a cruel side to Richard she hadn't seen before and didn't like to think existed.

She went home and opened the letter. So what if it was addressed to her doctor, it was about her and she had the right to read it. It was a bit of anti-climax. Just her details, date of birth, weight, height, allergies, a brief medical history and a note about how she had been trying for a baby without success for over one year. She found a new envelope and put the letter into it. The following morning she rang the hospital from work. She went to the boardroom and made the call from there. She didn't want any stray ears to hear what she was doing. She was given the name of a consultant who would be dealing with her case and a date for her first appointment. She was told there was a long wait at the moment and they could only see her in five weeks' time. That would be early May. Not as much of a delay as she had anticipated, but it was five weeks of twiddling her thumbs that she could have done without. She rang Richard and told him.

"The seventh of May at 11.30 – that's just over five weeks away. It's longer than I'd hoped for but hopefully things will have sorted themselves out and we won't need the appointment at all."

"Maybe, you never do know with these things."

The morning of the appointment dawned. There had been no change in circumstance and, as they got dressed and ready to leave for the hospital, Sinéad became convinced that something awful was about to happen.

"What if we know the doctor? What if he's our age and you were in school with him or something?"

"So what if we do?"

"Do you not think it'd be weird?"

"I haven't given it much thought to be honest." Richard was putting on his jacket and jiggling his keys at her to hurry her up.

"Well, what if we met someone we know? What if we met your sister or someone?"

"We're all there for the same reason – at least we'd have someone to talk to about it."

"What if we met someone going in for a baby scan or

something and they just assumed we were having a baby and then we had to tell them where we were going?"

"Sinéad, no one is going to come out and ask us why we're visiting the doctor. And if we see anyone we know we'll just smile and say hello. Stop panicking about it."

"I just have a really bad feeling, like this is all going to go wrong or something."

They got to the hospital in plenty of time. They parked and walked back to the entrance and took directions down to the HARI Unit. They booked in and were told to head to the waiting room where they sat in silence pretending to read the paper and ignoring the rest of the nervous faces around them. Sinéad stared at each face in turn from behind her magazine and confirmed to Richard that she knew no one.

"Then are you going to put the paper down from your face? You look like a skit of a private investigator."

Sinéad relaxed a bit, but that only highlighted a new problem. She needed to go to the loo. She didn't know where the loos were and the door was suddenly very far away. She tried to read her magazine and ignore her need but she couldn't read either. She was too jumpy. She couldn't concentrate. Her heart was pounding and her hands shook a little when she turned the pages. She was sure everyone else could see it and she became very aware of it. She stopped trying to read and instead looked around, taking in her surroundings. She listened to the staff outside in the corridor. They were in sharp contrast with the patients. They were all relaxed and full of smiles for everyone. They could be heard chatting about this and that. The patients on the other hand were quiet and shaky, sitting in a row, looking at the magazines and the posters around them. A door would open across the corridor and a man would call a name. Some woman would clamber to her feet and make her way out, followed in most cases by a man. Sinéad didn't know if she envied or pitied the women making their way into the surgery. She could still get up and walk out, tell the matter-of-fact girl in reception that it was all a big mistake and that they were going home again. Once they crossed the line and entered that office across the hall, then they were officially a couple with 'fertility problems'. They were one of the statistics, 'the ones' who needed 'help'. It was a frightening development and one Sinéad hated to admit to. It didn't fit in with her role in life; she was a go-getter, a leader. She decided what she wanted and made it happen; now here she was, needing help with one of the most fundamental things in life. Look around you and it seemed that every teenager in the city was pushing a pram, either that or about three weeks away from it judging by their stomachs.

Suddenly her name was called and it was too late; she couldn't escape. The blank faces looked around, wondering who Sinéad Kilbride was. She stood up and made her way out of the room, Richard following behind.

They walked into the office and the doctor introduced himself.

"I'm John Whitney, and you're Sinéad, I take it?" he smiled.

"Yes, this is Richard, my husband."

They all shook hands. Then they sat down, the doctor took out his pen and started to run it around his fingers.

"I don't want to sound pessimistic but I feel it is important that we all go into this with our eyes open and with realistic hopes. This is not a quick fix. You will both be going through some very emotional times – some of the tests we perform are not pretty. But they are necessary and you are not by any means the only people going through it. You've seen the waiting room. Call in any day and you'll see the waiting room just as full. You are not alone and there are wonderful support groups if at any time you feel overwhelmed by the whole process. And I have to tell you, a baby is never a guarantee. It's never a guarantee for any couple. People who get pregnant very easily have just the same probability of miscarriage as the ones who finally go with IVF. It's a fact and I think we should get it out on the table."

Sinéad stared at him, her stomach flipping. She had sort of believed it was a guarantee. She hadn't meant to pin all her hopes on this meeting, but she had.

"I'm sorry. I don't want you to think this is all doom and gloom – we have a very good success rate here. Taking into consideration your age, and the fact that you're addressing the issue early, not waiting until forty, I'd be more than optimistic on this one. Put it this way; at this point we have no reason to believe you won't be one of the ones who walk out of here in a year's time with a baby in your arms. But we need to be realistic and I need to know you are not pinning unrealistic hopes on us, on me. I'm just a man, and even with all our help, it is up to nature, to God, to whoever you believe in, just not me."

Sinéad looked at Richard. Again she wanted to make a run for it, out the window, up the walls, just away from this situation. Richard was looking at the doctor as if he was God. He was nodding at him and listening intently. He glanced at Sinéad and half smiled. It occurred to Sinéad that they might be coming at this situation from very different perspectives. She wanted a baby, end of story; she was here for no other reason. They could hang her from the light bulbs – if she walked out with a baby in her arms it would all be worth it. It looked like Richard was here to find out what was happening, why they were having trouble with this, what the problem was and how you spelt it. He'd look it up on the internet and get a man to come out and fix it for them.

The doctor looked at his notes, and began to talk again. "So, after that speech, is there anything you are unsure of?"

"Em, yes," Sinéad began to speak, her voice sounding small and far away, "these tests you're talking about. What happens? When do they start?"

"Well, we start with fairly simple ones: a blood test and a pelvic scan with you, a sperm test for Richard are usually the first tests we go with. But there'll be no tests today. Today is just a chat and a chance for you guys to ask any questions and think abut what's happening."

"No tests? But, Dr Whitney, I really want to get the ball rolling. I would like to get started straight away. If it's just a blood test and a scan, then do it now – there's no reason to wait."

"Well, we prefer to be completely happy that the patients' expectations are realistic before we start any treatment. We also need to do the blood test on certain days during your cycle – it's not just a case of any old time at all. We really should wait."

"Please, this is a hard enough process and we completely understand – a baby is not guaranteed to anyone. We understand all the facts – you're not a god. So, please, can we not prolong this any further?"

Sinéad knew she was playing hard-ball with the doctor and this was a thin line she was treading. If she overdid it just a step he could refuse to go any further with the tests. He could say they had unrealistic expectations and pull the plug completely, but she was hoping it would go the other way, push him to believe they were go-getters, who wanted to get the ball rolling at all costs.

The doctor looked at her, then at his notes again, then at Richard. "I see you are a manager in the bank. I presume you're used to getting things done fast. Well, here we can't work that way. Things move a little slower when you're talking about medicine. You have to understand; we cannot fast-track this process. I need to get some details on your history and then we'll talk more." He looked at Sinéad again. "You're what age?"

"Thirty-two." Sinéad sighed inwardly, she had pushed too hard. He was playing his own hard-ball.

"And Richard is?"

"Thirty-five."

"And you've been trying for a baby for how long?"

"About fifteen months now."

"And you've had no miscarriages, abortions, anything like that?"

Richard shifted in his seat and Sinéad glared in his direction before answering. "I have never had an abortion or miscarriage, but Richard and an ex had a situation in college."

The doctor looked up from his notes, his pen still on the page, mid-sentence.

"I was only nineteen and she was even younger – we had ourselves a weekend in London if you know what I mean." Richard felt himself blush.

The doctor nodded and made a note on his file. "Sinéad, do you have a regular cycle and when did you begin to menstruate?"

"Yeah, regular enough. About a thirty-day cycle. I started when I was about thirteen. Not very early but not that late."

"Great, that's perfect," the doctor smiled. "And what day of your cycle are you on today?"

"What?"

"The first day of your period is day one, the next is day two and so on until the first day of your next period. Could you calculate what day you're on?"

"Em, all right." Sinéad counted in her head. "Day twenty-one."

"Twenty-one?"

"Yeah, my last period was on the seventeenth of last month."

"Great," the doctor smiled. "Have you ever had any STDs, or infections that went undiagnosed for any length of time, either of you?"

"No."

"No."

"And have you any reason to believe you might not be ovulating or things may be slightly off, Sinéad? Sometimes the patient has a feeling or an idea and we can check that out first?"

"No, I'm ovulating each month. I bought those kits and they show every month, like clockwork."

"Right." The doctor looked at his notes and rapped his fingers on the desk for a second or two. "Well, we could get the ball rolling today, I think, but we need to be clear: there is no way to fast-track things around here."

He looked at Sinéad. She nodded.

"I'll call one of the nurses and she can take a blood sample from you, Sinéad. We'll get it checked for hormone levels. The first ones we'll check are your FSH and LSH levels. Then we'll do a quick scan and check your ovaries for cysts or anything that could be blocking the release of the egg. And, Richard, would you mind telling me, have you had intercourse in the last seventy-two hours?"

Richard and Sinéad looked at each other. Sinéad wanted the floor to open up and swallow her. Richard didn't look like he was too far behind her.

"Yes, I have," he replied.

"Right, well, we're going to need a sperm sample from you but I'm afraid we can't take it today. Could we make an appointment for you to come in at a later date and give a sample to be analysed?"

"Yeah." Richard looked mortified. "When will you need it?"

"As soon as possible would be great. While the nurse is taking Sinéad's bloods she can make an appointment for you. There's no need for me to be involved with that part of things. The nurse can organise it and test the sample for you."

Sinéad silently thanked God she was a girl and would never have to perform that kind of stunt for anyone.

A nurse came in and took Sinéad off to another room and took three vials of blood from her. She chatted merrily to another nurse while she took the blood and Sinéad took the opportunity to have a look around the room. The usual array of gloves, sterile needles and sample jars in boxes around the walls. In between the boxes and notices on the walls were pictures of babies, lots and lots of smiling babies. Plump faces smiling out from white towels. Sinéad looked at all the pictures, all these IVF babies, all the happy endings. Sinéad's heart was filled with excitement and worry in equal measure. Excitement at the prospect of a baby like that, one of her own! Her very own! And then the worry that it might never happen for them. What would she do if it never happened for them? If she was told by some doctor in ten years' time that it was all over. They had gone as far as they were willing to allow her go? What would happen? How could she deal with it? She looked back at the babies on the walls: they were gorgeous. She would just concentrate all her energy on them. She would have one of those babies, she had to – by whatever means possible, they'd get the happy ending. She was determined.

The nurse broke into her thoughts and told her they had all the blood they needed.

"Now your husband is having a sperm test, is he?"

"Not today, but he has to make an appointment to have it done."

"Grand, I'll go in and make an appointment with him."

She pulled a few pages from a file and went with Sinéad back to the office. She set a date with Richard and gave him a page with a list on it. They were all things Richard was to do and not to do in the days coming up to the test. Richard took the sheet and looked at the list, his face a studied blank.

"All right, we'll send that off to the labs and the results should be back in about three days. Hopefully there'll be no problem with it. Richard, while you're reading that list, Sinéad and I will just go into the next room and I'll give her a quick scan to look at her ovaries and check for cysts."

Richard nodded and went back to reading the list.

"If there's anything you need to query, just shout," the doctor said as he led the way for Sinéad. "Now, Sinéad, have you ever had a scan before?"

"No."

"All right, I have to ask, is your bladder reasonably full?"

"Yes, in fact it is." Sinéad had forgotten she needed to go to the loo – now the memory came flooding back in full Technicolor.

"Good, we need a full bladder. Now just lie back there and if you could open your trousers and pull them down just a little. This will be a little bit cold at first."

Sinéad watched as the doctor looked at the screen, a fuzzy screen with black spots was all she could make out but by the look on the doctor's face he could see a lot more.

"Everything looks fine here," he said. "Here we have your right ovary, nothing untoward there, and the left one looks perfect to me."

He pointed at the screen and Sinéad pretended she was following him. It was all good news so far, that was the important thing. They moved over to her womb and looked at that. It too looked perfect. He turned off the scanner and pushed it to one side.

"Everything so far looks fine to me."

"So what next?" Sinéad couldn't help feeling unsatisfied.

"Well, we've sent the bloods for analysis, Richard has an appointment for his sperm test and when we get the results of those tests we'll get a clearer picture of where we're going next. If that all comes back clear we need to do a few other tests."

"What kind of tests?"

"Let's just get the blood tests back first. There's no point in getting way ahead of ourselves."

"No, please, I want to know what happens next."

"You certainly do want to get things moving! Is this in every aspect of your life or just babies?"

"I'm sorry. I don't want you to think I'm a complete control freak. I am able to handle it when things don't work out, honestly! I just handle things better when I know what to expect. I'm one of those people who need to be as prepared as possible."

"You know there will be times in this process when

we'll all be blindsided by something. It could be something small, but we won't be fully prepared every time."

"I know that, but where I can be prepared I would prefer it if you told me what to expect. I don't want things to be kept from me. Tell me exactly how it is. I may cry or look shocked but I just prefer to know all the facts."

"All right, I'm getting a picture of the type of person you are and that's good. It's important to know. Is Richard the same?"

"Sort of, he likes to know the facts. He's not as pushy as me – he'd never have made this appointment. He'd just wait and see."

"That's very typical. Men do tend to stick their heads in the sand when it comes to their health."

"So getting back to the tests. What's next?" Sinéad smiled.

"You're some piece of work!" the doctor laughed. "Come through to my desk and we'll discuss it with Richard."

"Fine."

Back behind his desk, he continued. "All right, Richard, everything is fine with the scan, nothing to worry about there. Now, Sinéad was asking me what was next on the agenda. So, if all the bloods come back fine, then our next test is a little intrusive. We really don't like to discuss it before we have to."

"Please discuss it," said Sinéad.

"The next test is the post-coital exam. And it's exactly what you think it is. What we need you to do is to make love before your appointment, then not shower or go to the bathroom, just come straight in."

Sinéad gasped.

"I'm sorry – this isn't the most pleasant exam for you. We'll need you to come in and we'll bring you straight in and do an internal – in fact it'll be to all intents and purposes exactly like a smear test – we'll take a sample of the cells on your cervix and we'll check if the sperm is surviving in the vagina. Sometimes it doesn't and obviously that's a problem." He looked at Sinéad with a sympathetic smile. "The test can be performed by a nurse if you prefer."

"It's not who the person looking up my skirt is that bothers me; it's the fact that someone's looking up there in the first place."

"I understand."

"I don't think you do."

The doctor looked away and Sinéad was instantly sorry for snapping at him.

"Sorry, I'm just a little shocked," she said.

"If you want to call a halt at any point, it's entirely up to you. There is no obligation on you to do any of this."

"No, I want a baby. We both want one. I'll be fine." Sinéad sighed.

"Well, the tests results will be back within a few days. One of the nurses will give you a call with the results and we'll take it from there."

The doctor stood up and came around the table. He shook their hands as they headed for the door. "But we've made good progress today and everything is looking good at this point. We'll talk in a few days and go from there."

They left the hospital and got into the car.

"Jesus Christ, you should read the list of things I have

to do before I give this bloody sample. No sex, no caffeine, no hot bath, no alcohol!" Richard complained.

"Were you listening to him in there? Did you hear what we have to do next time?"

"Yeah, but we may not have to do that test at all. I have to go in there next week and toss off in the toilets!"

"You have to go in there next Friday and think happy thoughts in a private bathroom! I have to have people look inside me after we have sex! There is no comparison, Richard!"

"Yes, there is! Mine is just as embarrassing as yours will be!"

"No way, mate. Mine is way more embarrassing!"

"No way!"

"Richard, get over it! All boys love to toss off but there's no girl on earth who wants a strange man to check her insides after she has sex. It's not normal. Sorry for you, but tossing off is. You guys are always insisting that it is anyway!"

"Okay, sorry. Yours may be marginally more embarrassing. But hey, it may never come to it. They might find something on the blood tests and get that sorted out without ever having to go there."

"Jesus, what's worse? 'Yes, your hormones are askew' or 'No, your hormones are fine. Just go off and have sex there and we'll check you in half an hour'?" Sinéad buried her head in her hands.

"I'm sure it's not going to be like that. I'm sure it's very discreet and as painless as possible, Sinéad."

"It's going to be completely mortifying, that's what it'll

be!" Sinéad replied as she looked out the window, her heart pounding with pent-up frustration.

She closed it all from her thoughts and concentrated on the babies on those posters. This was just a small hurdle they had to face; it would be worth it and completely forgotten about when she got to hold her baby. A doctor's examination was nothing to worry about.

"Forget what I just said, Richard. I was just a bit panicky. It'll be fine. It'll be worth it to have it all sorted out," she said as she watched the traffic.

"That's right, babe. It'll all be over before we know it."

"And we'll be leaving that hospital with a baby, right?"

"A dead cert!"

The mood in the car lifted as they drove. It would be fine.

31

Richard and Sinéad went to the hospital the morning he had his sperm test. Sinéad insisted that she go with him. He wasn't overly keen on her being there.

"This is embarrassing enough without you sniggering about it outside the door."

"I won't be sniggering outside the door – I'll in the waiting room howling with laughter!"

"You're not helping."

"Go on, you big sissy," she smiled at him. "It's only a bit of fun on your own in a public loo!"

"Just call me George Michael!"

"Oh, George!" Sinéad smiled. "I was so sure I'd marry him, so bloody sure. It came as a complete shock to me that he was gay."

"It couldn't have."

"It did. I was that sure he'd marry me I thought he was just waiting until we met."

"He hadn't met the right woman because he hadn't met you yet?"

"Yeah, he still hasn't met me. I might be the girl to straighten his affections!"

"You think you could turn a gay guy straight? Do you understand that whole gay versus straight thing, Sinéad?"

"Of course I do. Oh listen, that was your name they just called."

Richard got up and followed the nurse out of the waiting room.

"Have lots of fun!" Sinéad whispered as he was leaving.

He ignored her completely.

Sinéad sat back in her chair and read a magazine. She looked around, taking in her surroundings more thoroughly this time. She was less stressed and was able to take in more. It was true what the doctor had said: the room was packed with people. All these people waiting to be told what was wrong and how it could be fixed for them. All these people with the same goal in all of this: they all wanted a baby. Sinéad realised she was not alone in this, there were plenty like her, and they came in all shapes and sizes and they all had their reasons for waiting as long as they did or ignoring the signs that something was wrong.

Half an hour later she saw Richard pass the waiting-room door and head for the reception. She jumped up and followed him out to the corridor. He was talking to a nurse who took his sample and labelled it. She thanked him and that was it – they were free to go.

"So that's it?" Sinéad said. "We can go now?"

Richard walked ahead of her along the corridor. "Yes, how fucking embarrassing was that!"

"What happened?"

"I'll tell you when we get out."

"You could do it, couldn't you? You didn't not do it?"

"I said I'll tell you when we get out!"

Sinéad rushed along behind him. He had handed the nurse a sample so it had all gone according to plan, so what could have happened? She moved faster, getting out to the footpath so she could hear what went wrong. They got into the car and Richard put his head in his hands. Sinéad was stunned. For a moment she thought he was crying, but thankfully he was laughing.

"So what happened?" Sinéad asked, relief flooding over her as she spoke. If he was laughing it wasn't so bad.

"To cut a long story short, I fell."

"You fell? Did you actually fall over or did you trip and steady yourself?"

"Actually hit the deck. No – in fact, I hit the wall and fell to the deck." Richard put his head in his hands again.

"Was this before or after the event?"

"After."

"So did you break the jar – or spill the – um, sample or what?"

"No. It did fall to the ground but it was okay."

"But . . ."

"But what?"

"I wondered about whether it'd affect the . . . you know . . . the guys." Sinéad smiled but Richard didn't find it funny.

"You're afraid they all come out with concussion? Swimming backwards and banging into the side of the Petri dish?" Sinéad nodded, smiling at him.

"No, it doesn't work like that. If that was the case, then drunk guys would be unable to get anyone pregnant and as we all know, drunk men are the ones who do it most often!"

"I suppose it is. I never thought about it like that. Anyway, what happened?"

"I was coming back out of the bathroom and I tripped over the step of the door. I fell head first onto the corridor. I banged my head and it stung like a bitch."

"Where?"

"Against the wall, I told you."

"No, I mean did you injure your head?"

He turned his head and showed her the huge bump on his forehead just above the hairline. "But that's not the worst part."

"What was the worst part?" asked Sinéad, alarmed again.

"Well, I wanted to just run out of the place – I mean I must have looked so ridiculous falling like that trying to save my sample – people were sniggering – but a nurse saw me bang my head and made me sit down for a while. I had to sit in the corridor outside the bathroom with the sample in my hand. It must have been the busiest corridor in the hospital, and the only loo in the building! People were coming and going like ants and everyone was looking at me and the fucking sample in my hand."

"Did you not put it in your pocket or up your sleeve or something?"

"No, I didn't. I never thought of that actually. I just sat there holding the bloody thing. Oh look, I never, ever want to do that ever again."

"Oh poor old you! I just hope you knocking them on their heads won't affect the sperm count. Anyway, if it comes back low they make you do it again. I read that on your little list."

"That was not a *little* list, and I will never do that again!"

"What? The sperm test or dropping your sample on the floor and giving your sperm the shock of their lives?"

"Both."

"Look, it'll be all right. It won't affect the test results and it'll be a funny little story you can tell at dinner parties. You can only tell our closest friends though! No one outside of Gavin or Luke!"

"This is a story I will not be dining out on, you can be sure of that!"

"Well, maybe you'll see things a little rosier when this whole thing is behind us and I'm pregnant."

"No, I'll never look back and laugh at that."

The Wednesday after the ill-fated sperm test was marked in pink highlighter in Sinéad's diary. This was the day she had to ring the hospital for their results. She was to ring any time between 1 o'clock and 4.30, which meant she was going to have to ring from work. She was not the least bit happy about that but she really needed the results so she had to ring. She decided to ring from the boardroom phone at 1.30 – that way most people would be on lunch and there'd be no one anywhere near the boardroom. She was sick as she got up from her desk and headed for the lift on her way to the boardroom.

"Jesus, Sinéad, are you feeling all right?" came a voice from a desk as she passed by.

"Yes, I'm fine," she smiled and kept going.

"Seriously, Sinéad, you look like you're going to faint!" the voice sailed after her.

"No!" She turned her head to see who it was that was shouting at her. "I'm completely fine, thanks!"

If Sinéad had been looking in the right way, if she had been walking and not almost running as she looked around her, she'd have seen her line manager come through the door carrying his lunch and an open can of Coke back to his desk. If she'd been looking in the right direction she'd have seen him before she crashed into him. She would have seen him before she mashed his sandwich all over her chest and spilt his Coke all over his. The sandwich – or in fact half of it – the half that wasn't pasted to her top, fell on the floor spilling its contents all around. The can dropped and spun in a circle spraying Coke all over their legs. People jumped up, grabbing their bags and screeching as their legs were sprayed with the coke. Her manager looked at his top and trousers, then at hers. He was annoyed, she could tell by the curl of his lip, but he was keeping a lid on it.

"Jesus, Sinéad, where were you off to in such a hurry?" he asked.

"Oh my God! Liam, I am so sorry!" she began but was interrupted.

"Sinéad, are you all right? Are you feeling sick?"

That damn voice was back. Sinéad looked around to see who it was. It was Ciara and she was coming down the aisle between desks with her concerned face.

"Yes, I'm completely fine, Ciara. I was just in a bit of hurry."

"Where were you off to in such a hurry, and looking over your shoulder?"

Sinéad was just about to answer with a smart 'none of your bloody business' but she realised that it was her manager who had asked the question, not Ciara.

"I was just popping out to make a call," she answered, cursing her inability to make up a lie in time.

"Why couldn't you have made it from your desk?"

"We're not meant to make personal calls from our desks..." Sinéad's voice trailed off at the end of the sentence. While that might be strictly true, no one thought for a moment that people didn't use the phone on their desks for personal calls. And if Sinéad didn't use hers then she was completely brainwashed by the company. Her manager looked at her and picked up his sandwich off the floor.

"While you're out there making your call, will you pick me up a sandwich then?" he said.

"Yes, absolutely, Liam. What do you want in it?"

"Chicken salad on white with butter and a can of Coke."

"I'm so sorry, Liam, I'll get it straight away."

Sinéad was mortified. She wanted to cry but she just kept moving.

"I'll be back in a few minutes, all right?" she called brightly as she walked away.

"And Sinéad," he called after her, "you do look very pale. Are you feeling all right?"

She swung around – stopping this time for fear of

bumping into someone else. "Pale? But I'm blushing! I'm so embarrassed."

"No, I mean this morning – you were looking a bit off." Liam smiled. "Anything we should know about?"

"God no, nothing like that!" Sinéad smiled back. She could feel her face flush even more and decided to get moving.

She hurried out the door and got into the lift. She jumped out on the second floor and rushed around to the boardroom. She was busy brushing salad and mayonnaise from her top as she walked in the door. She was pulling pieces of thinly sliced lettuce from her buttons as she rushed by the large table and went to pull the phone out of a cupboard in the corner. The phone wasn't there but the wire was. She pulled the wire to see where the phone was. Someone must have dragged it to the table and left it there. She looked up and to her astonishment there were five men sitting around the table, the phone in the middle of them and all five sets of eyes on her.

She screeched a little as she realised she was not dreaming, that this was really happening her.

"Oh my God! I'm so sorry!" she began.

"Can we help you?" one of the men asked. It was the managing director.

"No, I'm so sorry, I was . . . I'm just . . . I am so sorry, I should have knocked. Excuse me, I'm just leaving!" She turned and ran out the door.

She ran to the bathroom and stood by the sink with her hands shaking. After a minute or so she gathered her thoughts together and cleaned off her top. She stood in the bathroom for a while, waiting for the blush to leave her cheeks and for her heart to stop pounding. She wondered whether or not she was sacked. Perhaps she was, running into her manager and mashing his lunch all over her chest, and now walking in on the MD making a conference call of some sort and almost pulling the phone line from the wall.

Well, if they're going to sack you, you may as well make it worth their while, she thought.

She went out and sat on the steps outside the office and made the call from her mobile. She hated making important calls on her mobile – in the middle of town you could never be sure if you were breaking up or not. She dialled the number and gave her details.

The nurse who 'deals with all the blood tests' came on to the phone.

"Sinéad Kilbride?"

"Yes, that's me."

"All your test results are perfect. The hormone levels are perfect and your husband's sperm test is completely normal."

"So that's all good news?"

"Yes, it's perfect."

"So what's next?" Sinéad was so relieved she felt suddenly giddy.

"Well, according to your notes Dr Whitney has spoken to you about the post-coital exam. That's the next test we would usually go with."

"Oh Christ, I really hate the thought of that one." Sinéad's giddiness was all but gone.

"Look, Sinéad, nothing is set in stone and you don't

need to go ahead with any of these tests if you don't want to."

"I know, but we've been trying for almost eighteen months now – I really need to find out why this isn't happening for me."

"I understand but please don't feel pushed forward into anything you don't want to do. Would you like to meet with Dr Whitney again and talk it over with him?"

The nurse sounded so nice – she seemed to really care about Sinéad even though they were complete strangers. Sinéad thought for a moment about talking to the doctor again, but then decided against it.

"No, it's all right. That's just prolonging the agony. This test will have to be done, won't it?"

"It's up to you but, yes, at some point you will most likely decide to do the test."

"Well then, make an appointment and we'll get it over with."

"All right, how does the fifteenth of June suit you? At ten thirty a.m.?"

"All right, that's fine."

"What we would ask is that you make love on the morning of the appointment, not more than two hours before the appointment. Please do not bath or shower after you make love. The idea is we need to see what actually happens to the sperm, if you know what I mean. We need to make sure it goes where it should and if not what's happening to it."

"Oh God, say no more. Just make the appointment!" Sinéad laughed through gritted teeth.

"All right. But just remember what I said – if you want to cancel this whole thing it's up to you."

"Thanks."

Sinéad hung up, her emotions all over the place. Yes, this was wonderful news – there was nothing wrong with her or Richard.

But now they had to do this damn post-coital test.

She rang Richard straight away.

"Well, that's good news," he said. "The tests are fine, that's one hurdle over."

"Richard, we have to do the post-coital test now."

"The what?"

"The one we spoke to the doctor about."

"Oh Christ, Sinéad, I'm sorry, honey."

"Not as sorry as I am."

"Well, when is it? We'll get it over with as soon as we can."

"It's in two weeks. The fifteenth of June."

"Okay, well, we just have to get it over with and pray it comes back all clear."

Sinéad played with her computer all afternoon but did absolutely nothing. Five couldn't come quick enough for her. Finally she turned off her computer and headed for home.

She lay on the couch watching TV until Richard came home. Her heart was heavy and every so often she felt her chest tighten. As soon as he came in, a bottle of wine and a box of Milk Tray under his arm, she felt herself crumble and the tears fell.

He sat on the couch holding her while she cried. Again and again she asked the same question.

"Why us? Why do we have to go through this? Why can't we have a baby?"

And again and again Richard gave her the only answer he could.

"I don't know, babe. I honestly don't know."

32

Gavin had agreed that they would not talk about 'Babygate', as it was now being called, for six months. He had promised that he would leave Julie to think about it. He had promised he'd do it, but of course he didn't actually do it.

Three months later he was on about it again.

"Come on, Jules. It'd be a great idea. Give me one reason why we shouldn't have another baby?"

"I don't want another baby now. That's a reason."

"Why not? I thought we were having loads of kids? I thought you wanted to be a fucking Soccer Mom or whatever the word is? Why the change of heart?"

"Gavin, I have lived up to my side of the bargain. We have two small girls or have you forgotten about them? In your hurry to get a son have you forgotten about them?"

"They're getting older – Genevieve is almost two and a half. By the time the next baby arrives she'll be about three and a half. There'll be a huge age gap between them."

"What's huge about that?"

"I thought we were agreed that we'd have them close together and they'd be company for each other?"

"What? I never agreed to any such thing. We never spoke about the ages of the children. Anyway, Gavin, I'm working and I'm enjoying my job. I'm getting myself together here. I'm finally getting some time out to look after myself."

"Look after yourself? But you can have your hair done and your bloody nails or whatever on a Saturday morning while I take the girls to the park. What difference would a third baby make to that set-up?"

"It'd make all the difference! I don't want to get fat again or have to give up my job!"

"Fat again? You'd be pregnant – that's not fat."

"I'd blow up like a house again and I'd be another year getting rid of the weight again."

"And as for your job, it'd be no loss to give it up. It doesn't even pay a wage!"

"Yes, it does, and if I gave it up I'd have the girls back every day. We couldn't afford to have them in the crèche without my crappy job. And I wouldn't have the money to get my hair done on a Saturday either. Things would be very different around here if I didn't work."

"I can't believe it. I never wanted you to take that stupid job and now you're using it as an excuse not to have another baby?"

"*No, Gavin!* The job's not my excuse. I just don't bloody well want a baby right now. I asked you to give me time – I asked for six months!"

"Come on, Jules, it's not all up to you!"

"Gavin, if we go ahead and have this baby — let's just suppose we do — things would be so different around here. We'd have a third baby to feed, nappies, blue clothes if it turned out to be boy. We'd have to change the car and get a bigger one; we'd have to find one that could fit three baby seats in the back. I'd have to give up my job because we couldn't afford to send all three of them to the crèche. We'd have all three children back in the house. The girls would miss their little friends and all because you won't wait a year or two for the next baby? And you call me selfish?"

"Personally I don't see any problem there. Getting a bigger car, everyone does it. You giving up work, I'd love to see you give up that job. It's a waste of bloody time."

"It's my job, Gavin! It's my fucking independence. It's my escape from this damn house and the girls and this bloody kitchen!"

"Fine, have it your own way then!" Gavin sneered. "Be a shelf-stacker in Dunnes for the rest of your life. Put our family plans on hold while you climb your corporate ladder and some day you might just get to be a check-out operator!"

"Piss off, Gavin!" Julie hissed. "This is my job. I like it and it pays my bills. That's all I need and believe it or not I'm very happy. I will not have another baby yet, not for another year or two. You will not push me into having more children right now."

She stood up and left the kitchen. In the hall she saw her car keys. Without a further thought she picked them up, grabbed her coat and opened the front door.

"I'm going out. You watch the girls for an hour or so."

She saw the kitchen door swing open as she shut the hall door.

She got into the car and drove off, not sure where she was going but just that she wanted to get away from Gavin, the house and the children for a while. She drove up to Howth and up to the Summit. She sat there in her car listening to the radio, staring out at the lights of the city. She sat there, not looking left or right, ignoring the fogged-up windows of the cars around her. She couldn't help but wonder if any of the occupants of those cars would regret this trip in nine months' time.

She wouldn't, that was for sure.

33

The morning of the post-coital test dawned. Sinéad set her alarm for seven. When it went off she got up and showered. It was the longest, hottest shower she'd taken in months; she scrubbed and scoured her skin. There was no way anyone was looking at her unwashed body, no way in hell.

She dried her hair, smothered her skin in sweet-smelling lotion and got back into bed. It was functional and they barely looked at each other. Afterwards, Richard promised he wouldn't shower out of sympathy with her. They dressed in silence and went to the hospital. Richard held her hand as they waited for the doctor to call her name. Finally her name was called loud and clear. She got to her feet, knees knocking, and went to the office. The doctor was very friendly and ushered her into his surgery and into a small room at the side.

"Just slip off your trousers and underwear. And if you could just hop up on the bed, bend your knees, put your ankles together and let your legs relax. Just like a smear test, you know the drill? And there's a blanket you can cover yourself with there."

He left and she got undressed as fast as she could.

The doctor came back in a few minutes later and set to work. It was very like a smear and not quite as embarrassing as Sinéad had anticipated. But having said that, she hated every second of it.

"That's it. It looks completely fine and we got a great sample there but of course we'll have to look at it under the microscope before we give you the diagnosis."

He left with the specimen on a slide. Sinéad got dressed again and went to the doctor's office just as the doctor ushered Richard in the door.

"Well, it's all good news," the doctor smiled. "There's nothing wrong. Everything is where it should be and doing exactly what it should be doing. So that is great news."

"So what does that tell us?" Richard asked.

"At its most basic, the test tells us that the sperm has survived its time in the vagina and is completely fit for insemination, if and when it meets an egg. Sometimes the atmosphere in the vagina can kill off the sperm before they get any further, but that's not a problem for you guys."

"What is the problem then?" Sinéad asked. If she'd just had that humiliating test for nothing she was suing someone! And nice guy or not, Dr John fucking Whitney was first in line!

"You must understand that at the moment we are

simply checking off our list. We're going through the possibilities and at the moment you're coming up trumps in each test. We know that there's no abnormality in your hormones, your sperm test is perfect, you don't have ovarian cysts and now we've confirmed that the sperm is surviving into the Fallopian tubes."

"Are we ever going to find out what's wrong?"

"Sinéad, there may be nothing wrong. We do have cases where the couple have no medical reason for the infertility. I don't know if that's the case in your situation but we need to go down every avenue until we either find a reason or can confidently say there is no reason."

"What if there is no reason? What then?"

"If there is no reason for the infertility then there's no reason we wouldn't hope that it would rectify itself in time. Sometimes all the couple need is the reassurance that everything is in order."

"So what's next for us?" Richard asked, putting a hand on Sinéad's leg.

"Well, from here on in, the tests mainly focus on Sinéad. We can do one of two things, a hystero-salpingogram or HSG and then a laparoscopy."

"What's an HSG?" Sinéad asked.

"It's an X-ray. We inject dye into the Fallopian tubes and uterus prior to the X-ray. This dye runs through the tubes and we would check to see if the tubes were clear. If the dye runs through then it's all clear, if not we have a blockage."

"I've heard of a lap," Sinéad said.

"I haven't," said Richard.

"A laparoscopy is where a camera is inserted through

a hole in Sinéad's belly-button. We then get a clear view of what exactly is going on in the womb, tubes, ovaries etc. This is the one procedure where we put Sinéad asleep. We'd do it early in the day but it would still mean an overnight stay in the hospital."

"What would we do first?" Sinéad asked. After the test today nothing seemed quite so bad.

"I would suggest the HSG as it doesn't involve any operation. But this is just me. At all times you are the ones directing us. I will not push you into any procedure you're not completely happy with."

"After today's ordeal, nothing is too much for me. That was my all-time low."

"It's everyone's all-time low, Sinéad. You're not alone in that," the doctor said. "So do you want to go home, talk it over and make your decision? When you're ready give us a call and we'll book you in for the next appointment."

"Can we not just make the appointment now?" Sinéad asked.

"I would suggest taking a little time out. There have been a lot of tests and today was stressful for you. Why don't you go home and talk in the comfort of your own home? Call us in the morning to make an appointment."

"I think he's right," said Richard. "Let's just take a moment to talk, Sinéad."

"What are you talking about? Let's get this over and done with. Dr Whitney, I want the appointment made and the testing process to be over, as soon as possible. It's me that's being prodded and poked – let's get it over and done with."

Richard and the doctor looked at each other.

"Richard, are you happy to go ahead with the next stage?"

"Why are you asking Richard? It's me that gets injected and X-rayed. I want to get it over with!"

"This is a two-way thing, Sinéad," said Richard. "It doesn't just affect you – I'm here too and it's stressful for me too!"

"You haven't had to do anything! Anyway, it was you who were begging for this baby all along. Now that things are finally moving, you're acting like you don't even want it!"

"What are you talking about? I'm here, aren't I? I've done everything I've been asked to do. And what about you? Why the sudden change of heart? You never wanted a baby at all and now look at us, reading books, those predictor kits and now a fertility clinic! What's got you all maternal all of a sudden?"

"I'm thirty-three, Richard – most people get broody in their thirties." Then under her breath she muttered, "And most people's husbands have no problem getting them pregnant."

"I heard that! I'm the one firing on all cylinders here. We've had the proof of that. Twice."

Sinéad opened her mouth to attack him on the 'twice' remark but the doctor got there first.

"All right, guys, I think this really has gone far enough."

Sinéad nearly died. She'd forgotten the doctor was there and couldn't believe she'd just attacked Richard like that in his presence.

"There are a lot of issues and stresses on people in your position," the doctor went on. "I would again, please, ask you both to go home and have a chat. Get these issues – all of them – out on the table and decide where you want to go from there. And if you could just remember – this has an effect on both of you, even if it is just Sinéad going through the procedures. It affects everything and everyone. So go easy on each other."

"I'm sorry. You're right. I don't know what I was thinking," she replied, her cheeks burning. Why had she raised her voice like that in front of him?

"I'm very sorry, Dr Whitney," Richard apologised. "We shouldn't have got into that in front of you. I'm sorry."

"It's all right. It happens a lot. This is why we keep telling you: do not feel pushed into treatments you're not ready for. Go on home and relax, open a bottle of wine and order a Chinese. It always helps."

"Thanks," Sinéad smiled as they left.

They walked through the hospital in silence. They got to the car without a word passing between them. The car journey home was a mute affair but when they got in the door Richard broke the silence.

"We need to talk," he said as he went into the kitchen. "About everything, just like the doctor said. Everything needs to be laid on the table. All right?"

"Okay. I just want to go to the loo first."

When Sinéad came back to the kitchen Richard had boiled the kettle and he was making a few sandwiches. They made tea and brought the sandwiches over to the table and sat down.

"Do you want to get things started?" Richard asked.

"No, not really. I don't know where to begin," Sinéad replied.

"Right, I do. I have one question and it's bothered me for a while now. Why the sudden change of heart? About having a baby?"

"It's not that sudden, is it?" Sinéad asked.

"Well, you were dead against the whole idea of kids, then one day you just decided we *had* to have one *straight away.*"

"It actually wasn't like that at all, Richard. I wasn't charmed about the whole baby thing. I can think of more pleasant things to be doing with my time than getting fat and achy and stretch-marked and then there's the actual birth. It's not exactly a walk in the park by all accounts. But then I saw Annabel and Genevieve and how great they are and you were always cracking on about how great it'd be to have one and I suppose I just thought it'd be nice to have one of my own. I wasn't that worried or even bothered for the first while, but then about six or seven months in I began to think it was taking a while. Then Julie said there were great books out there and I decided to read up on it. Then I will admit things kind of snowballed a bit, but I don't think I became *too* obsessive about it."

"Too obsessive? You were buying little tests every month, lying on your back upside down in the bed, watching what we ate and drank and even what I wore. Just a tad obsessive I would say."

"Well, I suppose . . . I suppose . . ." Sinéad didn't know what to say. By that account she was a hair's-breadth from a mental institution. "I didn't mean to get so manic about it . . . it just sort of creeps up on you I think. That and the fact that doctor said I —"

She stopped abruptly, she'd never told Richard about the doctor all those years ago. She'd never mentioned it to anyone.

"What doctor? What did they say?" Richard was interested.

"Nothing, it was nothing."

"No, go on. Everything on the table, remember?"

"It was nothing – it makes no difference now anyway."

"What was nothing?"

"It was just something a doctor said in passing years ago."

"Go on."

"He just said that because my periods were irregular and I was having such a hard time with them that maybe I should be checked out. He wanted to see if there was anything that could be wrong with me."

"Anything wrong like what?"

"He wondered about my fertility, but at the time I was just a teenager and I never did anything about it. I think that was why I got worried so quickly when things didn't just happen straight away."

Sinéad was being overly casual about it; she didn't want Richard to give out to her about not getting checked out. It was no use – he was on top of her in a second.

"You were told to get checked out for infertility back in your teens? And you never got checked? And you never bothered to tell me?" Richard was incensed.

"I didn't think it was a big deal." As Sinéad spoke, she realised how wrong she'd been on that score. She absolutely should have told him about this from the start.

"No big deal? Sinéad, you knew I was dead keen to have children and you knew this might be a problem, and you said nothing?"

Sinéad felt cornered, and she hated being cornered. She came out fighting a completely different battle. "Well, you never bothered to tell me about the abortion! All the time we were together and you never bothered to tell me that!"

"That had no bearing on us trying for a baby. It was nothing to do with anything, Sinéad!"

"But it was important to me!" she lied.

"Why was it important to you? The only bearing it has on our lives is that it proves I can get a girl pregnant. It means nothing else."

"It has a lot to do with why you want a baby so badly. You want to replace the baby you got rid of!" Sinéad hardly knew where this thought had come from.

"No, I don't. It's been over fifteen years since that whole thing happened. It has no bearing on this baby at all!"

"Yes, it does! You may not want to face the facts but it's obvious that you wanted a baby so badly because you felt so guilty about the other one!" Now she was convincing herself.

"Listen, Sinéad, it may amaze you to hear this but I don't actually regret that abortion. I'm not thrilled it happened, it's not something I look back on and smile about, far from it, but I think we did the right thing. We were too young and it would have been the end of both our careers and Joanne's life if she'd gone ahead and had that baby. I am not replacing anyone. I want a child – plain and simple. I'm a grown man with a career and a home and a wife and I'd like to have a child. What's so hard to understand about that? Why have there got to be huge guilt issues to explain it?"

"Well, if you felt compelled to replace the child you lost, that would explain why there was such hurry on all of this," Sinéad said.

"A hurry? I've waited years for you! And now it's you who's putting the pressure on. I was always willing to wait until it happened naturally. I always assumed it would. Now you tell me you've had fertility problems since your teens and you never thought to tell me."

They were back on track again and this time Sinéad couldn't change the subject.

"I don't have fertility problems. The doctor wondered about getting some tests done, that's all."

"And what happened?"

"Nothing – my periods settled down after a while. You heard what my GP said – it sometimes takes a few years for these things to settle."

"What age were you when this was all going on?"

"I was nineteen and it settled down in my early twenties."

"Nineteen? When you said your teens, I thought you meant early teens – when your periods began."

"No, but they had always been very irregular." Sinéad

could see where his mind was going with this and it was an obvious conclusion. Why oh why hadn't she just got herself tested?

"That's a hell of a long time to be getting settled – what was it? About six years before you went to the doctor? Eight or nine years before they became regular?"

"I suppose, about that."

"Why did you never get tested? And why did you never tell me about this?"

"I don't know why. I just didn't."

"You just didn't what? Not get tested or not bother to tell me about this?"

"Both, but you make this sound very sordid. As if I did it on purpose to trap you into marrying me. I didn't think we'd have problems and then when we did I remembered the problem."

"I can't believe you didn't tell me any of this. Now I know why you were so eager to get to that fertility clinic. You've known there might be problems for years."

"I haven't, Richard. That's so unfair! I never thought it would turn out like this. I never in my wildest dreams thought we'd have to get help with having a baby. Please, Richard, please believe me about that!"

Richard sat for a long time staring at the table and then at Sinéad. Finally he spoke.

"I believe you never thought we'd need help on this. And I believe you didn't mean to get so obsessed about the whole thing, but I think the fact that you knew there might be problems and never told me is unforgivable. I really hate that you didn't tell me about that."

"I'm sorry. I never meant to hide it from you. I never thought it was going to be an issue. If I'd known back then that we'd be sitting here like this today, I'd have had every test they offered but the truth is I didn't. I'm sorry, Richard. Maybe I was in denial – I don't know."

Richard stood up from the table and put his mug on the draining board. "I hear what you're saying. I do. I just need to get out for a while. I need to clear my head. I can't talk about this any more today."

He left the kitchen and went into the hall. Sinéad heard the front door closing a few minutes later and his car drove off. She sat at the kitchen table, her head resting on her forearm. Before long she was fast asleep.

34

Six months had passed since Julie took off and went out to Howth. The trip had had the desired effect. Gavin was shocked into silence on the baby issue. Julie had come back home just before eleven. She'd gone to the fridge, opened a bottle of wine and poured a large glass. She'd gone into the sitting room, picked up the paper and sat back to read it. Gavin had watched her in silence. Anger and relief that she was all right prevented him from speaking to her. Julie for her part had nothing more to say on the topic. She was not having another baby right then.

But now it was six months later and the topic was rearing its ugly head again. Gavin was eager for a new baby and, although he was willing to leave the topic rest for a while, he was just as eager to start it up again.

They had gone out for dinner one Saturday night. Julie had taken the opportunity to dress up and wear her new sparkly top, a gift for herself from this month's hundred euro. Somewhere between the main course and dessert

Gavin had broached the subject. Julie was a bit giddy from the wine and high on the adrenaline buzz that being out gave her.

"Julie, it's been eight months. You have to realise I really want to have another baby. I think the timing is just right. The girls are out of nappies. Annabel will be going to school in eighteen months. Come on, Jules, I've been very patient on this one."

"Gavin, you've been pushy and sulky and argumentative for the last six months. You may not have said the sentence 'Let's have another baby' lately but it's been an underlying problem with you the whole time."

"Julie, I don't want another row about this. I really just want you to realise how important it is for me."

"Gavin, I get it. I've known for a while now, thanks."

"So what will we do about it?"

"I'll give it serious thought, Gavin, all right? Just give me a month."

Julie knew she was playing for yet more time here, but she wasn't sure she wanted another baby. She had said when they got married that she wanted at least four children and now Gavin was reminding her of this fact every time they spoke about the matter. She'd said a lot of things back then. She'd said she wanted to open her own café and travel to India before she was thirty. She hadn't done either of those things but Gavin wasn't reminding her of that every second, was he? She'd also said she wanted an eternity ring when Annabel was born. Four years later her finger was still naked. But Gavin wasn't letting this one rest. If she said no – which she could if she wanted, it was a free bloody world – it would only rear its head yet again in three months. She was thirty-two now. She'd be thirty-three when the baby was born, Annabel would be almost five and Genevieve would be four. Maybe it was time to be having another baby. By the time the baby arrived she'd have got used to the idea of a third set of lungs screaming for her. She'd give it some thought.

Julie and Gavin were sitting in the kitchen one night after the girls were gone to bed. Gavin had been dropping hints the size of elephants about the baby. Julie could feel her nerves tingle whenever he began to talk about it again.

Finally the time had come to make her decision. She had sat Gavin down at the table. He would have to listen to her and hear every word she was about to say. She needed his full attention. If they were having a third baby, they were having it on Julie's terms.

"Gavin, listen to me and hear me out before you get up on your high horse," she said. "This is what is going to happen. We will have another baby, just one. If it's a boy then I'll be happy for you. If it's a girl I will not be the least bit sorry for you and we will not have any more children. I am not some brood mare and I will not 'keep going' until you get yourself a son. You will be happy with whoever God sends. Three children, four if this is twins, is my absolute limit. After this I hang up my boots and you content yourself with three little Hurleys. Right?"

Gavin looked at her. "Can I speak yet?"

"No, I haven't finished. Now Annabel is almost four

and the baby will take at least nine months to arrive. This means Annabel will be almost five and will be in school. I will take my maternity leave and then go back to work. I'll be able to afford to leave the baby and Genevieve in the crèche. I like my job and I want to keep it, I'm adamant about that." Julie stopped and looked at Gavin. She'd finished talking but he was still waiting for permission to speak. "That's it, I'm finished. You can talk."

"That's great, another baby would be great. And you're adamant that it'll be your last one?"

"Unless at some point around my thirty-eighth birthday I have a fit of hormones and decide the world will end if I don't have one more baby. But I can't see that happening personally."

"All right, and you're definitely going back to work?"

"I'll be taking my full maternity leave, but yes."

"Do you really like your job that much?"

"Yeah, I do, sort of."

"Fair enough."

35

Julie had committed herself to trying for a third baby. She had a three-year-old, a two-year-old and now she was going have a new baby too. Was she mad?

Gavin was delighted. Why wouldn't he be? It may have taken a while but he was getting his way again. And boy, was he getting his way! They were 'baby-dancing' every time they looked at each other. Julie never had much trouble getting pregnant so she was relaxed about it. All this fuss would end in a few weeks if the past was anything to go by.

Before they started he had asked her when her period was due. One evening he rang her on his way home from work.

"Any news?"

"Yeah, we need milk. Annabel spilt an entire litre today. I could have killed her!"

"And the other thing?"

"What other thing?"

"Your period, have you got it yet?"

"Gavin, that's a bit personal!"

"Well, have you?"

"Yes, I got it yesterday, but Gavin, it's not really a topic I chat about."

"Yeah, but I'm just interested. We are trying for a baby after all."

"And if there is any news you'll be the first to hear it – but this is just intrusive, Gavin."

"What are you talking about? I have the right to ask."

"No, Gavin, you don't. That's just rude. You do not have the right to ask. When I get pregnant I will tell you straight away – until then please do not ring me to ask me about it. That's really a step too far!"

"All right, sorry. I didn't think it was, under the circumstances."

"Well, I think it was. Just get milk."

"Fine."

Julie hung up the phone, fuming with him. She wasn't being coy – that was a step too far. She had the right to some privacy and she would be insisting on it. She also began to hope that this baby would arrive sooner rather than later. This 'trying' business and Gavin's obsession with it all was too much, and it was only the second month. What would he be like if it took nine or ten months? Would she be filing for divorce on the day the pregnancy was confirmed?

Three months later she was surprised to find herself still not pregnant. It wasn't for lack of trying and suddenly

Julie found herself in unfamiliar water. She was one of the ones 'trying, but not getting pregnant'. It had been five months, not exactly time to call in the cavalry but it was a bit of a worry to her. She had really thought the baby would be well on its way by now.

Gavin was becoming truly obsessed by now. He was overbearing, watching her when she got drunk, 'advising' her on her diet, and watching the calendar, just as she'd asked him not to.

It was becoming a thorn in both their sides. One Sunday afternoon they were in the kitchen together, the girls were in the garden and Gavin had just boiled the kettle for tea. He came over with a mug of tea and some chocolate biscuits.

"There you go. Never say I don't spoil you!" he smiled as he put the biscuits on the table.

"Thanks!" Julie smiled, digging in straight away.

They sat in silence, watching the girls as they ran in the garden. Julie looked at Gavin; maybe they should have a chat about the baby situation. Something needed to be said and now might just be the time to say it.

"Gavin, I think we might need to take a step back from the baby thing. We both know that we can have children – so maybe we should just leave it a month or two and see what happens."

"I just don't want to let it go, not have the baby at all. Find ourselves out of time and always sorry we didn't keep trying."

"But, Gav, we are trying. This isn't calling a halt to it all. I'm just saying is let's stop the panic. I'm still only thirty-two, for another eight weeks anyway. It's been five months, but they've been stressful. We've had Annabel's birthday and the cast of thousands at her party, and then your uncle had his heart scare – maybe we're just pushing too hard on this."

"Maybe," Gavin sighed."

"We could do with taking a break. To tell you the truth I could do with a break from sex and a break away from here. A few nights away, down the country or somewhere. Without the kids. I think it would help us a lot."

"We have been a bit obsessed by it all, haven't we?"

"We? What's this 'we'? I never checked your dinner!"

"Yeah, I was bad. Sorry about that."

"You should be. I never want to have my dinner scrutinised again, understood?"

"Absolutely."

Julie went to the window and shouted to Annabel to stop pulling Genevieve's hair.

"And you want more of them?" she laughed.

"Not another Annabel, thanks. This house couldn't take another one of her!"

"This world couldn't cope with another one of her."

Julie looked back out and saw Annabel carrying the cat over to the swing, then trying in vain to make it sit on the swing. The cat had other ideas, jumped down and took off down the garden.

"Annabel! Leave the cat alone!" she called out the window, and only then realised that Genevieve was being very quiet down the back of the garden. "What's Genevieve doing?"

"She's fine – she's just eating the snails."

"Oh, Christ!"

Gavin was already out of his seat and running down the garden.

Genevieve was indeed trying to eat snails. They were all over her hands and there was one in her mouth. She was forced to spit out the one in her mouth and come in. They washed her face and hands and then they were at a loss. She looked up at them, a calm expression on her perfectly clean face.

"Did you actually eat one of the snails?"

She shook her head.

"Tell the truth. You're not in trouble."

She shook her head.

"Did you eat any of the other little animals out there?"

"A worm."

"Just one?"

"Yes."

"And do you feel sick?"

"No."

"Have you a tummy ache at all?"

"No."

Gavin looked at Julie. "I think she's fine."

"Me too."

"Well, Vieve, please don't eat anything else out there. If you're hungry just tell me. We'll get you something from the kitchen."

"Okay," she nodded solemnly.

They let her back out to the garden and she went on with her game. They watched her during the day but she was completely fine. The worm had had no ill effect on her; with a bit of luck it hadn't tasted nice and she wouldn't be eager to repeat the performance.

Julie and Gavin sat back that evening and laughed about it all, but in the Julie's head that old worry began to niggle again. The girls were good – yes, they were a handful and her job was time-consuming too – but she had the balance just right and had got to a point where she was having a little time for herself. Now they were discussing another baby, and she could just feel all her good work going backwards. She had committed herself to having this third child. Was she out of her mind? Would she ever feel completely sane again? Would she ever sit down again for that matter? Not for another two years anyway, that was a given.

36

It had been nine months since Julie and Gavin had decided to have that third baby. Julie knew because Gavin had been ticking off months in the calendar in the kitchen. He'd promised to stop fussing but of course in true Gavin style he'd just fussed in silence.

Anyway, it was nine months later when Julie began to feel that familiar tingling in her breasts and the sudden 'feeling' that something was different. Something had changed; she was content, almost smug in herself. There was something happening that was very personal. She knew what it was – a week before her period was due and she just 'knew'. She waited the week out and finally on Saturday morning she took the test. The blue line came as no surprise to her. It had taken nine months in all, an eternity for Julie but it was all over now, the test was positive and she called Gavin to give him the good news.

"Gavin!" she called.

"What?" he shouted from the kitchen.

"Come up here."

He appeared at the bedroom door, Annabel over his shoulder like a sack of coal, her pony-tail hanging over her face, her cheeks flushed and sticky face grinning. He looked at Julie and let Annabel slide to the floor. She lay there waiting to be picked up again, but when Gavin stepped over her she realised the game was over and began to whinge.

"Annabel, go and check what Genevieve's doing, will you?" Julie smiled at her.

"She's eating her breakfast." Annabel replied.

"Well, go down to her, will you?"

Annabel began to complain but then saw the expression on her father's face. She left and went back downstairs.

"Don't go down there and start fighting with her! I don't want to hear crying and roaring!" Gavin called after her. He turned to Julie. "What's happening?"

"I took the test and it's positive. I'm pregnant again."

Gavin hugged her. "That's fantastic! Jules, this is the best news!"

"Yeah, it is," Julie smiled, her stomach knotting as she spoke.

Another baby. Night feeds, nappies – that damn steriliser would be back. Another bloody baby.

The weeks progressed. By week eight Julie was back to throwing up after every meal and feeling generally like she'd been hit by a bulldozer. She was exhausted, all day everyday, sick to her stomach with exhaustion. She was only thirty-three, that wasn't old, but this time round her body was aching under the strain of this baby. It was taking all her energy. She spoke to the chemist; she didn't want to talk to the doctor. She was too embarrassed to tell her yet again that she wasn't fully prepared for another baby. She had taken all the folic acid, and had eaten well while they were talking babies. Why was she falling apart so early in this pregnancy? If she had lost it when she was pregnant with Genevieve she could have understood it, but she'd just put her head down and got on with it last time. This time she was gripped by – nothing. Nothing at all. When she thought about the pregnancy, that she should eat properly – eat fruit or not eat peanuts – she found herself slipping her hand into the bowl of peanuts anyway. She'd never have done that during the other pregnancies. Now she'd eat a handful of peanuts or have the second glass of wine when they were out, and she didn't feel guilty about it. She'd just think – what did she think? She thought nothing of it. She just took the chance.

As the weeks progressed she felt no better about the pregnancy. She liked the thought of the baby. She was a good mother so she was completely sure that when it was born and the baby was placed in her arms that everything would click into place. She knew that she'd love the baby when it arrived and she'd be good with it. She was good with children; she was just naturally maternal. It was as simple as that. She didn't worry that this baby would be unloved. Quite the opposite. This would be her last baby; with this baby came a release. She would never have to feel this morning sickness again, and she would never have to night-feed again after this baby. When this baby was out of nappies she would never again have to wash a dirty bum while feet kicked in the air and spread poo from their heels to their hands to their clothes and finally to the their face. She would be free of that steriliser. She'd be throwing it out when this baby was one year old – the day it turned one she was flinging it in the bin. Not selling it, not putting it in the attic to lend to anyone else – it was going in the bin. She hated that steriliser.

She went into the chemist's to talk to him about the tiredness and ask for a tonic or something to help.

"Is this your first pregnancy?"

"No, my third. I'm just finding it very difficult this time. I'm exhausted."

"Well, there really is nothing I can give you for the exhaustion, not while you're pregnant. It's just a side effect and it does pass."

"Is there nothing? No tonic? What about Pharmaton?"

"You can't take it while pregnant. The best thing is just to rest at every opportunity and take a vitamin supplement formulated for pregnancy. That's really all I'd be happy to give you without the say-so of your doctor. If you think this exhaustion is over the top, then talk to your doctor and see if you're anaemic or if there's another reason for it."

"Thanks. I've got lots of vitamins and stuff. I'll see how it goes this weekend and I might go to the doctor next week."

Julie walked out feeling sort of like she'd just tried to buy heroin and hard liquor. She was embarrassed, as if she'd done something wrong.

37

Julie had got to the magic three months. They had been to the hospital and had the scan. It confirmed only one baby and all was going perfectly so far. They got a photo of the baby and suddenly it began to feel very real to Julie. She sat in the car on the way home staring at the small grainy picture. This was a baby, its legs kicking and arms waving on the screen. She really had to take the time to eat properly and start seeing this baby as a person with needs. She had to stop eating peanuts and taking that third glass of wine. It was time to face up to the reality: this baby was on the way and she had been just as responsible as Gavin for its arrival.

Later that night she rang Sinéad to tell her the news.

"That – that's fantastic news!" Sinéad enthused and it would have been convincing to anyone else, but Julie knew her too well. She could hear the stammer.

"What's wrong, Sinéad? Are you all right?"

"Yes, I'm fine. I'm just surprised. You didn't say anything about another baby."

"Well, we were talking about it for a while and then it didn't happen as fast as it did with the girls. So we just decided to keep it quiet for a while and see what happened."

"Well, I'm very happy for you."

"Thanks, now tell me, what's going on? Why are you so unhappy?"

On the other end of the line, Sinéad was silent.

"Sinéad?"

Sinéad was staring into space, weighing up the options. Would she tell Julie what was happening? Would Julie understand? She'd had such an easy time getting pregnant.

"Sinéad?"

"Jules, can we meet up this weekend? I'd love a chat."

"Yes! That would be fantastic. Saturday?"

"Yeah, come over to me, would you? Could Gav take the girls?"

"Yeah, I'm sure he could. What time?"

"About one?"

"Perfect. See you then . . . but, Sinéad?"

"Yes."

"Are you all right?"

"Yes, I'm fine. There's nothing wrong with me. I'm just a bit down and I could really do with a girly chat."

"Okay, see you Saturday."

Julie went around to Sinéad on Saturday. She was nervous. She hadn't seen much of Sinéad recently, and when they did speak she seemed distant, as if there was something weighing on her mind. Something that was about to boil over at any moment but Sinéad seemed always on her guard so that it didn't. She was scared that Sinéad would tell her something awful. Something Julie didn't want to hear or perhaps shouldn't hear. She hoped it wasn't about her marriage. Richard and Sinéad were perfect for each other. They didn't always see eye to eye and they tore strips off each other when they fought, but really they were a great couple and Julie knew that Sinéad would be hard pressed to find someone like Richard again. But the fact remained that Sinéad was unhappy. She was reserved and lately when they chatted on the phone there were intervals of silence when Sinéad said nothing at all, just voicing a heartfelt sigh. Julie had wondered for a while if everything was as rosy in the garden as Sinéad said it was. There was no hiding the fact that Sinéad and Richard were throwing money at each other at the moment. They had got a huge conservatory added to the house and they'd taken weekends in Prague, Barcelona and Paris in the last three months. It was plain to see they were drowning some sort of problem.

She got out of her car and rang the doorbell. Sinéad answered and the problem stared both of them in the face.

Sinéad was tiny, painfully thin in fact – her size ten clothes were hanging off her and to Julie's eye she didn't look good. Her hair and clothes were pristine as usual, but there were bags under her eyes and she was gaunt-looking.

And for Sinéad there was Julie, her cheeks rosy, her stomach nicely rounded and she had that happy glow you get from a pregnant woman who's having a good day. She looked healthy and content. And pregnant. Sinéad swallowed hard on the lump that was rising in her throat and opened the door wide.

"Jules, you look fantastic. Congratulations!" She hugged her hard as they entered the hall.

"Thanks, I'm feeling good today, but let me tell you it's not been easy. I'm knackered all the time! I've had very little morning sickness so that's something to be grateful for but I am putting on a pile of weight again. In fact, I think this pregnancy has been the toughest of all so far. Today, though, I'm feeling very well and quite sprightly, which is nice!" Julie looked at Sinéad, taking in her gaunt face and her pained eyes. "Sinéad, you don't look healthy. I know I shouldn't say this but you're awfully thin. Are you all right?"

"Yes, I'm fine. I know I've lost a bit of weight but really I'm perfectly healthy. I'm a perfect specimen in fact!" Sinéad laughed but it was hollow and sounded almost belligerent.

Julie followed her into the conservatory. Her thoughts were diverted from Sinéad for a few minutes while she took in the sheer size and perfection of the room. It was huge, and furnished to perfection. Amazing what a difference no toys and clean hands can make to your furniture, Julie mused as she looked around her. The room was decked out with about twenty plants of all shapes and sizes, every shade of green with yellow, pink and orange flowers blooming around the room. The tiles were cream and instead of wicker furniture there were two large beige couches facing each other, one against the back wall, the other directly in front of it. Each couch had about seven scatter cushions of every imaginable colour lying around it, a coffee table between them with a standard lamp on either side of one of the couches. The room was huge and Julie could see there were smaller chairs over near the door facing the garden but they had been folded up and laid against the wall. There was music coming from somewhere but Julie couldn't make out where; it just sort of filled the air. Then she saw a speaker set into the wall above their heads, just above eye level – she looked around and sure enough there were four of them strategically placed around the room. Julie took in the whole effect; it must have cost a bomb for the furnishing alone. And she knew that it was all done in the space of a fortnight. They'd had the builders, painters and gardeners in one after another and now that they were gone the house looked like this. It looked as if the conservatory had always been here, or that it had arrived fully furnished and heated. Again Julie found herself wondering what it must be like to have the kind of money Sinéad and Richard seemed to take for granted. She felt the uncomfortable pang of jealousy creep over her chest. She hated the feeling; she hated feeling it about Sinéad most of all. In fairness, they were never showy about it, but they never worried about the cost of anything, and they rarely picked up a paint-brush themselves. They thought nothing of getting a plumber to look at a blocked drain, or ringing 'that guy' when they needed the spare room carpeted and painted. But the house was gorgeous and Sinéad loved it – she often told Julie she would happily live out the rest of her life in this one house. She said her heart lived in this house, and Julie found herself agreeing more and more. If your heart had to live anywhere, this house was as good a place as any. Julie glanced into the corners and wasn't the least bit surprised to see not a single dust bunny hanging out under the potted plants. This house was spotless. If I had money to burn and no small hands breaking everything in reach, this is the way I'd like to live my life, she thought. She looked up just as Sinéad came back in with mugs of coffee, sandwiches and chocolate biscuits. She put them down on the table in front of them and curled up on the couch, pulling a cushion around and bunching it up on her lap. She looked so thin and delicate sitting there, Calvin Klein would have snapped her up for one of those black and white adverts, the ones they film on a beach and that have nothing to do with the product they're selling. They just look like a daydream or something. Sinéad looked very pretty but Julie couldn't shake the thought that she looked too skinny, in fact she looked like a high-class druggie. Julie wondered if her friend was one of those new professionals who take cocaine at the weekends. It wasn't the first time Julie had thought this of Sinéad recently. She fitted the description: early thirties, money to burn, no kids and high on the old career ladder. She didn't want to think that way, especially about her best friend, so she cleared it from her mind.

"This is fantastic. It's huge!" Julie smiled.

"Yeah, that's the joy of a long back garden. We could make a huge room and not lose too much from the garden."

They looked out at the garden. Julie took a sidelong glance at Sinéad: her shoulder-bone was sticking out from under her top like a point. There was no fat and it looked almost like no muscle under her skin, just bone.

"Sinéad, I have to say this. You look far too skinny."

Sinéad looked at down at herself and nodded, stretching out her arm to inspect it. Julie looked at the skin hanging from it – it made her shudder.

"I know. I've lost a lot of weight. I've been stressed – things have been tough around here lately."

"Is everything all right with you and Richard?"

"Yeah, we're fine. We have our good days and we have our bad days but we're fine."

Sinéad looked out onto the back garden. "You know how it is – life doesn't always work like clockwork. And sometimes nobody can tell you why exactly."

Julie looked at Sinéad. She was trying but it was hard to follow this conversation. "Sinéad, what's going on? Are you or Richard sick? Is that what's happening?"

Sinéad still stared out at the garden as she spoke. "Sick? No, not sick exactly. Richard and I are perfectly healthy but we seem to be unable to have a baby." Her eyes filled with tears as she said it.

Julie felt awful. This was something Sinéad needed help with and Julie had absolutely no idea what to say or do for her.

"Oh Sinéad, I'm so sorry!"

"Yeah, everyone says how sorry they are, but we're the ones who have to live with the empty house."

"How long have you known this?"

"Well, we've been trying for about two years now."

"Oh, Sinéad!" Julie's heart sank for her, and here she was on her third pregnancy herself.

"Yeah, it was a bit of surprise when nothing happened, but you try not to panic, don't you? Then you think you're just nervous and that's stopping things happening, but after a while you have to admit there's a problem."

"And are you doing anything about it?"

"Yes, we've been in the Rotunda about it, at the HARI Unit. We've done every test known to man and the results keep coming back clear."

"So that's good news?"

"I suppose, but we still have no baby."

"What kind of tests?"

"Let's see, what have we done so far? Well, blood tests, semen analysis, scans, X-rays and of course the post-fucking-coital exam. The next thing is a laparoscopy next week."

"Hang on, post-coital exam? Dare I ask?"

"It's exactly what it says on the tin. We had to do the deed and have them look up my skirt!"

"Oh, Sinéad, I can't believe it!"

"I was a bit traumatised myself."

"And everything is coming back clear?"

"Yes, so where does that leave us?"

"And you've been doing this all by yourself? You should have told me."

"What could you do? There's nothing anyone can do for us."

"I don't know, but I'd have tried to be some kind of help, just someone to complain to if nothing else."

"You're up to your eyes with the girls and, to be honest, I've been steering clear of babies. I'm a bit off balance at the moment."

"Are they messing with your hormones?"

"No, not yet, but it's only a matter of time I'd say. I think they're running out of ideas at this stage."

"Is there anyone you could talk to other than me? Someone who's been through it too? Or hasn't any kids, if the babies are driving you insane? And I completely understand that, by the way."

"Thanks. You know I love the girls more than life. They're the absolute best, but right now I need to take myself out of their circle."

"In fairness you do."

"The hospital gave us numbers for support groups but I've never rung any of them."

"Why not?"

"I don't want to get involved with support groups. I don't think I'm that type of person."

"What type of person? A person who needs support during a stressful time? Are you a robot?"

"No, but I don't want to sit in a church hall, drinking weak tea and crying with a whole load of hormonal women."

"Is that what they do? Sit and cry in parish halls?"

"I don't know, but I have a dreadful foreboding about the whole thing. Like it would just be the most depressing bloody thing ever."

"But have you even asked what the meetings are like? Do you know where they really do meet up?"

"No, I don't want to ring in case they make me come to the meeting. Anyway I'm sure they all just talk about the various tests they've had and what's happening to them next."

"How do you know that?"

"I saw *About a Boy*."

"So did I, but what has *About a Boy* got to do with anything?"

"Remember that Lone Parents group? Remember how bloody depressing they all were?"

"Yeah, but surely that was fictional, that was for drama – it's not real!"

"How do you know? Maybe that's exactly what they're all like!"

"No way! The groups are there to help, Sinéad! Not depress you even more!"

"I'm not convinced and until I have it writing that they're not just a gang of hormonal women lusting after their doctors then I'm not going."

"Lusting after their doctors? What are you talking about?"

"I looked a group up on the net a few months ago and read one of those chat rooms. They were all going on about their doctors and saying how cute they all were."

"I think you may have stumbled into a joke chat room!"

"No, they began chatting about what some girl's doctor said about a course of drugs. He'd laughed off a side-effect and she was really offended, then they all started chatting about who had what doctor and who was the best one!"

"Well, who was?"

"I can't remember his name; it was some guy in the country. But his name was mentioned and they all practically fainted! I just assumed they'd all had their hormones jolted or something. I mean you should have read some of the gushing about these guys! That can't be normal!"

Julie took a biscuit from the plate. She remembered having quite a crush on her dentist once – it was back in the late eighties but she still remembered his name and had to smile. "Falling for your gynaecologist is not as mad as you think. Lots of women do."

"Did you? Is that why you keep rolling them out?" Sinéad grinned and Julie was relieved to see the pain fade away from her face as she smiled.

"No, I'd swear my guy was about seventy except he'd have retired by now. He's very old, so no."

"I see."

"What about your guy?"

"Dr Whitney? He's in his fifties, I'd say, but well preserved."

"And?"

"No. Not dreamboat material. Very nice but not a knee-trembler."

"Well preserved, fifties and very nice? I think we have crush material there now!" Julie laughed. "I think we'll be hearing a lot more about this Dr Whitney guy!"

"Do not hold your breath on that one!"

"It's entirely up to me what I do with my breath, thank you very much!"

They sat and laughed for a while. Julie was glad they were laughing but she was aware that things were edgy. And she knew that in this instance laughter was very close to tears.

"I hear what you're saying about the church halls and weak tea, but have you had any success at all on the internet?" Julie asked.

"I've read up anything I can about infertility, but it doesn't answer my questions to tell you the truth."

"What do you want to know?"

"What's wrong with me? What's happening in me that I can't have a baby? Will I ever be able to have a baby?"

"And this laparoscopy, what happens there?"

"They go in through a hole in my belly button and look with a camera at my womb and stuff. They want to see if there's anything wrong with me in there."

"What might be wrong? Your womb might be in the wrong spot or something?" Julie asked, then suddenly regretted the flippant sound in her tone. "Sinéad, I'm sorry, that sounded like I was taking the piss — I didn't mean it at all."

"I know. I thought pretty much the same as you when they said it first, but it seems they're happy enough that my bits are all intact — they just want to have a look at them."

"And when is this going to happen?"

"Next Wednesday morning. I have to go in at eight in the morning and I have to stay overnight."

"And will they tell you what they see before you go home?"

"Yes, if they can they will."

"Wow."

Again they were silent. Julie watched Sinéad as she stared into space. Her heart was full of sympathy for her but she knew Sinéad better than most people and she knew that she was proud and private. She wouldn't want Julie to spout clichéd niceties at her but Julie wanted to say something – she wanted to help her, but how?

"There's a website that might help you," she said. "I went on it when I was pregnant with the girls and it was great. There's a whole section on babies and another whole section for infertility and pregnancy loss and stuff like that. They have discussion boards where you can ask a question and people come back to you and try to answer."

Sinéad looked at Julie for a second, her eyes interested but her face a studied blank.

"Who answers the questions? A nurse or doctor?"

"No, just other girls usually. The people who post messages on the boards will be girls who are in the same situation and with the pregnancy boards they were great for just getting worries and gripes off your chest."

"And they have a separate one for infertility? Away from girls gushing about their babies?"

"Of course, they have! It's actually a really good site. It's Rollercoaster.ie. Have a read of it at least and if you don't want to add a note then don't. You can just read what everyone else is talking about."

"Rollercoaster.ie?"

"Yeah, try it out – if it doesn't suit you then just log out."

"All right, I might have a read of it." Sinéad smiled but she didn't think she'd actually go on the net and talk about it. It was far too private and what if someone recognised her? Someone from work who was on to look at the pregnancy pages? She'd never live it down.

They sat for a while longer, Sinéad looking out into the back garden lost in her own little world. Every now and then Julie would notice tears glistening in her eyes but she never actually cried. Julie felt so completely helpless. It was the first time in their lives that one of them had a real problem and no amount of shopping, bitching or drinking was going to sort it out.

Finally Sinéad spoke, still looking out the window – but a smile played on her face as she spoke. "Those nuns, I blame them."

"What nuns?"

"The nuns from school. Do you remember that afternoon that we were herded into the science labs and they played that video?"

"Oh my God, that one about the two drops of rain? Coming together and forming one drop?" Julie laughed. "I haven't thought of that video for years!"

"They practically led us to believe that if you sat next to a boy you got pregnant!"

"That's right! No real info. Just that if a man and a woman are married they have sex and nine months later the baby arrives. That was it."

"Yeah, they sent us out into the world clueless, and they sent home letters letting our parents know the birds and bees chat was all taken care of."

"But remember that poor Miss Hannon? She had to tell us about the period and sperm bits in religion." Julie took another biscuit, remembering the class and how embarrassed the poor teacher had been. "But she flew through it – just you get a period every month and once you start getting them you can become pregnant."

"But that's my point! They never said anything about some people will get pregnant again and again with no problem and some people will never get pregnant. For no good reason they'll just have some sort of glitch in their genes and that's that. We were never led to believe that anything might go wrong! Have sex and nine months later, hey presto, a baby!"

Julie sat for a moment, not sure whether to let her rant or try to calm her down. So she just looked at her with a sympathetic smile – at least she hoped it was sympathetic; she meant it to be but it maybe looked patronising. She stopped smiling, and took yet another biscuit.

"Why didn't they warn us?" Sinéad ranted on. "Why didn't someone take us aside and say this is what happens in most cases, but for about one in six of you there'll be no bloody happy ending! Why didn't they just give us a heads-up on the whole thing? Why did it have to creep up on us, out of the blue and give us such a horrible fright?"

"But, Sinéad, love, there's lots of things they could have said to us in school. 'By the way, one in three of you will have some sort of brush with cancer; one in five of you may have a miscarriage when you do get pregnant; some of you will die before you hit fifty; someone in the class might even die before they finish college and some of you will never meet that special person and will never marry at all.' They could have told us loads of statistics about what might happen. I could go home and tell my children all the same statistics, but why should I? What right do I have to scare them like that? What right did the teachers have to scare us?"

"But I was never told that this might happen. I was never warned!"

"But we were always talking about babies and how much we hoped we'd be able to have them. All through our teens we chatted about getting married and having children. We were aware of the problems some people have. We knew they existed."

Sinéad looked away, tears glistening again. "Yes, I knew it was out there – fertility problems were out there. Other people had them, people you felt sorry for but you didn't know them and they weren't real." She sighed and the weight of the world was in that one sigh. "I just never thought it would happen to me. Not me."

"I'm so sorry, Sinéad. I feel so guilty sitting here like this, with the girls at home and another one on the way. I had no idea what you're going through and I'm sorry." She put her hand out and touched Sinéad's leg.

Sinéad moved her leg just out of reach. "Sorry, I just can't handle sympathy at the moment. I'm really trying to keep it together here."

"Don't be trying to keep it together. This is me, Sinéad! I'll cry with you – believe me, if it was me I'd be hoarse from crying at this stage."

"You know me. I hate crying in front of people."

"I'm not people! I'm Jules, the one who cries at movies, adverts, happy endings. I'm always sobbing over something!"

"I just want to hold it together as much as possible. I may have to start telling people that we can't have children. I want to be able to say it without breaking down. I know that might sound daft to you, but I need to preserve some dignity."

"I completely understand not wanting to cry in front of the office or the girl in the Spar, but surely the best way is to get it out of your system now. Cry it all out and when it comes time to tell people you're all cried out about it."

"I just want to keep a lid on my emotions. I really am scared that if I start I won't stop."

"But, Sinéad, you have to cry – this is a huge shock for you. You must cry if you feel like it."

"Julie, I don't want to start crying! Do you understand what I'm saying? I know you cry at the drop of a hat but that's not me. I don't cry like you do! I don't want to cry like you do!"

After that outburst they both sat in silence, Sinéad glaring out the window, Julie looking at the tiled floor.

"I'm sorry you think I was bugging you to cry, but I do think you need to let it all out. That's all I'll say about it, Sinéad."

"I'm sorry I shouted at you. I know you think everything in this world can be solved with a hot bath and a good cry, but sometimes it can't be fixed. Sometimes nobody knows what's wrong and so they can't fix it anyway."

"Is that what you think? They'll never find a cause for it?"

"I don't know, but it's beginning to look like it. They keep testing and coming back fine. The doctor did say that sometimes there is no medical reason, just unexplained infertility. You just can't have children; no one knows why."

"In that case, have you discussed the possibility of never having children?" Julie's heart raced as she spoke – one word or syllable out of place and Sinéad might never speak to her again.

"No, I don't want to think that way, not until I absolutely have to. I'm just not ready to give up yet."

"Well good, that's the way to think until you're told different. Assume you can until they tell you for definite that you can't."

Sinéad went out to the kitchen and brought back more coffee. She sat down and poured them two large mugs.

"Well, to be honest I have thought about it. The 'no babies' thing – I have on occasion let my mind wander on it."

"Really?"

"Yeah, I don't like to think about it but, of course, I've wondered. Most of the time I can't bear the thought, but then other times I just think 'To hell with it, if I can't I can't!' I mean, look at my lifestyle – do I even want a child with sticky hands grabbing at the furniture?"

"You do have a wonderful life, Sinéad. You know that."

"I do, and having a baby would put an end to our weekends in Paris and my Saturday morning lie-ins."

"It would. It'd put an end to any rest and relaxation you'll ever plan to have again!"

"Inherently I think I'm a lazy person. I enjoy my rest and reading a good book on the couch all afternoon. Not to mention opening and drinking a bottle of wine on a Monday night if that's what I'm in the mood for. When's the last time you drank on a school night?"

"A school night? Jesus, well, before I got pregnant again, I maybe had a glass of wine with dinner now and again but I haven't polished off a bottle to myself since before Annabel was born. And of course, not while I was pregnant either."

"So three, four years?"

"Maybe," Julie buried her head in her hands. "I really have to start living again!"

"Well, as soon as this one is born you have to start drinking wine again!"

"I have to start doing lots of things again."

"Like what?" Sinéad sat up. She needed to hear that babies equalled bad-hair days and puke-stained jumpers. "What have you stopped doing since the girls were born?"

"Where do I begin? Okay, since I got my 'little job' I've been getting out a bit more and having my hair done and stuff. But before I got the job I hadn't had my hair done professionally for about a year,"

"What?" Sinéad put down her mug. "I can't believe that. I get my hair done every eight weeks, no matter what!"

"Well, that's what having a baby will do – you can

forget about your hair. And forget tweezing, bleaching or shaving too. I only get a chance to shave my legs once a fortnight – if I got hit by a bus tomorrow they'd honestly think they'd found the missing link if they had to take off my trousers!"

"Get lost! You cannot leave your legs get that hairy. Let's see!"

Julie pulled up the leg of her jeans and there it was: an ape's leg hiding underneath the leg of her Levis.

Sinéad began to laugh and rubbed her finger up Julie's leg. "That is vile, Jules. You know you're now a slob, officially."

"I've been a slob for almost three years – I could give a shit!"

"Okay, the not shaving your legs is gross – but if you're honest, Jules, that's just you being a lazy slob – you could run a razor over your legs in the shower every morning. You just don't bother!"

"I jump in the shower, get myself wet and jump back out. I have no time even for soap or shampoo, so forget about a razor! So that's my legs and hair – what else can I tell you about? Oh yeah, when the babies came I gave up putting on make-up."

"I noticed that but how did it happen?"

"When Annabel was born I stopped using it because I never had time to put it on, then Genevieve arrived and I had even less time. Then when Genevieve was about a year old I finally did start thinking about putting some lipstick on again. But by then my make-up bag was lost. I had to go out and buy everything again, mascara, foundation, lipstick, eyeliner – everything! Then about a month after I'd bought everything new I located the old bag – it was in the girls' Wendy House in the back garden. My old foundation was all gunk and clay-mixed and there was a row of dolls sporting my Elizabeth Arden lipstick as eyeshadow." Julie smiled at the memory – she had wanted to kill them both at the time, but she could see the funny side now. "Do you still want kids?"

"Keep talking. You're helping!"

"While I was pregnant with Annabel we went to the cinema every week almost. We were waiting for movies to come out. We knew all the trailers by heart. Then, when she was born we couldn't get out the door to even get a DVD. And of course Genevieve arrived within a few bloody weeks! And so we didn't get to the cinema for about eighteen months. And – I'll let you in on a very big secret here – don't tell Gavin you know this. When we got there and the lights went down, we both fell asleep. Both of us. We only woke up when the lights came back up. We were mortified! The people beside us were laughing their heads off at us."

"Jules! I don't believe you! You woke up after the movie – popcorn untouched!"

"And a very flat Coke sitting between us."

"Well, that's a first! I've never heard the like of that one before."

"And I can assure you, it won't be mentioned again! Gavin gets really embarrassed about it all for some reason and he will not mention it."

"I have no idea why. I think it's funny," Sinéad smiled.

"Some of it can be fun but there are tough times too

raising children. They don't come with manuals, and just because you're a woman does not mean you know what to do with them every minute of every day. And the first time they really get ill, I mean a temperature of over a hundred, vomiting and crying, it's usually in the middle of the night and you really panic inside if you can't get them to stop crying. And Gavin just sits there staring at you, expecting you to know all the answers. And then every cent I have is eaten up keeping the girls in shoes, clothes or toys. I work three days a week, and I have the girls in the crèche. And after paying their crèche fees, do you know how much I have for hair do's and fancy tops? I have one hundred euro. A hundred euro after a month's effort! Now I get my hair done every eight weeks and I spend a few hours by myself on a Saturday morning, so that's all right, but if something came up and the girls needed something I'd forgo my hair-do. And it gets worse! Before I went back to work – that whole time I was off work – I hadn't bought as much as a new T-shirt or a new pair of knickers! Every time I saw something I'd like to buy for myself, one of them needed a bloody new dress or some such crap."

"No way, you shouldn't have to do that. You need to look after yourself more, Julie."

"Well, I don't *have* to do it. It's my own fault to be honest. I feel guilty about buying myself anything if the girls need something too. If I don't have the money to buy all three of us a new outfit, mine goes back on the rail. It's not as if we're poor, far from it. Gavin makes good money and we can afford for me to stay home – it's not as if I need to work – it's just me really. I feel guilty about spending money on myself when the children need something. And now there'll be a third and I'll never buy myself another new top if there's a third pair of eyes watching me and asking for new shoes or something. And on top of all of that I have to give up my job – I'll be back in the house alone with all three of them with no way of getting out of the house. I just don't how I'm going to manage at all."

Julie sat there after announcing this. It was only when she looked at Sinéad that she realised something odd had just been said. Her eyes widened as she realised what had just come from her own mouth.

"Oh Christ, Sinéad, that sounded awful! I didn't mean it. I don't begrudge the girls anything and when the time comes this one will have anything it wants too. I love them. I honestly love them!"

"It's fine – I know you love them," Sinéad sympathised, but secretly she was astonished by the announcement. It wasn't so much the words, it was the cold, resigned tone Julie had used as she spoke, like she was hardened by it all. "But, Jules, if you really feel that badly about the whole situation then you need to stop spending on the girls and get yourself a few new tops and a pair of shoes or something. You need to pamper yourself too, Jules."

"I try to. It's just that every time I go to pick something up for myself, one of them needs a new dress, new shoes, it's a birthday or Christmas or Easter or something. There's always something they need, and that has to take precedence over whatever it is that I was looking at. I'd *like* a new top, but they *need* new shoes. And they're my children – I can't spend money on myself and let them go without."

"They have wardrobes that are overflowing with dresses and shoes and bedrooms piled high with toys, not to mention the playroom and the back garden covered in toys – they're not going without, Jules. You are!"

"Oh I'm fine. I'm just moaning. The poor little things, they don't realise they're such a financial drain! And they're not really. It's me. I spoil them."

Sinéad looked at Julie as she spoke. She was backtracking, Sinéad could read her like a book. Julie knew she'd said too much and was now back-pedalling like crazy to get herself out of the situation.

"Oh my God, this was not about me and the girls – it's about you and I was meant to be making you feel better!"

"It's fine. I do feel better. Just hearing about your hair and seeing the hair on your legs has made me wonder why on earth I'm allowing strange men to poke around under my skirt! I think I should stop complaining and enjoy my life!"

They laughed, but neither of them felt overly joyful.

"Sinéad, forget what I said. I should never have said it. I certainly don't feel that way, not about spending money on the girls. And I should never have complained about them in front of you. I'm sorry."

"That's all right. To be honest I prefer to hear complaints about them – you'd be surprised how awful I feel when people start going on about how wonderful and life-changing children are. It's a lot easier to hear people say they're horrible little money-grabbers!"

"Well, look at it this way: they are all of the above, they are a financial black hole, but you can't help but love everything about them. And when the time comes, you'll feel just the same about your baby." This time Julie took Sinéad in her arms and hugged her. "I have to go home now, but ring me at any time, day or night, and we'll talk."

"Thanks, Jules."

Julie left. Driving home she felt drained despite the level of caffeine in her body. It had been an emotional day. The announcement from Sinéad and the confession from herself. Thank God she had stopped short of telling Sinéad that she didn't particularly want this baby. That must never, ever get out. Too many people would be hurt and angry, not to mention the pain for the baby. But she still couldn't seem to whip up any enthusiasm towards this bump. As time wore on it bothered her – what if she just never bonded with this child? What if something went wrong and she forever blamed herself for it? What if she was to blame for it?

38

Sinéad watched Julie drive off, car horn tooting as she
went. She shut the door and went back to the
conservatory. She tidied up the dishes, washed down the
kitchen surfaces, tidied the cushions back on the couches
in the conservatory and stood back to survey her house. It
was gorgeous, not a cup or plate out of place, all the mod
cons and latest styles, everything just as it should be. She
could be standing in a lifestyle magazine. She opened a
bottle of wine, poured herself a glass and sat at the kitchen
table reading the paper. She read the birth announcements
at the back of *The Irish Times*. She liked to read the names
and snigger at people who took the announcement too
seriously. You should get charged double, she thought, if
you go in for comments like 'Our Raving Beauty' or
'And the Lord gave us a son' and what was going on in
Ireland these days if people were naming their children
Honey Jade Murray or Alfie Caleb O'Brien?

She finished the paper and the last of the wine. She

looked around her. The house was perfectly tidy. She wasn't hungry so she didn't want to start on dinner – anyway, Richard would be home in an hour or so, and maybe they could go out tonight. As Julie said, there'd be no time for herself once they had a baby, so she might as well enjoy the luxury of deciding to go out at the last second. It was almost six so she went into the sitting room and watched the news.

After the news on a Saturday night there was an early evening movie, one especially for children. Tonight it was *Stuart Little* so she settled back on the couch and began to watch. It was a daft movie about a couple who adopt a mouse, but the story touched a chord with Sinéad and somewhere between the opening titles and the first ad break she began to cry. A few minutes later it had nothing at all to do with the movie, Sinéad was just crying for Ireland. She hated it, sitting here in this perfect house, on her perfect street, with her beautifully styled hair, waxed legs and expensive clothes – she hated it! Her life was empty – it seemed perfect but it was a shell. It was a fake. She was a fake. Her life was meaningless – she needed to have a baby; she needed it. Her entire body ached for it. There was only so much she could buy, for herself or the house. Money was not the answer to this problem. She wanted to hold a baby of her own. She wanted the morning sickness, the stretch-marks and the kicked ribs. She wanted it all; she needed to have a baby of her own.

She sobbed for it. With all her heart and soul she sobbed. She couldn't stop, not even if she wanted to. She cried and cried. So much so that she didn't hear the door open and Richard come in.

Suddenly he was in the hall and calling her name. She couldn't stop the croak in her voice as she answered him and he came straight in.

"What's wrong?" he asked as he sat beside her on the couch.

"I'm miserable!" she sobbed. "I need a baby – I just need one so much!"

Richard sighed, and looked towards the TV. "Christ, Sinéad, I don't know what I can say to you. I want a baby too, and we're trying. It'll happen. It has to happen."

"But what if it doesn't? What if we never have a baby?"

"We could adopt, or foster, or maybe just fill our lives some other way."

"I can't. I can't fill my life. I've tried. Look around us: we've a show house and four bedrooms that we can't fill. And there's not a city in Europe worth talking about that we haven't spent a weekend in. We have great jobs, fancy cars, but it all means nothing to me. I've tried to fill my life with shopping, the gym and my job – I can't do it any more. I don't want to just fill my life, Richard! I want to be able to relax, to sit back and enjoy my life. I'm filling every inch of space in my life for fear a few spare moments will allow me to think about the baby we can't have!"

"We can have children, Sinéad. We can. All the tests are coming back clear and we have no reason to believe we can't. We just need a bit of help and we're getting that now."

"If we can have children, then why am I not pregnant? What's going wrong?"

318

"I don't know." Richard took her in his arms and held her.

She cried until her eyes and cheeks were swollen and her face was stained red from tears and rubbing. She couldn't go out now even if she wanted to. She looked as if she'd just gone ten rounds with Mike Tyson.

They ordered a pizza and Richard opened a second bottle of wine. They lay on the couch, both of them too upset to watch what was on TV. But Richard pretended he was dug into *Parkinson*. At least, if he was watching it, Sinéad would stop asking him what their future held. At that moment, and for a while now, he had no idea what the future held for them.

One thing was certain, Sinéad needed to talk to someone who could help her, and he couldn't. He really needed to come home at night and not have to scrape Sinéad off the floor or talk her down from whatever ledge she'd got herself out on during the day. It might sound cruel but he was struggling too and he didn't have the strength right now to hold both of them up. It was all he could do to hold himself up these days.

39

Sinéad went to the hospital on Wednesday morning. She was booked in for her laparoscopy at 9.30. She changed into the surgical gown and waited in the room to be called to theatre. As she waited she listened to the sound of her stomach rumble. She was fasting and by 9.15 she was starving. It was after eleven when the nurse finally took her down to the theatre. She explained on the way down the corridor that there had been three emergency Caesarean sections that morning.

"That's what babies are like though!" she laughed. "They all throw a strop at the same time and have to be dealt with! But sure they're all fine and wonderful now, mammies and babies all back on the wards doing grand."

"Great, what did they have? Boys or girls?"

"You know, I haven't a clue. I don't work on the baby wards at all so it's only the rare occasions we hear the outcome. Only if there's a big emergency or something."

They came to a set of doors that told them there was

no admission beyond that point. So they sat on the corridor and waited. After a few minutes Dr Whitney came out, all smiles in his green scrubs.

"Sinéad, sorry about the delay – you've been told about the rush of emergencies we had this morning? So everyone is running late. I'm just waiting for the theatre to be disinfected and we'll be straight in. Is there anything that you're unsure about? Any questions?"

"No, I'm fine. I'm just hungry at this stage," Sinéad smiled.

"I'm sure you are – well, this will be over in twenty minutes and you should be back on the ward within an hour. We'll get you tea and toast then, all right?"

Sinéad nodded. Tea and toast sounded like a birthday feast to her right then. The doctor disappeared back in through the doors again and was gone. A few minutes later someone came out and called them in.

Sinéad was led to a theatre and helped onto an operating table. About five people worked around her for a few minutes and then one man stepped forward and asked her to count backwards from ten.

"Ten, nine, eight, sev –"

And she was gone.

She woke up in a different room. People were talking and moving around in the other corner. She lay there looking at the ceiling, unable to move that well.

A nurse noticed she was awake and came over.

"Hello there, are you awake?" she smiled.

"Did it go all right?" Sinéad asked, her voice weak.

"It's all over and it went fine. We'll have you back in your room in two minutes and the doctor should be in to you in an hour or so."

They moved her through the corridors on the trolley and back to her room. She was helped back to bed and given tea and toast just as she'd been promised. Then she was left alone. She sat up in the bed and devoured the toast. When it was eaten and the tea drunk, she looked around. It was a bright day and the room was very warm. She could hardly believe it when she noticed it was only 12.15. It was still so early in the day. She rang Richard and let him know it was all over and she was back in her room.

"Great, I'm glad it all went fine. Will I come in and see you at visiting time?

"Absolutely! I expect to see you here bang on six o'clock."

"All right – I might not be there for six but I should be there by 6.30."

"That'll have to do, I suppose!"

"But Sinéad, give me a shout when the doctor comes around and tell me what he says, won't you?"

"Of course, I will."

"And don't forget – this is just another test that is going to come back all clear. Don't be worrying about it."

"I won't."

Sinéad hung up and turned to put her phone on the bedside locker and, as she did, she got a stabbing pain in her stomach.

"Ouch!" she said aloud.

How stupid! She'd forgotten that she had stitches in her stomach. She lifted her gown and looked at the bandage. No blood – that was a good sign. She hadn't pulled or burst anything, but her stomach burned with pain. She looked at the bell. Should she push it and tell a nurse? She tossed it around in her head and finally she pressed the bell.

"I twisted to put my phone on the locker and I hurt my tummy," she said.

"Oh, you silly old thing! I know, it's easy to forget – let's see if you've pulled stitches."

The nurse pulled up her gown and looked at the bandage, poking and pressing a little.

"No, you're fine. You've just pulled it a bit and made yourself sore. I'll get you some painkillers. Which would you prefer – Ponstan or Solpadeine?"

"Solpadeine."

The nurse came back in and gave her the tablets and a glass of water. She took them and within five minutes the pain was gone. She lay back on the bed, careful of her stomach, and read her magazines cover to cover. Then she turned on the TV and watched an episode of *Dallas* that she found on one of the stations. She looked at her watch and saw it was 3.30. She wondered if she was going to have to stay overnight. It mightn't be that bad after all. She couldn't remember the last time she had lain in bed all day and watched TV. She opened her bag and found a packet of Polo mints – she put them on her bedside locker and turned up the TV.

There was a knock on the door and in walked Dr Whitney.

"Hi there, Sinéad. How are you feeling?"

"I'm fine. I'm a bit sore but the nurse gave me painkillers and I'm a lot better now."

"Great, the pain should ease off in the next few hours but it will be tender and sore for the next few days. Take it easy and take a few days off work – you have had surgery this morning."

"I will. Don't you worry about that!"

"Now, the thing we want to discuss is what we found in there this morning."

Sinéad sat up a little. Finally it appeared there was a test they hadn't passed with flying colours.

"We found what I thought we might find. I'm afraid we located many areas of endometriosis around your womb and ovaries."

"What? Endometri-what?"

"Endometriosis – you obviously haven't heard of it before?"

"No. What is it?"

"All right, don't panic. It's not the end of the world. The condition is actually quite common. A huge percentage of women have it. This is where tissue similar to the lining of the womb, the endometrial layer, forms outside the womb. It can form anywhere in the pelvic cavity, but in most cases it is on the outside of the womb and around the ovaries and can even wrap around the bladder. In your case we noted it outside the womb and on your right ovary. Have you ever taken the contraceptive pill?"

"No, I tried but I got all sorts of side effects, and every make of Pill I tried seemed to make me worse. So I was never on it."

"That's a very big pity. You see, we often prescribe the Pill for women with endometriosis as it controls the growth and in some cases clears it up. But in this case we obviously can't give it to you."

"So what happened? The lining of my womb is on the outside? What does this mean?"

"It means that pregnancy is difficult – not impossible, but difficult. We would be concerned that a fertilised egg could embed not inside but outside the womb. That would be obviously death for the baby and also, very serious for you if undetected. Are you familiar with the term ectopic pregnancy?"

"No."

"It's where a pregnancy becomes established outside the womb, most often in one or other Fallopian tube. If that happens we have no option but to take the tube out. So in the case of someone with endometriosis we have a greater concern that this may happen."

"Can it be cured?"

"Endometriosis is not a disease. It's a condition. So you have this condition. It is treatable but we're not going to be able to cure it as such. You have always had this condition and you will continue to have it."

"What do you mean? Is there nothing you can do for me?"

"There are a number of things we can do, short of actually curing the condition."

"I've never heard of this thing, so excuse my ignorance but will I be very sick? I mean, will it affect my health?"

"Well, it may give you some discomfort or even pain around your menstrual cycle and of course it affects your ability to get pregnant – also, some women may suffer from fatigue – but other than that there should be no ill-health or sickness. It has been described as the 'Silent Enemy' and that's actually because most women diagnosed with it are completely unaware they have it. They may have heavy or painful periods but that's about it. So no, Sinéad, this condition will not affect your health adversely."

"All right." Sinéad looked down at the bedspread. She was trying to keep all the information in her head while not letting it get to her too much. "So what can we do to treat it?"

"Well, there are a number of options. Firstly, we can do nothing at all. This condition impinges on your ability to conceive, but it doesn't necessarily stop it entirely. So you can go off today and carry on trying for a baby with no further treatment if you like. Secondly, we can treat it with a drug called Decapepyal. This drug would stop your menstrual cycle; it would put your body through the menopause for all intents and purposes. We would put you on this course for about six months. We make your body believe it's going through menopause and this stops the ovaries from ovulating each month. This in turn stops the womb from building up lining, and the idea is that the lining thins out and sheds from outside the womb. Lastly we could go in for further surgery. This would involve using a laser and burning off the endometrial layer. But, as I've said, none of these procedures will completely cure the condition."

Sinéad sat there, trying to take in and hold on to the information. The words were blurring together: menopause, endometrial layer, laser, ovaries. It was too much to take in.

"This menopause business – what happens after the six months on the drug? How do you reverse the menopause again? I mean could my body be forced into it and then no one be able to jump-start my system again?"

"No, there is no possibility of that happening – your body will begin to menstruate again once you stop taking the Decapepyal."

"And what would happen with the surgery?"

"We would go in and use a laser to burn away the endometriosis, but I'd be unhappy to go straight into surgery. We prefer to think of surgery as a last resort."

"What do you suggest I do?"

"Personally I would advise going for the drug treatment. It takes a few months but it works. Given your situation, where we're dealing only with the endometriosis, with no tube blockage or ovulation problems, I would be happy that with this treatment you could go away and get pregnant then without any further intervention."

"No further intervention. It sounds very serious."

"It's a serious business, this baby stuff. Very close to the heart!" Dr Whitney laughed.

"So when will we start this drug treatment?"

"Well, let yourself heal and rest after this surgery, talk

to Richard about the whole thing and we'll talk again when you come back to me for your check-up."

The doctor made to gather his things and leave.

"So it was my fault all along," Sinéad said quite suddenly.

"What?" Dr Whitney turned back to her.

"We're having these problems because of me. We're jumping through hoops and it's my fault."

"Sinéad, for your own sake, don't start pointing fingers and assigning blame here. You did nothing to cause this – no more than if Richard had a low sperm count. It's no one's fault here. If you start faulting each other now you're done for. Remember that."

"I can't help it. This is all new to me – it's just hard to believe there's something wrong with me."

"I know it's hard, but please remember what I said – do not assign blame here. You did nothing wrong. It's not your fault."

Sinéad suddenly wanted to get away from this room and hide away in her own bed.

"I'd like to go home."

"I do have to keep you here overnight, just for observation. But if you feel good overnight, then we can let you go home in the morning."

"All right."

"It's not so bad – just lie back in the bed and watch TV for the afternoon. Get a good night's sleep and you'll feel rested in the morning. Believe me, sometimes a day's rest is the very best medicine you can get."

"Thanks, Dr Whitney."

"Not a problem." With a smile, he left the room.

Sinéad rang Richard and told him the news.

"Please come and see me as soon as you can. I really don't want to be here on my own."

"I'll be there by six, don't worry – I'll be there within two hours."

When six o'clock finally rolled around Richard was at the door, a stash of trashy magazines and a box of chocolates under his arm. He came in and sat on the chair by her bed. She went through everything she could remember about the conversation. All the treatments and the fact that there was no real cure for this condition. Richard listened as she spoke and sat silently as she cried her eyes out.

"It's my fault! It's my entire fault!" she complained through the tears.

"It's not your fault. It's no one's fault, Sinéad."

"But this must have been what that doctor suspected all those years ago – why he wanted to investigate! And I said no! I'm sorry. I'm so sorry!" she sobbed.

"Sinéad, Sinéad, don't worry, love! We'll be all right, just wait and see. We'll have that baby really soon," Richard said, praying that it would be true.

40

Julie decided to take Sinéad's advice. She was right – it was high time she went out and blew a few euro on herself. She got up early on Saturday morning and gave the girls their breakfast. Then she told Gavin she was heading out for the day.

"Grand, I'll see you later," he replied, misunderstanding. "I'll be back around five and then maybe we'll order in a Chinese and get a DVD?"

"Five! Back from where?"

"Golf. I told you last week I was going to be going out with the lads this weekend."

"I didn't hear you. I thought you could take care of the girls."

"Oh shit, no way. I can't take them golfing with me and I can't cancel. Jules, I've been really looking forward to this. I never go out with the lads any more."

"Fine," she replied but her heart was like lead. There was no point in fighting this one. Gavin was off on a golf outing and she would have to look after the girls. Sometimes you could stop for a row, then other times there was no point. There was no point to this one – she'd just lose and there'd be a bad atmosphere all day. She'd have to bring the girls with her or else forgo the entire trip. She wondered which one was the more appealing prospect. A day in the house with two hyperactive children or a day in Liffey Valley with two hyperactive children? Neither sounded like much fun but she needed to get out of the house. She was feeling claustrophobic so she decided to get out and go shopping. In the car on the way over to the shopping centre she explained to the girls as nicely as she could that it was Mammy's day out and they were just along for the ride.

"Mammy has to buy some things for Mammy, so this is Mammy's turn to go shopping. We'll buy things for you girls next time we're shopping. Is that okay?"

They nodded.

"So please, don't start asking for things in the shops. Mammy will buy you things next time."

"Can we get a food, Mammy?" Annabel asked.

"Yes, of course. We'll get a McDonald's if you like – would you like a burger and Sprite?"

"Yummy!" they both chorused.

"Okay, we'll get lunch and then Mammy will buy some Mammy stuff. It'll be a fun day out, won't it?"

They nodded more vigorously.

They got to the centre and queued for the cash machine. Then they walked around for a while, Genevieve in the buggy and Annabel walking alongside. They scooted from shop to shop and Julie looked at every type of top she could see. She wanted to try some things on, but with the girls there she couldn't. She didn't trust either of them to sit still while she changed and the thought of racing around a shop half-naked trying to catch them made her blood run cold. She held a pink top up to herself in one of the mirrors and stood for a moment deciding if she liked it. She turned this way and that, then suddenly caught sight of herself in the mirror. She was pregnant. She was fat, and she was shopping in the skinny section of the shop. Could she possibly have forgotten she was pregnant? Could it have slipped her mind? Does it slip a girl's mind that she's almost five months pregnant? That was another moment when it hit her full force: this baby was a distant unreal figure to her. It wasn't even an imaginary baby to her. It simply didn't exist. She stared at herself in the mirror, her cheeks flushed pink as she looked at her reflection and realised that soon she would be heavily pregnant and she still hadn't noticed. And despite all her best intentions she still wasn't eating well or saying no to that glass of wine.

She looked around the shop but there was no maternity section so she left. She went to another shop and headed straight for the maternity rails. The clothes were pretty but she still felt as if she was buying tents. Everything seemed so wide. She picked up a few tops and brought them to the register.

As they were rung up the girl behind the counter smiled at Annabel. "Helping Mammy shop today?"

"Yes," she nodded solemnly, "all the money is for Mammy today – there's no money left for us today."

Just as Annabel spoke, Julie opened her purse and

crumpled twenties and fifties sprang up. There was not actually as much money as it looked, but Julie could feel the girl's eyes rest on the money as Annabel's small voice rang in her ears.

"Annabel! That's not true!" Julie laughed as she handed over the money.

"Yes, it is. You said we couldn't ask for anything today because it was your day for Mammy-shopping."

"Anyway, you don't need anything. You've lots of clothes and toys."

"But Genevieve's shoe is broken and my skirt has a hole. The one I always wear has a hole."

"Annabel!" Julie was scarlet at this stage. People behind them were watching intently and the girl at the checkout was listening to the exchange.

"Really, that was one skirt and I told you to throw it in the bin and no one's shoe is broken!"

"Yes, it is – here!" Annabel picked up Genevieve's foot and showed the assembled crowd that the buckle in her shoe had broken off.

"When did that happen?"

"Yesterday, when you were on the phone."

"Why didn't you tell me?"

"We showed it to you and you told us to go away."

Genevieve nodded and said, "Go 'way, girls. Mammy's on the phone!"

Julie was being hanged, drawn and quartered here. She looked at the girl behind the counter. "I was only on the phone for five minutes. My friend is going through a rough time and I needed to talk to her."

The girl unsmilingly handed back her change and her tops in a huge carrier bag. Julie was sure they had been put in the biggest bag available to make it look like she'd just bought up the shop floor.

"Come on, Annabel. Will we go to McDonald's now?"

"Are we allowed?"

"Yes, of course we are. Remember I said we'd have a treat in McDonald's if you let Mammy do her shopping?"

"Oh goodie!"

They left the shop, every eye burning a hole in the back of Julie's head. She could just hear the mobile phones dialling Childline as soon as she left.

They sat in McDonald's, the girls spilling most of the contents of their burgers all over the table and playing with some plastic dolls they'd just got from their Happy Meal boxes.

"Annabel, mammies are allowed to go shopping from time to time. Mammy doesn't have to buy her children something new every time she goes out. Sometimes we need to buy some clothes for ourselves."

"I know."

"So there's no need to tell everyone that we have no money. We have lots of money but we're just buying Mammy clothes today. All right?"

"If we have lots of money, can I have a new skirt?"

"New shoes!" Genevieve put in.

"No, next time we go out we'll get you new shoes and skirts." Julie decided to stick to her guns. This was her shopping day and she'd not be forced into buying the girls things today. They didn't need them.

"When?"

"Next time we go shopping I'll get you a new skirt and Genevieve some new shoes."

"Next time?"

"Yes."

"Okay," Annabel nodded.

They finished their food and gathered up the toys.

They went into the next shop and Julie looked around. They passed the children's department but Julie kept on going.

"Mammy, skirts!" said Annabel, pointing.

"Not today, next time."

"But my skirt!"

"Shoes!" Genevieve shouted.

"No, this is Mammy's day out. Remember we talked about it?"

"But we could just get a skirt, a pink one," Annabel whispered.

"No, we're not getting anything for little girls today." Julie stuck to her guns, but could feel in her heart it was a stupid thing to do.

"But what about my skirt?" Annabel said a little louder.

"You have lots of skirts with no holes."

"But that was my favourite."

"It was not!"

"I need a new skirt!" Annabel knelt down on the floor as she began to wail.

"Annabel, get up off the floor!"

"I want a skirt!" She threw herself down and lay flat on the ground.

"I will not be buying you anything if you don't get off the floor."

Annabel stayed where she was, crying loudly.

"Fine, stay there!"

Julie went to walk away, but in this day and age leaving a little girl alone on the floor in a shop was not the safest thing to do. So she walked a short distance away, then looked back to see Annabel's eyes following her. But she never got up.

"Annabel, come on. Get up!"

"No!"

Julie walked a few steps further and pushed the pram around a rail of clothes. Genevieve got upset when Annabel went out of sight. She began to cry. That was all Julie needed, both of them in tears.

She stepped back around the rail. "Annabel, get up. You're making your sister cry."

"No!"

"Right, that's it!" Julie rushed back, grabbed Annabel by the arm and pulled her to standing. "We are going home. Our day out is over and you are to blame, madam!"

She straightened up and pulled Annabel out of the shop while pushing the buggy with her other hand. They walked out of the centre and out to the carpark, packed up the car and drove off.

As they sat in the queues of traffic at the toll plaza, Julie drummed her fingers on the wheel. She hadn't bought any make-up, or new trousers and she hadn't picked up a nice snack from Marks and Spencer. She'd been hasty and cranky with Annabel. They could have just left the shop and gone somewhere else – they didn't really need to go home. She had in fact cut off her nose to spite her face as they say. Annabel was looking out the car window, tear-stains on her cheeks and her face flushed. She sighed deeply, very deeply for a four-year-old.

Julie studied her from the front seat but said nothing. Annabel was not aware she was being watched. She tipped her trouser leg, then the frill on the hem of her top. She ran her finger over the frill again and smiled to herself. She smiled for an imaginary friend and kicked her leg out to show off her shoes. There was something so innocent in her gestures and something so girly about her frilly top and pink shoes as she sat and admired them that Julie's heart melted. It was only 1.30, they still had plenty of time and, let's face it, she hadn't bought a lot of clothes – she still had a few quid in her purse!

"Annabel, do you really need the new skirt?"

Annabel looked up and nodded. "I really need a new skirt, Mammy. Skirts are my favourites."

"All right, we can drop into Blanchardstown and pick up a skirt then."

She knew she was giving in to the child, but really, she felt so sorry for her. Genevieve was asleep in her car seat. Julie glanced back at her. She'd have to buy her a pair of new shoes – if they were broken they really needed to go in the bin.

Julie pulled into the carpark in Blanchardstown and looked around for a parking space. When she finally found one, about a mile away from the centre, in behind a small group of shops, she took the girls out of the car and put

Genevieve in her buggy. She walked back to the shopping centre, pushing one child, pulling the other as she dawdled along the path.

"Annabel, get moving!" she said as she stopped for the third time along one stretch of path.

"Can I pick these flowers?" Annabel asked.

"No, they're for a display."

"If I only pick one?"

"No."

"Please can I pick a flower?"

"Annabel I said no."

"Not fair!" Annabel complained as she walked on, looking back at the flowerbeds of tulips that spelt out Blanchardstown Shopping Centre.

They made their way into the centre where literally hundreds of women laden down with bags, buggies and children walked towards them. Julie wondered if the centre was in fact closing: everyone seemed to be leaving. She looked behind to see if the shutters were closing, she was so sure there was a mass exodus in progress. Behind her a trail of equally harassed-looking women walked in, each one pushing a pram or trying in vain to control uncontrollable children who were screaming for everything they saw.

She decided to rush to Dunnes, pick up a skirt, a pair of shoes and leave. She walked into Dunnes: it was like World War III in there. Then she saw a sign swinging from the rafters: 50% off everything in store.

"Oh Christ!" she groaned as she went to turn the buggy around. "Sorry, but we're not buying anything in here today."

This was a crowd she did not feel up to struggling against. But then a coat caught her eye, a cream mac with big buttons and a flowery lining. How much was that?

She went over and looked at it – it was down to thirty euros. It was her size. This was fate. She picked it up and joined the queue to buy it.

"What are we doing?" Annabel queried.

"We're buying this coat for Mammy."

"But we're here to buy me a skirt."

"We will after we buy this."

"You said we were buying nothing in here. How come we're buying you a something?"

"Because I saw this and I need a coat."

"Can we buy me just a skirt?"

"We'll buy it in another shop."

"Which shop?"

"I don't know. We'll look around."

"Can we look over there?" Annabel pointed at the Children's Department.

It was black with throngs of people, pushing and shoving.

"It's too busy in there."

"Can we just look?"

"I need shoes!" Genevieve shouted. "I need shoes!"

"I need a skirt!" Annabel reminded everyone.

Julie could see this turning sour very quickly. She was irritated by Annabel already and people around them were taking a huge amount of interest in the comments of a four-year-old. She could see the woman behind her watching the whole exchange, her head moving from person to person as they spoke.

"Oh fine then, we'll look for a skirt," Julie said as she pushed her way through the crowd and left the queue.

They got to the Children's Department and pushed their way through the crowds. People everywhere were pushing and shoving in front of each other. They fought over the tiniest amount of rail space and clothes were being discarded on the floor as shoppers located a better bargain. Julie hated this type of shopping and she never went near the January sales for just this reason – no item of clothing, for no giveaway price was worth this amount of trouble. She kept a close eye on Annabel as she looked at the rail and tried to concentrate on looking for a suitable skirt, but all the while she could feel people brushing up against her back and she got the horrible feeling she was being rubbed against by the wrong type of person. She looked around, glaring at a small boy whose head had accidentally just bumped off her bum as he passed. She was mortified when the child looked up at her and smiled his apology.

"Oh sorry, love," she said, but his mother had herded him off in another direction, glaring back at Julie as she walked.

She turned back to her rail and noticed that Annabel had disappeared off to another rail close by.

"Annabel, stay here! Stay with me!" she called.

"Look at this one!" Annabel shouted back, picking up a bright pink miniskirt with cream dots on it. It came with really big knickers in the same design. Julie took a closer look at it. When did they start making miniskirts for four-year-olds? Ones with knickers to match?

"That's a very short skirt," she smiled as she took it from Annabel.

It was only when the skirt was in her hand that she noticed it was for a nine to twelve-month-old. They were in the nursery section. She moved over to the children's section and they tried to locate a similar type of skirt for a four-year-old. There were none to be found. There were a hundred skirts and dresses of all colours and designs, but none to suit Annabel's exacting taste. About ten skirts were selected and returned to the rail for various reasons. Too short, too grown-up-looking, the wrong colour, a footprint on the back of it.

Finally they located a skirt that fitted all the criteria. It was pink, had a frill or two and hung to the acceptable level between knee and hip. It was machine washable and heavy enough to withstand a few knocks and bumps.

Then they headed for the shoes and located a pair for Genevieve. It was a much easier task than looking for anything for Annabel. Genevieve was a much easier-going person than Annabel. She tried on a pair of shoes and twirled in front of the mirror and nodded. That was her shoes bought. Annabel set her sights on a pair of sandals in bright pink to match her new skirt.

"Can I just have these to match my dress?"

"No."

"Please, look, they have flowers on them."

"No, Annabel. We bought you your skirt."

"Mammy, they have flowers and look, they say Barbie at the back. *Pleassse!*"

"No."

"But *pleeeeeasssse!*"

Julie looked at the shoes: they cost a tenner. That was nothing really, and not worth the row that would ensue if she didn't get them.

"Oh fine, give them to me. What size are they?"

"I dunno." Annabel handed over the shoes and together they searched for the correct size.

After what seemed like an eternity they located one pair in Annabel's size and they all headed to the till. It took forever for the cashiers to get through the crowds. They kept stopping and having to call managers to fix the prices on the things.

Finally all the purchases were bagged up and they left the shop. They were leaving the shopping centre as far as Julie was concerned. They'd spent far longer than she'd expected in there as it was.

"Mammy, I'm hungry," came a voice from somewhere close by.

"Jesus, Annabel, are you ever satisfied?" Julie replied, not trying to hide the irritation in her voice. "I'm sick of the constant requests from you!"

"It wasn't me. I never said anything," Annabel said, her voice quivering.

"Who said they were hungry?"

"I did!"

"It was Genevieve!" Annabel started to cry. "Why are you giving out to me?"

"I'm not. I'm sorry, Annabel. I'm just tired." Julie tried to calm Annabel down. She really didn't need a screaming child on her hands. "I'm sorry. I didn't mean to be cranky – Mammy's just tired out today."

"I'm hungry, Mammy!" Genevieve repeated.

"Okay. We're going home now and I'll get you some dinner when we get home."

"I'm too hungry, Mammy."

"I'm hungry too," Annabel whimpered.

Julie checked her watch: it was almost four. They hadn't eaten in over four hours. Maybe they were hungry.

"All right, what do you want to eat? Not McDonald's, you've had that already. A sandwich maybe?"

"A cheese sandwich?" Annabel asked, perking up a bit.

"Yeah, a cheese sandwich!" Genevieve clapped.

"All right, we'll get some sandwiches and orange juice."

It being late on a Saturday afternoon, they queued for half an hour, squashed into a tiny table in the corner of a ludicrously expensive restaurant and ate cheese sandwiches and orange juice by three. Even as they sat there happily chatting and eating their food, Julie knew it was only a matter of time before the dreaded sentence was uttered. Then there it was.

"Mammy, I need the loo."

They tidied up their wrappers and food and made their way to the bathroom. Another long queue, watching children dance around in an attempt to stop from wetting themselves, ignoring the terrible smell that comes from every public toilet.

And then there was the awful comment from every cubicle as the occupant opened the door and the next person raced in: "Sorry, it won't flush."

The person on her way in would stop in her tracks and look nervously at the toilet seat, only to decide it was worth a chance and she'd go in.

After what seemed like an eternity they were sorted out, hands washed and dried, and ready to head for home. The girls were exhausted and slept all the way. When they got home it was after six and Julie put them both in the bath and into their nightclothes. Then they all sat down and watched the Big Movie on TV. By the time Gavin came home the girls were asleep on the couch and Julie wasn't far behind them.

Gavin carried the girls up to bed and when he came down they ordered a Chinese and Julie lay on the couch. She had a glass of white wine and savoured every sip of it. As she lay there she wondered about coming clean and telling Gavin about the fact that she had forgotten she was pregnant, that she had looked for ordinary clothes and was annoyed that the clothes were too small. She glanced at Gavin as he watched TV and ate his takeaway. She weighed up the options but decided against it. What was the point in telling him? He'd either treat her as if she was losing her mind and insist she spoke to a psychologist or he'd pat her on the head and use it as an excuse to patronise her for the rest of the pregnancy.

Either way, it was probably best that no one knew about any of this. She'd just pray that when the time came she'd bond with this baby as quickly as she had bonded with the girls.

41

Julie had an appointment to have a scan when she got to week twenty.

A few days before her appointment she had a very busy day, running from place to place.

First she dropped the girls to playschool. They had both graduated from the crèche a few months before and were now playschool girls. Then she ran to the supermarket and did the weekly shop. She dropped some clothes in for dry cleaning and then came home. She put away the groceries, then unloaded the washing machine, put clothes on the line and refilled the machine with a new load. She raced out and picked up Genevieve from the playschool and on her way home picked up some wine that she'd forgotten to get in the supermarket earlier on. She went back out an hour and a half later to collect Annabel from her new little friend's house. They had met in playschool and had bonded instantly. Now they spent a couple of hours each week in one another's house after playschool. They walked to the park and the girls played in the playground for the best part of an hour while Julie watched them from a bench near the swings. She read the paper as they played. It was the first time she'd sat down that day and without even realising it she sat with her hand on her bump, casually rubbing it.

She had sat there for a few minutes when it occurred to her that she hadn't felt a kick lately. Her heart leapt crossways as she thought about it. Had she felt one yesterday? She'd been very busy all day but surely there'd be some kick or thump? This baby had begun to kick around at about fifteen weeks and she had felt a kick or a prod most days, in fact lots of them, every day. Today there was nothing, and she was really trying to remember if she'd felt anything yesterday. At that moment her mind was a blank – she couldn't remember feeling anything at all. She pushed her tummy a little to see if anyone would push back. Nothing. She poked a little harder, ignoring the sound of her own heart as it thumped loudly in her ears.

She poked again, still nothing. She waited, trying not to panic as she sat there. She wanted to go home and drink a glass of Coke – the caffeine and sugar in the Coke would wake the baby and jolt it into action. She wanted to lie down on the couch and wait for the kicking to start but she couldn't do that at the moment. The girls would be looking for dinner when they got home and then they'd be playing for a while and it would be much later before she could lie down in a quiet room. What if there were no kicks then? What would happen then? What would she say to Gavin?

She tried not to panic, but her heart was racing and the

guilt over not noticing the lack of kicking was already starting up.

Later that evening when the girls were in bed Julie had drank three glasses of Coke in quick succession with no luck.

That was a full day without a kick. She had to tell Gavin. This had never happened to her before – the girls were such kickers, both of them.

"Gavin, I think we have a problem," she said as she walked into the sitting room. "I haven't felt any kicks all day and I'm after drinking about a litre of Coke and still nothing."

Gavin looked at her, concern on his face, but he wasn't panicked about it. "No kicks at all?"

"Nothing, and I was pushing my tummy earlier to see if it would move at all, but nothing happened."

"What should we do?"

"I don't know." Julie could feel herself panic.

"Ring the doctor, explain what's happening and ask him if he'll see you sooner."

"It's after nine. He'll be gone home."

"Well, ring the hospital. Ask if you can come in and have a scan."

"They don't just scan you like that – the scanning unit closes for the night."

"Well, will you ring them and see what they say?"

"All right."

Julie rang the hospital; she was a bit embarrassed that she'd not done it already. It seemed like a logical thing to do now that Gavin had pointed it out.

The nurse in the emergency room was very nice. She

asked how far along Julie was, had she had any bleeding, and when was the last time she felt a kick. She advised that Julie should come to the hospital straight away.

Gavin rang his mother and she came straight over.

Just before they left for the hospital Julie ran to the bathroom. When she got there was another shock in store for her. Blood. Lots of it.

She came out of the bathroom and got straight into the car. She told Gavin on the way into the hospital – she hadn't wanted to say anything in front of his mother. She was enough of a busybody. She'd be on the phone to her daughters talking all about it.

Forty minutes later Julie was sitting in the emergency room with a monitor strapped to her stomach, listening to the familiar whooshing sound. She listened as the nurse located the heartbeat and the monitor picked up and counted out the beats per minute.

"There it is!" The nurse smiled. "That's a fine heartbeat."

The nurse handed her a monitor with a button to press on the top of it.

"When you feel any movement press that button," she said.

Julie took it in her hand and waited, then waited and waited. Nothing, no movement, no kicks. The nurse came back and checked in on her.

"Nothing at all?"

"No."

"Baby may just be asleep. But there's the heartbeat, beating away nicely, exactly as it should be. You say there hasn't been any movement yesterday at all?"

"No, nothing that I can remember."

"And anything today?"

"No, nothing at all."

"Well, the baby is alive, that's the main thing. We are concerned that it hasn't moved and of course about the bleeding. I'm going to call your doctor and see if he wants to talk to you. But don't worry. Your baby is alive and there's nothing to panic about. But first, can you take me through your day yesterday. Was there anything that we should know?"

"No, nothing unusual. I was very busy in the morning but by the afternoon things were back to normal."

"No falls or bumps, no moving heavy furniture?"

"Nothing."

"No unusual stress or strain on yourself?"

"No, no more than usual."

Julie never mentioned the fact that this entire pregnancy had been a strain. That she'd been stressed from the word go, that she never really wanted this baby, that she felt she'd been forced into it by her spoilt husband, that he'd wanted a boy and would stop at nothing to get his way.

Julie never mentioned that she was completely numbed to this baby. So numbed in fact that while she was out shopping last week, she had forgotten she was pregnant, completely forgotten about it – looking at fitted trousers and tops and wondering why nothing seemed to fit right. How could it have slipped her mind for the last five months? Any woman who has ever been pregnant will tell you that it's ingrained in your mind from the moment that a positive result is confirmed. From day one you're planning ahead and thinking about what this baby will be, who it will be and what it might look like. You never forget about it. You never forget you're pregnant, do you? She'd never forgotten while she was pregnant with the girls. Not even Genevieve and let's face it there was reason enough there to want to forget. The fact was she didn't though. But she forgot about this baby.

The nurse broke into Julie's thoughts when she said that they might need to keep her in overnight. Just as a precaution. They really needed to keep an eye on things to be sure the baby was in fact still moving. Julie listened but didn't really take it in. A night in bed to herself, with no one to get up for in the middle of the night, would be very nice indeed. It was only when her consultant appeared in the room in his jeans and a T-shirt that she realised maybe things were a little more serious.

The baby was alive, its heart was beating fine. She watched the monitor as it read out the beats per minute for a long time. The doctor felt her tummy and pushed down hard here and there. Then he went outside and spoke to the nurse for a moment. They came back in and the doctor explained that he wanted to bring her upstairs to the Foetal Assessment Unit and have a look at her baby on the monitor there. He was concerned about the blood loss and the fact that the baby was not moving.

They all went upstairs. The nurse went ahead of them and had a machine turned on and ready to go when they arrived. She put the cold gel on Julie's tummy and the doctor scanned her. He worked busily for a while, measuring, moving, twisting and prodding. He printed various pictures and looked at the placenta for a long time. It all seemed perfectly fine. The placenta was in the correct place but the baby was not moving at all. They sat for a moment staring at the screen, almost as if the doctor didn't know quite what to do next.

Then there was a sudden and very definite kick. Julie gasped and the doctor pointed to the screen at the same moment. The baby kicked again and that was it. Baby had woken up. Baby was completely fine, kicking and stretching as they looked on.

The doctor sat on the bed beside Julie and read her notes, then he asked a few questions of his own.

"If a person loses the amount of blood you seem to have lost tonight, with no real reason for it, we are concerned about a placental abruption, but from the scan it seems to be fine. We have no idea why this happened, or if it could happen again. Just to be on safe side we're going to keep you here overnight. We are concerned that if we don't know why it happened it could happen again. We'd rather just watch you here for a few hours."

"All right. Just for tonight?"

"At the moment it's just tonight but we can't say for definite. We'll need to look at things in the morning before we can let you go home."

"Will I be on bed-rest for the rest of the pregnancy?" Julie was listening to the doctor more intently than she had listened to the nurse and so it had just dawned on her that there were twenty-two more weeks of this pregnancy – that was a lot of bed-rest.

"Hopefully not, but if we need to we will have to prescribe bed-rest."

"I have two small children. I can't be on bed-rest."

"You and that baby are my concern. If bed-rest is what it takes, then I'm sorry, bed-rest it is."

"I know." Julie tried to backtrack – she didn't want the doctor to know there was anything unusual about her feelings for this baby. "Sorry, I don't mean to sound like I don't care but the logistics of complete bed-rest! You have no idea!"

"Look, we'll see how things pan out tonight, then we'll talk about bed-rest. In the meantime we'll move you to one of the wards and get you settled in."

After he left, a nurse came over and took Julie out and into a ward across the corridor. Gavin followed them in.

"Julie, you poor thing!" he said. "I'll get you an overnight bag. I'll just grab some things from the house and come straight back."

"Thanks."

Julie sat on the bed watching Gavin leave and felt like a little girl again. It was lonely and scary to suddenly find yourself in hospital like this. Only two hours ago she was wondering what to watch on TV tonight and now here she was, sitting in hospital, alone.

She looked around and caught the eye of a girl in the bed across the room. She smiled and looked around at the rest of the girls. Various smiles and various bump sizes stared back at her.

"Got a shock, did you?" one girl asked.

"Sorry?" Julie looked around.

"When they told you that you have to stay in. It gives you a terrible shock, doesn't it?"

"Yeah, this is my third and I never had to stay in hospital before."

"This is my second and I stayed here for the last three months on the first. I think I'll be here for the long haul again this time."

"Is it very boring, the bed-rest?" Julie asked.

"*Yes!*" came the reply from every bed.

An hour later Gavin came rushing back into the room, an overnight bag in one hand and a bottle of Sprite in the other.

"Jesus Christ, Julie, I couldn't find anything in the house. It took ages to find your stuff – when did you move it all around?"

"I never moved it around, Gavin – you are unbelievably crap at packing, that's all!"

"Well, I brought you in everything I could think of."

"Did you bring in a toothbrush?"

"Yes."

"Toothpaste?"

"No – do they not have it here?"

"No, Gavin, they don't."

"Do they have a shop?"

"I'm on bed-rest!"

"Shite, I'll go and get you some. I'll be back in a few minutes."

The next morning the doctor came back to have another

chat. This time he was a lot happier. There had been no further bleeding and he had been reading her file and had just one question.

"You were out with the children yesterday?"

"Yeah."

"And were you very busy? Carrying bags, rushing around?"

"Yes, I was going all morning – the supermarket shopping, dropping the kids to school and picking them up again, walking with them. Why? Do you think I caused this bleed?"

"I think you may have burst a blood vessel in your groin or pelvic area."

"What?"

"You said there was no pain at all and, if you were struggling with shopping bags as well as two children, it is quite possible and in fact probable that that's exactly what you did."

"I burst a blood vessel?"

"It's the most likely cause – a sudden heavy bleed with no trauma to the baby at all, no pain and no repeat bleeds. I would be happy with that conclusion."

"So what now?"

"Well, I'll let you go home but you must take it easy for the next few days anyway and if possible take it easy for the next few months. We'll monitor you from here on in but hopefully it was an isolated incident."

"So I can go home?"

"Yes, you can."

"Great.

Gavin collected her at eleven, took her home and she lay in bed for the day. Gavin's parents kept the girls for the night and Gavin danced attendance on her all day. When the girls came home Julie's mother arrived to look after them. By the end of the week Julie felt a hundred times better. So much so that when things finally went back to normal and she was left alone with the girls, she could hardly believe how much work was involved in looking after them.

42

Sinéad was back in Dr Whitney's surgery for her post-op check-up.

"I was sore for a few days but I'm completely fine now," she told him as he looked at her stomach and asked how she was feeling in general. "And just to let you know, we've had a long chat about the next move and we've decided to go with the drugs and menopause."

"All right, I think it's the right thing to do."

"It may be the right thing to do, but I still feel weird about drugging myself into menopause to tell you the truth."

"I understand." He helped her to a sitting position. "We'll talk about it now in a moment. I'll go through the whole procedure with you. Your stomach looks perfect and there is very little scarring there at all. I'm very happy with that."

They went into the other room and sat at the desk with Richard.

"I understand that you've decided to go with the

course of Decapepyal and I think you're doing the right thing," the doctor said, bringing Richard up to speed and getting straight down to business.

"So what happens next?" Richard asked.

"Well, the course involves three injections of a drug called Decapepyal. Sinéad would go to your GP and get the injection every four weeks for about three to four months. The injection is into the leg given every month on day two of your cycle. By that I mean day two of your next cycle and every four weeks thereafter – your cycle would of course be stopped during the treatment. I would give you a prescription for the injections and your family doctor can administer them."

"So that's it?" It seemed sort of easy to Sinéad.

"Well, that's it treatment-wise, but there are side effects and they're not pleasant."

Sinéad sighed inwardly. This was no news to her. In fact, what part of the last few months did he think had a pleasant side effect?

"What kind of side effect?" she asked.

"Well, you are putting your body through the menopause. So all the side effects of that: hot flushes, loss of libido, dryness of the vagina and mood swings."

"Oh Christ," she said aloud. "Sounds charming!"

"I know, it's not pleasant but it's only for a few months and then it's all back to normal," he smiled. "So what I want you to do next is make an appointment with your GP. I'll give you the prescription for the Decapepyal and if you bring it with you on the day, your doctor can sort it all out for you."

"It sounds too easy," Sinéad smiled. Glad for a change that something did.

"Well, as I said, it's just an injection once a month for three months but you are putting your body through a major upheaval. There will be side effects and all I'd say is go with the flow and be easy on yourself for the next few months. Now is not the time to go renovating the house or taking on a new job."

They left the surgery and headed for home, happy in the knowledge that things were for now moving forward. This was going to be a long few months and Sinéad couldn't help but calculate in her head that Julie's baby would be born slap-bang in the middle of this whole process. Just another little treat for her to endure, as if all of this wasn't tough enough.

It took forever for Sinéad to get her period after the laparoscopy. The doctor had told her that things would be messed up for a few weeks and to be honest it came as no real surprise to her. But the waiting was a killer. She watched her body for signs but none came, then one day she went to the loo and lo and behold there it was. No bloated feeling, dull ache or crankiness – it just arrived. In the end it had taken only five weeks, but they were five long weeks. At least it meant that she could get started with the injections.

She rang the doctor and explained why it was she needed to see him the next day.

She went in after work and got the injection. He went

through all the ups and downs and side effects of the drug. She'd heard them all before and thankfully there were no surprises there.

It took about a week for the first side effect to kick in. It was a hot flush and Sinéad honestly thought she was going to suffocate. She was in the car coming home from work when suddenly she felt like there was no air; she felt her heart begin to thump as her face began to burn up. She looked at the rear-view mirror, expecting to see her face scarlet but it was fine. A little flushed but nothing extreme. She opened the car window and took a long drink of her mineral water. Thank God she had some in the car – to think she almost left it in the office tonight! She looked at other drivers. It seemed odd that they weren't aware of her sudden panic – had it not registered on her face? She looked at the woman in the car next to hers and then in the mirror at the man talking on the phone behind her. Seemingly not. As quickly as it came on her it began to subside. Then it was gone. She felt a lot better and cooler. She pulled the window up again and relaxed. As it turned out this was the first of a barrage of hot flushes over the next four months.

She got home that night and told Richard all about it. It was the first time it had happened and it was news. In a strange way it was a bit exciting – it was proof that things were beginning to happen. She was being put through the menopause and it would hopefully fix everything and, who knows, next year they could be playing happy families with the best of them. It would all be worth it.

Later that evening she got another hot flush. She was in the sitting room watching TV when it hit her.

"Hey, Richard! It's a hot flush!"

Perhaps they were two of the stupidest people on earth, but they got all excited about it.

"Wow, what does it feel like?

"Really, really hot. Like being in a sauna – you know, the real dry hot air? Oh my God, the heat! Am I all flushed?"

"You're a bit red but not that much. I wouldn't notice it if you hadn't said anything."

"Really, I feel really hot. Will you get me a drink?"

"Yeah," he raced out and came back in with the water. "Have you still got it?"

"Yeah, I hope it goes soon." Sinéad was beginning to feel a bit panicked; it was too hot in here. She drank down the water and it began to subside. "Oh thank God, it's going away."

Richard watched her as the flush left her cheeks and she began to relax until it was completely gone.

"Phew! I'm glad that's over!" she smiled.

"Wow, so you're really going through the menopause then?"

"Yeah, I'm getting all the symptoms anyway."

"That's mad!" he said more to himself than to her.

"Yeah, it is mad," she replied, but her heart was still pounding. Even though she knew it would only last a few minutes it was still sort of scary as she was going through it. They carried on watching television.

On Thursday night they were watching *EastEnders* when Sinéad felt the tell-tale signs coming over her.

"Is it very hot in here all of a sudden?" she asked.

"No, not very," Richard replied lazily.

"I'm red-hot," she said fanning herself with a magazine she found on the floor. "Oh wow, the heat! Do I look flushed?"

"No, not really."

"Well, I am. I need a drink. Will you get me a glass of water?"

Richard returned to the sitting room with a glass of water. Sinéad drank it down in one, but it didn't help – the air was still hot in her nose.

"Oh God, it's still really warm. Can we open a window?"

"Yeah, if you want." He hesitated.

"Richard, will you open the window?"

"Fine." He went to open the window.

Before he got to it the hot flush began to subside, the air was cooler and the room wasn't as stuffy. She could breathe more easily.

"Oh it's going away. Thanks be to God for that! You don't have to open the window."

Richard was in the middle of opening it. "Do you want it open or not?"

"No, it's fine. Close it again."

Richard closed the window and came back to the couch. His irritation was noticeable to Sinéad but she ignored it.

"Was that it?" he asked. "Does it only last a minute or two?"

"Yeah, but that's enough!" she laughed in exasperation. "It's a pretty long few minutes for me, I can tell you."

"Yeah, but I mean, is it over? That's all there is to it?"

"Yeah, but Richard, it's not an enjoyable experience."

"I believe you, but I just thought it'd be worse than that."

"Well, sorry to disappoint you – I don't writhe around in agony if that's what you expected."

Richard shrugged and carried on watching TV. Sinéad stared at the side of his head for a few minutes. Was he for real? She'd just had a hot flush and he shrugged it off because it wasn't 'extreme' enough for him.

A fortnight later the hot flushes were old news. They were coming thick and fast and Richard was not bothering too much about them any more. He'd see them and knew the drill: Sinéad got hot, flushed a little and then it went away.

43

Sinéad found the next few weeks very tough. It wasn't so much the side effects themselves, it was the fact that they came upon her without warning. It was manageable when she was at home or out shopping, but work was a nightmare. She hadn't told any people about what was going on, just her immediate boss because she needed the time off and some understanding when she came back to work. So now there she was, sitting at her desk battling with hot flushes that were coming on her without warning, and in the already dry air of the office it was suffocating. And then there was the vaginal dryness . . .

Also, the mood swings were kicking in. She was tired a lot and as a result her fuse was shorter than usual. She was usually the epitome of calm and good sense in the office but she could very often feel her hackles rise.

She was short with Laura for no good reason on one occasion. Poor Laura had asked for a day off. It was coming up to the Bank Holiday and she was seven months pregnant. She had asked Sinéad if she could have the Friday off and make a long weekend of it. She acknowledged that it was short notice but she was hoping that it would be okay.

"No, Laura, it's not okay!" Sinéad snapped. She could see the shock register on Laura's face but she carried on. "You can't just come in on Tuesday and expect to get Friday off. I know you're pregnant but I can't make exceptions just because of that."

"Oh, all right, I just thought I'd take the chance." Laura smiled but her eyes were hurt and angry.

Sinéad realised a little too late that she'd overreacted to the simple request but she was not about to apologise. It wasn't her who'd come in looking for a day off at the last second. She wasn't bending the rules, baby or no baby. She ignored the fact that it was a mood swing she was having, just slammed her folder shut and hammered at the keyboard for a few minutes before taking a walk down to reception and back. When she got back she was still agitated but she didn't feel so argumentative, so that was better.

As bad as things were in the office they were a hundred times worse when there was a meeting of any kind going on. If anyone got up her nose in any way she found it impossible not to let it show. Things that should have gone over her head completely – pen-tapping, heavy breathing and God forbid anyone should have a cough or a sniffle. Sinéad would glare at the offender with a belligerent eye until they noticed her and stopped whatever misdemeanour they were carrying out.

And there was no feeling on earth like a hot flush in a stuffy boardroom, stranded miles from the door, water out of reach, with your face and neck on fire. It was a nightmare.

Home was her sanctuary. She could snap at Richard and lie on the couch moaning for hours without any real consequences. He knew what was happening, he knew it was only going to be for a short while and most of all he knew why it was happening.

Then, about seven weeks into the whole procedure, Sinéad hit a brick wall. She was well and truly menopausal. She had the libido of a wet tea bag. They were watching TV late one night and, during an otherwise middle-of-the-road type movie, a very racy sex scene began. It was a bit of a surprise as there was no real introduction to it and no, it was not a porn movie they were watching. Richard sat up a little, taking a keen interest in the proceedings. Sinéad watched with only a vague interest.

While it was in full swing she sat there watching and finally had to announce, "I don't know. I might as well be watching *Coronation Street*."

"Really?" Richard sounded surprised.

"Yeah, nothing whatsoever."

"Bummer," he laughed.

Sinéad smiled as he laughed but her head was troubled. She didn't appreciate Richard's flippant laughter, but she let it go.

And she didn't appreciate he found the vaginal dryness problem funny either . . .

A few days later she was in the doctor's office getting

her second injection. They were fine as injections went but she hated the sight of a needle. At this stage her period was all but a faint memory and she was getting more used to the hot flushes. They didn't fill her with quite the same panic as they had done before. She could just open a button, take a drink and wait it out. Her moodiness was under some control too. So she was feeling okay about it all. Also, it was month two now – just one more injection and the whole thing would be over. She came home that evening to find Richard in the kitchen. He was reading the paper, drinking coffee and he'd made a bit of snack for himself. They hadn't been to the supermarket for a fortnight and the kitchen was not very well stocked at the moment. Sinéad saw his sandwich and suddenly a toasted cheese sandwich sounded like a really good idea. She went to the fridge and found it was empty. He'd used the last of the bread, the last of the milk and left a mouldy edge of cheese-back instead of throwing it away.

"Ah Christ, did you eat all the food in the house?" she complained.

"No, I made a sandwich."

"What's this? Why didn't you just throw that bloody cheese out, Richard? And is there any milk left? Is there no milk for my tea?"

"If there's no milk in the fridge then no, we've no milk left."

"Why did you use the last of it?" She could feel her voice tighten as she spoke.

"What's wrong with you today? It's not my fault you haven't been to the supermarket in months and it's not my fault you had to get that bloody injection today. Don't go taking it out on me!"

"I'm not taking it out on you! I just want a bloody cup of tea when I get in. Is that too much to ask for? After I've been in work all day and then at the doctor's being injected with some bloody awful hormones! All the things I've been through and you just go and drink the last of the milk!"

This row was not about the milk and they both knew it. They should have just backed off but they were both too wound up by the last few months.

"It's not my fault that you have to go and get those stupid injections. It has nothing to do with me! You're like a fucking maniac these days. I can't take much more of the snapping and demands from you!"

"You treat me like I should keep going as if there's nothing wrong. I'm just about keeping it together here. This whole bloody procedure is a nightmare but you wouldn't know anything about it. You never ask me how I feel. I come in and you don't offer me as much as a cup of tea!" She was suddenly sobbing, her legs went from under her and she slumped to the floor, her head buried in her hands. "I hate this! I hate the way I feel and I hate that you just ignore it all and laugh about the hot flushes and the no sex drive! I hate it all!"

Richard had jumped up when she fell to the floor. He thought she'd fainted but then realised that she was just crying. He stood in the middle of the kitchen, just looking at her. Sinéad who was always such a tower of strength, now was just a tiny frail little girl lying on the kitchen floor sobbing.

"I thought you didn't want a fuss. I thought we weren't making anything of it and just waiting until it was all over," he explained.

"You keep laughing at me when I get a hot flush and you thought it was funny to buy that KY Jelly last week in Boots when I was getting my vitamins. You just treat me like it's all a joke and nothing to get upset about. I am upset. I'm devastated! Look at me! I'm thirty-four and I've been wishing for a baby for two years now! And Julie's having her third baby next month and I'm still waiting for my baby!"

"I'm still waiting too," Richard sympathised, but that was only a red rag to a bull.

"Don't you think I know that? I feel sick about it. Every day I feel sick to my stomach that it's my fault you have no children!"

"Listen, I'm not getting at you here, Sinéad. I'm just saying you're not the only one in this – I'm here too."

"But it's my fault, and you make fun of it!"

"I don't make fun. I don't mean to make fun, Sinéad. I was being silly buying the KY jelly – it was a joke, a stupid one, but I had no idea how badly you were taking all of this. I'm sorry."

Sinéad sniffed loudly as she began to pull herself back together. She wiped her eyes with a tissue she found in her pocket. "I can't bear this feeling. This useless, broken feeling. It makes me so angry to feel like this and there's no way out. I just have to keep going. I have no choice any more."

"You have a choice. You always have a choice. If you

want to stop the whole thing right now and call a halt to
the injections I'll respect that and we'll get on with doing
other things."

"I couldn't do that. I couldn't just say no to the help
now and then complain about the fact that I've no
children later on. At least this way, if we're still looking at
each other when I'm forty odd, I can say I tried everything.
I couldn't bear it if I looked back in years to come and
regretted stopping the treatment."

Richard sat on the floor beside her; he looked at his
beautiful, together wife and thought how lucky any child
would be to have such a wonderful, kind mother, not to
mention such a good-looking one. She was a real catch
and between them they would get her the baby she so
badly desired. If they had to look into foster care they
would. They would go down whatever road they had to.
Sinéad needed this to work out. She needed a baby,
preferably one of her own but if that didn't work out
they'd have to adopt one, from here or overseas. Only now
did he realise how much she was willing to go through to
have one.

Sinéad looked at him, her eyes fixed on him. "What
demands do I make on you?"

"What?"

"A while ago you said you couldn't take any more of
'the demands'. What do I demand?"

"Nothing, I was just annoyed."

"No, go on, what do I do?"

"It's nothing – you used to ask me to get you water
and open windows and get you ice cream when you were

having flushes and you were snappy when you were having a mood swing. I was just annoyed about it."

"You were annoyed because I asked you for a drink of water?"

"No, it wasn't any one thing – it wasn't the water or the snapping. It was all of it together."

"I didn't realise that I was so snappy. I knew I was bad but I didn't think you minded too much."

"I am only human, Sinéad. I hate being ordered around as much as you do."

"Sorry."

"I'm sorry too."

They sat on the floor for a while before moving out to the conservatory and lying on the couch listening to music. They opened a bottle of wine and drank it together. Things were quiet that night and they went to bed early.

Richard slept like a baby but Sinéad was struggling to get comfortable. The hot flushes were really bad at night. She fought with the duvet all night.

44

Julie had been resting as best she could for the last three months. She was now thirty-seven weeks pregnant. There was no further bleeding which was good news but she was tired and heavy and wanted this baby to be born, sooner rather than later. The girls were very excited about the baby and they kept a close eye on Julie. She couldn't go to the bathroom without an escort. They would come straight in to the bathroom and sit on the floor beside the bath. At first Julie was mortified and found it hard to go to the bathroom with them there. But as the days went by she began to get used to the constant entourage.

It was getting to the point where if she stretched, sighed or rubbed her back the girls became concerned. They would follow her from room to room asking her if the baby was coming.

"Are you okay, Mammy?"

"Yes, I'm fine."

"Are you having the baby?"

"No, not yet."

Her due date was still three weeks away. She was giving the girls their breakfast when she got a sharp pain in her side. She winced a little but kept going. Then a few minutes later she got another one. She wondered about it but decided to ignore it. She was there by herself with the girls – she really didn't need it to happen right now. Anyway, she never came early. Well, she never had before, but there was always a first time.

And for the first time ever Julie went into labour three weeks early. She knew what was happening as soon as she got the fourth sharp pain. She checked her watch when she got another pain, ten minutes. Another pain and this time it was about eight minutes.

"Shit," she thought aloud, "why right now, when I'm here with the girls alone?"

She rang Gavin. He was only after getting to the office, he hadn't even got to his desk, but he was turning around to come home as he spoke. He was facing into rush-hour traffic though and he'd be a while getting home. Julie decided to get her neighbour just in case she had to taxi it to the hospital alone.

Ellen raced up the drive with her daughter under her arm. "Are you okay?"

"Yeah, Gavin's on his way, but I thought just in case he doesn't get here and I have to grab a taxi you could watch the girls until he shows up."

"No bother. Do you want to go and lie down? Have you a bag packed?"

"Yes, it's in the bedroom. I'll get it."

"You stay right where you are! Do you want to lie on the couch for a while? I'll get the bag and look after everything."

"Thanks, Ellen, I'll just sit down for a few minutes. The girls are just finishing their breakfast and after that they usually go out the back and run around for a while."

"Grand, I'll look after everything."

Julie sat on the couch, but the pains were very close and very painful so she stood up. It was easier to walk around. She was circling the sitting room when Ellen came back in.

"Who's looking after the girls while you're in hospital? Have they bags packed?"

"No, but Gavin's Mum is taking them. They'll be going over to her for the day but she'd coming back with them tonight and she's staying here for a few days. It's easier to do it that way. It's a nightmare packing for kids. They need so many changes of clothes. This way they have everything here."

"Grand, are you very sore? Want a cup of tea?"

"No, I'm fine," she began but stopped. "Actually, a cup of tea would be great!"

Forty minutes and several cups of tea later, Ellen and Julie were in the sitting room. Ellen was sitting in the armchair drinking tea and Julie was walking in circles while holding her mug. The pains were coming very strong by now and Julie was really wondering about that taxi option.

"Come on, Gavin! Where are you?"

"I think you might have to take the taxi, Jules. I couldn't deliver a baby by myself. I'd be useless."

"You'd be useless? I'd be a basket case! I have no intention of giving birth in this room!"

The car pulled up outside and Gavin jumped out.

"Oh thank God!" the women chorused as one. "Gavin, we're in here!"

"Traffic!" Gavin shouted as he raced into the room. "What's happening?"

"Oh, em, nothing much! I'm in labour for the last hour and Ellen is terrified that she'll have to deliver the baby on the hearth-rug!"

Gavin raced around the house, bundling the girls up and putting them in the car. Julie sat in the car waiting for him. She winced as she sat in the front seat and when she then glanced into the back there were two sets of eyes staring at her.

"Are you having the baby, Mammy?"

"Yes, I think I am, Annabel."

"Are we going with you?"

"No, you're going to Grandma's."

"Will we see you after?"

"Yes, tomorrow."

Suddenly the sound of crying was heard in the car. She looked around and saw Genevieve crying.

"What's wrong, honey?"

"Is the baby hurting you?"

"No, of course not."

"Then why have you the hurting face on you?"

"The baby isn't hurting me. My tummy hurts a bit but the doctor will fix that up when I get to the hospital."

"How?"

"He'll give me medicine."

"All right. And you won't have the hurting face any more?"

"No, not once I get the medicine."

Genevieve looked at Julie closely, as Gavin locked the door and put her bag in the boot.

They drove to Gavin's mother's house and dropped the girls off.

"Hurry, no chatting to her!" Julie shouted out the window as Gavin herded the girls up the driveway.

The journey into the hospital was always going to be fraught. Julie was in pain and wanted to get there without stopping or going over any bumps in the road. Gavin was excited and chattered a lot, never hit the brake and took off over every pothole and speed ramp in the city. It was as if he was looking out for them as he drove. They got to the hospital and like old pros went straight to the emergency room; they knew the drill and Julie answered all the questions, even offering answers to questions the nurse forgot to ask. Things moved very fast and four hours later Julie was sitting in her room, a glass of Diet Coke in one hand and her mobile phone in the other, texting everyone in her phone book to tell them the good news.

"Baby boy, 8lbs 7oz.

Cute as a button, no name as yet."

She turned back to Gavin who was walking around the room carrying his son in his arms.

"What are going to call him?" she asked.

"I have no idea. I still like Rex," Gavin said as he watched the baby yawn.

"We are not calling the baby after a dinosaur. I like James."

"James is all right, but Rex Hurley sounds great. How about Rex James?"

"No, I'm not having Rex. Pick another name, Rex is not happening."

"Why not? I let you pick Genevieve and I'd never even heard of it before."

"You had so heard of Genevieve before. Anyway Genevieve is a pretty name, Rex is a dog's name."

"Rex is a boy's name, but if you really hate it I'll think of another one."

Julie was really beginning to regret ever telling Gavin that if it was a boy he could choose a name. To be honest she'd got such a pink vibe from the baby that she thought it'd never come to it. She vaguely wondered if the pink vibe meant this little boy was going to be gay. She dismissed the thought – so what if it did? She looked at the top of his head as Gavin passed the bottom of the bed on his third lap of the room. Black spikes of hair tufted out from his blue blanket.

Suddenly it hit her. "What about Harry?"

"Harry Hurley? You are joking, aren't you?" Gavin laughed.

She hadn't thought of that, damn it – she'd really liked Harry all of a sudden.

"I have it and I will not be moved!" Gavin announced. "Max James Hurley!"

"Max? Max Hurley?" Julie tried the name out for a while and to her surprise she didn't hate it. Admittedly it wasn't exactly setting her alight with joy, but it was better than Rex anyway.

"Yeah, I think it's great. Baby Max Hurley, Mr Max J Hurley – yeah, it'll get him from childhood to adulthood. I love it and you said I could choose the name."

"I suppose I did. All right, Max it is then."

"Well, hello there, Max!" Gavin said holding up the baby in the window.

"Can I hold him now? I haven't seen him since he was all cleaned up." Julie smiled.

Gavin came over and laid the baby in her arms.

"Here he is – Max Hurley!" Gavin beamed.

Julie held him close and studied his small face. He was fast asleep as she held him, but his face was so pretty, like a little girl in fact. She loved the look of him; she loved the smell of his head and the feeling of holding such a small bundle. She looked down at him and felt the familiar surge of warmth that she got when she held the girls. It would be all right. She loved Baby Max. She breathed a silent sigh of relief as she sat there. Thank God she'd told no one how she felt about the pregnancy. It was all over; she was finished having babies: no more stretch-marks, no more antenatal classes and no more carrying around a sack of potatoes up your jumper!

And most of all, the end was in sight for that damn steriliser! In twelve months it was going in the bin.

"So have we decided on Max for definite then?" Julie asked.

"Absolutely."

"The registry girl will be around in a while and we can't change it once she has him registered."

"I won't change my mind."

"Right so, Max James." Julie's stomach knotted slightly. Did she like the name? Oh God! She didn't like the name!

She looked at Max. His eyes blinked open and locked on hers.

"Max?" she said as she looked at him, "Is that your name?"

The baby stared up at her.

"Yes, I suppose it is." She smiled at him as he closed his eyes again.

45

Sinéad knew it was coming. Julie's due date was just around the corner and she never went too far over, but when a text arrived in the middle of Tuesday afternoon she realised she was not prepared. She was delighted for Julie and Gavin – Gavin had wanted a boy so badly. He had only been talking about it last week so she was glad for him. And she was thrilled for Julie, but Christ, did it all have to happen right now? She had been feeling very weepy for the last few days and the hot flushes were losing their novelty value. In fact she was sick of them. She still hadn't told anyone in work about what was going on. She knew the doctor had been right when he said that it was no one's fault and that she should not apportion blame, but it was hard. It was very hard for her not to blame herself, and it was very tough to admit to herself or anyone else that she had a problem. Sinéad had always been so capable. Learning to drive, she'd taken off with no problem; she'd passed her test first time. College had been plain sailing, as was getting a job and then holding down her job. Climbing the career ladder had been so easy. But now, the most fundamental of things – having a baby, and she couldn't do it. She was still stunned and embarrassed that she was having trouble. She told no one in work; she didn't want the sympathy or whispers. What *they* didn't know wouldn't hurt *her*.

But that text stung her. It stung her as sharply as a dagger in the chest. Of course she replied to the text. Sending love and kisses to the new baby, baby number three. She sat at her desk staring into space as the text flew across her phone screen and the message came up that it was sent. She sat there for a while looking at Julie's text: *baby boy, no name yet.* No name? Why no name? Would they not have talked and talked about names for the last nine months? She would, if she ever found herself in the wonderful position of choosing a name for her own baby. She'd have a name picked for months in advance. Why had Julie not chosen a name? Sinéad felt a twinge of irritation pass through her; it prickled her chest and made her eyes sting with tears. Then she realised it was not irritation that stung her eyes, it was jealousy. For the first time in years, possibly ever, she was jealous of Julie. She swallowed down hard on that particular emotion – it wouldn't help anyone. Her phone rang, jolting her from her thoughts. It was Julie.

"Hey! Thanks for the text!" Julie said.

"No problem, I really am thrilled for you, Jules. A boy!"

"Yeah, a big lazy boy, here asleep in his cot."

"So fill me in on all the details!" Sinéad rallied, her friend's happiness infectious.

"Well, it went fine. No problems, a very quick labour.

Although I did kick the consultant in the arse by accident!"

"Oh Christ, Jules! How did you do that?"

"My leg was dead from the epidural and it was heavy, I was holding my leg up the way I was told to."

"Oh yeah, I remember you telling me that one. Very classy!"

"Listen, you have no idea how classy it is when you drop your leg and you've to grab at it before it overbalances you and you fall off the bed! Anyway, my leg dropped and it's a dead weight so I couldn't control it. I kicked the consultant bang on the arse. I was mortified!"

"Oh my God! What did he say?"

"Nothing, he just smiled and moved to the side. I was scarlet! I kept telling him I was sorry, but he kept saying it was fine."

"Oh poor you, Jules!"

"I know, if it's going to happen to anyone it'll happen me!"

"Anyway, what does Baby Boy look like?"

"Oh he's fabulous! Loads of jet-black hair – his name is Max by the way."

"Max? That's gorgeous."

"Do you think so? I'm not one hundred per cent on it, but Gavin loves it and I told him he could pick the name if it was a boy. And he picked Max. I'm lucky really – he had wanted Rex."

"Oh no, not Rex! Rex is a dog's name!"

"Tell me about it, not to mention the fecking dinosaur. I don't love Max, to tell the truth, but it's not bad and I'll get used to it."

"You will, and you'll love it!"

"Well, when are you coming in to see me?"

"Eh . . . I thought I might wait till you come home, Jules," said Sinéad hesitantly. She couldn't bear to face into a maternity hospital just then. "Is that okay?"

"That's no problem. I completely understand. Anyway, I'll only be here for a couple of days and all the family are chafing at the bit to have a look at him. He's only the second boy in the family after all the girls. Did you know I have seven nieces and only one nephew?"

"Really? Seven?"

"Yeah, so there are nine granddaughters and up until this afternoon only one grandson. So Max is a bit of an auld novelty!"

"Well, I'll be there first thing when you get home. I'll be the one waiting on the doorstep. I can't wait to have a look at him!"

"Well, if you're just sitting there, would you mind letting yourself in and tidying up a bit while you wait?"

"Hey, no problem!" laughed Sinéad. "Anything else you want me to do? Book you in a massage? Hire a nanny? A maid? A personal trainer?"

"I knew I could depend on you! But, seriously, I'll expect to see you just as soon as I get out!"

"Sure – just text when you're getting out and I'll be there!"

Sinéad hung up. She opened her emails and read through a few but she couldn't concentrate. Finally she grabbed her bag and went for a coffee.

She went around to the canteen and sat in the corner.

She stared out the window as she nursed her coffee. Someone came and sat at a table close by; she didn't really notice them until she looked up and saw that it was Laura. She looked pale and tired – Sinéad remembered the request for that Friday off last month. She was still embarrassed to think back on how she had bitten Laura's head off. This was her opportunity to make amends.

"Laura!" she called.

Laura spun around. Her cheeks pinked as she registered it was Sinéad.

"Sorry, I just thought I'd grab a quick cup of tea. I'm not feeling great today. I said it to the girls and they said it was no problem to take five minutes."

"No! It's not that at all. I don't mind you taking time out. Sure look at me, I'm doing the exact same thing. I wanted to say sorry about the other day."

"What other day?"

"That time you were looking for the Friday off."

"Oh, that was ages ago. It's all right." Laura smiled.

"No, I was in a really bad mood and I took it out on you. I felt awful about it. I just wanted to say sorry."

"That's all right. I'd forgotten all about it to be honest."

They sat there for another few minutes in silence.

"So, how long more have you got?" Sinéad asked.

"Another two weeks in work and then two weeks at home."

"I bet you can't wait."

"I can't wait to have work over, I can't wait to have the labour over, I can't wait to have it all over!"

"I'm sure! A friend of mine just had a baby today."

"Really? What did she have?"

"A boy, Max."

"And was it her first?"

"No, her third. She has two little girls, so they're thrilled with the boy."

"And she called him Max?"

"Yeah, have you names chosen yet?"

"Oh God, yeah!" Laura looked away for a second and then back at Sinéad. "It took a fair while for us to have this baby, so I've had a few names on my list for ages. We're calling it Luke if it's a boy and Ella if it's a girl."

"They are really beautiful names. I love Ella."

"I do too, I'd love it to be a girl, not that I'd be disappointed with a boy! As I said, we've waited a while for this person so I don't care what it is."

"Do you mind me asking how long you were waiting?"

Laura flushed a little. "Well, it took about two years."

"Really! And then it just happened like that one day?"

"Yeah, I wanted to get checked out, but my husband was adamant that we didn't need to. We just kept trying and finally it worked!"

"You're very lucky," Sinéad smiled.

"I know." Laura got a little more self-assured. "Do you think you might like to have a baby some day?"

"Yeah, we'd love a baby, but it's not as easy as we imagined."

Sinéad realised what she'd said just as the words left her mouth. She couldn't believe it – she'd just blown her cover, just like that. She looked at Laura, but Laura wasn't horrified nor was she laughing at her. She was just nodding sympathetically. But the sympathy wasn't hard to take. It was nice. It was soothing.

"The amount of girls with bumps in here you'd think it was as easy as falling off a bike, but if you actually chat to some of them, they'll tell you it took for ever to get pregnant. Loads of them took months and months; some of them even took years, way longer than me even," Laura said, matter-of-factly.

"Really?" Sinéad smiled, happy to hear she was not alone. "I look around here and I see nothing but bumps. I was beginning to think it was something in the water."

"No, it's not the water! I've been drinking it for years!" Laura laughed. "It's something different entirely!"

"Maybe that's where I'm going wrong then! I was keeping off the water!"

It felt really good to laugh and joke with someone. Someone who'd been where Sinéad is now, trying in vain for that elusive baby.

"Have you been trying for long?" Laura asked.

"Yeah, we've been through the mill. I have endometriosis but before it was diagnosed we were tested for lots of things."

"My sister-in-law has that. She had two children though so don't give up hope. Are they treating it for you?"

"Yes – do you know much about it?"

"I know a bit. Have they given you that drug called Dica something or other?"

"Decapapyal, yeah, I'm just finishing up on taking that one. It made me really moody – that's why I snapped at you the other day."

It was so wonderful to talk to someone who knew a bit about it and wasn't shocked to hear what she had to say. They sat for forty minutes just talking about babies and the ups and downs of trying to conceive. They only noticed the time when one of the girls came around to the canteen, concerned for Laura.

"Thank God! I thought you were giving birth in the toilets somewhere!" she laughed as they all went back to their desks.

Sinéad felt a huge weight was lifted off her shoulders as she got back to work that afternoon. Of course, it had helped to chat to Julie but she was so happy to talk to someone who had a little knowledge about it and who had been through a long wait herself. And just to hear that girls in the office were having trouble too, that it wasn't all plain sailing for everyone else.

Misery really does love company, she thought to herself as she opened her diary and made a note that Max had been born.

Going home in the car that evening Sinéad was stuck in the usual horror jam that is Dublin at six o'clock on a weekday. Her mind wandered to thoughts of Julie and baby Max. She liked the name. Hurley was a difficult name to match anything much with – Gavin Hurley sounded kind of cool, but let's face it Annabel Hurley sounded just a bit ridiculous to Sinéad's ear. Anyway, back to Max. She couldn't wait to see him. Though visiting other people's new babies was an increasingly fraught thing with her. Especially as Richard would talk all the way home about how much he was looking forward to having a baby of their own.

She would find it very hard to listen to that kind of talk at the moment – his excitement and optimism about the new treatment killed her.

She watched the lights change from red to green and looked at the car in front of her. No one was moving. People were jammed into the yellow box and blocking up everything. Usually it drove her to distraction – she'd be fuming and cursing everyone around her – but tonight she was calm. She didn't realise it until the lights went red for a second time. She hadn't moved an inch and for some reason she hadn't hit the steering wheel. She was calm. It wasn't for a few minutes more that she realised she wasn't as tense as she had been about Max's arrival. She'd been upset in work, but now she could think of him without feeling that pang of jealousy and she was really looking forward to seeing him. The sick, nervous feeling that usually accompanied these trips was gone. She was just plain excited to see him. Granted she didn't feel too much like going to see him in the hospital, but that was not just about seeing babies – it was also because hospital visiting hours were a pain in the arse.

But there was more to it than the visiting hours and baby Max. She sat there watching the traffic inching by her and somewhere inside she felt a warm glow. It started in her stomach and radiated through her whole body. She knew at that moment that she would have a baby. Maybe it wouldn't be this month, maybe not for a long time, but someday she would have a baby of her own. It would be her turn to have people come into the hospital and congratulate her, and other women would get all clucky when they saw her baby. Maybe it was because she had finally come out and told someone else about the problem, maybe it was because the person wasn't surprised and hadn't found it easy to get pregnant herself. Maybe it was because she had just come to the realisation that, just as a watched pot never boils, perhaps a prodded Sinéad never gets pregnant. Medical intervention works for lots of people, but it doesn't work for everyone. It was possible that she was just one of the ones it didn't work for. She was never going to get pregnant while doctors and nurses, no matter how well intentioned, were looking over her shoulder and ticking off boxes.

She always thought she'd go to the ends of the earth to have a baby, but as she sat there, a new calm coming over her, she realised that no, she was not willing to go too much further on this one.

She was in the middle of her menopause treatment and she wasn't going to stop in the middle of her treatment and she knew the doctor had one more trick up his sleeve after that. She'd see it through to the end of that process but she was not going to start a new one. She was beginning to realise she'd had enough.

She wasn't giving up on having a baby, far from it. She still wanted one more than ever. She was giving up on testing and prodding and the possibility of IVF. She wanted to be left alone.

She wondered what Richard would make of it. She

ran through a few conversations in her head; none of them worked out too well.

This menopause would last another month or two and then the doctor was talking about a course of tablets for six months. Maybe she'd wait to see how they worked out. You never know, she could be pregnant by then and the IVF conversation would never have to happen.

She should maybe think more about this before she sat Richard down for the long chat. But something in her had changed. She had come to a realisation: Sinéad and the medical profession were going to part company for a while.

46

A week later Max and Julie were back at home. Most of the visitors had come and gone, leaving bags of blue clothes and blue balloons all over the house. Annabel was very taken with her baby brother or at least his boy's bits anyway.

She was now four years old and was taking her role as the eldest child very seriously. She came to the door with Gavin as people arrived and took the gifts, putting them in a bundle on the floor in the sitting room. Then she took the visitor by the hand and led them to Max, wherever he was at the time, whatever he was doing at the time. So far Julie had been caught breastfeeding by Gavin's best friend, her parents-in-law and her neighbour from three doors up.

This time it was her brother and his wife. The screeches from both Julie and her brother were blood-curdling.

"Annabel! I'm feeding the baby!" Julie screamed as her

brother realised what exactly he was looking at and rushed backwards from the room, knocking his wife against the doorframe as he exited.

"Sorry, sorry, Jules!" came the ashamed voice from the other side of the door.

"Sorry! I'll be with you in a minute, Dave!" Julie shouted back and cringed for the next ten minutes as Max drank greedily.

Then she got herself together and reappeared with an embarrassed smile.

"Sorry about that, I was just feeding him," she told them.

Annabel came straight over and stroked Max's face as she advised everyone that Max was very small and that only Mammy and Daddy were allowed to hold him. Then she looked to Julie for back-up.

"That's right, only Mammy or Daddy can hold him," Julie smiled at her.

"Max is a boy. He has a boy's bit on his bottom," Annabel continued. "And sometimes he pees right up in the air and last night he peed on Mammy's face."

The smile froze on Julie's face. "Annabel, that's enough!" she said, trying to push the child away without actually toppling her over in front of anyone.

"He did, and you said 'Fuck!'" Annabel continued, her face a picture of innocence.

"We don't talk about people peeing, Annabel – it's rude," Julie said. "And don't use that other word."

"The word you said?"

"Yes."

"But you used it!"

"Yes, I shouldn't have – anyway, we don't talk about people peeing."

"Yes, we do! You told Daddy. You said to him that Max peed in your face. You talked about it!"

"Annabel, where's Genevieve? Go and find her for me, will you?" Julie said, trying to get rid of her as fast as she could.

"It's all right – she's in the sitting room," Annabel dismissed the request.

"What's she doing?"

"Watching *Scooby Doo*."

"Would you like to go in and watch it too?"

"No, I'm helping with Max."

"I don't need any help just at the moment, honey – when I do I'll call you."

"Are you sure? 'Cos I can help."

"Yes, I'm completely sure," Julie smiled at her.

"All right!" Annabel skipped off into the sitting room.

The room exhaled with relief. She was the most unmerciful gossip of a four-year-old. There was no knowing what she might say or who she might hang next.

When she was safely ensconced in front of the television Julie let the others hold the baby. She watched the door as they held him – even though she was a bossy little know-it-all, Julie still felt she shouldn't undermine Annabel in front of anyone. If Annabel believed no one but Julie and Gavin held Max then Julie was happy for her to carry on believing it. It also meant Annabel was happy not to hold him and the longer that could continue the better.

47

Sinéad went to see Julie and Max after he came home from the hospital. Julie was right. He was absolutely beautiful. As often as they both saw it, neither of them could really believe how small a new baby was. Even Max, who had been the biggest of Julie's babies, was a tiny little bundle in their arms. Gavin had taken the girls out for the day so it was just Julie and the baby. Sinéad was silently pleased about that; the girls might be a lot of fun but Annabel was at that age where she insisted on asking really embarrassing questions and also where she demanded an answer. Not only that, she wanted a real answer and you couldn't fob her off with a shrug or a smile. She was a small private investigator and everyone who entered the house was a suspect in her little mind-game.

Just last month she had cornered Sinéad and asked her why her hair was a new colour.

"I got the hairdresser to make it a different colour."

"Why?"

"I just wanted a change."

"And do you like it better that colour or your old colour?"

"I like it this colour."

"Really?"

"Yes."

"With the yellow bits in it?"

"Yes," Sinéad felt herself blush a bit as Annabel pointed at her highlights. "Did you like it the old colour?"

"Yes, I don't like the yellow bits."

"Really?"

"Annabel, that's very rude. You can't tell people you don't like their hair," Julie said as she walked into the room.

"I can if it's true. You can't tell lies. It's bold."

"You have to be polite – you can say you like the old colour better, but you shouldn't say you don't like someone's new hairstyle."

"It's all right – I'm not the least bit offended. She's just a child," Sinéad put in, mortified.

"No, Sinéad, I don't want her to just announce she hates a person's hair or clothes. She has to be told that's wrong."

"But why can't I tell the truth?"

"You might hurt someone's feelings."

"But I'm bold if I tell a lie."

"Yes."

Annabel was confused.

Sinéad had to stifle the laughter; Annabel was in fact learning one of life's harshest lessons. You're damned if you do and you're damned if you don't. And the poor child was completely confused.

Thankfully Annabel, Genevieve and Gavin were all at the zoo today and Sinéad was relaxing in the kitchen with Julie as Max slept in his basket in the corner.

"So, how are things going with you these days?" Julie asked.

"I'm fine. The injections are over, so I'm officially over my menopause treatment. I still have the hot flushes and stuff, but it's almost over. I'm actually just waiting for my periods to start up again."

"And what happens then?"

"The doctor said that he'd put me on this stuff called Clomid. It increases your fertility supposedly. It makes you ovulate."

"I didn't think that was your problem."

"It wasn't, but the doctor seems to think it'd be a good idea just to boost my system for a while. The only thing is, it can overstimulate your system and it increases the chance of twins and triplets."

"So, Jesus, you could find yourself with a gang of babies!"

"Yeah, I'd find myself on one of those programmes on *Discovery Health* about people who have seventy kids!"

"It never rains but it pours for some people!" Julie grinned. "But seriously, Sinéad, how are you feeling about all of this?"

"The menopause was hell, the hot flushes were a nightmare and I was a moody cow, but it's over now and I'll be a lot better once my periods are back on line and we're all down to business again. The doctor seems optimistic that I'll get pregnant by myself so I'm happy about that."

"That's great news. He doesn't think you'll need IVF and stuff?"

"No, he's happy. So we're happy."

They sat in silence for a while listening to Max sleep.

"I'd forgotten how they snuffle and grunt when they're new." Julie smiled as she watched him.

"I had no idea they did. I thought he had a cold."

"No, they all do that. Then their lungs clear and they sound normal."

"And how are you settling into a new baby all over again?"

"The night feeds are definitely harder this time. I'm feeling awfully tired all the time. I don't remember this level of exhaustion with the girls, but who knows? Maybe I was worse with them and I've forgotten."

"Well, you're older now. I'm thirty-four now."

"Oh please! Don't start telling me we're over the hill!"

"We most certainly are not over the hill, but we have to realise we're not the youngest of the group any more. In work I'm one of the older crowd now – where I used to be one of the youngest managers now I'm one of the average ones."

"I know – when I went to the hospital this time round I was definitely one of the older ladies. I was by no means the oldest but there were a lot of twenty-somethings sitting around."

"When did that happen? When did we become the

older generation? I don't remember getting that memo!"
Sinéad laughed.

"I have no idea, but we became the older ones
somewhere along the line. We're in our mid-thirties. I'm a
mother of three, I drive a people-carrier and I shop on
Wednesday mornings while the girls are at the crèche.
When did I become such a stay-at-home-mom?"

"I know. Richard and I are officially 'DINKIES'. We're
not in the age group who just haven't had kids yet – we're
in the official age group to qualify as Double Income No
Kids."

"Oh God, when did our lives become like this? I never
really noticed until one day last week when I was struggling
with the girls and Max, getting them all into the car, and
I said to them to put their fingers on their noses while I
closed all the doors. My father used to say that to us when
we were kids. I was left there thinking, I haven't even
become my mother, I've become my father!"

They both laughed at this. Julie's father was a very
austere cranky man and not a bit like Julie at all.

"You have not become your dad! No fear, Jules!"
Sinéad laughed. "But really, here we are complaining that
we've become all grown up and sensible, but would you
really want to be back there in your twenties, going out
clubbing, looking for Mr Right? Dressed in the height of
fashion even though you were freezing your ass off?"

"No, absolutely not. I'm very happy with my lot in
life. I have everything I wanted, the children all safe and
well, this house is great and in a great location and I love
Gavin. So no, I'm happy."

Sinéad began to laugh, "So are you telling me that if your Fairy Godmother showed up tonight with three wishes in her pocket, you couldn't think of a thing to wish for?"

"Well, three wishes from a Fairy Godmother, now that's different!"

"So what would you wish for? Now you can't wish for a man or money, don't forget that!"

"I'm not looking for a man, although some extra money now, that would be nice."

"What would I wish for, I wonder?" Sinéad looked down at her cup. She knew exactly what she'd wish for.

"Well, you wouldn't have to wish for a man or money. You've got both."

"Yeah, I've got them covered."

"I'd probably wish that I'd had a bit more of a career before I got married – but that would be in the past – can I wish for something in the past?"

"Well, let's say you can. Go on!"

"Okay – so, a bit more of a career, and maybe waited till I was bit older before we had the children. Not much older, but maybe until I was about thirty or so."

"Really? I thought you loved the fact that you had them when you were in your twenties?"

"I love them and I don't regret them, but I would maybe have liked to wait a few years to have them."

"Would that be a wish then?"

"I suppose it would. So, I wish I'd waited a while to have the children, I wish I'd spent more time on my career before I gave it all up to be a mammy – and I wish I'd known what the houses prices were going to do and bought a second house seven years ago!"

"Well, I'm with you there, but my wishes would be kind of opposite to yours. I wish I hadn't given my all to the damn job. I wish I could just switch off and go home at five. I wish I could have children without the prodding and poking I've been getting lately and I wish I'd started the process back in my twenties so that time wasn't an issue now."

"Time is not an issue, Sinéad – you're only thirty-four for heaven's sake! That's not old! People are having babies, their very first babies, at forty and over now. Don't be thinking you're over the hill just yet!"

"I know, but we've been trying for over three years, that's what it does to you. It makes you feel very old."

"You are not old."

"Sometimes I feel it – I feel menopausal for God's sake!"

"You are menopausal!" Julie grinned and they both laughed.

48

Sinéad waited another five weeks and finally her period made an appearance. For the first time in four years she did a merry little dance when it finally showed up. She went back to the doctor as she had been told to and he gave her the prescription for Clomid. He told her to get it as soon as possible and then start taking it on day three until day seven of her period. He listed off another round of side effects from it. Sinéad sat there giddy with excitement. She had been through all the side effects at this stage and nothing surprised her. This time she was having a baby. She was sure of it. This Clomid was going to get her the baby she wanted – who knows, it might even get her twins!

She took the tablet on day three and was relieved to find her head didn't explode and her hands didn't begin to shake or anything awful. Two days later she began to feel the effects of the drugs. She was sitting at her desk and her phone rang. It was one of the line managers and they wanted to know how far along she was with a report she was doing. Sinéad began to answer and soon realised her words were coming out much faster than she wanted them to. She stopped and began again: she was still flying through the conversation but at least the words weren't as jumbled as they were at first. The manager on the other end listened, and then asked her to repeat some of it. She repeated it in just the same rushed tone as she did before. He thanked her but she could hear the irritation in his voice. She wasn't doing it on purpose but he obviously thought she was.

All that afternoon she felt jittery, as if she'd got too little sleep or too much caffeine. And her voice, it was coming out at a mile a minute, she couldn't slow down. She wondered if this would go on for the full month or just while she was taking the dose. Would it be over in three days?

No, it wasn't. It was less pronounced and her speech slowed but the jittery, cat-on-a-hot-tin-roof type of feeling didn't stop. And it got worse. She was irritable again; the mood swings were back with a vengeance. She was short with Richard even when she didn't mean to be and she had all this pent-up energy. She would come home from work and want to get stuck into sorting out the box-room. She'd decide over dinner that she wanted to pull all the old boxes from the top of the wardrobe and tidy it all out. Then she'd be annoyed with Richard when he'd come in tired and watch TV instead of helping her or if he blankly refused to get involved at all.

"I'm not going up to the attic and bringing down a whole load of boxes for you to go through."

"I think we could really use the space up there much

better – we could fit a load of the boxes from the spare bedroom in there if we just moved things around and then we'd have so much more space down here."

"We don't need any more space, Sinéad. We have four bedrooms and all of downstairs. We have loads of space in this house."

"What are you getting at? We have loads of space and no children to fill it? Is that what you mean, Richard?"

"Oh Christ, is this what I've to look forward to for the next six months? You, biting my head off every five minutes?"

Richard left the room.

"Do you think I'm happy like this? Do you?" Sinéad shouted after him, her voice high-pitched and her hands shaking with adrenalin.

God, she hated being so cranky all the time but she couldn't help it. She hated being so out of control of her emotions and her body. She hated this process, but she kept going in the constant hope that all of this would bring them the baby they wanted. So what if she was moody for a few weeks? By next month she could be pregnant, then Richard would move any box she wanted.

Three weeks later Sinéad got her period. She was furious. All her good intentions and excitement when she was prescribed this drug, it was all for nothing. It hadn't worked. She sat at her desk, fighting back tears of frustration. She felt like ringing the doctor and complaining about it. She knew that was just the anger though and that she'd never actually ring the surgery and make the complaint. An hour later she was at a meeting and fighting her corner about staffing levels in her department. She needed two new bodies and the powers that be thought she could keep going with things as they were. She knew full well there'd be a revolt if the work-load was not lightened soon, so the conversation was heated. She was not walking out of this room with less than the go-ahead to start interviews for two new recruits. Two hours later she walked out with the confirmation that she needed and the go-ahead to recruit two new staff members with the possibility for three if the work-load continued to increase as it had. She went back to her desk to start the process when she got a call to reception. She went down to find a lovely bouquet of flowers waiting for her. They had a message from Richard inside.

"All in good time, my love. R"

She beamed at the message. He was so right. So what if it didn't work first time round? The doctor had prescribed her this Clomid for six months. There were five more months to go, and any one of those months could be the one.

She went back to her desk, thrilled with the flowers and given a new lease of life by the message. She sat there looking at the red roses and sprays of babies' breath. She had been looking at it in her usual way. As in all things she'd been convinced that it would work immediately, that there'd be no waiting around. She always assumed that things would click into action as soon as she decided they should. She had to let go of that; things don't work first time every time. Let's face it, she should have known that better than anyone, but no, in her heart she was still expecting things to get moving immediately. Richard was right. She would have to start looking at life from Richard's point of view: it would all happen in its own good time.

Three months later things hadn't changed. Sinéad was really trying to keep a clear perspective on things. Richard was still painfully optimistic and that actually made it harder for Sinéad at times. She knew she shouldn't – the doctor in the Rotunda had been adamant about not laying blame – but she couldn't help it. Especially when she had to find Richard, wherever he was, in work or in the garden or just watching TV and tell him again that it hadn't worked again, that next month they were again back to the drawing board. She knew she shouldn't blame herself but she did. It was her condition that was causing all this grief and lately she could see that it was getting to Richard. He was finally letting the smile slip, letting the disappointment show in his eyes. She felt awful for him, she felt guilty and as she sat there with him, rallying them both and shrugging off the disappointment again, she realised how their positions had changed in the last few months.

Richard had been the tower of strength and now he was crumbling. She felt awful to see him weaken and then fall in front of her. There was no joy in seeing the pressure finally get to him. She had sometimes wondered, during those months and years of trying and testing, why he never seemed bothered that it took forever for things to happen. In her darker moments she wanted him to crack, show some kind of strain, anything that would prove that it wasn't just her who was completely and utterly wrapped up in this process and feeling every single moment of it. And now it looked as if he was cracking, and she hated it. She couldn't bear the guilt. Every time it didn't work the first thought that entered her head was 'This is my fault. I'm so sorry about this'.

Things were turning around all right. It was now Richard who kept saying that they had given their all to the process, had performed on cue, abstained when required and put Sinéad's body through all kinds of procedures and even the menopause for God's sake. They should really be reaping some reward at this stage. It was only fair, as childish as it seemed to say this aloud. This whole process was so unfair. It wasn't fair that they were still waiting, after all they had been through.

It was now Sinéad who was being philosophical about the whole thing. They had tried and tried on this one. If after all of this there was no baby, then so be it. Finally she was beginning to see a future that wasn't so bleak. It might not involve a baby of their own but it was by no means bleak. They had a beautiful house, great jobs, plenty of money and, if they had to take the baby thing off their list of must-have items, then so be it. Sinéad would get a dog or maybe two dogs and lavish all her motherly attention on them. It wouldn't be the end of the world. She could fill her time with other things, most of her time anyway. She'd do what she could, if it came to it. She'd do her best, if there was no baby.

If they had to admit defeat on this one. If they had to.

49

When Max was five months old, Sinéad got a phone call.

"Hi!" Julie sounded upbeat.

"Well, hi there!" Sinéad smiled.

"How is everything with you?"

"I'm fine. How are the children?"

"They are hale and hearty. Annabel is doing my head in with all the bloody talk. She's talking from morning till night! If it's not about her Montessori teacher, it's about her little friend Ella who owns a dog. Oh yeah, I think we're going to have to get a dog! She's grinding Gavin into the ground about it."

"A dog? Three small children, a dog and a main road? Have you thought that one through, Jules?"

"Listen, we've tried to talk her out of it. Her birthday is coming up and all she wants is a dog. Ella has a dog so she wants one too."

"And you are aware that the dog won't stay in the toy-box in a month or two? It'll be around for a hell of a long time."

"Yeah, we've thought it all through. We'll get a small one, a Jack Russell or something and Gavin will take it for walks with the girls. It'll be a hassle and we have thought about it for a while – but really if she wants one that badly . . ."

Sinéad wondered about how spoilt Annabel was going to be allowed to get, but she put the thought to the back of her mind. Julie was a good mother – just because she indulged her children a bit didn't make her wrong. But Sinéad couldn't help notice that Annabel was indulged to a far greater extent than anyone else.

"I know you think I'm mad," Julie continued, as if reading Sinéad's mind. "I know I give in to Annabel a lot, but I can't help it. I suppose I still feel sort of guilty that she missed out on being the baby when Genevieve arrived so quickly."

"Julie, I will not listen to this one again! How old will Annabel be next month?"

"Five."

"Exactly! She's five years old, and she has everything she wants and more. She did not miss out on anything by having a baby sister early. She was lucky. Genevieve was a great little addition to the family and a great pal for Annabel when they were tiny. Stop the guilt trip!"

"I know I should. I just feel bad. I can't help it."

"Please, Jules, I mean this from the heart. If you don't stop soon you'll make her spoilt to the point where there's no going back. There is nothing on earth so awful as a spoilt woman!"

"Sinéad, she's only five, not exactly a woman!"

"You know what I'm saying. She'll be a spoilt child

and in time a spoilt woman. And there is nothing worse."

"Well, she's getting the dog anyway. We've already promised it to her, so we can't go back on our word."

"Well, enjoy your new dog. Annabel won't be the one walking, feeding and cleaning up after it."

"I know, but what can we do?"

"Do you want me to answer that one?"

"No!"

"Anyway, apart from Annabel and the dog, how are Gavin, Max and Genevieve?"

"They are doing really well. In fact, the reason I rang was to tell you that Max is being christened on Sunday week, the seventeenth, at three in Corpus Christi Church. Will you be there?"

"With bells on!"

"Great and there's one other thing I wondered about."

"What?"

"Would you and Richard like to be godparents? I know it's short notice, but Gavin and I have been thinking about it for a while. I wanted you to be Annabel's godmother but I had to ask Lynn, and then Gavin had to ask his sister to be Genevieve's. Would you like it?"

"Would I like it? I'd be honoured! Oh my God! I can't believe it. Richard would be thrilled. He has one goddaughter and he heaps the attention on her, so he'd be really delighted. Thank you so much!"

"Thank you! I'm so relieved. It was really late notice and I was afraid you wouldn't be able to make it."

"As I said – we'll be there with bells on!"

"Thanks, so that's Sunday week at about a quarter to three."

"Don't worry, we'll be there. Do I get to hold the baby at the font?"

"No, you just say that you'll stop him from joining a cult or doing drugs and stuff!"

"I'll do my best on the cult thing, but I can't promise you anything!"

"If my darling son shows up after shaving his head and piercing his lip, he'll be moving in with you until the hair grows back and the lip heals, right?"

"Wait and see if it suits him – he might look good!"

"A pierced lip? And you think he'll look good?"

"Okay, I better shut up or you'll get Annabel to be his godmother!"

"She's beginning to look like a really good alternative!"

"I'd better get off the phone, but I'll be in Drumcondra on the seventeenth, never fear!"

"Thanks! See you then if I don't see you before!"

Sinéad went off smiling to herself. She had never been asked to be anyone's godmother. She was going to be the best damn godmother in the world. There'd be nothing that she wouldn't do for Max. He was her godson. She rang Richard, told him, and he was just as pleased as she was.

"And they want me to be the godfather?"

"Yeah!"

"Fantastic, I can't wait. Do I get to hold him during the christening?"

"No, we just get to condemn the devil and stuff."

The christening went off without incident. Richard and

Sinéad stood up and denounced Satan, promised to defend Max to the end of the world and look out for his spiritual welfare from this day forth. They did get to hold him; they had a few photos taken with him. They were like children, taking it in turns to hold him. Sinéad smiled for the cameras and held Max close as he smiled up at her. Then she handed him back to his parents and they went up to the altar with the other parents and had photos taken and certificates handed out. Babies were blessed and elderly priests tipped babies' small heads all over the place. Again and again, Sinéad heard the words "What a beautiful baby!" or "God bless this child always!" or "Is it your first?" drift down the aisle. Clusters of happy families smiled down at white satin bundles and small children were hushed and reverend when the priest approached to speak to them. She watched Julie's mother wipe away a tear as she took Max from Julie. Julie smiled and hugged her mother and they both shed an embarrassed tear as they smiled down at Max with his fists waving.

Sinéad took a sideways glance at Richard, just as she had on Julie's wedding day. He had become older. Of course he had. There were a few extra grey hairs on his temple, and his laughter lines were a little deeper than before, but he was perfect. In Sinéad's eyes he was still as wonderful as the day she married him. More so in fact. They had been through the mill and they were still together, still strong and they had an understanding now. They had both been through the wars. Just because it was Sinéad who had actually been prodded and poked, it didn't mean that Richard hadn't felt the hurt and embarrassment. She was his wife and there were men looking at her under a microscope. And he had been helpless to do anything about it. She held his hand, breaking him out of whatever daydream he was having at that moment. He looked at her and she noticed his eyes were glistening with tears.

"Are you all right?" she asked.

"Yes, I'll be fine," he smiled.

"It'll be all right, Richard. We have each other, and I love you very much."

"I love you too, Sinéad. I really do. But what if it never happens? What if we never have this happy ending?"

"We'll get our happy ending, Richard, even if it doesn't involve children. We're both healthy and young. There is more to life than a baby. We have to just keep remembering that."

"Young? I'm almost thirty-seven, we've been trying for years and we're no closer to a baby than we were when we started. Holding Max today, it just really brought it home to me more than ever how much I want that. I want what Gavin and Jules have."

"So do I, but maybe we should start looking at the alternatives. If it doesn't happen, then what? Would you ever be happy to just leave it?"

Richard looked down, rubbing his eyes with a tired gesture. "We'll have to – sooner or later we're going to have to. You're thirty-four now – we have four, five years ahead of us."

"But maybe I don't want to spend the rest of my youth chasing the dream. Maybe at some point I'll want to call it a day."

Richard looked at her as if she was a stranger. "Are you saying you don't want a child any more?"

"No, far from it! But I just want, I don't know. Maybe we should talk about this later."

"No, what are you saying?"

"I just think I'm coming to a point where I might want to say stop. I might, not yet, but some time in the future I might."

Richard looked down. "I see. Maybe we should talk about it later then."

"Richard, I'm not saying we should stop today or even anytime soon. I'm just saying that I don't want to keep going and going until we can think of nothing else."

"We'll talk later."

"But if we can't have a child, then maybe we should focus on other things, go out and enjoy ourselves a bit more."

"Sinéad, please, I don't want to talk about it here and now."

"I'm just making the point."

"I hear you. You've made it. You want to start looking at other alternatives. I get it." Richard rubbed the side of his head in an irritated gesture.

He was closing down. She hadn't meant to bring it up right there and now she was sorry she had. She didn't know whether to apologise or say nothing at all. In the end she said nothing, just sat there quietly beside him.

They both looked up at the altar, at Julie and Gavin and their ever-growing family. Sinéad watched them talking to Genevieve, her small face animated as she told them her story. Who was she kidding? She still wanted this happy ending; she wanted it with every fibre of her being. She needed it. She had a month of this Clomid left and she was going to make it work.

50

Sometimes Sinéad felt honestly as if God was laughing at her. She remembered as a young girl, while in school and even into college, sitting at the kitchen table with her mother as they discussed what Sinéad wanted to do with her life.

Sinéad had wonderful plans: careers and travelling, huge houses in expensive locations, husband and children. She had it all planned out – the locations, number of children and husband's occupation changed through the years, but she was always adamant that she would have it all, money, husband, children. Her mother would smile as she listened to the pipe dreams.

Sinéad would become indignant. How dare her mother laugh at her plans?

"I'm not laughing at your plans, darling. I just think you should have a little more flexibility in them."

"What do you mean?"

"I just think you should leave some things in the lap of the gods."

"I have it — I want three children and I'll let God decide if they're boys or girls!" she'd laugh.

"Ah, you'll learn," her mother would laugh and carry on with whatever bit of work she was doing at the time.

"I'll learn what?"

"Well, a great bit of wisdom my grandmother told me when I was just a little girl was this — and you'd do well to remember it yourself. She said: 'If you want to give God a laugh, tell him your plans'. And that bit of advice has got me through many a tough decision."

"What are you talking about?" Sinéad dismissed the comment, as was her way at sixteen.

"I'm saying you can have your life planned to the last moment, what you'll do and who you'll meet, what you'll eat and where you'll live. God has his plan for you, my girl. He's the one who decides who does what. Wait and see."

"Well, he can't stop me from planning. And I plan to have a great job, travel the world and meet a very rich man and marry him."

"I really hope you get all you wish for, I really do, but be prepared to fall for a poor guy and live in a flat in Mullingar. You can never guess who you'll fall for."

"I think I'll stop myself from falling for a poor culchie!" Sinéad laughed. She may have been only sixteen, but she knew she would never be happy living in poverty somewhere.

"You might just be very happy with that 'poor culchie' as you say!"

"Doubtful, when there's a rich doctor in the offing!" Sinéad grinned.

As a young girl she had always been so sure of herself and her plans. Now she wasn't so sure. What if this was God laughing at her? What if he gave her all the things she wanted, with a small catch at the end? Everything she wanted bar the children – they had always been last on her list of must-have items. What if God had just ticked off her list and put a line through the children? And what if she was so busy with Richard and making money that she hadn't even noticed? It looked like that was exactly what had happened. Here she was into the last month of her Clomid and still no baby.

Richard was gone from disappointed to despairing. Last week Sinéad had come in to the sitting room with the news that all the testing and timing and lying flat on her back with hips tilted hadn't worked. Not to mention all the candles they'd lit in every church around the city. They had practically set their local church ablaze. And again, she was coming down the stairs with the horrible news that it hadn't worked. She felt so guilty and, when she told him this time, he'd actually cried like a baby. He'd sobbed and she'd held him in her arms and listened as he cried. She felt so helpless; she couldn't do anything for him. She couldn't give him the one thing he wanted most of all in the world. It was breaking her heart and watching him become more and more unhappy about it was making things worse. She had never really lost the guilt about the situation but watching him lately had only increased her sense of guilt and anger about the whole thing.

She decided then and there she'd give it this one last

month and then it was over. She was never going back to the HARI Unit; she was never having another doctor, no matter how well-intentioned, prod her with a needle or put on a glove and stick his hand up her skirt. The only man who was coming anywhere near her from here on in was Richard. She'd had enough of the testing, the poking and everything else that went with it.

But, more important, she'd had enough of the endless hoping, the endless waiting, the repeated disappointments, the increasing wear on the nerves.

She'd had enough, and, whether he knew it or not, so had Richard.

She'd give it one more month and then she'd talk to Richard about it.

She had a feeling he wouldn't be happy, but in the long run she really believed it was for the best.

That's not to say she wasn't willing to give this last month her all. She was determined to give it a go. It was her last month of Clomid and there was no reason to believe that it wouldn't work out this month.

"Richard, I was thinking about this whole thing, and maybe we need a weekend away," she said one evening as they watched TV.

"I'm all ears," he said as he watched *Scrubs*.

"I was thinking a weekend in Kilkenny or somewhere, dinner and wine somewhere really nice and back to the hotel bar for a few drinks. What do you think?"

"Sounds like a dream."

"And no worrying about timing or sex or any of that, just us having a weekend away."

"That sounds nice."

"I'll see what I can book."

"Great."

Sinéad got them a weekend in Kilkenny the following week and they did just what they'd agreed to do. They drank lots of wine, ate out each night and stayed in bed till late in the mornings. They did chat about the baby thing though, even though it was one of the things that they had agreed would be off limits. But over dinner on the Saturday night Richard brought it up.

"Remember at the christening that time, what you said about wanting to call it a day?"

"I never said that. I said I didn't want to keep trying and trying until we were both over the hill. I want to be able to enjoy some of my youth."

"What do you mean by that?"

"I mean I would love it to work out, but if it doesn't I don't want to keep flogging the dead horse. Especially if the dead horse is me," Sinéad replied.

"So, we have this last month of that Clomid stuff. Then what?"

"Then nothing," Sinéad shrugged, her voice resigned. "We're on our own again. I could go back to the doctor and see what he says, or go back to the Rotunda and see if they have any more tests up their sleeves."

"What would you like to do?"

"I'd like for it to work this month. I'd like to see those two blue lines on that pregnancy test."

"And if not? What then?"

"Richard, this is our weekend away. I thought we were trying to forget all about it."

"This is important. We need to be together on this, whatever the decision."

"Well, I have been thinking about it as it happens."

"And?"

"And I don't think you'll like what I have to say."

"Just tell me what it is then."

Sinéad took a sip of her wine and looked at Richard. Was he ready to hear this? Maybe he was. Either way she'd have to tell him sooner or later.

"I really think that if this doesn't work out . . ." She looked at him again – was he really ready for this? Here goes nothing – he asked the question after all. "I think I'd like to leave it, at least for a while. I'm not ready for IVF. I don't think I ever will be. I think we've gone as far as I'm willing to go on this."

Now that the words were out of her mouth she felt the cold terror grip her insides. What if Richard was thinking the opposite? What if he was ready to go for anything as long as it got them the baby he wanted? What if he was furious with her?

Richard took a sip of his wine and put the glass back on the table. He looked around the room for a moment, taking in the other customers. It felt like an hour before he finally began to speak again.

"I think you're right actually," he said. "I think we have

gone as far as we really need to go with this one. I was never overly keen on IVF, and I really couldn't stand back and watch you put your body through much more quite frankly. And it's not just your body; it's everything. I've looked up on the *net* what this IVF involves. It's a nightmare: injections every day, scans and egg retrievals. This whole process has been a huge strain on us. I think we're fucking amazing for getting through it without killing each other. Honestly, I feel like we've been living on a rollercoaster for the last six months. I am so stressed out, all the time. It's like I never get a full night's sleep. You know the feeling? I go to bed every night and I'm too exhausted to think, never mind anything else. And in the morning I just feel the exact same way. I feel like I've had too much caffeine and then a few minutes later I feel like I did when I used to stay up all night when I was in my teens. You know that slow-motion, freezing-cold sort of tiredness? I think we both need to just unwind a bit. It's been tough on me, but I can only imagine what you're feeling like. "

"Oh thank God! I thought you'd be furious."

"Me? As if it would be my place to be furious? You've done everything you can for this baby. You've had all the tests, all the treatments and that whole menopause thing was just too much for me. I couldn't have done it. It messed up your hormones, your emotions and you just dealt with it all. You kept right on working and shopping and being Max's godmother and everything. You just kept right on going. I could never have done it."

"Yes, you could. You could have if it meant a baby in the end, and I believed it would mean a baby. That was what kept me going. But living on a rollercoaster – I know exactly how you feel – that tired, slow-motion feeling. I've had that coupled with that jittery, talking-too-fast and shaking-hands thing. As well as the menopause of course, the hot flushes and everything else. I am completely wrecked. There are some days when I actually think my brain has finally given up the ghost. I think it's actually fried, then an hour later it's kicked into overdrive and I'm back talking too fast and jumpy. Then those mood swings! I don't know how anyone put up with me in work at the height of my 'menopause'. At least you knew what was happening; the guys in work knew nothing. I just kept bouncing off the walls for no reason on them. I mean, seriously, my head is wrecked."

"Well, I think you're amazing. The lengths you went to, to fulfil our dream of a baby of our own."

"Let's not throw in our towels just yet. It could happen this month!" Sinéad smiled, hoping against hope that it would work.

"Even if it never works, I still want you to know this: I think you're amazing."

"Thank you," she smiled as he refilled their glasses. "You know, the truth is, I never really lost that horrible guilty feeling about all of this. It was my endometriosis that stopped us having children and maybe if I had allowed that doctor to investigate all those years ago –"

"No! Sinéad, you can't think that way! Don't let yourself think that way. Remember what the doctor kept saying – it was no more your fault than it would have been mine if I had a low sperm count. You have to let go of that guilt, and anyway, you did everything you could to reverse the condition."

"I suppose I did, but I still feel guilty about it all."

"Please don't. I don't feel in any way aggrieved about this, not towards you anyway."

"I know, Richard, I know."

"Well, as you say, don't throw the towel in just yet. We still have one more month of this Clomid and after that we have the rest of our lives, isn't that right?"

"Yes, we still have this month, and then who knows!"

"But we're decided that this will be the last test or drug you have to take. After this we'll just see what happens."

"Yes. This is the last treatment I put myself though."

Sinéad sighed heavily. Other than actually being pregnant, this was the best outcome she could have wished for. Richard was not annoyed or upset; he looked almost as relieved as she did about it. They were closing a chapter of their lives, that was for sure, but they both seemed ready to do it.

"I'm really glad we had this weekend, and this chat," Richard said after a while. "I think we're making the right decision on this case, Sinéad."

"I think so too," Sinéad said, "but I don't think it'll be an easy transition to make. I mean after all the testing and timing and stuff. I'll find it hard to leave it all behind!"

"I think you'll make that transition much easier than you think. You'll suddenly realise what a lot of time and effort you spent at it all these years."

"Maybe you're right." Sinéad grinned and added, "But,

hey, don't drink too much – we still have this month and I might still need your services tonight!"

"I should hope so! Did you see how much this weekend is costing us? I fully expect to get a bit of the bold thing this weekend!"

"The bold thing! Why do you constantly refer to it as 'the bold thing'? What age are you? Fifteen?"

"I'm whatever age you want me to be, sweetheart!" Richard gave her a mischievous smile as he bit into his tiramisu.

They took every spare second over the weekend and all through the following week. If this was their last month they were going to make the most of it. Sinéad turned off the computer at five and raced home every evening. They had a full week of early nights. And Sinéad tilted her hips and lay with her legs in the air for over twenty minutes each night. They hoped against hope that it would work out this month, but neither one spoke too openly about their hopes.

In the end their weekend away didn't work out, neither did the legs in the air business. Sinéad broke the news to Richard yet again. This time however he was resigned to it.

"So be it," was all he said.

"Are you okay?" she asked.

"I'm completely fine. I'm glad it's over. No more of that waiting and wondering, right?"

"I suppose so, no more waiting and testing." Sinéad felt

a pang of deep pain as she spoke, a pain that stung deep in her heart. So this was what it felt like to give up. She'd never given up on anything before, never ever. She'd never admitted defeat before and here she was admitting defeat on the most important fight in her life.

"Are you all right, Sinéad?"

"Yes, I made this decision and I'm going with it. It'll just take a few days to sink in, that's all."

"We made the right decision. How long were we going to keep this up?"

"I know, I know."

"We'll be fine, love," he said and kissed her.

Some time later, seeing him immersed in the TV, she tentatively said: "I think I might call over to Jules. I think I need to talk to a girl about it all."

Sinéad got in the car. She didn't ring in advance, she just drove. She'd take her chances on Julie being in or not. It was as much for the drive as anything else she was going over.

When Julie opened the door to Sinéad, she threw her arms around her.

"You must have read my mind – I was just wishing for a girly chat! I'm alone! Gavin has taken the children to his mother's to give me a break!" .

"Thanks, that's the best hello I've ever got around here!"

"Well, call over more often," said Julie as she ushered Sinéad in, "especially when the children are here doing my head in. I'd sleep with the milkman if he agreed to take them for the day sometimes!"

"Does the milkman know you feel this way about him?" said Sinéad as she plonked herself down on the couch.

"No," said Julie, joining her, "but I feel the same way about the postman, the canvassers and even those annoying people who come around and shove junk mail in your letter box."

"I will be seriously worried if you mention that small bloke from the Church of the Latter Day Saints!"

"Listen, if he arrived on a bad day I'd give it serious thought! You have no idea what it's like trying to keep the peace between two small girls and a boy who pees on everything!"

"No, I have no idea at all, and it looks like I never will." Sinéad smiled but her heart groaned under the pressure on her chest. It came out in a strangled kind of sound.

Julie looked at her and without a second thought hugged Sinéad so hard that the tears spilled down her cheeks.

"Please, Jules, I really don't want to cry about this," she said as Julie hugged her harder.

"You've been putting a brave face on all of this for far too long. You need someone to hug you and you need to let it all out."

"I have cried a river in private for this baby, but it isn't happening and we've gone as far as we can without resorting to IVF. And I don't want to. I really can't do it."

"I think you've made the right decision then. If you really feel IVF is a step too far for you, then you have to stop. How does Richard feel about it?"

"He's all right about it. He seems resigned to just stopping the whole charade."

"And you?"

"I know why we're stopping, but I hate it. I just feel so defeated about it." As Sinéad spoke the tears streamed down her face again. "I'm sorry. I didn't mean to come over here and cry all over the place."

"Sinéad, I'm actually glad you're finally admitting it's such a big deal. You just sit there and have good old cry. I'll get us a cup of tea."

Julie arrived back with a bottle of wine, two glasses and a packet of Sensations crisps.

"What happened to the tea?" Sinéad asked.

"Ah, I thought we could do with a bottle of wine instead."

They opened the wine and drank it; then they opened a second and talked for hours. They talked about babies and pregnancy and Julie told her all about the nitty-gritty details of labour and delivery. They laughed about Julie's various embarrassing situations and how, after the baby was born, Julie had not forgotten about them. Yes, the children were worth it, but given the choice she'd have much rather she hadn't done various things in the delivery suite. Kicking the consultant was just one thing on the list, throwing up all over herself after she got the epidural was also on the list and cursing at a very timid midwife was another of her shining moments. She had spent the whole hospital stay after having Genevieve trying to ensure that nice nurse heard how sorry she was. Then there was the wonderful moment when Genevieve was only a few weeks old and Julie took the two babies to Blanchardstown Shopping Centre. She had a twin buggy that she couldn't work. She had battled with it for about ten minutes, trying to open it. Three hours later she was again fighting the good fight with the bloody thing, this time trying to close it. She was trying to get home for feeding times and Genevieve was beginning to scream in the back seat. Julie could neither open nor close the damn buggy and in a fit of rage had kicked it around the car park before getting out her mobile and ringing the shop that she bought it from. Luckily the shop happened to be in the centre. She controlled her voice as best she could and asked if someone could come out and help her close the buggy. The girl who answered the phone explained that she couldn't leave the shop floor.

"Look here, you," Julie spat. "Either someone comes out and helps me close this fucking thing or you're gonna get it fired through your front window. I have two small children in the car and I really need to get home to feed them. Now get out here and help!"

The girl had high-tailed it out of the shop and into the car park. It took her all of three seconds to close the buggy. She opened and closed it again and again just to prove to Julie the bloody thing worked. Julie stood there watching her, her face burning and tears stinging her eyes. She was furious. What was she doing wrong the whole time?

"There is a knack involved, madam. Maybe you should practise opening and closing it," the girl had said.

It was the wrong thing to say.

"Do you honestly think that, looking after a seven-week-old baby and a fifteen-month-old child all day, I have time to then go and open and close this stupid buggy all night? Is that what you think I should be doing in my spare time? Do you not think you should stock a buggy that's easier to open and close, one that doesn't require a 'knack' or a fucking degree in engineering?"

The girl had turned and run off before the buggy was actually fired through the window. Julie packed up the stupid buggy and drove off cursing everyone and everything in her path.

It was just what Sinéad needed, to hear about the underbelly of childbirth and child-rearing. If she had nothing else, she had the knowledge that she wouldn't have to undergo any of that palaver!

She stayed in Julie's for about three hours until Gavin and children arrived home. They were all exhausted and the girls were so tired they didn't even complain when they were told to go to bed. They just kissed Aunty Sinéad goodnight and headed off.

Sinéad called a taxi just after eight – she wanted to leave Gavin and Julie alone. The children were in bed and Gavin had come home with a bottle of nice red wine under his arm.

Julie walked her to the door and hugged her as they said goodbye. "You look after yourself, and remember you're making the right decision!"

"I know, I'll be fine, I just need a few weeks to get used to the idea."

"You'll get used to it. It's the right thing to do, Sinéad. It'll all work out in the end."

Sinéad got into the taxi and went home. Richard was

watching TV and drinking brandy when she got in. He poured her a large one with a little Coke and she sat down beside him. They talked into the night about all kinds of things. What they thought of the traffic in the city, where they might go for holidays this year and how much everything in Ireland cost. It was much later when they finally got onto the subject of babies, and what they'd do with themselves now that children appeared to be a quickly fading hope. They talked about it for a long time, but they didn't really come up with any big plan. Just that they were finished with trying.

It was sad night. Even though they'd both known it was coming, it was sad. Their hopes were coming to an end. A baby was no longer on their agenda. They were a childless couple; there would be no christenings, no first day of school, no graduation dances and no grandchildren. Nothing.

It took about three months for Sinéad to finally give up hope on having a baby. She had stopped testing and working out dates, but she hadn't stopped hoping. They say hope is the last thing to die and they're right. Richard checked in on her a lot in the beginning. He watched over her. She could sometimes see him watching her as she took off her make-up or put on her moisturiser. She'd smile at him and tell him she was fine. He'd claim he wasn't watching her, but she could see him and he knew he'd been caught. He'd just laugh and carry on reading or watching TV or whatever it was he was doing.

He had been great in the beginning though, just at that

time when Sinéad needed help in giving it all up. He'd listened to her as she cried her eyes out at the prospect of no children. He held her hand and told her he loved her when she panicked about the future, just the two of them, no children just the heartfelt longing that she sometimes felt would never go away. Even when she was an old lady, sitting with Julie watching Julie's grandchildren as they played – would she still long for children even then?

It was Richard who finally threw away all the books and the ovulation kits and the pregnancy tests and the charts that Sinéad still kept under the bed. He came in one night after a particularly bad day and threw them all in the bin.

"If we really have given up on all of this then we need to clear the decks," he announced as he threw the last few tests in the bin.

After that night the house felt almost as if it had been exorcised; the last remnants of the haunting were gone and the house was finally clean. They could get on with other things without opening a press and having baby books fall out on them. They could turn that corner now.

Sinéad felt stronger, her life was not as hollow as she once believed it was.

It was time for some new challenges.

The garden was as good a place as any to start. So they threw themselves whole-heartedly into that for a few months. It was perfect timing: it was springtime and the weather was just right for garden work. They bought plants and shrubs, trimmed borders, cut back overgrown bushes and bought garden furniture.

When everything had been planted, tidied and set in just the right position, they stood back and surveyed their handiwork. It had taken them five months to get the garden just perfect but it had worked and now when people came over they gasped as they looked out at the garden. It was fabulous, a real little haven, away from the hustle and bustle of the busy street outside.

Sinéad was very proud of herself, even if most of the heavy lifting and planting had been done by Richard. She had overseen the whole process and she had supervised it very well.

She wondered what she might tackle as her next project. She looked around the house. The kitchen and sitting room were fine, the conservatory was perfect so she wasn't touching that. Her bedroom was always good for a spruce. Yes, next project was definitely her bedroom. Then the boxroom, in fact the whole upstairs of this house was in need of a good going over. There were projects lined up until next Christmas!

51

It had been seven months since they had decided to call a halt to the whole baby process. It was late on a Sunday afternoon and Sinéad was lying on the bed in her newly decorated bedroom. The sun streamed through the window and the room was beautifully warm. Richard had finished cutting the grass and was watering the plants they'd spent the last bank-holiday rowing over. Sinéad had wanted to put them in front of the window so that she could look out at them from the conservatory, but Richard, being the level-headed one, had read the instructions and pointed out that they needed shade. In front of the conservatory they were in direct sunlight. The battle had been fierce but logic prevailed and they were now planted down near the back wall. It was a compromise of sorts: Sinéad could actually see them from the conservatory though she had to turn her head to do so and, even with the door open on a fine day, she couldn't smell the wonderful fresh scent they gave off.

In hindsight it was probably for the best; in the fortnight that the plant was there the increase in bees in the garden was worthy of comment. Richard had threatened to ring *Mooney Goes Wild* on Radio One.

"There's the phone then," Sinéad had tutted, still smarting over the fact that the plant was far away from her.

"I might – if they haven't fallen off in numbers by next week, I will."

"It's June, you big eejit! It's bee season!"

"And if you'd had your way they'd be in here day and night!"

"What are you talking about?"

"I mean, if you'd planted that bush right here by the window like you wanted to, there'd be bees and wasps setting up home in the kitchen. We wouldn't be able to open a window in the back of the house!"

"Go away! Dick!" Sinéad laughed.

Four years ago, when they began to talk about having a baby, it would have been hard to imagine that they would be here all those years later with no baby but happy. Enough was enough and, once they'd got used to the idea of not having children, it was easier to live with than either one had imagined. In some ways it was actually a relief.

They had sat together crying and talking about it all for weeks after they made the decision. They both cried a lot, for all their lost hopes and all the fears for the future. Sinéad had been very scared they would have a long and lonely future.

Now here they were seven months later and they were happy, their days were full and life just as hectic as it was before. To the outside world things hadn't changed. If a baby was not to be, then there would be other things in their lives.

When Richard had thrown away all of Sinéad's books and ovulation kits, she had poured them both a very large glass of wine.

"If I never have sex again I won't particularly care!" she announced.

"What? Don't be rash now, love!" Richard laughed.

They were happier now than they'd ever been. The great white elephant that had been sitting in the room with them everywhere they went for the last four years had finally slung its hook. Things would be easier from now on. From now on it was just the two of them, no hidden agendas, just them and they were a team.

Sinéad drifted off to sleep for a few minutes. She'd been busy in work over the last few weeks and she couldn't seem to get enough sleep lately. She woke up and listened to Richard in the kitchen. He was making a start on dinner – she should go down and help him, but she'd just take a few minutes to rest here first. Half an hour later Richard woke her up.

"Dinner will be ready in a few minutes – would you like a glass of wine?"

"Mmm, that sounds nice." She stretched and sat up.

"Grand, I'll have one ready for you downstairs."

She went into the bathroom. She looked at her face: it was sunburnt from being out in the garden earlier on. She opened the press under the sink and rooted around for after-sun cream. As she did she found a pregnancy test buried deep in at the back. She pulled it out and looked at it. One that had been missed in the big clear-out. Kneeling in the bathroom like this, holding the test in her hand, she realised how things had changed and how much more relaxed she was about everything. No more counting days, no more marking up calendars. Where was she in her cycle this month? After all the years of testing and checking had she really forgotten it all already? This time last year she could have told you where she was on her cycle at the drop of a hat, but right now she was lost. Granted she'd just woken up and was feeling groggy but still . . . When was her last period? She thought back. It was just before Richard's mother's birthday. They'd been out for a meal, so when was that? It was the ninth of May. It was the twelfth of June now. Could it be nearly five weeks ago? It was last month anyway, that was for sure. Five weeks . . .

Seven months ago she would have been trembling with excitement. Her period was late and that might mean . . .

Would she take the test just for laughs? She looked at the expiry date on the back; it wasn't out of date for another year.

Honestly, what were the chances of it being positive? But it was here in her hand, her period was late and it seemed like fate.

All right, she'd take the test but if it was negative she'd just forget about it. She wouldn't get upset or anything.

But her hands were shaking as she opened the package. This was pure silliness now, she was just doing it for a laugh, but . . . what if?

She washed her face and put on the after-sun while she waited for the test to give its result. She looked at her face in the mirror, flushed with sun and excitement. This was complete madness.

She scolded herself in the mirror. "Do not get your hopes up. Why would it have worked now if all the doctors and drugs in Dublin couldn't sort it out last year?"

Then she looked at the test, her heart pounding hard.

There were two blue lines, clear and distinct. Two of them.

She grabbed the package and read the back.

She picked up the stick and raced to the kitchen.

"Richard, don't pour me any wine!" she shouted as she ran down the stairs.

"Why not?"

"Because I'm pregnant!" she shouted as she burst into the kitchen.

"You're what?" he shouted, his face a mixture of joy and complete confusion.

He was so confused he tried to hug her while holding a pot full of pasta.

"Drop the pot before you hug me!" Sinéad beamed, her head light with giddiness.

He put the pot on the counter and hugged her. They hugged and hugged.

Then Sinéad sat down at the kitchen table, her knees weak from the excitement. She put the test down in front of them. The two lines were still there, as clear as they were when she first saw them. They both stared at the test for what seemed like an hour but might have been closer to twenty minutes.

"When is it due?"

"I think it's due in February."

"So what do we do now?" Richard asked, still staring at the stick.

"I'll go to my doctor and have it all confirmed and then we wait for nine months!"

"We need to get a few books, read up on what you can eat, what you can't eat and you need to start eating properly. None of these Chinese takeaways for you any more!"

"I'll look after myself – you don't need to concern yourself on that one!"

"What if there's something wrong with the kit?" Richard suddenly asked. "It's been there a while."

"Do you think?"

A few minutes later Richard was in his car heading for a late-night pharmacy.

Fifteen minutes later Sinéad was doing the test again.

She was still pregnant.

They grinned from ear to ear as they sat and ate dinner, reheated by microwave, of course. Sinéad couldn't finish hers, she was so excited.

After dinner they retired to the sitting room. Sinéad lay flat along the couch with her feet on Richard's lap all night. They talked about when it might have happened. Was it the night of his mother's birthday? Was it the afternoon they painted the bedroom and just for laughs took break in the middle while they waited for the paint to dry? Was it that night they had a row over the broken glass in the sitting room?

Did it really matter when it had happened? It had happened and that was all that mattered. They both grinned from ear to ear as they sat and watched TV together.

"What will we call it?" Sinéad asked. "I really like Christian if it's a boy."

"Christian Greene? I don't think so, Sinéad. It sounds daft to me."

"Well, what names do you like then?"

"I've always liked the name James to tell you the truth. But I have no idea," he smiled. "But seriously, let's not get ahead of ourselves just yet. It's very early days."

"I know it is, but I can't help myself! I've been planning names and birthday parties for four years!"

"Well, wait till you get it all confirmed and then we'll plan to our heart's content."

"I have to tell Julie. I'm not waiting until the twelve weeks to tell her. I'm telling her in the morning, after the doctor's appointment."

"It up to you. I'm keeping it quiet until twelve weeks, but if you want to tell Jules it's up to you."

"I have to – just Jules – no one else!"

When Sinéad came out of the doctor's the next day she rang Richard and confirmed all the news. Then she rang Julie.

The scream of joy could be heard all through the city.

Sinéad cried with joy as she sat in the doctor's carpark and Jules jumped around the kitchen in Drumcondra. They both beamed down the phone through the tears.

"I do hope you'll ignore all those silly little stories I told you about the births and stuff. I was exaggerating the whole thing really!"

"Julie, I couldn't care less. Give me an epidural and a bikini wax beforehand and I'll be all right."

"Oh yeah, make sure you get the bikini wax, Sinéad! Let's not forget the wax!"

"I will never forget to wax, darling – you're the slob around here!"

"I can't wait to ask you about your waxes when this baby is six months old!"

"Oh my God! A baby, I'm finally having a baby!"

"I couldn't be happier for you!"

"I couldn't be happier for me either!" Sinéad grinned as she wiped the tears away and started the car.

She smiled through the tears as she drove off to her new life.

A life where she actually had everything she ever wanted.

A life where she and Richard had a baby of their own.

THE END

Direct to your home!

If you enjoyed this book why not visit our website:

www.poolbeg.com

and get another book delivered straight to your home or to a friend's home!

www.poolbeg.com

All orders are despatched within 24 hours.